The Fires of Sinhala

COLIN DE SILVA

GRAFTON BOOKS

A Division of the Collins Publishing Group

LONDON GLASGOW
TORONTO SYDNEY AUCKLAND

Grafton Books
A Division of the Collins Publishing Group
8 Grafton Street, London W1X 3LA

Published by Grafton Books 1986

British Library Cataloguing in Publication Data

De Silva, Colin
The fires of Sinhala.
I. Title
823[F]   PS3554.E837

ISBN 0-246-13052-0

Set in 11 on 13 point Garamond by Columns of Reading
Printed in Great Britain by
Billing & Sons Ltd, Worcester

To
Beatrice Clara de Silva,
wife, mother and human being
without peer

Some Important Sinhala Monarchs

VIJAYA 483-455 BC
see *The Founts of Sinhala*

DEVAM PIYA TISSA 247-207 BC
Introduced Buddhism to Lanka

ELARA 145-101 BC
ABHAYA GAMINI 101-77 BC
SADHA TISSA 77-59 BC
see *The Winds of Sinhala*

AD

QUEEN ANULA 12-16

GAJABAHU 174-196

BHATIKA TISSA 203-227

MAHASENA 334-361

BUDDHADASA 380-409

MAHANAMA 409-431

DHATUSENA 460-478

KASSAPA 478-496

MOGALLANA 496-513

PARAKRAMA BAHU I 1153-1186
Founder of Polon-naruwa

PARAKRAMA BAHU VIII 1484-1518
Ancestor of:
DHARMA PARAKRAMA BAHU IX
WIJAYO VI
BHUVENAKA BAHU VII
MAYA DUNNE
RAJA SINHA I
see *The Fires of Sinhala*
The Last Sinhala Lions (to follow)

ACKNOWLEDGEMENTS

My deep appreciation and thanks go to:
Grafton Books for its faith in me, particularly to my editor, Anne Charvet, for her unfailing courtesy and professional support; the editorial staff of Grafton Books for excellent editing;

Dominick Abel, my literary agent, for invaluable assistance with a re-write of the original manuscript;

Heidi Helm, for research into Portuguese trading, ships, armament, and dress;

Marcia Krueger, whose devotion to my work once again went beyond the line of duty, in typing several revisions of the manuscript, often meeting impossible deadlines and in making useful suggestions.

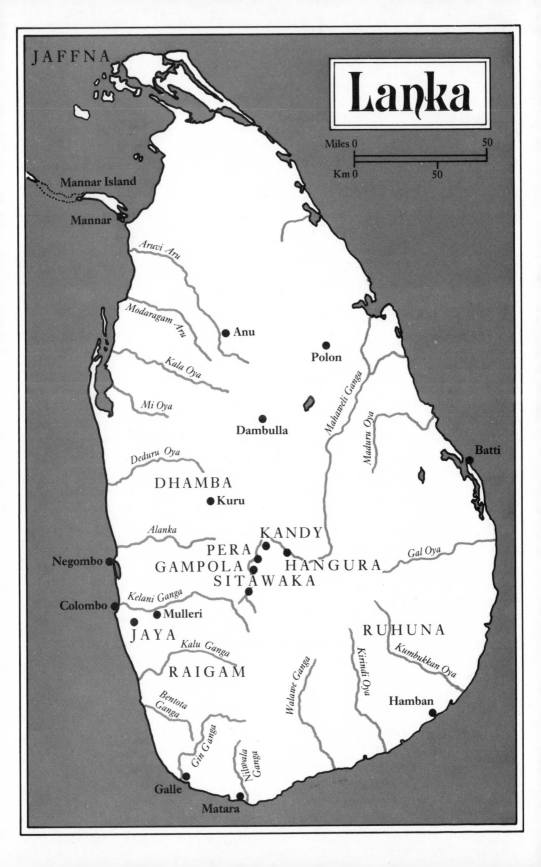

PROLOGUE
Monday, 11 February 1521

On board the Santa Caterina, *flagship
of Admiral Lopo Soarez de Albergaria
of the Imperial Navy of Portugal*

Excited yet nervous, he stood alertly behind his father, on the
poop deck of the flagship. At almost eighteen, Fernao Soarez de
Albergaria was a midshipman and had already seen combat
under his father in Sumatra and Diu, but those had been police
actions. Their presence in the port of Colombo today was to
force a landing.

How effectively would the mob of bare-chested Sinhala and
turbaned Moors, now crowding the wharves and screaming
defiance through the silver sunlight of morning, oppose the
landing? Their angry shouts, hoots and jeers did not exactly
promise a welcoming party.

Fernao was surprised at their conduct, for the island of Lanka
had a culture and a recorded history going back two thousand
years. Its principal inhabitants, the Sinhala, or lion race, were of
Aryan stock originally derived from the early Caucasian settlers
of North India. Now here were representatives of an ancient,
cultured people hurling crude epithets across the murky waters.
Ado Suddho! 'Hey, you white fellows . . . We'll have your livers!
Step ashore and we'll cut your cocks off and stuff them in your
mouths.'

And yet he must expect opposition. The *Santa Caterina* was
the first European vessel ever to enter Colombo harbour. It had
led the remaining sixteen warships of the flotilla commanded
by his father, to anchor in arrowhead formation, which
permitted direct communication between the vessels and

11

simultaneous broadsides. The natives could not know that they came in peace, for trade, and that if they had intended conquest they would have first pulverized the city.

The people of Lanka had no experience of cannon and the fearsome armament of the flotilla meant nothing to them. So it was not only the first warmth of the day that started prickles of sweat beneath Fernao's close-fitting blue tunic, and his tight white pantaloons. It was fear.

He raised his eyes to his father's massive back. Though Fernao himself was six feet tall, the admiral towered over him, a magnificent figure in a close-fitting doublet of dark blue with puffed sleeves and gold facings over a high ruffed white cambric shirt. The slashed maroon breeches, holding up white nether-hosen reaching the thighs, revealed long, sturdy legs, the knee garters adorned with gold buckles. For all his great bulk, the old sea dog stood springy on the balls of his feet, right hand inside his doublet, left hand lightly on the belt of his sword, in the loose-kneed stance of those accustomed to roll with the ship.

The admiral half turned. 'I've allowed them an hour,' he said, 'to reveal their hands. If they make one wrong move, I shall pulverize them with a bombardment the like of which the Indies has not experienced since we first sailed here with Vasco da Gama. If they merely make threats, we shall go ashore peacefully.'

His ice-blue eyes, their black pupils piercing as a hawk's, held nothing but cold contempt for the clamorous mob ashore. The rugged features, face carved in marble, skin shot with tiny red veins, nose patrician, the long hair and square beard white-blond from exposure to salt air and sunlight, inspired confidence, restored courage.

Fernao knew he had inherited those ice-blue eyes, but the rest of him, the slender build, fair skin now tanned by tropical sunlight, black hair, were all from *a mae*, his mother. The straight nose and fine facial bones had made him look almost feminine until a couple of years ago. He recalled with angry disgust the night an officer had made advances to him while he lay sleeping. He had almost gutted the man with his knife and it

12

had not taken long for word to get around the *armada de alto-bordo*, the high seas fleet, that the admiral's son was not to be taken. Strange how such incidents came to mind at the oddest moments.

As for his father's threat of a bombardment, it took Fernao back in time. His father had sailed with Vasco da Gama out of Lisbon in 1497 on the historic voyage around the Cape of Good Hope which had opened up the sea-route from Europe to the eastern seaboards of Africa, the Middle East and on to India. He himself had been born in the year in which his father had returned with Vasco da Gama to India, 1503. *A mae*, his mother, whom he had worshipped, had died of consumption when he was six. His father, who had been a captain with the *armada* of the *Estado da India* at the time, had secured a transfer to the home fleet to look after Fernao, his only child. They had lived together in the huge family mansion near Lisbon, but his father was away so often that most of Fernao's lonely upbringing had been in the hands of his governess, Pia, and his tutors. When he was twelve, his father had him admitted to the naval academy, and as soon as he completed his training, his father had requested transfers for them both to the Indies fleet. Shortly afterwards, his father was promoted to admiral for his brilliant participation in the bombardment and capture of Ormuz in the Persian Gulf.

Though Fernao's ambition as a boy had been to join the university and become a writer, his father had discouraged it so firmly that he never dared to broach the subject again. Once in the Indies, his sensitive spirit had at first recoiled against the killing, the blood lust, the brutality, but this reaction had slowly been dissipated through the years of active service by the sense of power that firearms and military might had brought. Today, his only concession to his artistic yearnings was the private diary he maintained.

Now, as he glanced shorewards, Fernao heard a sudden sharp rise in the clamour of voices from the wharves. In contrast with their packs of belligerent humanity the harbour's arc was peaceful. A buff-coloured beach was lined with grey wooden wharves. Beyond were red-tiled warehouses, at the entrances to which covered bullock wagons and open carts were lined. In the background, the city was pretty, with red- or white-tiled roofs nestling amid lush green branches.

'Someone is inciting those stupid natives,' the admiral declared.

Fernao's stomach clenched. Many of the men on the wharves were now brandishing spears and swords. Their clamour was deafening. The men on the ship's deck began to answer back but were quickly stopped by the sharp command of an officer. 'Hold your tongues and your fire, soldiers! Don't shout them down, wait till you can shoot them down.'

'I'll ask you to remember that we need our military domination only for trade,' Admiral de Albergaria said flatly to his son. 'Only trade can support the expense our Emperor Manuel bears at home and in the outfitting of our fleets, and turn him a handsome profit. We use force to ensure that our treaties are kept. Sixteen years ago the Sinhala king executed a *carta* of commerce promising our King two elephants and a cargo of cinnamon each year, and gave us the right to erect a factory in the capital port of Colombo.' He turned and raised a finger. 'We are here today to exercise that right.'

Fernao knew the purpose of the mission already from briefings before they left Goa, the Portuguese enclave on the west coast of India. He had secretly wondered whether Galle on Lanka's southern coast would not be a better location for the factory. It was there that Captain Lorenzo de Almeida had caused a stone pillar with a cross on top to be erected on a green headland thrusting into the ocean. It carried the Portuguese Quinas, the royal arms representing the five wounds of Christ and the thirty talents of silver for which he was sold. De Almeida sent a message to the King of Lanka, saying that the treaty between the two countries would last as long as the cross remained standing. He also left behind two Franciscan friars, Father Juan and Father Perez, who desired to carry the Catholic religion to the natives, and a young nobleman named Duarte de Brito, whom he appointed the Portuguese trade representative. They had remained as King Dharma's guests all these years and had been a great source of intelligence to the Viceroy in Goa.

14

'I have a special and important role for you in this country,' his father gruffly interrupted Fernao's thoughts.

The boy's heart leapt. Suddenly it seemed as if all the great events of Portugal's trading history had conspired to bring him to Colombo on this exciting day.

Today was the eleventh day of February. On 13 March he would be nineteen. A great future lay before him, thanks to his father. A spasm of guilt intruded. He admired but did not love the powerful man at his side.

Monday, 11 February 1521

In the Great King's palace at Jaya, about seven miles from the port of Colombo

He was thrilled when his father invited him to stroll in the palace gardens, immediately after breakfast. Men such as General Prince Maya Dunne did that only with grownups they could trust. Since this was Prince Tikiri's sixteenth birthday, his father's gesture must be a sign that he had entered a man's estate, for the general was not given to romping with children.

They paced the shady avenue bordered by tall *na*-trees, whose green and pink leaves were gently riffled by a breeze, white blossoms scattered on the brown dirt. Prince Maya Dunne came directly to the point. 'Today,' he stated abruptly, 'you have reached the age at which Sinhala princes enter manhood. The times are such that you must start preparing yourself for military battles ahead.'

His father was Commander-in-Chief of the armies of the Great King of Lanka, which gave him the added name Seneviratna, because the station entitled him to carry a jewelled sword. In Lanka, royal birth entitled one to a gold sword and family tree, noble birth to silver. Petty nobles had to use brass, commoners less. His father and he were of the royal Sita Waka clan. The Great King was his father's uncle. His father had arrived last night from Sita Waka, two days away on easy horseback, to greet him on his birthday.

Being the third son, his name was Tikiri Bandara, which

15

meant the youngest prince. After his older brothers died, he was sent at the age of seven to live in the Great King's palace in Jaya, to pursue his princely studies and learn the martial arts and sciences. So many deaths in his family. His mother had died eight years ago and his elder sister, Mala, just last year, after which his younger sister, Princess Padma, was sent to the distant city of Anu to be brought up by royal relatives.

They said that he looked like his father. He loved that, for his father was a slim man, tall and erect, over six feet in height, with a pliant sword-blade of a body. His long, shining black hair, shot with silver, hung down at wide shoulders, which tapered to a narrow waist. His clean-shaven face was well-chiselled, the features elegant and cast in the Arya mould, with tight muscles and a straight nose, the nostrils lightly flaring. His mouth was wide and generous, the jaw strong with a cleft chin, his colour Sinhala gold, for the stock was pure and went back through many centuries of royalty. In his white silken *dhoti* and short red tunic brocaded with gold, General Prince Maya Dunne looked every inch a soldier and a prince.

The morning sunlight lay shredded silver-gold on the avenue, but tenderly upon the green lawns bordered by great beds of russet-leaved canna plants, topped by orange flowers. Spiked scents of yellow *kapuru*, wild marigolds, were rustled by a light westerly breeze. His father glanced upwards at the screech of mynah birds as they passed a flame tree, then sideways for his son's reaction.

Prince Tikiri hid his surprise, held his peace, for want of something to say, but his pulse quickened.

'You have become an expert horseman,' his father continued, 'and your swordplay is as good as any. You are a fine wrestler, and reported to have a natural flair for military tactics.' He paused and they stopped to face each other by common consent. 'You are mature beyond your years. I am told that you think and reason like a grown man. All this is to the good, because it points to the great destiny that has been prophesied for you since the astrologers first cast your horoscope. The future of our family is in your hands. You are first and last a Sinhala. I command you to place honour above all things, always, especially above money, greed and personal ambition. Live by the Arya code which is your heritage. Be ready for action.' The fine black eyes invited a response, man to man at last.

'But *thatha*, father, are we not at peace?' This was all he could think to say, though his heart was pounding with joy at the praise and excitement at the promise for the future.

Unexpectedly, his father exploded. 'You dare call this pallid situation peace?' His black eyes flashed; his expression grew so hard that Prince Tikiri quailed. 'I thought you'd have more sense.' He lowered his voice, but continued with controlled anger. 'We have a Chola king in the north; Moors dominate the seaports through trade; the former granary of the east is held to ransom because it depends on rice imported from Cochin. Sinhala are divided into three sub-kingdoms, with their own sub-sub-kingdoms, different races, languages, religions: a people exploited, subdued, devoid of pride! News came last night of the return of the barbaric *parangi* sailors, whites who have established a reputation for senseless brutality in the Indies. Chola, Moors, *parangi*! The only way we are going to stop foreigners dictating to us is by uniting all the Sinhala kingdoms – in fact, instead of merely in name as now. Divided, the foreigner will rule.' He ended abruptly.

Prince Tikiri could tell that the arrival of the white men had triggered his father's concern. Such fears were obviously not confined to the general, for there had been an atmosphere of doubt and unease in the palace that morning, with courtiers whispering to each other on the verandahs, attendants gossiping in knots and tension among the guards. 'The Portuguese are not a leading power in Europe,' he volunteered instead, eager to show off knowledge gained from his *parangi* tutors, Father Perez and Father Juan. 'They may well have to withdraw their forces to face King Henry VIII of England.'

'An astute observation, Prince, but make no mistake, Lanka faces the power of Portugal today. And we will meet other difficulties later, when the greater powers of Europe discover the fortune which Portugal has been amassing in the Indies and speed in this direction to make this region their new battleground. For the present, I will not allow the Portuguese to turn Lanka into a trading station such as Goa.'

'I'm with you, *tha*.'

His father clapped a hand on Prince Tikiri's shoulder, squeezed once and let go. It was their first physical contact he could remember, and the feel of his father's *prana* through his being made him tremble. The general had always been a remote person, not given to displays of emotion, conveying his love by unfailingly doing his duty by his children. Prince Tikiri had never loved the man more. 'How can we unite Lanka, *tha*?' he inquired.

'Only by force of arms.'

'But the Great King is dedicated to the methods of Lord Buddha's Doctrine. He will not permit. . . .' Prince Tikiri stopped short before the fiery expression in his father's dark eyes.

'The Great King can continue being a *dharmista* ruler and acquiring merit for his next birth. Our highest loyalty to him must be manifested by doing whatever is necessary to unite the country for him, regardless of our own *kharma*.' His father paused. 'I shall send for you when the time is right,' he concluded. 'Meanwhile turn your endeavours towards becoming a commander.'

'Of course, *tha*. You will send for me within this year perhaps?'

The general shrugged. 'Who can tell when? All I know is that the day will surely come.' The bushy black eyebrows lifted, that quizzical smile Prince Tikiri liked so much touched the sides of the firm mouth. Their eyes met, glowing like twin lights from opposite doorways. At long last, he and his father had something tangible binding them. They nodded and, man to man, turned to resume their stroll.

'If the Portuguese get a foothold here, they will do more than give us two friars and an agent. They will use their religion to divide and their friars to fry us!' the general declared.

'Why should religions divide people, *tha*?' Prince Tikiri inquired. The person he liked best was a Catholic, after all. 'Don't they all teach people to be good?'

The general seemed about to give the answer, but changed his mind. 'You are a thinking person,' he responded. 'You have been taught the principles of all religions, so I want you to work out for yourself what a man's choice of religion reveals. That choice reflects his thinking, feeling self, his temperament, involving differences more basic than the race and language to which men are born. The Moorish religion, Islam, preaches an eye for an eye and a tooth for a tooth. Its followers call people of other faiths infidels and have no hesitation in slaughtering unbelievers. Judaism is the only means by which the Jewish people have been able to survive in a hostile, envious world. The Hindus believe in *dharma*, the duty of birth and office, so strongly that they would butcher anyone to fulfil that duty. The Catholic religion is meant to be one of love, yet many Catholics in power believe in one thing and practise another and their conduct towards people of other faiths has often been barbaric. All these religions are willing to use any means for religious ends, whatever the original teacher intended.'

'Isn't Lord Buddha's doctrine different?' Secretly Prince Tikiri believed that its insistence on non-violence had emasculated the Sinhala lions.

'Lord Buddha's teachings are unique. Buddhism is neither a religion nor a philosophy, nor even a way of life, but rather a manner of living. Highly individualistic, it requires Right Conduct, the means being all important for each person's salvation. You will be faced with a choice soon.' The general eyed his son squarely but with a hint of sadness and compassion. 'Do you take the sword or follow the Doctrine?' A sober note had entered his voice. 'Whichever you choose, I say, let it be to the ultimate degree, an *arahat* in the battle against the senses, or an invincible warrior in battle against men.'

'You know the course I must take in my life, *tha*,' Prince Tikiri responded quietly. He grinned impishly. 'Since you desire me to be invincible, I suppose I simply will have to be!'

19

PART ONE

The Dragon and the Knight

CHAPTER 1
Monday, 11 February 1521

Fernao directed his attention to the twin-muzzled culverin at the bows of the *Santa Caterina*, the gunners standing by, piles of cannon balls within easy reach. These deadly new weapons afforded a tremendous feeling of security, although he still felt some compassion for those who suffered a bombardment.

'Never forget that it was the need to mend the family fortunes that brought me to the Indies in the first place,' his father broke in. 'If birth is to be effective, it must be backed by wealth. Countries are no different. Portugal has twenty to fifty years more of trade monopoly in these waters before the sharks of Europe enter them. Even today, France, Spain and England would send their ships speeding here if only they knew the way!' He barked a short laugh at his jest. 'Venice, the Netherlands and our own Portugal are the richest nations in Europe because we have steered clear of political expansion and concentrated on trade.'

Fernao had heard that the crowned heads of Europe contemptuously referred to his own King Manuel as 'the grocer', because he traded in spices while they sought conquest.

'What about Holy Church, sir, and the conversion of the heathen?' he inquired. 'Aren't we here to spread the Gospel too?'

The admiral smiled cynically. 'Holy Church teaches the natives to kneel and close their eyes in prayer, the more easily to steal from them. No, my boy, the Church has become so corrupt that it has provoked opposition in its own ranks. The Reformation movement of that renegade friar, Martin Luther, will shake Holy Church to its foundations. Forget about Holy Church unless it can be used for financial gain.'

The facts hit Fernao in the pit of his stomach. What was he

doing here on this flagship? What else were they all here for, but money? If he had other gods, other ideals, why had he not jumped ship and somehow returned to Portugal? Here he was, at the threshold of his life, perverted to other causes because he had not possessed the courage to become a writer. His course was irreversible. At that moment, he grew up and became involved.

'You are a grown man now.' His father's words seemed to come from a distance. 'I have plans for you, arising from our visit to this country, which I shall reveal to you before the day ends, which make it important that you understand the true nature of your mission.' An unwonted kindly note entered the craggy voice. 'I could have given you a long lecture on honour and the Code of the Cavaleiro, but as your father, I have told you the truth instead, and as your admiral, I expect you to follow it. I'm sorry. I wish we lived in a different world.'

The stark truth flung at him without pretence caused the stirring of something more than respect and affection for his father within Fernao for the first time in years. Before he could even identify the feeling, however, the admiral turned round abruptly, as if embarrassed by his frankness, and directed his whole attention to the city.

Sensing that the period of waiting was over, Fernao followed the movement of the great blond head as it surveyed the scene once more. To the left of the foreground, due north, was the mud-brown of an estuary; then came a white sand beach fringed with green coconut palms. The arc of the harbour shoreline with its grey warehouses and wharves was in the centre, with a small headland fringed by black rock escarpments due south. In the middle distance behind the headland was a silver lake bordered by swamps, small white-washed houses with red Calicut tiled roofs clustering in dark green groves of trees surrounding it, a white bell-shaped *dagoba* beyond, its spire thrusting towards the blue sky. The heart of the city was in the centre middle distance. It consisted of brown bazaar streets flanked by buildings, a green mosque with a gold-painted minaret near the lake. Palanquins, wagons and carriages moved on the streets, along which masses of people were hurrying

23

towards the port in response to news of the arrival of the flotilla. And no wonder, Fernao thought, for Colombo has never seen anything like it. His eyes shifted to the background, left to right, a more distant view beginning to shimmer with the risen sun. A muddy river separated swamps from bright green deserts of ricefields, patched with shadowy oases of coconut palms, blue hills in the distance, an idyllic scene in a beautiful country.

The admiral's gaze moved back to the left foreground and settled on a green hill devoid of houses.

'H'mm!' His grunt was one of satisfaction. 'No sign of any real opposition other than those screaming natives on the wharf, so why not give ourselves a welcome and them a warning with more than a single shot across the bows! This country has never heard a cannon or musket fired. About time it came of age. Summon the gunnery officer.'

'Aye! Aye, sir!' Fernao stiffened in salute, touched his forelock. He ran forward, turned around and slipped lightly down the aft ladder to the main deck.

Officers and men gazed curiously after him as he sped past. He found Lieutenant Leopold Nantes seated on a pile of cannon balls by the twin fore culverins, chatting to two sailors while his gunners stood at their posts. Most of the master gunners in the Portuguese Navy were of Flemish, Dutch or German stock. Nantes was no exception. A roly-poly man, Flemish by birth, his shiny cheeks and artless smile hid one of the coolest, most deadly artillerymen in the world.

'These guns are the newest cocks,' Nantes was bragging. 'They can fuck up those buggers screaming on the wharves from long range. Their fourteen feet length gives them deadly accuracy. They are of 32 calibre. Since you bloody sailors are merely windmakers, let me tell you that's over five inches in girth. Imagine being fucked up your arse by one of these as you run away!' He grinned, picked up a cannon ball and fondled it lovingly. 'Look at this iron baby. It weighs seventeen pounds. Feel its power. We stick these balls down the muzzle of the cock to eject. A bombardment can shatter fortress gates or rampart walls. How's that for laughs!' He gave a great guffaw.

The sailors guffawed with him. They relished the Master

24

Gunner's salty language. Now they turned at Fernao's approach and their movement attracted Leopold Nantes' gaze.

'Ah, the admiral's whelp!' Nantes exclaimed. The cannon ball clattered as he dropped it back. He rose to his feet, gave an exaggerated salute, then grinned maliciously at Fernao's cold gaze. 'The whelp's not built like the sea monster,' he observed. 'But by the stigmata of Saint Francis he has the same cold fish eyes. Well, what can we do for you today, young sir?'

Secretly Fernao had found the Gunnery Officer's crude speech and blasphemous oaths amusing. He kept a straight face, however, as he stated shortly, 'You're to report at the double to the admiral on the poop deck.'

Nantes took off at a run. On the bridge, he came to attention in front of the admiral and gave his smartest salute. 'Lieutenant Leopold Nantes, chief gunnery officer, reporting as ordered, sir.'

Admiral de Albergaria eyed the man before him. 'I have an interesting assignment for you, lieutenant,' he finally declared. 'You shall signal the *Vera Cruz* and the *Flower-of-the-Sea*, on the extremes of our flanks, to fire two synchronized broadsides each from their starboard and larboard guns. They will fire into the shorelines, maximum range, directly south and north, close enough to the land not to damage any ships or boats, merely to break up rocks and create spectacular water-fountains. If those damned natives on the wharves don't heed the warning and take to their heels, a few rounds of direct fire will make them scurry!'

He must have observed the look of disappointment on the lieutenant's face for he half-smiled sympathetically. 'The time to pulverize Colombo may not be far away, lieutenant. Be patient. Meanwhile, as a test of your skill, I shall also give you a land target for a salute from your culverins.' He pointed with his left hand. 'Look background left about five hundred yards at the solitary hill feature just south of the estuary.' He waited for the gunnery officer's gaze to lock. 'At its centre is a small green grove. You will observe that it has no houses.' He noted the lieutenant's nod. 'It is part of the grounds of the port governor's mansion. Simultaneously with the second broadside, have each of the two fore culverins of the *Santa Caterina* fire a single shot

25

into that grove – a salute to the governor, shall we say?' He paused to ensure that Lieutenant Nantes had taken in what he said. 'You will have no opportunity to test for range or straddle, but it is essential that you hit your target without destroying property or taking human lives. We are ostensibly on a peaceful mission here, in furtherance of our treaty with the King of Lanka. I shall expect your first broadside in seven minutes, the second five minutes later.'

'Aye! Aye, sir!' The lieutenant saluted. 'Permission to retire.'

Signal flags began flapping from ship to ship. The clank and creak of wheels announced the movement of the culverins on their base plates for sighting their targets. Every move was carried out with clockwork precision. And why not? Most of these men had sailed the Indian Ocean together for over twelve years. A bloodthirsty bunch, delighting more in plunder than in trade, sea warfare was their chosen profession and they had proved themselves the best in the world at it.

'Let us hope the cannonades will enable us to land unopposed,' the admiral said over his shoulder.

'They don't seem to have a fort or any cannon ashore,' Fernao responded. 'Nor even a proper army. Just that rag-tag bunch of workers brandishing their outmoded weapons on the wharves.'

'They don't have a fort in this city.' Fernao was surprised at how much intelligence his father had gathered. The three *compadres* in the palace had done their work well! 'Once we complete our factory and build the fort, we can supply it by sea and be invincible.'

'Build a fort, sir? But that's not in the treaty.'

'In the modern world, treaties are interpreted by artillery and musket,' the admiral replied. 'As for right, the stronger force always prevails and what prevails eventually becomes what's right!'

How about the moral force of our sweet Lord Jesus, Fernao wondered, but with a strange objectivity, almost as if he were paying lip-service to a concept foreign, at that moment, to a mind seething before the prospect of a display of military might. Aloud he said, 'So that's why you directed us to carry building material and artillery in the holds.'

26

'Not to speak of a *terco*, a regiment of seven hundred fully trained infantrymen.' The admiral must have sensed some of Fernao's inner feelings for the first time in his life. He half-turned again towards his son, his hard features softening. 'You must realize that we are dealing with a bunch of barbaric brigands who would slit the throats of our civilian traders and rob us blind if they had half a chance.'

'Aren't the Sinhala supposed to be a civilized race of gentle disposition, sir, much given to honour during a recorded history going back over two thousand years?'

'Their history is galley garbage, spilled by their own monks. The Sinhala are supposed to be the lion race. Admittedly, they've grown decrepit with age, but there's still some spirit left in them. They could be formidable opponents if they would only unite. That's the trick of it, my boy. All these Eastern races are governed by the feuds of power-hungry families, as Europe used to be. Armed might and guile can certainly support us, but our best course is to exploit the existing divisions of the heathen so that we can rule their many millions with a few thousand soldiers.'

The thunderous roar of cannon firing their broadsides from either flank of the flotilla crashed into the conversation, blasting Fernao's eardrums, and tingles of burnt gunpowder soon overlaid the air.

CHAPTER 2
Monday, 11 February 1521

Standing at her bedroom window in the cottage she and her father occupied in the Jaya palace seven miles east of Colombo, Julietta de Brito did not see the early morning sunlight. Her father's words at breakfast had vividly brought back the past. What did the future hold? She was fourteen now. She had been only seven when she discovered, in the most cruel fashion, what was unusual about her.

Her father, a *fidalgo*, Duarte de Brito, had arrived at the port of Galle, about sixty miles from Jaya as the crows flew, in 1505, with Captain Lorenzo de Almeida. When the squadron left, Captain de Almeida had directed her father to remain behind as the trade representative of the Viceroy, promising to return soon. It had been weeks before the Sinhala conducted her father and two Catholic friars, Father Juan and Father Perez, to the court of the Great King in the Jaya palace where she was born two years later.

Even before she was born, her father had become a commercial advisor to the Great King of Lanka in his Jaya palace and therefore a respected member of the court. No one, not even her father, would speak about her mother, who died in childbirth. Julietta assumed that she had been from one of the few European families in the Indies, a *castico*. As she grew up, she refrained from asking her father questions because she had developed feelings of guilt after she came to learn how children are born. Had she somehow been responsible for her mother's death? So child though she was, she concentrated on doing her best to please her father, playing the role of the woman of the house in the Jaya palace grounds, with two Sinhala servants to look after all their needs.

She was thought to be pretty by everyone in the court. She had even received some paternal attention from the king, but her favourite was the handsome young Prince Tikiri Bandara, with whom she and other princes attended the court school, learning Latin and Portuguese from Father Juan, European history from Father Perez, Sinhala from the Venerable Buddhist *bhikku*, or monk, Narada, and mathematics from the Arab *imam* in whose country the science originated.

Her increasing popularity had excited the envy of Prince Tikiri's sister, the Princess Mala, who joined their classes in Sinhala whenever she visited the court.

One day seven years ago, following a lesson in which she had excelled and the Ven Narada had given her much praise, Mala insisted on accompanying her home. She remembered the noon hour, with the sun beating down fiercely from a burnt blue sky on the red flagstone walkway. Mala was fifteen at the time, a brown-skinned lump of a girl with strangely thin, sparse hair and a voice, sharp as an arecanut cutter, that matched her disposition.

'It is good that you are doing well in your studies, for you can become a Catholic nun some day,' Mala remarked, as they walked side by side.

'I shall not become a nun,' Julietta replied seriously. 'I shall meet a handsome prince and get married.'

'Ho! ho! ho! Listen to her.' Mala stopped in her stride, pointed a derisive finger at her. 'Who in Lanka would want to marry a *parangi*, let alone you? Do you know why we call you *parangi*?' A vicious note had entered her voice.

Innocently, Julietta shook her head.

'It's because your skin is white like the patches that Sinhala with the white leprosy disease have on their skin. You *parangi* are all tainted with the disease.'

'Not at all,' Julietta retorted hotly. 'Father Juan says that everyone in the European countries is white-skinned because of the climate.'

'You are stupid to believe the lie of another *parangi* who has the same disease. It is a filthy disease that the *devas* inflict on the accursed and all *parangi* are therefore tainted persons. Why, a decent Sinhala would not even spit on you, leave alone touch you.'

29

Tears sprang to Julietta's eyes. She brushed them aside. She would not allow this sinful person to get to her. A fierce rejoinder rose to her lips, then she remembered the teaching of Christ. She calmed down suddenly and said a silent prayer to the Virgin Mary for help. 'I am a Christian and I forgive your cruel lies,' she finally replied in gentle tones. 'Now, if you will excuse me, Mala, I must hasten home and attend to my duties.' She turned and took off at a run.

'You are not even a *parangi.*' The words reached her loud and clear, in silver tones scarred by rust. 'You are a *lunsia*, half-caste. Your mother was a Sinhala whore whom your father took to his house to appease his lust and whose brother killed her for giving birth to you!'

The words shattered the sunlight into fragments as Julietta ran on, but the hideous truth penetrated later, after she had questioned her father that night. Then her entire world shattered. She wondered why the Blessed Virgin had given her this tragedy instead of the succour she always sought. 'Holy Mary, mother of God. . . ' She must be a sinner.

Her father swore that her mother was no whore, but a Sinhala woman of lowly estate whom he had come to love. It was love alone that mattered to Christians. But Julietta already knew that the Sinhala despised people of mixed birth, though their kings encouraged foreigners to take local concubines. She would be an outcast in this society when she grew up. Gone were her dreams of a handsome prince. For a while, she blamed her father and hated him for it, but he was always so kind and gentle, seemed so much to need her in his loneliness that she could not sustain her resentment. Yet the grievous wound remained and deep within her a bitterness against life that sometimes manifested itself in withdrawal from her father. At those times the hurt look on his lean scholarly face made her fiercely glad, for which cruel streak she prayed to the Virgin Mother for forgiveness.

From then on, shame made her run home from school every day, caused her to avoid playing with other children. She could not know that those children who liked her took her attitude for racial superiority, fair skins being highly thought of in the

30

country. All she knew was that at times she felt like the lepers in the Holy Book who warned normal men, shouting 'Unclean! Unclean!' She threw herself into her studies and determined that she would indeed become a religious some day. She had no calling, but she had no alternative either.

It was then that Prince Tikiri began to give her more and more attention. She sometimes thought that he knew all.

The next year, Mala died of a disease that was said to have been the cause of her sparse hair, a disease as incurable as her spite. If only Mala had held her peace long enough. Why did she have to tell the truth and die? But Julietta was practical enough to realize that she would have learned the truth some day. She even came to be grateful to Mala for having brought it to her notice early enough for the pain to wear away, though the shame remained.

Prince Tikiri drew even closer to her after Mala's death. He made special efforts to be with her, showered her with little acts of kindness, gave her fruit and flowers, even presented her with a little brown and white puppy on her last birthday. Her favourite times came to be when he sat on her front doorstep, idly drawing patterns on the sand with a stick, telling her of his country's history, its anguish which he so keenly felt, and of his dreams.

Father Juan, the friar, befriended her, but in such a strange, condescending way that she believed he must despise her for being a *mestico*. Yet whenever he spoke of Portugal, it seemed a fairytale land to her, Lanka being her own reality.

This morning, all she looked forward to was meeting Prince Tikiri. At fourteen, she had faced up to the fact that she loved the prince, but her love was hopeless. Far from considering marriage to a foreigner, and a half-caste at that, Prince Tikiri merely needed her as a sister.

She sighed. Life was so difficult, she had best concentrate on the present. It was Prince Tikiri's sixteenth birthday so she must look especially pretty for him. She walked back to the looking glass on the dressing table in her tiny bedroom.

Her new blue pinafore dress, ordered for her by the Sinhala *duenna* of the court, fitted her slim figure to perfection.

Beneath the high white lace collar, her breasts were beginning to swell. That had begun after the bleeding last December, just when she and *o pai*, her father, were getting ready to celebrate a quiet Christmas. She had been shocked and horrified when it occurred, thinking the bleeding would never stop. She remembered the bloody bed-sheets and bandages with disgust. Even the assurances of Menika, the scrawny, grey-haired widow who cooked for the household and had been like a mother to her, had produced scant comfort.

Once again she had felt unclean, physically unclean this time. Menika had said that attaining womanhood was a proud event which the Sinhala celebrated, but she had only wanted to hide her new shame. Word got around, however, perhaps because Menika boasted about it, and people, especially men, started treating her with greater deference; but she had still not become accustomed to the cramps she experienced every month. 'Be glad to have them,' Menika advised her with a cackle. 'It's when you don't and you're not married that you have to worry!' She still didn't quite understand what Menika had meant.

She now inspected her face closely. It had developed a glow since she became a woman. Small and oval, with the complexion the Sinhala poets called *ran-thambili*, pink-gold king coconut, a very fair skin beneath which were the light brush strokes of a rose glow. Two tiny freckles on her right cheek enhanced a flawless complexion. Her eyes were wide aquamarines, shaped like almonds, her curly hair, already hanging beyond her tiny waist to the flaring hips, was of darkest auburn. She was tall for her age and would grow taller. Her father had told her that she took after his side of the family.

She knew she looked like a princess. She knew this from her father's book of paintings. At least she could always act like one, even if she never had her prince. The thought brought burning tears to her eyes. She fought them back.

Patting a wayward strand of glossy hair in place, she glanced briefly outside, took in the confirmation of a clear day. She would not need her palm umbrella. She turned to leave for school. As she stepped into the sunshine, she remembered her

32

father's final remark at breakfast that morning.

'Everything will change for us today,' he had stated. 'Especially for you. All to the good.'

'How, Father?' She had no hope for herself, though she asked.

'You'll see.' His mouth tightened in that withdrawn way which always made further questioning useless.

Monday, 11 February 1521

My father's words had me curious as to what attracts people to different religions, and thinking to start with a Catholic, I made my way through the Jaya palace to Father Juan's room. Built according to traditional Sinhala architecture and set in the midst of extensive gardens containing cottages for staff, the palace had a great open courtyard by the front entrance gates to serve the public, their vehicles and mounts, at the audience hall. Behind was a centre courtyard with four sets of residences, the king's and queen's quarters and the male and female quarters respectively, each with its own centre courtyard adorned by bathing pools and fountains in ornamental pleasure gardens. As palace guests the two Catholic friars had been allocated rooms not far from my rooms, but there were restrictions on the extent to which they could ply their religious trade.

I knocked on Father Juan's door and the familiar booming voice called out, 'Come in!'

The friar rose from a *prie-dieu* at the far end of his sitting room, placed before an altar above which was a silver crucifix. To the left a painting of a certain St Francis adorned the white plaster wall. Father Juan and Father Perez claimed to be of this saint's Order. The altar contained a blue and white statue of the Madonna before which two tapers burned, emitting a smell of wax. Father Juan smiled when he saw me standing at the entrance. He had a beautiful smile, pearly white teeth shining between the trim dark moustache and beard. He was a slim, small man, five and a half feet tall, with pointed features, his short dark hair shot with copper tints but with a circular bald patch at the back of the head which he called a tonsure and claimed to be a necessary symbol of belonging to an ecclesiastical order. Since the Buddhist *bhikkus* shave their heads completely as evidence of their rejection of life's vanities, I have concluded that Catholic friars shed only a patch of their vanity! Father Juan wore his usual white cassock with a braided black linen belt. His tanned skin contrasted sharply with large eyes of the palest yellow, the pupils so black and penetrating they could disconcert.

'Ah! Happy birthday! To what do I owe the pleasure of this visit, prince?' The friar spoke fluent Sinhala.

I gave him our traditional greeting, palms together held up to my chin as I would for a teacher. By Sinhala custom, I would have held them at forehead level for my parents, the *bhikkus* or the king and above the top of my head for Lord Buddha or the *devas*. 'Thank you, Father,' I stated. 'I would like to ask you some questions on religion before our classes start.'

The friar's eyes lit up. 'Sit down.' He indicated a wooden settee by the wall and drew up another for himself. The cooing of doves made me glance out of the open window to a peaceful morning scene. Green treetops blended into a clear blue sky. A fountain sparkled, its water splashing pleasantly.

'What do you wish to ask me, Prince?'

I came directly to the point. 'This is something I have to work out for myself, Father, but I would like some help from you. It seems to me that, while all religions teach men to be good, not to kill, rob or steal, to be truthful and fruitful, the most bitter conflicts in the world are not those of race or culture but those between people of different religions. Why should this be so?'

His yellow eyes quickened with interest. He was about to answer, but pulled back. The teacher came out. 'Let us examine your question together,' he suggested.

'That is what I too desire, to seek the answers myself.'

'Let us start at the beginning. What do the Christians say of creation?'

I was rather proud of my memory.

'In the beginning, God created the heaven and the earth. And the earth was without form and it was void; and darkness was upon the face of the deep. And the spirit of God moved the face of the waters. And God said, Let there be light. And there was light.'

34

'We Christians will not accept any other concept of creation.' His voice boomed out surprisingly harsh. 'We will not even hear or speak of other, heretical beliefs. There is only one God, our God, and only one way to salvation, through His Son, Jesus Christ.'

Surprised at his dogmatism, for he was usually the most open-minded of men, I had a glimmer of understanding as to just how deep religious conflicts can arise. But why was Father Juan unusually dogmatic today? 'Are you saying that you find it easy to accept a person of a different race, or colour, because there is no changing these things, of a different language because you can learn to speak it, but the one thing...'

'Precisely,' the friar interrupted. 'There can be no argument about the truth.'

Was that, I wondered, why the Muslims had shed so much blood? They believe in Allah, one God, like the Christians. They even acknowledge Jesus as one of the prophets. Why then had these two religions been so militantly opposed to each other? An answer struggled to surface in my mind, but I was not wise or deep enough to force it out. 'Have you studied the Hindu theory of creation, Father?' I inquired instead.

'I have no interest in it.'

I came to learn of this man, I thought. He has taught me the Bible and Christianity without attempting to convert me – he would never dare attempt that in our Buddhist court – but the first time I really ask him questions about other religions, I find him implacable. Twin streaks of cunning and devilishness moved me to quote the Rig-veda:

'*Darkness there was at first concealed in darkness: this all was infinite Chaos.*

'*All that existed then was void and formless: by the great power of warmth was born that unit.*

'With such a similarity of ideas as to creation, why must Christian and Hindu quarrel?' I inquired with apparent innocence.

He had flushed in anger, his thin lips tightening even before I finished speaking. 'I will not listen to such heresies,' he declared. 'It is a mortal sin. You came here to seek advice, not to utter iniquity.'

35

I was seeing a new Father Juan. It was obvious that he was releasing deep frustrations, long pent up. For the first time I realized how frustrating the past sixteen years must have been for this missionary priest. 'I am sorry, Father,' I apologized.

He smiled and relaxed. 'You must understand that it is indeed a mortal sin for me to listen to primitive, ungodly blasphemies,' he declared. 'The devil has spawned his creatures in Europe in modern times. A man named Martin Luther has even challenged the Church and now faces a Bill of Excommunication. Another apostle of the devil, named Erasmus, has published a New Testament. The forces of the anti-Christ have suddenly multiplied and must be destroyed. So, in our country, Portugal, we have begun what is called the Inquisition, which exposes the heretical beliefs of people, purges them by fire in a ceremony called *auto da fé* and seeks at least to fit them for Purgatory since they have no hope of reaching Heaven.'

Men have been conquered by fire and sword, but cleansed? And how could Father Juan claim his religion as the only means of salvation when he would not learn about other religions? Did his Inquisition fit the philosophy of Jesus Christ, who said that not one sparrow falls to the ground without God observing it and that when an enemy strikes you on one cheek, you should turn the other cheek?

My thoughts were interrupted by the faint rumble of distant thunder from the west. I glanced up. Sunshine still lay lightly on the air, upon the leaves and the grass. The patch of sky within my vision remained a perfect blue. Whence came the thunder? I noted Father Juan listening too, not curiously but intently.

Within five minutes another peal reverberated in the distance. A strange expression crossed Father Juan's face. It seemed almost like triumph.

Why, I wondered, should Father Juan rejoice to hear a storm approaching from the west?

36

CHAPTER 3
Monday, 11 February 1521

'The monsoon rains are not due for three months at least, Father,' I ventured. 'And there is not a cloud in the sky. Why then do the heavens rumble?'

The friar's features became a mask. 'What you hear is the thunder of man, not of the heavens, though man might well use it for God's work.' He paused, gave his old, sweet smile. 'Many cannon in unison have fired what we call broadsides. I . . . uh . . . guess they come from foreign warships in the port.'

Having heard of the destruction which the big projectiles called cannon had wrought in India, I could not restrain a quiver of anxiety. These weapons are rather like catapults, only incredibly more fearsome because they are thick metal tubes which hurl iron balls several hundred yards. Foreign cannon in Lanka!

My stomach churned. 'My father told me of the arrival of the ships. Does it mean we are being invaded?'

'I doubt it.' Again that secret smile. 'Since we have heard only two salvoes, they are probably salutes, one for the king of . . . er . . . the country to which they belong and one for the Great King of Lanka.'

We were interrupted by an urgent knocking at the door. Father Juan rose to his feet. 'Come in!' he called.

The door opened. An attendant, clad in the palace uniform, white pantaloons and red tunic, stood at the entrance. He bowed low, hands to forehead, then addressed me. 'Your father, General Prince Maya Dunne, desires you to join him in audience with the Great King.'

Was there a new respect in the man's eyes because he was addressing a prince about to have discussions with the sovereign? My alarm vanished before a feeling of elation. I glanced at Father Juan, hardly believing my good fortune.

37

The friar smiled encouragingly back. 'You have arrived at manhood, Prince,' he stated. 'I know you will accept your new estate with dignity.' He paused and a twinkle lit his eyes. 'Life always seems to thrust something ahead of your studies, Prince, does it not? Up to now it has been the martial arts. Now, it is obviously some affair of State that must certainly take priority over your books. You are excused attendance at our morning session.' He turned his gaze on the attendant. 'Why don't you leave now and inform the general that the prince is on his way to the Great King's audience chamber?'

'Yes, sir.' The man bowed again, closed the door behind him.

'Well, Prince, we did not exactly conclude our discussion on religion, did we?'

I was too excited even to think about it. 'I hope we can do it some other time, Father,' I responded, before remembering that there had been no discussion at all, merely Father Juan laying down the law.

The friar glided up to me, gripped me by the shoulders and stared at me with those pale yellow eyes, his gaze so intense that I felt like a small animal transfixed by a leopard. 'You have always shared your dreams with me, have you not, Prince?'

For the first time in the nine years I had known Father Juan, I felt uncomfortable. 'Yes, Father.' I turned my head to avoid the close personal contact and the friar's bad breath.

'You must always feel free to share your secrets with me, especially now that you have grown up. We of the Church are ever available to those who need counsel and succour, advice and spiritual upliftment. As you know, by decree of the Great King, we are forbidden to convert our pupils to the Catholic faith, only to teach them the religion, but several hundred of your fellow countrymen have voluntarily accepted Our Lord and we say Mass and conduct our services regularly in the community hall of the Jaya village.' His grip tightened. 'Father Perez and I feel that we are bringing light to the darkness of many lives. Soon, we hope to have our own church building and we shall make it a most magnificent structure, worthy of Our Lord. You are undoubtedly approaching a position of responsibility in this kingdom, Prince, so before you leave promise me one thing.'

By this time, I was ready to promise anything if only I could get away without being rude. 'Certainly, Father.'

'Come and share with me this opening at long last of your future.' His voice deepened with earnestness. 'I am so happy for you, I want you to tell me all that you discuss with the Great King.'

'Of course, Father,' I replied without thinking. A noisy chirping made me glance towards the open window. A single black and white magpie was perched on the sill, cocking his head sideways to peek inside. A single magpie is a bad omen. Having delivered its message, the bird flew away.

Father Juan shook me once to obtain my attention. 'You will share every detail with me? I want to be a part of the glorious future that awaits you, Prince. I don't believe in astrology. My faith in you is based upon knowledge. I know what lies ahead.' His eyes crinkled in a smile; the intense look had left them. 'There now, you have the confession of one whose whole life must be spent sharing, not achieving.'

'I'll be glad to tell you all that takes place,' I replied, eager to get away. 'And I do appreciate your interest and faith in me, Father.'

'Good.' He released me, made the sign of the cross over my forehead, then leaned forward and kissed me on the top of my head in benediction. I was amazed, for it was the closest that anyone had been to me physically. I felt an access of affection for the friar in spite of his offensive breath.

Perceiving my feelings, not the revulsion, he smiled broadly. 'You'd better hurry,' he urged. 'Go with God.'

I gave him salutation and hastened down the open corridor, which led into the front verandah of the audience hall, trying to produce the right combination of speed and the decorum expected of princes who do not run in public, except, I supposed, when fleeing from defeat in battle! There was an inner tension in the saluting attendants and sentries I passed, especially in the courtiers who gave me friendly greeting. My cousin, Prince Vidiye, who had just married the daughter of my father's oldest brother, Prince Bhuvaneka, emerged from the audience hall. He was a huge man with enormous, staring black eyes in a heavy face. A terrific warrior, at twenty-six he was already an army corps commander. Dressed in dark blue pantaloons and gold tunic, his gangling, loose-limbed frame prevented him from looking smart and soldier-like.

The prince blocked my way. 'Where are you going in all this hurry? To wage a one-man war against the invader?' He threw back his head and a deep belly laugh emerged from him. 'Let me at least wish you a *subha* birthday.' His smile beneath the great, black moustache somehow lacked sincerity.

'Thank you, cousin,' I replied. 'I'll talk to you later.' I could not resist the urge to brag. 'I'm already late for an audience with the Great King.'

'Oho! He's reached manhood today and already the Great King waits for him,' Prince Vidiye told his companion, a lantern-jawed captain, whose name I could not recall. 'We must not detain His Approaching Majesty.' He gave an exaggerated salute, stood aside, and with a mocking grin, waved me on.

The hum of excited voices within the audience hall reached me. A guard captain saluted. I was indeed expected.

I entered the audience hall, glanced briefly up towards the tiled roof, perhaps twenty *ratana* tall, then walked between the great soaring columns of brown teakwood intricately carved at the cornices, marching in orderly rows like lines of soldiers on parade, my sandals clacking on the floors of white mountain crystal.

It was a glittering scene. The hall was crowded with courtiers, talking to each other in low voices. I could tell their concern. Most were dressed in brocaded tunics and pantaloons of shiny red, blue, green, or gold, with white satin here and there marking the more elegant. Jewels sparkled on tunics, sword hilts and curving shoes. How would these peacocks face battle?

On a platform at the far end of the hall, I caught the gleam of the golden Lion Throne of the Kings of Lanka, the arms and head-rest studded with gems, surmounted by the white silk, gold-tasselled Umbrella of State. On a gold table at the right of the throne were the Royal Sword, its scabbard gold, the hilt set with precious stones, the golden Sceptre and Crown, sparkling with the *navaratna*, the nine gems, red rubies, blue sapphires, green emeralds, purple amethyst, brown tourmaline, yellow topaz, pale aquamarines, cat's eyes and flashing white *diamanthi*. In front of the throne was the royal footstool, also of gold, upholstered in crimson velvet which had been a gift from the Portuguese naval captain who visited the port of Galle in 1505. It was my father, the aristocrat, who advised the Great King to use the velvet for this piece of furniture, so that he could symbolically place his royal feet upon the offering of the powerful *parangi*!

Several of the courtiers nodded to me as I was led past them, but most were too engrossed in their discussions to notice me as we passed through a door at the left rear of the platform and headed for the audience chamber.

The captain knocked and was bidden to enter. The door opened to a small room, with high grilled windows revealing the blue sky beyond. As I entered, the rich, strong scent of sandalwood incense assailed my nostrils.

Looking very calm, the Great King was seated on a carved black ebony chair at the far end of the room, behind a small ebony desk, matching the floors of black and white mountain crystal. The walls of the chamber, painted a creamy colour, were adorned with dark brown, red, yellow and orange tapestries of Buddhist *bhikkus* and nuns.

A moon-faced man of over seventy, the Great King was dressed soberly in white tunic and pantaloons. His bald head and benign expression made him look rather like Lord Buddha. He had never married and was held to be a *dharmista*, a just ruler dedicated to the Doctrine.

Appropriately enough, to his right was an altar lined with red satin on which was placed a gold image of Lord Buddha seated in the lotus pose. In front of the image were several incense holders of brass, pale grey smoke curling up from the glowing joss sticks placed in them. At the king's left, three men were seated on ebony settees. The brother of the Great King, my grandfather, Prince Wijayo, a well-built, silver-haired man, with the fine features of the family, his face unlined though he was well over sixty, sat immediately next to the Great King. Next to him, my father's older brother, the daring Prince Raigam, small and slender, with lean features, wore his customary devil-may-

41

care expression. Beside him sat my father, very relaxed, knees slightly apart, right leg slightly outstretched, left leg drawn in. My father's oldest brother, Prince Bhuvaneka, was conspicuous by his absence. No loss, I thought, for he is a weak man, cunning and ambitious.

A sudden silence fell on the room when the guard captain made obeisance and announced me. Four pairs of eyes were turned in my direction. With no other movement or speech, the effect was that of a mime play.

When I rose from making obeisance, I could feel the Great King's large, dark eyes boring into me, though my own gaze was fixed beneath the level of his head, as was the custom.

'Come in, Prince,' the Great King commanded. He motioned with the back of his hand for the captain to retire. 'Stand there and let us get a closer look at the new man in our Court.' He nodded to a position across from his desk.

It is frightening for a boy to be standing in the presence of any king, still less to be the subject of the ruler's close scrutiny. I felt the sweat breaking out.

'Look us directly in the eye,' the Great King commanded.

I stuck courage into apprehensive guts and raised my eyes to meet the Great King's penetrating gaze. It seemed to pierce my every veil so that I wished I could look away. As the long seconds passed, a thudding began in my ears, my throat ran dry and the air before me started to quiver. I am my father's son, I told myself desperately and I quail before no man. I held the Great King's scrutiny boldly.

'You have bred an unusual cub.' The King softly addressed my father. 'The blessed gift of the inner sight tells us that he will fulfil the prophecies.' He sighed unaccountably and gestured with his hand. 'You may stand there beside your father, Prince, and listen to our deliberations on this momentous occasion, as a birthday token.'

'Thank you, Sire,' I murmured hoarsely and backed away to stand beside my father.

'Oh and by the way, we have another small token of our affection for your father and you,' the Great King proceeded, his eyes brightening. 'He is called Rama. You know him, we understand. He is your very own charge henceforth, Prince.'

My heart leapt. Rama was a black Scindhi thoroughbred in the royal stables. Just four years old, he was already seventeen hands tall, of lithe muscle, especially in the rear haunches, glossy coat, proud tail carriage and smooth movement. He would be a great war-horse soon. I fell to my knees in obeisance. 'Sire, I am your humble, obedient, most grateful servant!' I exclaimed earnestly. 'I shall serve you unto death, if need be.' I rose to my feet again, eyes shining.

'Serve us unto life instead, riding your noble steed to glory,' the Great King suggested, that amused glint again in his eyes. 'Well, my lords, now that the bright sentiments have been expressed, let us get down to dark reality. We have already discussed the arrival of the seventeen *parangi* ships and you have had time to think. What do you all advise as to the possible intentions of the *parangi*? Prince Wijayo?'

'I think the *p-parangi* p-plan an invasion, Sire.' My grand-father's stutter had become more pronounced in recent years. 'They would not c-come in such strength merely for t-trade. We should conciliate them. We d-do not have cannon and muskets, so their d-display is p-probably meant to impress and intimidate.'

'And you?' the Great King's eyes slid towards Prince Raigam.

'We may be impressed but we are not intimidated.' Prince Raigam, a man of few words, spoke quietly. 'If the *parangi* come in peace, we shall receive them in peace. If they attempt invasion, we shall fight.'

'As good Buddhists we should avoid bloodshed and try to do good,' the Great King responded. 'And what does our general say?'

'We should first determine the intentions of the *parangi*,' my father counselled gravely. 'I understand their seventeen ships are heavily armed with cannon and laden with fighting troops. If their intent is military, we cannot oppose a landing. I doubt that such is their plan, however, since they would otherwise have sailed in with all guns firing, as they did at Kilwa and Cannanore many years ago. If we do have to fight, it cannot be within range of their ships' cannon. Let us await their move and act

43

accordingly. I have, however, placed the army on full alert. We have twenty thousand men ready for action.'

'Our palace and fort are so c-close to the p-port of Colombo', Prince Wijayo grumbled. 'If you will recall, Sire, I advised several years ago against the m-move to Jaya.' He stared pointedly at my father who had sided with the Great King in that decision. 'The m-move has m-made us vulnerable.'

'Such moves do not make us vulnerable,' the general snapped back. 'Only disunity and lack of courage can do that.' An unusually harsh note entered his voice, though he was speaking to his own father. 'Besides, we can hardly repel an armed invasion today by reverting to the advice you gave years ago.'

'Enough, gentlemen,' the Great King commanded with gentle sternness. 'General Prince Maya Dunne is right on all counts. We direct the three of you to leave for the port immediately and assess the situation. You had best travel without escort so as not to give the impression of armed response. Besides, the people must not be agitated any more than necessary. Already they quote traders from India as saying that the *parangi* wear jackets and hats of iron, rest not a minute, and are supposed to eat hunks of stone and drink blood.' His smile was cynical but kindly. 'Presumably some kinds of bread and wine. More importantly, the sound of their cannon is said to be louder than thunder when it bursts upon the Yugandhara rock. These weapons fire great balls of iron that travel many *gawwa* and can shatter fortress gates and pulverize ramparts. Our instincts tell us, however, that our visitors mean no harm, for they value trade above conquest.' Again that cynical smile touched the sides of his mouth. 'Go now and report back to us before nightfall.'

'Should we not take one or all of the p-palace *p-parangi* to act as f-friendly emissaries or at least as interpreters?' Prince Wijayo inquired.

'We think not,' the Great King replied unhesitatingly. 'They may be more useful here as hostages.' What he had abandoned on the field he had obviously compensated for in cunning. 'General Prince Maya Dunne, you shall take your whelp with you on this mission. He has learned the *parangi* language from

44

the friars for over five years now, so you can use him as an interpreter if you meet the inv...the visitors.' His face had become bland and unconcerned.

CHAPTER 4
Monday, 11 February 1521

The royal school was a low brick building in the Jaya palace grounds, with open verandahs and half-walls on all sides. It had four classrooms, in the centre of which was a fully enclosed common room for the teachers, including Father Juan, Venerable Narada the Buddhist *bhikku*, the Muslim *imam*, Mohideen and Father Perez. Julietta had always thought it a pretty building with its lime-plastered walls hidden by yellow oleander, and a red-tiled roof, set in the shade of tall flame trees whose blossoms scattered the green lawns.

Apart from Julietta, the school had about thirty princes and princesses as pupils, varying in age from six to sixteen. The classrooms were assigned broadly to each of four age groups, the youngest group being from six to eight years, the oldest being from twelve to sixteen. The teachers rotated between classes, hourly, from nine in the morning till noon, when the younger pupils ended the day's work, while the older boys went on to the military schools after the noon meal, except on Saturdays when European history was taught by Father Perez in the schoolroom. Only the Venerable Narada ended his teaching day at eleven o'clock, so as to finish *dana*, the single meal that *bhikkus* eat daily, before noon.

Prince Tikiri was always so punctual at school that Julietta was disappointed and a little hurt when he was not in the classroom ahead of time that morning, to have his usual chat with her. She found their daily talks all too brief, but today was very special because it was the prince's birthday and she had brought him a present of a painting she had done on canvas. She couldn't wait to unroll it for him. She also wanted the prince to see her new dress.

She had heard from her servant, Menika, that the prince's father had arrived in the palace the previous night, so perhaps he was detained by the general. Menika knew such things because a palace is a hot-bed of gossip, where few comings and goings pass unnoticed. Julietta thought with a blush of the crude statement that a man can pass wind in the east wing and people will be laughing about it in the west wing before the sound reached there!

Then Father Juan, who took the first session, announced importantly that Prince Tikiri would not be attending school that morning because he had been summoned to an audience with the Great King. Julietta's heart sank and her eyes prickled with tears for the second time that day. She would be sweaty and dishevelled by the time the prince saw her. Supposing she never saw him today? The thought made her throat tighten, but it also produced the determination that she would see him somehow, even if it meant invading the male quarter of the palace. She offered a silent plea to Sweet Jesus and the Blessed Virgin to help her.

'Julietta, I asked you a question.' Father Juan's voice intruded upon her prayer.

She rose to her feet. 'I am sorry, Father,' she apologized. 'I was not listening. Please forgive me and repeat the question.'

Father Juan's pale yellow eyes flashed and he stuck both thumbs inside the black cord belt of his white cassock as he was wont to do when he was put out. 'Inattention is the greatest . . .' he began, then paused. 'You look specially beautiful today, Julietta,' he observed. 'Your blue dress reminds me of one I saw in the Lisbon palace years ago. Who gave it to you?'

'The *duenna* had it made for me, Father.'

'How did she know to make the pattern?'

'I gave her a painting from one of my *o pai*'s manuscripts.'

'It certainly becomes you. Is there any reason why you should wear such a beautiful dress to school? It is more fitting for a ball, if you were grown up enough to attend one.'

Julietta felt the blood mantling her cheeks. She blushed easily. 'N-no reason, Father . . . except that I think it is pretty.'

The pimple-faced Princess Devi tittered, to be quelled by a stern look from Father Juan. 'This is not a *nadagam*, theatre, Princess,' he admonished in prim tones. 'It is a schoolroom.

47

You are not permitted to titter or smile. You must learn deportment as well as language in my class.'

The princess relapsed into a sulky silence.

'Well, Julietta, you are growing up to be a young lady of great beauty. You should use your talents for the greatest good.' His pale yellow eyes became so hypnotic that it caused a spurt of alarm in Julietta. 'I want to see you privately when we close at noon.' He smiled through his beard. 'Now to the question you did not hear because your thoughts were elsewhere.'

His look told Julietta he knew where they had been and she became embarrassed and confused. All she could do was to stammer, 'Y-yes, Father.'

'I have more than one question for you. First, what is *auto da fé?*'

'It is the Act of Faith in Europe, whereby Jews and other heretics are burned to death or made to undergo some other public condemnation.'

'Good. You see how easy it is when you pay attention. All right. What is a *cartaz?*'

'A licence issued by the King of Portugal to permit a ship to sail the seas and trade.'

'Excellent. One final question. What is *limpeza de sangue?*'

Had a merciless look flashed at the back of those yellow eyes? Oh cruel friar, why should you ask me of all people this question? She knew there had to be a reason, but could not fathom it. 'Purity of blood from a religious and racial standpoint,' she replied hoarsely. And knew that her classmates were eyeing her with scorn and amusement.

'Precisely,' Father Juan said. 'You have done well indeed, Julietta.'

Julietta passed the rest of the morning in a daze. She tried hard to pay attention lest she be admonished again, but her eye kept darting towards the flagstone pathway along which Prince Tikiri would come. All she saw was white-gold sunlight, black mynahs and grey doves flying from tree to tree, two gardeners sweeping the lawn with long *ekel*-brooms made of the spines of coconut leaves. Scrape, scrape, the brooms went, to the scrape of the misery inside her. When the yellow-robed *bhikku* emerged to walk away from the schoolrooms, he seemed a lonely figure, as lonely as she felt.

Father Juan had the whole morning session with them that day, but he did not ask her any more questions. He finished a few minutes early and the students stood up respectfully to bid him farewell. 'Thank you for the lesson, Father,' they said in unison, as he had taught them.

'Thank you for your attendance, my children.' Father Juan made the sign of the cross over them.

'Wait for me, Julietta,' he commanded. 'I shall walk home with you.'

Both Catholic priests had a habit of pacing rather than walking. *O pai* told her this came from their years in the cloisters of seminaries, meditating or debating. Julietta felt as much frustrated by the slow pace as by the friar's presence. She had hoped to spend the meal hour seeking out Prince Tikiri in the palace.

'What is that scroll, my child?' Father Juan inquired gently.

Julietta blushed to the roots of her auburn hair. 'It's . . . it's, nothing, Father.'

'A very tangible nothing,' Father Juan commented drily. He glanced sideways at her. 'I venture to suggest it's one of your paintings?' He looked away, but his deep voice had given the last word the inflection of a question that brooked an answer.

'Y-yes, Father.'

'You are a good painter. It is a talent that comes from a sensitive, artistic spirit.' He glanced at her again. 'Why did you not show us the painting this morning?'

Julietta had no reply. She merely stared at the path, her mind spinning, her heart heavy.

'Aren't you going to share it with me at least? Why don't you unroll it?' He paused in his stride and faced her.

Something broke within Julietta. She liked, respected and even feared the friar, but this painting had been a labour of love for her prince and he had to see it first. She clutched the scroll fiercely to her breast and all feeling fled, other than the need to protect what she had done for the boy in her life. 'No, Father, I'd rather not.' Then, as her courage mounted, 'I painted this for

49

Prince Tikiri, especially for his birthday. He has to see it first.'
She awaited Father Juan's outburst.

The friar's laugh rang out instead. 'Ah! You are romantic and sentimental too, I see.' He nodded his head. 'Good. Very good.' He reached out a hand to grip her shoulder. 'You are in love with the prince?'

Julietta looked him squarely in the face. 'Yes, Father,' she replied and suddenly felt a great sense of release.

'Is the prince in love with you?'

'I don't know, Father. We have never spoken of it.'

A look of pity briefly crossed the friar's eyes. 'A hopeless love?'

She could not hold back the sobs that jerked out of her. He reached out and held her then. He smelled of sandalwood lotion and stale underwear. His breath was bad, but the feel of him was comforting. No man, not even her father, had held her before.

'My poor child,' he said. 'How my heart goes out to you. I too knew such a love once . . . a long time ago . . . in Lisbon . . . before I entered the seminary. So I understand what you are undergoing, because I too was far beneath the lady, a princess of the royal blood.' He released her, held her by the arms, his eyes searching every contour of her face.

With the instinct of a woman, she knew he was searching for his lost love. She began to see Father Juan in a new light, as a human being capable of love. It made her feel a warm empathy towards him. We are one in our hopelessness, she thought. 'Was she beautiful, Father?' The words were a whisper.

A gentle wind rustled the branches overhead, shimmering the dapple of sunlight and shadow that lay on the path. 'As a cool mountain breeze on a warm night,' the friar responded. He sighed. His eyes drifted past her, looking back through time. 'She even wore a blue dress such as yours one day.' He pulled himself together abruptly, his deep voice became strong again. 'But such thoughts are sinful, for every moment of my being is now dedicated to God. Even that sad past has but strengthened me for His work.'

Hot tears prickled her eyes and she brushed them away with

the back of her hand. 'I'm sorry, Father, but I'm glad you told me.'

'It was God's will that I tell you, my child. I believe that one reason why He inflicted the loss on me long ago was in order that you and I can better understand each other today and dedicate ourselves to His work.'

'How can I do that, Father? I am but a single girl, a half-caste by birth, an outcast of the people around me.' She could not keep the bitter note from her voice. 'I was fourteen years old last October, an age by which most of the maidens of the Jaya palace are betrothed and many a peasant girl in Portugal has, I understand, consorted with a man.'

His grip on her arms tightened and he shook her once, earnestly. 'Don't you see that it makes you special, Julietta? Instead of bemoaning your fate, rejoice in your estate.'

She looked at him in wonderment. 'How may that be, Father?'

He released her arms. 'Do you not remember that the Blessed Mother was a virgin? Have you ever thought how she must have been reviled by her fellow man, what doubts they must have cast upon her chastity when she conceived Our Lord before knowing her husband, Joseph?'

'No, Father,' she whispered. Now it was her turn to stare beyond him into the past, but she was penetrating the centuries, understanding, accepting, not rejecting. When she looked at him, it was with determination. 'You are right. I have been blind to God's purpose. You are his emissary on earth. What does he require of me?'

She listened silently, but with growing surprise, barely aware of the golden sunlight, while Father Juan told her of the sad state of the new Catholic Church in Lanka, of heathen doctrines that blasphemed God's word, of the devil's representative, the Great King, who had forbidden direct conversions. She had never dreamed that the usually calm, imperturbable priest had feelings that were so deep and yes, so bitter.

'These are the acts of heretics.' His voice was kept deliberately low, but its intensity was the more disturbing in consequence. 'Father Perez and I, of the True Faith, have waited long for the day of Our Lord. I believe it has arrived at last and I

51

am glad you are ready for His work. Do you know why I asked you those questions in class?'

Julietta shook her head.

'*Cartaz* is more than a licence to sail the seas and trade in them. Its significance is that it derives from the authority of a Christian King, to whom God has given that authority. I believe that *cartaz* implies God's mandate, given to *our* King in Portugal that the Catholic faith be established throughout the world. Do you understand?'

Julietta thought it best to nod, though she had not quite grasped the friar's meaning.

'The other question was the meaning of *auto da fé*. You have to be a fit vessel for Our Lord's guidance. The process of cleansing you began when I asked that third question, for it is only by the recognition of the blood within you, by an acceptance of your God-given estate, and through the confessional, that you can be cleansed and prepared for your life's work.'

A silent voice within her warned that this might be some trap of life, but she was swept away by the friar's intensity.

'What would you have me do, Father?' she inquired humbly.

He lowered his voice and told her.

Monday, 11 February 1521

Following our audience with the Great King, it was agreed that, in order not to show any signs of alarm, we would depart leisurely together on horseback shortly after the noon meal. The timing well suits my grandfather, who is a *buth-billa*, a rice lover, I thought, as I hastened towards the schoolroom, hoping to catch Julietta. He would rather have a meal in the palace than the sort that would be served at the little inns in the tradesmen's quarter of Colombo. Then I became so engrossed with reflecting on Julietta that I barely identified the people I passed.

When I first saw her, young as I was then, I had a strange sense of knowing her, but I was also smitten by her beauty. Not even my sister, Padma, was so fair, or so bright. Those sparkling aquamarine eyes reminded me of the sunlight glancing off the shallow seas of the east coast. There was something different about her too, the way she held herself, the way she walked, that set her apart from the other girls in the school. I would steal glances at her whenever I could without being observed. I soon discovered that she was also very game and even matched some of the princes at sports. She became the only person in the world with whom I had any real personal conversation.

There came the day when Mala was so cruel to Julietta and bragged about it afterwards. 'I made the *lunsia* think', she informed us with malicious glee and I felt revolted, ashamed and sad for Julietta. I had never accepted the snobberies of the court, the belief that distinctions of birth and caste are 'essential to preserve the structure of our society', as a nobleman once told me. From my earliest years, I had observed and experienced true nobility from the humblest of servants and witnessed uncouthness and vulgarity even from those of royal blood. Besides, my father's soldiers were all of different castes and we were all equals. I believe it is only weak men who need to fall back on birth for their standing.

Realizing that my fellow princes and princesses looked down upon Julietta, I felt an overwhelming desire to protect her, the more so because she had begun to avoid contact with everyone, like the lepers in the Holy Bible, and hastened home after school every day. At first, she did not respond to my overtures, but I persisted and before long we became friends. I knew from the start that I felt more than friendship for her, but what it was I could not identify. It made me wonder whether I had known her in previous births. After Mala died, Julietta became more comforting and thoughtful towards me. I found myself thinking of her frequently and in my imagining, especially before I fell asleep, I would conjure up incidents where she was in danger and I would ride to her rescue.

Once Julietta became a woman, the proprieties would normally have decreed that our friendship cease, but no one dared oppose a prince of the royal blood, so our communion continued, only I now felt a new and different kind of attraction towards her in addition. This was more physical, the desire to reach out and touch her, moments of drawing hidden magnetism from her body and wondering what it would be like to hold her. I was still a virgin, though being big for my years this was not through lack of covert offers from some ladies of the court. My sexual adventures were therefore confined to encounters with myself and to my dreams, most of which were of sensation and ended with my awakening in disgust at the wet and the smell of raw emission. Yet I never thought of Julietta sexually, only loved it when our eyes locked so sweetly, and some magic would pass between us before we both looked away, happily embarrassed, she blushing like the rosy skies of eventide.

The sun was warm overhead. As I absently greeted a gardener weeding a bed of giant red cannas, I remembered a love story of antiquity. Prince Saliya, the only son of my hero, King Abhaya Gamini, whose winds of Sinhala had united Lanka seventeen hundred years ago, had seen Asoka Mala, a maiden of the Chandala, the lowliest caste, in the palace gardens and fallen in love with her. Though he incurred his father's wrath and banishment, he gave up the succession to wed her.

I determinedly thrust the recall aside. I was not Prince Saliya, but a reincarnation of his father, with a destiny to fulfil that went beyond my own life to the lives of millions of Sinhala and the future of the kingdom for generations. I would win the succession and place myself in such a strong position that the people would have to accept Julietta as my queen. Such a simple solution, it seemed in my youthful ignorance. I strode on with a springier step.

I saw Julietta and Father Juan engaged in earnest conversation and it reminded me of my promise to tell the friar what transpired during my audience with the Great King. I would speak to the friar later and be noncommittal with my information. Now, wanting to avoid him, I cut across the lawn, doubled behind the schoolhouse and made towards Julietta's house to intercept her when she finished with Father Juan. A hedge of red hibiscus screened me from view.

Within minutes, Julietta came down the path, looking very serious. I jumped out, saying 'Hoi!'

A gasp escaped her. Her eyes widened. 'Oh Prince Tiki-tiki!' The pet name was one she gave me long ago. 'You frightened me.'

'You should only be frightened of *avatars*.'

'You haunt me all the time.' The words escaped her without thought and I felt my heart dilate with joy. 'I thought I was not going to see you today of all days and I was miserable.'

'Would you have pouted?'

'And stamped my foot too!'

'Then you are being yourself!' We laughed together. I noticed her dress. 'What a pretty dress you are wearing. It makes you look like a princess in the paintings you showed me.'

Her face turned rosy pink, stirring me. She swung around graceful as a dancer, the blue skirt flaring. 'See, I had it made specially for your birthday.'

My heart was full. 'Oh, Julietta.'

'And I also brought you a present.' She proffered a scroll.

I opened it and sunlight fell on a knight riding a black horse. The rider was clad in the garments of Julietta's country, his sword drawn to slay a dragon. He was rescuing a lady in a dress exactly like the one Julietta was wearing. I took in the picture, capturing every detail. These were the images of my dreams, but my heart sank. The prince must be a *parangi*.

'Do you like it?'

'Yes, yes, I do.' Then, anxiously, 'Who is the maiden?'

'Guess.'

'It's you.'

'Of course.'

I hesitated, love making me diffident. But the need to know caused me to plunge on, fearful that the knight might be someone else. 'And the man?' I tried to sound casual, but my heart stopped beating for her reply.

Her brown eyebrows arched in surprise. 'Why you, of course, dear Prince Tiki-tiki. Who else could it be?'

Now I could hear my heart pounding. 'I love you, Julietta!' I exclaimed involuntarily.

A little cry escaped her. The beautiful eyes widened, then shone with joy. 'I love you, my prince.'

I dropped the painting to hold her, not caring whether we were observed. Her hair smelled of sweet sandalwood, her soft body sent fire through me. A gentle thigh touched mine and I felt my organ fill and start to rise. My mind awhirl, my body aflame, not knowing what to say or do, I kissed her head. She turned her face upwards, her eyes wide, sparkling like the blue waters of the palace pools. I kissed her soft cheeks, drawing my breath in. She returned the kisses on both my cheeks. Her breath quickened, started to come from somewhere deep inside her, smelling fragrantly of the *valmi* root. My organ was so fully erect now it hurt. My body cried for more. I went wild and started to fumble at her.

The whinny of a horse from the distant stables streaked into my blurred consciousness, intruding through the mist of my desire. I was due to ride to Colombo soon.

I released Julietta, pulled away, picked up the painting. It tore my heart to see the disappointment in her eyes, their whites reddening with tears.

'I have to leave on a mission with my father,' I explained quickly. 'I cannot keep him waiting. I shall return tonight and see you tomorrow at school.' I paused, reached out and touched her cheek. It was soft and smooth as a rose petal. 'Be here for me. I am yours and you are mine now!'

'Of course I shall be, Prince. Go with God.'

My heart bade me remain with her, but some stronger, deeper compulsion pulled my feet away.

CHAPTER 5
Monday, 11 February 1521

The wharves had cleared as if by magic as soon as the broadsides were fired, with people scuttling for cover, the crowds pouring into the port back-tracking in hurried flight.

The admiral directed Fernao to summon Captain Juan Oliveira, a big, burly naval officer whom an attack of cholera in boyhood had rendered completely bald. The captain had anticipated the summons and was standing by on the fore-deck. He strode forward eagerly, ahead of Fernao, and listened impassively to the orders for him to lead a landing party of fifty men ashore. As he listened to his father, Fernao concluded that the admiral must have had complete information as to what military opposition, if any, could be expected, long before they set sail from Calicut. He had a shrewd idea as to one of the sources.

'Get your corselet and helmet,' the admiral directed Fernao, after the captain departed. 'You shall accompany Captain Oliveira ashore. It will be a good experience for you. Besides, your knowledge of the Sinhala language may come in useful if you meet someone in authority.'

Someone in authority? More likely a hail of spears and arrows that don't speak the Sinhala language, Fernao reflected as he hurried below decks to his cabin.

The wharves were still empty, the city streets deserted, when he returned to the poop deck, but the sense of unseen people watching from the shelter of the warehouses made his skin prickle.

Led by Captain Oliviera, the party of fifty men started going down the ship's ladder. Neatly dressed in blue and red uniforms, bandoliers across their chests, muskets in hand, they moved with such precision and practised ease that Fernao felt a thrill of pride at being a part of them.

He glanced at his father. The admiral stood on the bridge in his characteristic pose. He was sweating in the fierce noonday sun but gave no evidence of discomfort. Fernao was sweating even more profusely in his leather mail, the iron helmet uncomfortable on his head.

It was time to leave. The admiral returned his salute formally. He was not going to treat his son in any special way on such an occasion. Fernao clambered down the poop-deck ladder. Captain Oliveira was on the main deck counting the heads of his men who were climbing down the two ship's ladders in single file. He raised thin black eyebrows when Fernao marched up to him, halted and saluted.

'Sir, the admiral has directed me to accompany you ashore.'

The captain returned his salute smartly. 'For what purpose?' His sharp blue eyes conveyed that he did not care for interference.

Fernao thought quickly. 'I don't know, sir, but I expect it is because he thinks I can learn more from you than by remaining on the flagship.'

An expression of surprise shot through Oliveira's face, then the sides of his eyes crinkled in a slow smile. 'Crafty little bugger, aren't you? For that smart reply you shall sit next to me in the leading longboat.' He indicated its stern thwart.

Within minutes, the two longboats were being rowed over sun-glinting waters towards the main wharf. It was still deserted but the feeling of watching eyes persisted and the black sails of crows wheeling above the warehouses made the scene eerie. The wind had dropped, the air was hot and humid, the rowers were soon sweating with their exertions.

The boats ground against the sides of the main wharf. The rowers shipped their oars and two men in each boat rose to their feet, grappling hooks raised like dancers in a ballet.

This was the moment. Fernao's breath caught. He released it with a conscious effort, eyes scanning the wharf and the shoreline. Nothing happened.

The fifty men landed with speed and precision, trotted to form lines two deep along the sides of the wharf, muskets held at the port position, iron helmets and corselets gleaming dully in the sun. Fernao leapt lightly ashore and stood stiffly to attention, raising his hand in salute when the captain came ashore.

The burly captain assumed the at ease position, hand on sword hilt, and gazed down the wharf towards the warehouses. 'We are here on a trading mission, *comprades*,' he declared to his troops. 'Your presence as an armed escort is meant only to deter the natives. We have scared the shit out of them already, so let's have no bloody nonsense from you unless we are threatened. Midshipman de Albergaria and I will now walk to the warehouses and find someone to carry a message to the port authority.' He addressed the sergeant. 'Have the musketeers follow us in double column, then form two deep again at the base of the wharf, to give us cover.'

'Sir!' The sergeant turned and began shouting his orders.

Captain Oliveira stumped up the wharf, shoes clacking on grey wood. Fernao followed. He had a weird feeling that something was about to happen.

They clomped to the base of the wharf, the men plodding behind them. They paused to allow the men to form lines again. Then Captain Oliveira started making for the nearest warehouse some forty yards away. The sunlight was pitiless now, shimmering in waves before them before alighting on the white coral roadway. Sweat was streaming down Fernao's face and back. His head felt hot, the stink of dry fish, garbage and copra was overpowering. He glanced up at the sky. It was a burnt blue canopy without a trace of a cloud. The sad caw of one of those crows disturbed an ominous stillness.

One moment there was no trace of human life and the next, men materialized as if from nowhere. Captain Oliveira halted abruptly. Fernao's heart thudded and came to a stop.

There were hundreds of them in groups outside the nearest warehouse, dressed in Moorish costumes, dirty white *dhotis*, brown waistcoats and matching headdresses. Those in the rear held bows at the ready, arrows to strings, or brandished spears. Those in front carried long, wicked looking scimitars. Could fifty muskets hold them back?

Monday, 11 February 1521

To my joy, Rama was saddled and being held by a groom in the palace courtyard, to which I hastened without lunch. I ran to the horse, barely acknowledging the greetings of the grooms. Rama was mine, gleaming with the black beauty of a dark, luminous night. Forgetting all the admonitions as to how one should approach a horse, I rushed impulsively up and threw my arms around Rama's neck. He gently stamped a hoof, cocked an ear at me.

'You're mine, you're mine,' I whispered.

Rama seemed to understand. He twisted his neck around, nuzzling me, his nose cool and wet. I released my hold, grasped his noble face with both hands and looked into his eyes. What large, beautiful, melting eyes horses have, but especially my Rama. A gush of gratitude for the Great King flooded me as I placed my cheek against Rama's.

'Ah! Your love affair has begun already.' It was my father's voice.

I knew immediately on whose orders Rama had been saddled up for my ride. I turned to give my father the customary greeting of worship. 'You were kind to arrange for me to ride him today, *tha*. I know you did it. Thank you.'

'It was the least I could do, since I did not have a birthday gift for you.'

'You have given me greater gifts today, *tha*, so don't feel bad.'

'I never feel bad about such things, Prince.' His tone was kindly but decisive. 'Each of us gives as we desire, so I won't match gifts in the giving or the receiving. The meal a poor man may provide can be more than the feast of a king, and a single act of thoughtfulness better than a kingdom.'

'I shall think on it, *tha*, but riding with you is the most precious thing I have received today.'

'Especially when you are riding your very own horse, Rama!' he retorted drily. He half turned at the sound of approaching footsteps. 'Ah, here come our companions.'

I gave my grandfather, Prince Wijayo and my uncle, Prince Raigam, filial greetings. They inspected Rama closely.

'A f-fine horse,' Prince Wijayo observed, stroking his silver beard. 'He shows great p-promise. H'mm.' He circled Rama, who stamped his foot, impatiently this time. 'P-powerful legs, excellent carriage, t-tail well up without any ginger in the rear, I assume!' He guffawed at his own joke, a reference to horse traders who placed ginger in the anus of sorry nags to bring their tails up. He cleared his throat with a great w-roo-omp. 'Count yourself lucky, young man. No one gave your grandfather this kind of p-present when he was your age. No, sir, I had to work for everything I needed.'

I knew that nothing could be further from the truth, but merely smiled in acknowledgement.

'A magnificent steed,' Prince Raigam stated in his usual laconic fashion.

Mounting up, we clippety-clopped our horses line abreast through the open courtyard towards the entrance gates of the palace, my father and grandfather in the centre, myself on the left flank and Prince Raigam on the right. I felt very important as we acknowledged the salutes of passersby and hoped that Julietta could see me riding my very own horse with some of the most important people in the land. I would have told her about the Great King's gift but more important things had happened. Julietta loves me, Julietta loves me, the horses' hooves seemed to echo. Feeling that she must be watching me, I sat erect in the saddle, relaxed my shoulders and thighs, lifted my chest and rode more proudly, soon fitting easily into Rama's smooth motion.

We walked our horses through the entrance gates and broke into a posting trot when we entered the long avenue of green *na* trees that led through the citadel to the west gate. The citadel of Jayawardena Pura was surrounded by earth ramparts manned by soldiers. Riding past residences, we soon reached the great citadel gates, solid brown teakwood, ribbed with iron, but open, as always during daylight hours. The Great King did not fear assassins.

The sentries presented spears as we rode past. We clattered over the wooden bridge that spanned a murky moat surrounding the earthworks, then headed down a long avenue of spreading

61

cassia trees. Shredded sunshine beneath the green branches made running mosaics of light and shadow as we rose and fell in our saddles, the wind of our movement cool to the face though the park on either side of us was noontide warm. The township appeared immediately ahead, long rows of the red-tiled roofs of the tradesmen's quarter to the right of the main avenue, whitewashed public residences to the left. The city was laid out in the traditional four quarters around the citadel, so behind us, south of the main avenue, were the noblemen's residences, with the quarter for priests, temples and schools on the north side.

The full glare and heat of the afternoon greeted us as we rode into the city's broad avenue and were caught in a babel of sound: the cries of vendors, the shouts of children, the rattle of cartwheels, the clatter of bullocks' hooves. We passed rows of shops offering bolts of multi-coloured cloth, glittering trinkets, shiny pots and pans, red and yellow fruit, green vegetables, piles of foodstuffs, red onions, white garlic heaped in wooden bins. The sides of the street were crowded with people talking earnestly in groups. The women wore saris, or cloths and jackets of light green, blue, and red, the men dhotis of various colours, mostly with white *kurthas*, overshirts. The few Mouro we saw were dressed in their traditional dark waistcoats. We were well known, so people respectfully made way for our passage, even carts and palanquins drawing to a side.

The grey battlements of the fort loomed up, dotted with soldiers in white pantaloons and red tunics. The captain of the guard, a swarthy bow-legged Sinhala veteran, recognized my father and saluted smartly. Sentries came to attention as we rode beneath the shadow of the granite archway.

Then we were in the open sunlight, clattering across the causeway spanning the wide, outer moat. As always, I noted the long still shapes of crocodiles with fascination. Intended to deter attackers from swimming across, the reptiles lay still, like great, grey logs basking in the sun. I shortened my reins, settled in my saddle, to join my companions in an easy canter. Rama had a soft mouth, responded readily to the aids and moved so smoothly that I had no difficulty sitting well in my saddle, moving with him from the waist down.

The highway ran past a small, shimmering lake, then through green paddy fields, dark groves and scattered brick houses with white country-tiled roofs. It being siesta hour, we passed only a few people and the occasional trundling bullock cart. Cantering due west for less than an hour, we reached the outskirts of Colombo. The city had developed around the needs of the harbour without much overall planning. Its paved streets were almost deserted. Everyone is either sleeping or hiding, I thought; and here are we, heading for action. That is the privilege of leaders. The nebulous mission suddenly acquired definition. There was danger ahead. Excitement sparkled my blood.

The port stables were located at its fringe, where the warehouses commenced. We dismounted in a large, dusty courtyard filled with bullock carts and wagons in orderly rows. Pi-dogs lay around, sleeping chins on forepaws, bare-chested grooms squatted in their noonday torpor.

The chief groom, a tall wizened man wearing a white turban beneath which his left eye was blind, approached. 'Water and rub down the horses,' my father directed him. He extended four coins to the man.

We walked side-by-side towards the harbour, were soon in its medley of smells, cinnamon, copra, dry fish, onions, heavy oils and the undefinable dank of sea odour. A faint breeze attempted a journey inland but petered out with a sigh.

'I d-do not hear the usual sounds of the p-port,' Prince Wijayo remarked nervously. 'And there isn't a soul around.'

'What did you expect?' the general retorted.

The ominous calm lying over the entire port sizzled into my stomach as we proceeded steadily beneath fierce sunlight in the confined spaces between silent warehouses. Through a gap in the buildings, I got my first glimpse of the great *parangi* warships riding the shining brown waters. A spasm of fear at their sheer size snaked through me. They looked so commanding, menacing, the great brown prows thrusting towards the city, the dark snouts of what must be their cannon pushing through the bows. I had never seen a cannon before, nor ships of such monstrous size.

'Foreign warships in our sacred waters,' my father muttered.

63

He glanced at me, pain in his eyes. I knew what he was thinking. Nothing would be the same for us ever again.

'Where is everybody?' Prince Wijayo demanded of no one in particular. He tripped over a large lump of coral. '*P-para-parangi!*' He cursed. 'But for them I'd be enjoying my afternoon siesta. I'm n-not getting any younger, you know.' And again, this time irritably, 'Where the d-devil is everyone?' As if to answer him, a brown and white pi-dog rose and slunk away, tail between its legs, from its own siesta in the sun.

We had the real answer when we rounded the next set of warehouses and saw the wharves and seafront.

Two lines of *parangi* soldiers in red and blue uniforms, brown leather corselets and iron helmets, were drawn up at the base of the main wharf, the first line kneeling, the second standing. Iron sticks – those must be their muskets – were levelled at groups of silent Mouro confronting them, brandishing swords and spears.

We ground to a halt and watched, spellbound. The twang of bows was followed by the hiss of arrows and the shoosh of spears. The *parangi* lines did not waver.

'Fire!' I understood the order of the great, burly man, who was obviously their leader.

The muskets of the kneeling line of *parangi* flashed and rattled, emitted puffs of smoke. The advancing Mouro fell like rotten fruit, screaming pitifully. I had never seen anything like it. People point sticks at their enemy, flame, smoke and a hideous rattle as of fire-crackers erupt. Men die.

Terror struck me, like one of those musket shots.

'D-d-d-dear *d-devas*, an action and we are not even armed,' Prince Wijayo stuttered. 'Let us d-depart.'

'By the devas, no,' my father ground out.

His words and his fearless expression drained the terror from my body. My blood began pounding with anger, defiance, I know not what. I only knew that I would have to learn to face these muskets with but a sword in hand and a mount between my legs, if I was to be of any use to my country and myself.

CHAPTER 6
Monday, 11 February 1521

The river breezes that blow along the re-entrant of the valley at
this time of the year to merge into the cool of the mountains
had suddenly dropped. The palace of the Kandy sub-kingdom
was so warm and close this afternoon that King Wira, seated in
his reception chamber adjoining his private dining room, was
obviously irritated. A red-brick verandah ran all round the
King's private quarters, which were built around a flagstone
courtyard, in which a fountain listlessly splashed. 'This damn-
able heat takes away the enjoyment of a good meal,' the King
grumbled, through his betel-chewing. 'Jaya is seventy miles
away in the low country, yet it must be cooler there. Imagine
that low-country bastard calling himself the Great King and
enjoying such a fine, cool palace while we *radalayas*, Kandyan
royalty, swelter in the heat of this building.'

His voice has grumbly undertones even when he is not
complaining, Prince Kumara thought. Its natural quality is that
of sluggish sewerage trickling through an iron grate. And he
will continue bellyaching until he dies. Until he dies! There was
the catch, for his father would probably live for ever. Kandy was
the sub-kingdom of the central highlands of Lanka. Like Jaffna in
the north, which was ruled by the Chola sub-king, and the
Sinhala sub-kingdom of Ruhuna in the south, it owed allegiance
to the Great King in Jaya, but the prince believed that he could
do something about that if he could only become king.

'The problem is we are too divided to become rich,' King
Wira declared. 'Every chieftain wants his own little empire in his
mountain fastness and his neighbour's if he can steal it. Three
sub-sub-kings in the up-country alone.' He paused. 'But why
spoil a good meal with talk of wretches who make poor
company?' He lay back on the gold silken cushions with a sigh,
rubbing his round belly in satisfaction at the noon meal just

ended. He double-burped. 'A good burp brings back the taste of the food you've just enjoyed,' he declared. 'It's like tasting the meal all over again.' He sniffed the air, relishing the smells of the curry and spice that still clung to the room. 'Food becomes more important as one gets older, but by the devas, it makes the day seem even hotter.' He raised a pudgy hand and clicked his fingers at the attendant standing beside him. '*Adey kolla*, wield that fan faster. It's not your lifeless cock!'

The plump, silver-haired servant, Lamaya, murmured an apology and moved the large palmyrah-palm fan faster.

Squatting on a wide, red-cushioned settee across the room, Prince Kumara studied his father with dispassionate interest. This pot-bellied man was all that lay between him and real power, for he was King Wira's only child, with but one half-sister whose husband was not a man of ambition or drive. Unfortunately, his father was middle-aged and in good health. Not a single strand of grey disturbed the dark, well-oiled hair tied in a knot at the nape of a bull neck, or the black moustache sprawled across the moon face. Large bulging eyes, with a slight glaze over them, completed the picture of a self-indulgent ruler who symbolized to Prince Kumara the failure of the Kandy people ever to rule the entire country of Lanka. For the present he had to humour his father. 'It's our family pride too that causes the divisions, Sire,' he volunteered. 'It's almost as if we have to pay a price for our birth and breeding. Those low-country fellows have nothing to be proud of because they mix marriages like pi-dogs breeding in the marketplace.'

'A nice turn of speech, Prince,' King Wira responded drily. 'But hardly comforting.' He surveyed the young man with some satisfaction. '*Adey*, you are a worthy product of the noblest Kandy family. You are not only clever, but you also look good. You have inherited the gold silk skin of our people, your mother's large brown eyes, your grandfather's elegant nose and ... er ... your father's resolute chin. A little more height and broader shoulders and you would have ... ' He paused, a sudden thought seeming to strike him. His glance became so penetrating that Prince Kumara felt a stab of dismay. 'You have sharp white teeth too! We hope you will not use them to chew off your poor father's head!'

'Now why would you say a thing like that, Sire?' Prince Kumara parried. 'All my fortune and any strength I have can only come from you. Have I not been an obedient son all these years? Don't you trust me?' He assumed an air of injured innocence.

'*Adey*, people of strength and ambition are only subservient until they are ready to act,' King Wira retorted. 'Our up-country people uniformly stab one another in the back, or cut each other's throats. As for trust . . . ' He shrugged beefy shoulders. 'How to trust anyone when you are a king?'

Prince Kumara had discovered through the years that he could simulate emotion almost at will, except on the rare occasions when he was so upset he lost control over himself. Brains were more important in life than brute force, pretended humility more effective than arrogance, and cunning the best way to succeed. One had to discover the weaknesses of others and exploit them. The look he now gave his father was one of pained submission, his silence that of loyalty unfairly questioned, especially in the presence of a palace servant.

King Wira understood. 'Keep it that way,' he advised softly. 'You are our only son and will inherit the throne some day, but don't get impatient.' He directed a stream of red betel juice expertly into the brass spittoon beside him, reached out to a gold stand beside him for another chew.

A discreet knock sounded on the door of the dining chamber. 'Who the devil can that be?' the King demanded irritably. 'On such a *musala*, accursed, hot day we should be left undisturbed at mealtimes.'

'It must be something important, Sire.'

'If it were really important, they'd be breaking the door down, Prince. The knock sounds more like news that a eunuch has borne a child. Ho! ho! ho!' He always laughed at his own dry jokes, his bare pectorals shaking like brown *dodol*, jelly. 'Well, let us see whether it's a boy or a girl. Ho! ho! ho! *Adey, kolla*, see who it is,' he directed the old servant.

The attendant stopped waving the fan, laid it on the red and blue Pahlava, Persian, carpet that adorned the brown flagstone floor. He made for the creamy satinwood door and opened it, while the king scratched his hairy chest.

The brawny guard captain, clad in the green *dhoti* and white tunic of the palace uniform, stood framed in silver-gold sunlight pouring on to the open verandah and courtyard behind him. He was accompanied by a wisp of a man clad in blue pantaloons and white *kurtha*, overshirt, with a small rat-like face and small rat-like whiskers. Dust-strewn, soaked with sweat, the man was near dead on his feet.

Captain Banda saluted while the stranger sank to his knees, touching his forehead to the floor.

'Sire, this man is named Gunaya,' Captain Banda reported. 'He is one of our ... ahem! ... ' he cleared his throat, ostentatiously glancing at Lamaya. 'He is one of our men in Colombo. He insists that he has news of utmost importance, for your royal ears alone.'

'Ha!' The king let out his breath impatiently. 'It is always of the utmost importance when people wish to intrude upon a ruler's few moments of hard-earned rest. We slave for this kingdom and for our people night and day. Surely ... ' He stopped abruptly. '*Adey*, we remember this man.' His interest had obviously quickened. 'His news could indeed be important. Come forward, fellow. You may leave, Captain Banda. You too, Lamaya.'

Gunaya stepped into the shade of the room.

'Give us your news, fellow,' King Wira directed sharply, when the others had left and the door was closed. 'There's no need for the usual formalities and flattery.'

'Sire,' Gunaya began, then had to clear his throat before bringing the words out. 'A fishing boat spotted seventeen great *parangi* warships sailing towards the port of Colombo early last morning. I rode day and night to bring the news.'

Prince Kumara was amazed at the change in his father. There was no trace of indolence in his manner and his eyes became sharp as spearpoints. 'What do they intend?'

'I don't know, Sire. I left Jothi and Palitha to bring you more news in a second and third relay, but deemed it my duty to inform you of the arrival of the ships forthwith, using our prearranged changes of horses to get here the sooner.'

King Wira seemed about to admonish Gunaya, but he held back. Gunaya had ridden seventy miles in about thirty-two hours, no mean feat considering that the last twenty miles of the journey involved a stiff climb through mountain passes.

'You have done well,' King Wira observed grudgingly. 'You shall be rewarded for your diligence. Any other news?'

'No, Sire, but Jothi should be here by tomorrow evening and Palitha the following night.'

'Good.' King Wira scratched his chest again, absently this time, his brain obviously working at a furious rate. He rang a small bell on the table beside him and the silver-haired Lamaya reappeared at the door. '*Kolla*, see to it that this man is fed, clothed and looked after. Give him a room for tonight.' His gaze returned to Gunaya. 'You shall go back to your post tomorrow and keep delivering prompt reports, but before you leave, tell us, did the *parangi* ships have the big guns they carried when they came to Galle sixteen years ago?'

'So the fisherman said, Sire, but he did not stay to count the guns lest the *parangi* seize him and drink his blood.'

'Drink his blood?' The king inquired incredulously. 'What kind of talk is that, fellow?'

'The *parangi* are reported to drink blood, Sire.'

Prince Kumara leaned forward and whispered in the king's ear. 'I have read that the wine they drink looks like blood, Sire. They claim it is the blood of their Lord Jesus, who died for them on a cross.'

'The right colour for blood, but a silly colour for wine,' the King remarked. 'All right, you may both leave now.'

The men made obeisance and departed, closing the door behind them but leaving the high odour of Gunaya's stale sweat in the chamber. King Wira absently seized a toothpick from the betel stand and started chewing it. 'Well, Prince, what do you make of it?' he finally inquired, holding up the chewed pick as if it were a taper.

'Seventeen ships suggest that the *parangi* mean business, Sire. As you know, they have been threatening this a long time and you have encouraged it.'

69

'Business is all they care about, Prince, if reports from Calicut and the Malabar coast are accurate. They already have the power to enforce trade with their cannon and firearms. We wonder what these weapons look like. No matter. All the white man wants is control of trade to accumulate wealth. Bah! They are no more than jackals, stealing the leopards' kill.'

'They also steal men's minds, Sire.'

'What do you mean?' King Wira glanced sharply at him.

'I think they want to spread their religion, which they call Catholica, Sire.'

'All this talk of a man who would save the world by being nailed to a cross! After these many centuries of religion, the world is further away from saving than ever before. I hear that the two *parangi* priests in the Jaya palace even preach of a single God. Anyone who believes in such a God must be fundamentally weak.'

'Not so, Sire. Their God is reported to be a source of strength and inspiration to the *parangi*.' The glimmer of an idea appeared briefly in Prince Kumara's mind.

'Now how do *you* know, Prince?' King Wira inquired petulantly, then suddenly seemed to remember. 'Oh yes, you *should* know. You are the great scholar of the family.' He pondered awhile. 'What are you thinking?' he suddenly shot out.

Prince Kumara decided to play to his father's character, for the old man, having afforded his son the education he himself had not received, resented him for it at times. 'I'm thinking, Sire, that you are very learned and wise. I'm thinking how *you* are reacting to this situation, now that the *parangi* are obviously here to stay, for why else would they come in such force?'

A cunning gleam entered King Wira's protuberant eyes. 'All right, if you're so smart, tell us what we are thinking.'

'I believe you will contact the *parangi*, who convert the Indian populations to their Catholic faith in order to make them better Portuguese than Indians. These converts give loyalty to the Portuguese king, rather than to their own rajas and the Zamorim. By this means, the *parangi* divide people to rule them with the mind and a few thousand soldiers. I am thinking that you, being a wise king, are already planning how to treat

70

with the *parangi*, for if we can ensure that they extend their stay in Lanka, we might be able to use their power . . . '

King Wira caught on, ' . . . to extend the Kandy kingdom to the uttermost ends of this blessed island,' he interrupted triumphantly. 'You are smart to be able to read our mind.'

'And you are so wise, Sire, to have such a fine mind,' Prince Kumara declared, with seeming admiration.

'That is why we are the king. You are lucky to be able to learn from us.' King Wira glanced up impatiently at another timid knock on the door. 'See who that is.'

Prince Kumara strode to the door and opened it to find the old attendant standing on the verandah, an apprehensive look on his time-weathered face. He made obeisance, then rose to his feet. 'Good news for our king,' he quavered.

'Enter,' King Wira called from inside. 'If we must be interrupted during our rest watch, let it at least be with good news. What is your news, *kolla?*'

'Your royal daughter in Pera *deniya*, flatland, delivered a lusty baby boy last night, Sire. The official messenger is on his way, but I just had the news from my son, who's a servant in your royal daughter's mansion, and came visiting me.'

'Did you say our first grandson is a "lusty" baby?' There was a note of pride in the grumbly voice.

'Yes, Sire. Reportedly fair of skin too.'

'On the ears? That's how one tells, you know.' King Wira glanced at Prince Kumara. 'All babies come out flushed with their exertions and therefore looking fair. It's an even more devilish business coming into this world than living in it or going out! The edges of the ears alone indicate the true colour.' He paused, chuckling maliciously. '*Adey*, perhaps your nephew will be fairer than you.'

More competition was the last thing Prince Kumara wanted. This baby had been born on the same evening the *parangi* arrived. Prince Tikiri of the Great King's palace had been born the same day the *parangi* first arrived in Lanka, in the port of Galle, sixteen years ago. Omens gave people wrong ideas. He had always considered Prince Tikiri, whose horoscope was well known to predict great things, as his most likely rival in the

71

fulfilment of his ambitions. The new baby could be another possible rival. He hid his feelings behind a smile. 'I hope the baby will be even fairer than me if that would please you, Sire.'

'You are a good son.' King Wira glanced back at the attendant. 'You may leave, *kolla*. We thank you for the wonderful news. A grandson at last!'

When the man had departed, the king remained lost in thought, his bulging eyes reflecting concentration. 'Great news today, great events ahead.' The words seemed to escape him involuntarily, almost dreamily. 'You shall leave tomorrow on a journey that might last several days, Prince Kumara.' He smiled to himself. 'The *parangi* should have an emissary from the Kandy sub-kingdom . . . secretly of course. Meanwhile, it's time you paid your respects to that *pathaya* low-country fellow, in the Jaya palace.'

CHAPTER 7
Monday, 11 February 1521

My father and my uncle exchanged questioning glances. None of us showed any trace of fear, which I can hardly say for my grandfather, who was sweating more profusely than warranted by the heat. My father nodded. He had obviously made up his mind. 'Let me handle this,' he directed, then glanced at me. 'I'll need you as an interpreter, Prince.'

I was about to step forward when a thunderous roar made me pause, my heart thudding against my ribs. Curious whistling noises arose, then a series of tremendous thuds and crashes, followed by the rattle of buildings and the sound of flying debris. The roar was more deafening than the thunder of a hundred monsoons.

Before my ears stopped singing, I knew that the ships had fired their big guns. It was the most terrifying experience of my life. Not even my new-found courage thwarted my first instinct, to turn and run, like some of the Mouro whom I saw through the dust and confusion, their cries of terror mingling with the shrieks of men in mortal agony. Instinctively too, I glanced at my father for protection. He stood there, unafraid, one hand on his hip, calmly surveying the scene. Suddenly, shame at my cowardice engulfed me. The price of honour could always be death. And in returning my fleeing courage to the sticking point, I learned not to be afraid of firearms; they are no more than another form of the death-dealing I knew I was destined to face. Fear, yes. To be overcome by it, no.

My father waited till the groan and creak of buildings in anguish and the clamour of the Mouro began to subside. 'Let us hope that since the enemy is fleeing, the *parangi* will be satisfied with one volley and one broadside,' he commented. 'Come with me, Prince. We have no time to lose.' He started walking towards the wharf.

Many of the Mouro had vanished, but some, braver than the rest, were regrouping. The weapons of the standing line of *parangi* were levelled in their direction. The kneeling line of *parangi* were reloading their muskets. Wisps of smoke from their volley still curled faintly in the air. I realized with horror that, to them, my father and I were also the enemy. Those muskets could shatter our bodies.

It needed more than courage from me, it required desperation to walk towards a score of muzzles that could belch fire any moment. I found that desperation in my love for my father, in his example, in my need to support him. Perhaps too, in some hidden urging of my destiny. Knowing that these moments would make or break me, I followed my father's footsteps, wondering what he thought he could accomplish single-handed.

We strode confidently forward, our feet crunching on the white coral. Ten, twenty... one hundred paces. The burly *parangi* captain was about to give the order to fire again when a young man standing beside him grasped his arm urgently, said something to him, pointed in our direction. The captain glanced towards us, hesitated.

We kept walking towards the *parangi*, watched by hundreds of human eyes and the screeching crows wheeling overhead. The tension was unbearable, the grim-faced enemy awaiting the order to fire. A strange acrid stink, like that from firecrackers, only more pungent, reached me. My mind suddenly accepted the situation. I was no longer afraid. A feeling of invincibility swept through me. I would not come to any harm.

A few more steps before my father stopped and I stood beside him, feeling naked and vulnerable, like a man who sees a rogue elephant move its ears forward, the warning that it is about to charge. The *parangi* were alert, suspicious. The tense silence was ponderous, hardly broken by the slap and wash of wavelets on the shore. All attention was now centred on the slim, elegant figure of my father, obviously a man of consequence, standing there imperious, unafraid. At that moment, I worshipped him.

A wounded pi-dog's whine broke the stillness. It had barely

ended when my father began to speak, the sound of his voice like someone bidding a storm to be calm. 'I am General Prince Maya Dunne, commander-in-chief of the armies of the Great King Dharma Parakrama Bahu IX, supreme ruler of all the kingdoms of Lanka.' My voice carried the same ring as his when I translated into the Portuguese language. The *parangi* were obviously surprised to be addressed in their own tongue; their captain listened intently. 'There will be no more violence in the Great King's dominions,' my father continued. 'The Great King welcomes the ships of the King of Portugal which have arrived in our waters on a peaceful mission. He will surely regret any offensive action taken in his port by foreign traders, who shall be severely punished. I am here to assure you that the officers and men of your fleet will be afforded every courtesy and hospitality before you resume your journey.'

Neatly put, I thought. My *tha* has brains as well as courage.

'I am Captain Juan Oliveira, an officer of the Navy of His Imperial Majesty, King Dom Manuel I of Portugal. I offer your Great King and you personally, General, thanks for your kind welcome.' A grim note entered his voice. 'It is a little more cordial than that which was afforded us by the bloodthirsty Mouro blackguards behind you, who attacked us though we landed peacefully.' He paused to allow his words to sink in. 'You are a brave man, General. We Portuguese respect and admire such courage. You will doubtless observe that we have suffered no casualties, while many a Mouro assassin has taken his defiance to the heretics' hell that awaits them all. Admiral Lopo Soarez de Albergaria, who commands our flotilla, has directed me to explain our mission to someone in authority. Your presence is therefore doubly fortuitous. I assure you there will be no more violence on our side, unless we are provoked.'

'Thank you.' My father turned to the remaining Mouro clustered around the warehouses. 'Begone!' he commanded them, flinging the back of his right hand outwards as if flicking away flies. 'Take your dead and wounded with you.'

Half-turning, I was surprised to see the Mouro meekly obeying his command, like pi-dogs shrinking away from a master's blows. They were not responding merely to my father's

75

order, I knew, but also to his position and reputation. Yet this was another lesson I had learned today, how authority can be exercised without bluster. The Mouro mercenaries had been regrouping even though they had suffered such unexpected losses, so my father's intervention was timely.

'You can have your men stand at ease,' my father bade the *parangi* captain.

The man's answering smile was cool. 'We are already at ease, General. I would have you know that the Portuguese military relax even in battle formation, with guns in their hands!'

'And I say we will not have any military in battle formation in this country, except the Great King's men.' My father's eyes were hard as the iron helmets of the Portuguese as he squared up to the captain. I heard the gentle wash of waves on the shoreline again, the peaceful sound incongruous.

The two men gazed at each other in a sudden clash of wills. Tension mounted once more, yet now it emanated from the *parangi*; my father was easy and relaxed.

As I expected, the *parangi* was the first to look away, his gaze flickering momentarily sideways. A short laugh escaped him. Knowing he had won, my father was gracious and spoke first to save the man embarrassment before his troops. 'Please reassemble your men and inform your admiral that General Prince Maya Dunne,' he half turned towards me, 'his son and interpreter, Prince Tikiri Bandara, his half-brother, Prince Raigam Bandara and the Great King's brother, Prince Wijayo Bahu, will receive him within two hours at the residence of the governor of the port of Colombo. A guide will await him here. He may bring his staff and a suitable armed escort of not more than fifty men. His safety from and to his ship is guaranteed on my sacred honour.'

My father turned away without awaiting a reply, as one who is used to issuing commands and being obeyed. The *parangi* captain, for all his arrogance, being accustomed to receiving commands, gave the order for his men to stand at ease.

'Let us leave immediately, before his brains take over his instinct,' my father bade in an undertone.

I was about to turn away when my attention was attracted by a

76

gaze intent upon me. An overpowering compulsion took my eyes unerringly from the captain I had been addressing to its source.

He was a young man of about my age, dressed in the blue *parangi* uniform. He wore a leather corselet, held a long naked sword in his hand. He was tall and slender, with tanned skin and dark brown hair beneath an iron helmet. Separated from him by less than fifty paces, I stared into his eyes. They were paler blue than aquamarines, yet piercing as hailstones in the high hill country. An eerie feeling streaked through me, causing me to shiver in the afternoon sunlight. As we stared at each other, suddenly we were in silent battle, for he knew me and I him, from some dim distant past and certainly from the future.

'Come, Prince,' my father commanded.

I turned away, though I wanted to continue the battle of the eyes and win.

Monday, 11 February 1521

Fernao watched the retreating figures of the four Sinhala with conflicting emotions. A part of him was relieved that the brief action had ended without any casualties among his men, but a part clamoured for the action that might have been. He felt like a man who had been soaring up, up, up on a swing, reaching for the danger of the skies almost, only to be suddenly jolted back to safety. It left him in a state of suspended emotion, of frustration at non-fulfilment. While he had been tremendously impressed by the courage, daring and quiet authority of the Sinhala general, the general's son had left him disquieted, with a feeling of past battles yet to be joined. What did it mean? Where did his future lie? He could not escape the absurd thought that it was in this moment. Strangely, the encounter sent his mind spinning back many years.

The peasant youth, twice his age and size, with sun-burned skin and unkempt hair, cannot know that he belongs to the great de Albergaria family, owners of the village and the entire district. All the lout sees is a neatly dressed boy of about eight sitting on a gravestone in the village churchyard. From as far back as he could remember, Fernao had enjoyed the peace and solitude of this churchyard, where he dreamed of those who lay buried beneath the gravestones, conjuring up stories about their lives. Here, he listened to the rustle of the green elms before a gentle wind carrying the scent of wild roses and sometimes heard the music of the church bells. This was his escape from constantly watching eyes in the mansion.

'Gimme that scarf,' the lout says, his voice as uncouth as his appearance. He reaches out to grasp the blue silk scarf about Fernao's neck.

Fernao instinctively recoils, not in fear but with disgust. A resoluteness, chill as the grave, sweeps through him. 'Do not touch me.' The command comes out cold and quiet, the voice of royalty, one of the de Albergaria, whose motto is: Let no man seize what is mine with impunity.

The boy faces him squarely, hands on hips, laughing scornfully. 'Lord high and mighty, be it?' He bows, mocking, hands still on hips. 'Well, lord, now I 'ave bowed to thee.' A ferocious grin twists the coarse features. 'Gimme that scarf.' His voice has risen, ugly.

At that moment, the ice enters Fernao's heart and takes over his whole being.

Hours later, the friar finds the lout sprawled behind the gravestone, unconscious, blood clotted on his head.

Fernao never quite remembers his thoughts, only the sequence of events. A cold, deadly purpose had guided his actions. A quick survey for something to attack with. A deadly kick to the crotch and a swift leap sideways when the lout closed in. The exquisite feel of the rock in his hand when he reached down and grasped it. The wonderful sensation rippling from his arm through his entire body when the rock smashed into the lout's head. The sheer joy at seeing a fallen enemy. The temptation to smash that head again and again, beat it to a pulp.

Curiously his rage had not been red but white, an aware rage that made him hold back and saved him from committing murder. No one ever discovered what had happened to the lout and the youth never told.

So it had been for Fernao thereafter, whenever someone assailed the dignity of his person. Right down to the night he took a knife to the Portuguese officer who had tried to fondle his genitals while he lay asleep.

'Dreaming again,' Captain Oliveira broke into the past. 'You're a strange bugger. Regular knot of the old rope. I'll say this for the admiral.' A note of admiration entered the husky voice. 'He is a master tactician and deserves every honour he has received.' He paused. 'Now don't you go repeating that to him, Middie, for I want no man to think I'm currying favour. Never needed it all my life. I'm a self-made man.' He shook his head. 'Sending us ashore like that, having all the flotilla's starboard cannon trained exactly where a surprise attack could come from so we'd be covered, timing it all. Superb.' He turned towards the flagship, saluted. 'That's for you, my admiral. I'd follow you to the gates of hell.'

A thrill of pride shot through Fernao as he surveyed the captain's burly back. It was followed swiftly by an iron resolve. Some day, men will say that of me too. He barely heard Captain Oliveira bellowing the order to return to the longboats, for he turned to face the direction in which the four Sinhala had now vanished. Only their auras remained, locked somewhere within him, and they brought back the feeling of disquiet while his eyes attempted to pierce the blinding sunshine, the empty air, searching for an answer that was not there.

Monday, 11 February 1521

Father Perez was conducting an unscheduled lesson in European history that afternoon. He was a short, rotund friar. Thin lips caused a perpetual smile on his round, rubicund face, which was generally sweaty, his odour being invariably so high that, as now, it reached the front row of students, where Julietta sat.

He had been speaking of the armed might of the European powers and Julietta had slowly begun to feel that he was trying to intimidate the class. 'So you see, the people of Portugal are descended from the early Huns, who invaded...' A strange rumble in the distance caused Father Perez to pause in the middle of the sentence, '...the Iberian peninsula,' he concluded. 'Those are the sounds of their guns!'

The sound came from the west and, aware that Prince Tiki-tiki was visiting the port with his father, Julietta was instantly terrified. Knowing how brave her prince was and how ruthless her people could be, she visualized him leading Sinhala soldiers against the warships and being blown to pieces. The shock was so great that a wave of dizziness swept her. Half-rising, her eyes wide, nostrils distending, she clutched the empty air vainly for support, then sat back on the settee with a thud. The impact revived her but not before a dozen pairs of eyes swivelled in her direction. The entire classroom remained thus while Julietta tried desperately to compose herself, her eyes on Father Perez. Something told her that beneath his observation of her, he was listening... listening for more. Minutes of silence passed, then Father Perez strode over to her, placed a hand on her shoulder. 'Are you all right, my child?' he inquired. His normally high voice had risen a shade higher. 'What ails you?'

'Yes, Father, I'm all right. Please forgive me. It... it must be the heat.' Her heart was still pounding fiercely.

'The *parangi* is a sissy,' Prince Tissa, sitting behind her, remarked under his breath. 'She is scared of noise.' Prince Tissa was jealous of her successes as a student.

Ignoring the remark, Father Perez looked down at her curiously, his bright blue eyes sharper than she had ever seen them. He seemed about to speak, but decided against it. Releasing her shoulder, he calmly announced, 'This has been an unusual day. The class is now closed and will re-open tomorrow morning as usual. You may return to your homes.'

The students leapt to their feet. Being well-trained, they did not display indecorous joy at the cancellation of the last period, but began filing away, slates in hand, in orderly fashion.

Julietta remained seated, struggling to master her fear.

'I'm sure Father Juan will want to see you, Julietta,' Father Perez said softly. 'So why don't you remain here until I send

80

him to you?' Without waiting for a reply, he waddled out of the room, bandy-legged.

Unable to move in any case, Julietta simply sat there, terror rising and falling within her. From the depths of her mind, a horrible realization was also beginning to emerge. If her people, the Portuguese, killed a Sinhala prince, perhaps four princes, the proud Sinhala would retaliate and war would result. Father Juan, Father Perez and *o pai* had always impressed on her that her only loyalty must be to her God, her Christian faith and her own country. For the first time, she began to see the possibility of emotional separation from the people with whom she had lived all her life. It was a dread prospect, not because of her personal safety, but because she loved the Sinhala people.

She heard Father Juan's familiar tread clacking on the flagstone floors. She opened her eyes and found herself staring directly into his pale yellow ones, their black pupils piercing her very soul. A shiver of apprehension ran through her.

'Father Perez tells me you nearly fainted at the sound of gunfire in the distance,' Father Juan observed, his booming voice surprisingly low. 'You are not normally given to terror. On the contrary, you have always been calm in the face of danger. What's the difference today?'

Julietta noted the absence of the familiar 'my child' from Father Juan's speech. The friar's whole bearing made her want to clam up, some woman's instinct warning against him, in spite of the closeness, warmth and understanding of their encounter that morning. 'Nothing, Father. I just felt faint and breathless. Probably because of the heat.'

'Have you recovered now?'

Julietta found that Father Juan's attitude had brought up some inner resources of strength within her. 'Yes, Father. I'm quite all right now.'

'Then stand up when you talk to me.' His voice was stern, almost brutal.

She sprang to her feet, hurt, bewildered. She stood as tall as him, unable to remove her gaze from those magnetic eyes. As she watched transfixed, his gaze seemed to move forward, recede, move forward, recede. The eyes began to whirl round, then stopped, the black pupils holding her like a transfixed animal.

'Lying is an offence against God.' His voice seemed to come from a distance, yet it was compelling. 'Lying to one of His holy priests is a mortal sin. Why are you lying to me, Julietta?'

She felt herself completely under his domination. 'Father, I am sorry. I have sinned and I seek forgiveness.'

'God forgives the sins of those who confess, Julietta, but for absolution there has to be truth. Why were you afraid of the cannonade?'

Some deep, desperate feelings of loyalty to the prince she loved came to the fore. She could not divulge what he had told her without his permission. 'I . . . I can't tell you, Father.' The words came out in a whisper, the desperate gasp of the creature transfixed.

His gaze intensified, became terrible. 'Do you want to be banished from Holy Church, to have your soul condemned to eternal hell-fire and damnation?'

'No, Father.' She was so terror-stricken her dry mouth could barely utter the words.

'Those who have not seen the way of Christ have to endure purgatory before going to heaven, but they at least have a chance of being cleansed to join the communion of Saints.' He lowered his voice. 'You are a baptized Catholic,' the words came hissing out. 'Your soul will be condemned to hell for ever.'

'No, no, Father. I beg you to forgive me.' She was in a bath of sweat, the tears pouring from her eyes, her nose running. 'I will tell you.' She paused, reflexively rubbed her nose with the back of her hand. 'Prince Tikiri, his father, his grandfather, and his uncle, Prince Raigam, left for the port this noon. I was afraid the sound of the guns may mean a battle between our two peoples . . . that . . . that Prince Tikiri may have been killed.' Surprisingly, she felt somewhat better at having shared her fears with someone, anyone.

'Is that all you know?'

'Yes, Father, the prince and I had but a few minutes in which to talk before he had to leave.'

'When did he see you?'

'Immediately after you and I spoke this noon.'

'Where?'

'On the path leading to my house.'

'Oh!' Father Juan's gaze relaxed, his expression became thoughtful. 'How could he have got there without crossing my path?'

'I d-don't know, Father. He appeared suddenly from behind the hibiscus bushes.'

'I see.' Father Juan seemed to make up his mind. 'The prince appears to confide in you.' His usual kindly tone returned. 'Don't worry about his safety, my child. A single salvo doesn't mean a battle. My present concern is about your honesty. You promised you would tell Holy Church anything you discovered.'

'I did not want to betray the prince's confidence.'

'You would rather betray God.'

'No, Father.' Inspiration seized her. 'If the prince knew, he would never confide in me again.'

A look of contempt flashed across Father Juan's face. 'Such a poor deception, Julietta. Does not God see what is in your heart?'

She blushed with shame, looked down, unable to speak.

'Henceforth, you will come to me with any confidence the prince may share with you, anything that pertains to the future of our country, Portugal, in this island.' His raised voice boomed with authority. 'Remember what I'm going to tell you now every conscious second of your life, Julietta. A blessing has been extended to the heathen by the divine will. At long last, the kingdom of God is at hand in Lanka. You have a noble role to play in the future that has opened today. You shall play it as I dictate. You shall tell me everything Prince Tikiri says to you.'

'Yes, Father.' She looked out in the direction of the hibiscus hedge. With a stab of apprehension, she noted the bare-chested Sinhala gardener digging a nearby flower-bed. He had not been there a few minutes earlier. Had he heard the friar's mandate and her agreement? Oh well, it did not really matter, because the man could not have understood the Portuguese language in which they spoke.

CHAPTER 8
Monday, 11 February 1521

At thirty-one, Aisha was the chief wife of Abdul Raschid. In 1504, she had been formally given to Abdul in marriage by her older brother Paichi Markar, the most powerful Mouro trader in Calicut. Since the eighth century the followers of the Prophet Muhammad, who originated in Arabia, had spread their religion by conquest until they had established an empire that stretched from Spain to the Moluccas. Aisha and her brother claimed a tenuous descent from Mahmud of Ghazni, the Afghan ruler who, several hundred years earlier, had swept into India through the north-west passes with such incredible ferocity and ruthlessness that the name of Mahmud had come to stand for the quintessence of Muslim brutality. Mahmud established the city of Lahore as the capital of the Punjab, pillaged India and took its treasures back to his homeland.

Four years after her marriage, observing how the Portuguese had recently captured trade in the Indian Ocean, mainly at the expense of the Mouro, Paichi Markar noted that Lanka was the only country that had been spared the attentions of the newcomers. He therefore posted Abdul Raschid and Aisha to Colombo to administer and develop trade between that country and the Middle East. Aisha knew that Paichi's faith was in her, and not in her husband who was a good man but did not have her determination and drive. Though she punctiliously observed *purdah*, always wearing the robes and black *yashmak*, she managed to wield power from behind the scenes – or rather the veils, as she often thought with sardonic amusement.

It was in Lahore that Mahmud of Ghazni had seeded Aisha's early ancestor, but the family subsequently moved further and further south in tandem with the successes of various Muslim generals, commencing with Muhammed Ghuri. This Muslim conqueror of the twelfth century had trained bodies of

84

mounted archers to wheel and turn, feint and retreat, then circle around for surprise flank attacks. At the battle of Tarain, he inflicted such a crushing defeat on the Rajput armies of India that according to a Muslim historian 'a hundred thousand grovelling Hindus swiftly departed to the flames of hell.'

Bearing as she did the name of the wife of the Prophet Muhammad, in whose arms he had died, conscious of the blood of great leaders flowing in her veins, the fact that she was a woman in a man's world had not in any way diminished the feelings of power that surged through Aisha's body. She believed that only a person's spirit could create servility or inferiority. So her brains, her courage and merciless diligence, backed by mercenary guards, helped consolidate her brother's trading empire in Lanka, side-stepping the military ascendancy the Portuguese had established in the Indian Ocean from the Middle East to the Moluccas.

After they settled in Colombo, her husband took three other Muslim wives. She had readily granted her approval to these marriages for they freed her from wifely duties so that she could direct all her energies to the expansion of the trading empire she had created with such fascination and delight. She had been able to bear only one child, a fine boy named Ali, now fifteen, for whose future she was equally ambitious.

Everything had been very orderly until last night, when she received news of the arrival of the Portuguese fleet. Though she feared neither man nor woman, only Allah, the one God – at times not even Him, though she had accepted *Tawhid*, the Oneness of God, the Omnipotent, Omnipotent Sustainer of the World – the news had hit her hard. She lay awake most of the night, her mind whirling with possibilities and plans and especially glad to be free of her husband this night. Muslim men bound by Sunna, the tradition and practice of their faith, must bestow their sexual attentions equally on all their wives. Abdul had never succeeded in making her think of these attentions as favours. On the contrary, she had experienced no sexual stimulation since her bud was circumcised. Her sex life, therefore, merely consisted of servicing her husband diligently according to the custom and pretending to be satisfied, though she could not care less about the whole silly performance, the groans, the sweaty, writhing bodies and the final revolting odours of climax. All this fuss, merely for a few seconds of ejaculation! It simply did not make sense to her, but it was the will of Allah, so she complied.

When she arose that morning, she had counselled her husband not to panic, to leave matters to her. He had readily agreed, but when the Portuguese fired two salvoes shortly after they anchored in the harbour, he had become frantic. It seemed obvious that the salvoes were merely salutes and a tacit warning, but he rushed to the port to find out what was happening at first hand.

Aisha was surprised when her husband did not return for *zuhr*, the noon prayer, but assumed that he must have observed it in the mosque not far from their home. She had barely finished her own prayers, facing the *quibla*, the direction of Mecca, reciting the *fatihah* as prescribed, in a low voice, when she heard the thunderous roar of another cannonade. For the first time that she could remember, she knew alarm. Strong-willed as she was, however, she controlled herself, deliberately inducing an icy calm.

They lived in a large, luxurious Moorish-style mansion in the Muslim quarter of the city about a half-mile from the port. It fronted the green lake and adjoined the quarter of the slaves and mercenaries, some of them black. The house was built around a large centre courtyard which had marble floors, a bathing pool painted turquoise and a fountain. Orange, tangerine and red *jambu* trees offered shade and nesting places for mynah birds, grey doves and bee-eaters. An aviary beside the sleeping quarters ensured trills, whistles and birdsongs from yellow and blue and white budgerigars all day long and a wake-up call at dawn. The women's quarters were off the rear verandah serving the courtyard and opened out to a spacious pleasure garden totally secured from the public gaze, the domain, or prison, of Abdul's other wives.

Aisha had left word with the head servant of the house that she desired to see her husband immediately upon his return. She awaited him in the privacy of her reception chamber. This

86

was a large room floored in squares of pink and white marble, with filigreed marble screens lining the back wall. The green and red Persian carpet on the floor was flanked by green and white silken divans. Low ebony tables inlaid with mother-of-pearl on which braziers of highly polished brass glowed with incense, emitting tiny curls of smoke and scenting the room with attar-of-roses, served the divans.

Her husband waddled in. Aisha rose gracefully to her feet and knelt to him. When she straightened up, she was only about three inches shorter than his six foot two, but her figure was slim, her skin perfectly white, her long hair black and curly, whereas the man standing before her was big and flabby, though only forty years old. He was completely bald, his face fleshy, the lips hanging free like his bare pectorals, which were adorned by three gold necklaces.

With good living Abdul had degenerated from a handsome young man to a gross middle-age. It did not take a closer look for her to realize that he was agitated.

'Would you like some refreshment, lord? Have you had your noon meal?'

He responded with vigorous shakes of the head, jowls quivering, as she waited for him to open the conversation.

'A terrible thing has happened,' he finally jerked out. 'Disaster.' He looked at her appealingly with those small pig eyes that frequently go with gross-looking men. 'The seventeen *parangi* ships were drawn up facing the warehouses.' He was trying to brazen something out. 'There seemed to be no undue signs of activity on board and we... uh... decided on a bold move to frighten them off.' He paused, a sickly grin crossing his face. 'I had Captain Majid collect five hundred of our Moorish mercenaries armed with spears, bows and arrows and hide them in the warehouses fronting the shore. Then I ordered him to muster every available worker and dock rat on the wharves and get them to shout, jeer and intimidate the *parangi!*'

Abdul must have observed Aisha's eyes flash, for he hastily apologized. 'I know, I know now it was a mistake. I know only too well. A landing party from the flagship pulled towards the wharf in the middle of the first watch after the noon hour. The

87

parangi soldiers . . . uh . . . only about fifty of them in number, came ashore with their captain and another young officer. Majid lost his head. Thinking he would really show the *parangi* our power, he ordered our mercenaries to fire volleys of arrows at the intruders and to charge them.'

Incredulous, Aisha felt her whole being go bleak. 'Why would Majid do such a stupid thing?' she demanded. She refrained from asking who had really given the order. 'Didn't he know how cruelly Vasco da Gama blasted Calicut when the Zamorin opposed him?'

'Majid is a pig's offal . . . er . . . ' He corrected himself. 'Was.'

'Was?'

'Yes. The accursed *parangi* shot back with their muskets and the ships suddenly fired a salvo. Majid and about thirty other mercenaries were killed. We were left with several more wounded and a great deal of damage done to our shorefront warehouses.' His eyes filled with tears, his cheeks started to quiver.

The true test of a leader is a cool head in a crisis. 'What happened then?' she inquired.

'Some of our men fled, leaving behind several wounded. Others were regrouping when . . . er . . . Allah warned me to get away from the scene.'

'And that was all? The *parangi* stopped firing then?'

'Er . . . yes.'

She knew he was lying, but before she could probe further, a discreet knocking sounded on the open door of the chamber. A veiled female attendant was standing diffidently on the verandah. 'What is it, Mariam?' she inquired. 'I thought I told you we were not to be disturbed.'

'I beg your ladyship's pardon, but a messenger has brought an urgent message for his lordship.' Head bowed, she proffered a sealed parchment scroll with both hands. It was a very official looking document.

Glancing apprehensively at Aisha, Abdul held out his hand. Aisha made a quick decision. 'I'll take it,' she declared.

'Give me that scroll!' Abdul commanded when Mariam had gone.

'No, husband. Let me read it out to you.'

'Give it to me!' His voice was raised in anger. 'Or by Allah . . . '

'Yes?' Her voice whipped out the question, deadly chill.

Their glances crossed. She felt iron in her veins and it showed in her gaze. Only the chirp of lovebirds broke the silence of the battle.

She won. 'All right,' Abdul said weakly, 'I'm tired. You can save me the trouble.'

For a few seconds she stared at him, experiencing a sharp inner yearning for a man who could battle her and win, dominate her so that they could stand side by side and conquer the whole world. Then the feeling was gone. Leadership is only for the lonely. She broke the seals and opened the scroll. Holding it up to the afternoon sunshine that bathed the verandah, she read:

'General Prince Maya Dunne, Commander-in-Chief of the armies of the Great King, hereby summons Abdul Raschid, trader and leader of the Mouro community in Lanka, to the residence of Prince Maitri Pala, governor of the port of Colombo, at the end of the second afternoon watch this day, to give evidence at an inquiry into certain acts of violence committed this afternoon in the port of Colombo against Portuguese guests of the Great King.

'The said Abdul Raschid is further commanded to bring with him any witnesses who can give evidence as to the people and circumstances that caused this event and details of all parties guilty of breaching the Great King's peace.'

Her fingers felt nerveless as she finished reading the summons, but once again Aisha maintained firm control over herself. She heard the breath leave her husband in a great gasp without any pity for him.

'Dear Allah, what shall I do?' He could barely whisper.

She had not come thus far to lose. 'Did you say Majid is dead?'

'Yes.'

'Did anyone other than Majid hear your orders to him?'

'Er . . . n . . . no.'

'Are you sure?'

'Yes, I'm positive.' He must have seen the drift of her questions, because he soon began to recover. Finally, a slow smile played on the sides of his mouth and a look of cunning crossed his eyes. 'Dead jackals do not betray the kill, eh?'

'Precisely.' She paused and made up her mind. 'You need have no fear of this official inquiry, husband, for I shall accompany you as a witness.'

Monday, 11 February 1521

We returned to the stables to recover our horses through cheering crowds who were pouring back on to the streets. Cries of 'Maya Dunne Jayewewa!' rang out, much to my grandfather's disgust, I am sure, and my father's secret embarrassment.

The governor's mansion was on a hill at the northern end of the harbour in the area known as Mutu Vella, because gems from a sunken trading ship were once washed to its shores. The port's governor, Prince Maitri, was a cousin of the Great King. We sent a messenger ahead on a fast horse to advise him of our visit and another bearing my father's summons to Abdul Raschid, the Mouro leader, at his home near the Slave Island.

'I wonder how Maitri is taking all this?' Prince Raigam inquired as we trotted side by side through glaring sunlight along the ocean-front road.

Prince Wijayo snorted in derision. 'N-nothing upsets him. He is n-not known as a m-man of action. He g-got this appointment b-because he is in the Great K-king's favour.'

'He was appointed governor becaue he is one of the most trustworthy men in the country,' my father countered. 'With the volume of trade handled by the port and the heavy expense of maintaining it, the Great King needs every *tola* of revenue he can generate through customs duty, taxes and levies. Honesty is therefore more important here than action, which Prince Maitri can always generate through his deputies.'

My grandfather clucked impatiently but made no further comment. I wondered what he would do if he ever became the Great King, which could well happen if our present king died before him. For by Arya custom, a ruler with no children is succeeded by the oldest surviving brother.

The great wooden entrance gates of the mansion, ribbed with iron, were closed. We knocked and were identified through a peep-hole by the guard captain. He shouted for the guard to turn out and the gates grumbled open with a squeaking of hinges. A winding brown cobblestone driveway, flanked by stately, green *ashoka* trees with spacious gardens extending on both sides, lay before the grey granite mansion with its red Calicut tile roof on the crest of the hill. As we trotted towards the mansion, a breeze fanned us from our left, where the deep blue ocean, flecked with white wave-caps, spread towards a shimmering horizon. Bringing the faint sounds of human voices, the laughter of children and the smells of cattle dung from newly manured flower beds, it taught me for the first time that the life of the people goes on while dramatic events seethe and swirl around them. A thought emerged which my mind was still too immature to shape into certainty: that life is a whole to which each individual contributes, so that if one person dies, the life still goes on.

Rounding a bed in the driveway, we saw the two-storey mansion more clearly now, splashed by the afternoon sun. It was surrounded by tall green flamboyant and tamarind trees, so that it was completely hidden from the harbour while still having splendid views all round.

To our surprise, Governor Prince Maitri awaited us on the top step of the front entrance, with grooms, servants and guards in attendance. He was a tall, gaunt man, with a long neck and a prominent voice box, very loose-limbed, about forty years of age. His skin was dark, the hatchet face pitted with pock marks, but the teeth shone pearly-white when he smiled his greeting. He was simply dressed in white tunic and pantaloons, with no adornments or weapons. If there was any jitteriness on the part of his retinue, he had probably dispelled it with his calm.

The grooms hastened to hold our horses' heads as we dismounted, Prince Wijayo with a grunt of satisfaction. Governor Maitri stepped down to salute us as we chorused our *auybowans*. He gripped me by the shoulders. 'Well, well, well.' His favourite phrase. 'So you have come of age, Prince Tikiri.'

91

His voice was very deep, slow-moving, seeming to come from the pit of his stomach. 'Happy birthday and welcome to the world.'

'Thank you, uncle,' I replied, sinking almost to my knees, hands to my forehead in the traditional greeting.

'You have bred a fine whelp by all accounts, cousin Maya,' the governor observed. The way he looked me over, we might have been meeting only for the first time, though I had often spent weekends at his mansion. 'The young man is growing up the spitting image of you in looks, Maya, a great handicap, I'm sure!' He paused. 'Well, judging from today's events, we are going to need men like him.'

'The country is always in n-need of good m-men,' Prince Wijayo intervened pompously.

'I presume you are aware of everything that has taken place?' my father inquired.

'Pretty much.'

'As our messenger must have conveyed to you, we would like the courtesy of your mansion to hold an inquiry into the actions of the Moorish trader, Abdul Raschid, which could have precipitated armed conflict between us and the *parangi*, or, at the very least, reprisals from them. We have also invited the *parangi* admiral here tonight.'

'My home is yours to command, cousin.' Governor Maitri's smile became grim. 'I presume we will give them dinner? Good. It shall be arranged. Meanwhile let me show you their warning.'

'What do you mean?' my father demanded.

'You will see. Please follow me.'

He led us along a red brick-paved walkway to the corner of the mansion. As we broke through an opening in a thick, mock-orange hedge through which the path led down to shady groves, we could see the entire harbour spread below us. The great *parangi* warships, dark-painted, dominated its gleaming waters. The whole scene was unreal, like a painting or a tapestry, but the threat was very evident.

The governor headed for a shadowy grove of jak-trees halfway down the hill. Three bare-chested gardeners, their skins burnt black by the sun, laid down their digging tools and made obeisance. Governor Maitri pointed towards two great white scars topping the trunks of the tallest jak trees and the mass of fallen branches in the grove below us. 'Two rounds from their big guns shattered the tops of those trees,' he stated. 'From all that distance away, so accurately!' He shook his head in wonder. 'We could really be in trouble. You can imagine our surprise when we heard the two salvoes and the second one sent cannon balls whistling towards us to crash in the grove. We thought at first that they were shelling the house, but soon realized that the salvoes were fired into the ocean with only these two shots directed here, as a warning.'

'D-damned lucky they d-didn't get your house,' Prince Wijayo commented. 'We shouldn't f-fool with these people. Let us just g-give them whatever they want and send them away.'

'We must first find out what they want,' my father retorted. 'Those are the Great King's orders and that is why we are meeting them this evening.'

'If we run away like pi-dogs with our tails between our legs, the whole country will run,' Prince Raigam commented.

'I d-don't like it,' Prince Wijayo muttered, fingering his grey moustache.

'Sena, you and Podda bring up those cannon balls,' the governor directed the oldest gardener.

Two of the men hastened to the edge of the grove and returned carrying round, iron objects in their hands. It was the first time I had ever seen cannon balls. I wondered at weapons that could hurl these rounds such a distance so accurately. This was the real power, concentrated into a single weapon instead of being borne by thousands of bowmen, cavalry and infantry, catapults and battering rams.

In that instant, I realized not only that the destiny of Lanka had altered this day, but that the country would need muskets and cannon for its survival. How to get them was the question. I had been told that the *parangi* manufacture the weapons secretly in their home country and never make firearms in their distant possessions. The very next moment, the tiny shoot of an idea sprouted in my mind, like the birth of the first green onion

93

I ever planted in the soil of my ancestral home. It produced an intense desire to hold one of those iron cannon balls in my hands.

As if in anticipation, my father offered the ball he had been holding. 'Feel the weight of this, Prince.'

I held the messenger of power and doom in my hands. It was vibrant. Its strength spoke to me from my palms, through my arms and my entire body. I am what you need to fulfil your destiny, it said.

'We d-don't have the time to f-fool around,' Prince Wijayo complained. 'Let us g-go in, b-bathe and g-get ready. Nephew Maitri, you will surely have some refreshment f-for us?'

Reluctantly I handed the cannon ball back to the gardener. I did not want to let it go. My father had been watching me with a strange intensity.

Monday, 11 February 1521

My room in the governor's mansion was the one I had used on previous visits here. It had boarded floors and was located on the upper storey, facing south-west, with a sweeping view of the harbour. After a visit to the bathing enclosure, I donned the change of clothing laid out for me on the divan bed, a tunic and pantaloons of white satin, my thonged black sandals cleaned. These mansions always carry some spare clothes but I was fortunate in that one of the governor's four children, all of whom were holidaying in their country residence at this time, was a young man about my age and size.

I stood by the window gazing down at the painted Portuguese warships on the painted Sinhala ocean. Their presence was an affront to me and to the entire nation. For the first time since morning, I had leisure to take in the enormity of the event. Fury seized me.

But my attention was diverted by voices on the paved, grey courtyard below. A lean, dark man, with a silver moustache and beard, his long hair gathered into a knot at the nape of his neck, was chatting with two red-uniformed guards. I recognized Kodi, perhaps the leading wood and metal worker in the country. It

94

was said that Kodi and his staff could manufacture anything from a sword to a ploughshare, a rain gutter to a chariot, everything a ship required. He and I had shared many a talk and even a dream or two together. My heart leapt and I was about to call down to Kodi when caution intruded. Instead I whirled round, raced out of the room, walked more sedately along the corridors, slipped down the stairs and casually made my way outside.

Kodi was still chatting with the two guards. His face lit up when he saw me. I returned his salutation, pretending to be surprised. The two guards saluted and moved away.

'How good to see you, young lord!' Kodi exclaimed.

He was well over sixty but his face was unlined, though his back was bent from years of labour over forge and workbench. 'It is your birthday too, is it not? I hear you and your honourable father have done brave deeds today.'

I shrugged, somewhat embarrassed. 'My father did it all. I merely followed.' I noticed the guards were out of earshot, but still kept my voice low. 'I'm glad you are here, Kodi, because there is something I want to ask you, something terribly important for our country, for the Sinhala nation, for history . . .'
I paused to take a breath before my own rush of words and he smiled humbly, obviously arrested by my earnestness.

'Down there are seventeen *parangi* ships.' I nodded towards the harbour. 'They have enough firepower to dictate anything to us. The only way we will stop them is if we have the firepower too.'

His brown eyes quickened with interest, then it was his turn to shrug. 'They have developed their weapons secretly through the years, young lord. We do not know those secrets.'

'If you had a musket and a cannon, could you not produce exact replicas?'

'I can produce anything made of wood and metal if these old eyes can see the original and these hands can feel it.' He held up long, tapering fingers, the ends strong and spatulate. 'But I have heard tell that the *parangi* never allow any native of the countries which they invade close to their weapons.'

Excitement had seethed within me at his boast. 'Listen, Kodi.'

95

I was holding his keenest attention now. 'You and I have talked in the past about how to build an organization that will provide a ready supply of weapons and equipment to a regular Sinhala army. We have even shared a dream, have we not?'

He swivelled his head to stare at the warships. The western sun caught the clean-cut profile, seeming to make it glow. He turned his gaze on me again and sighed. 'We have indeed, young lord. There is nothing I will not do for the country.'

'All right then, perhaps we can start in a small way. Here is my plan.'

He listened attentively, nodding his head, alternating between eyes downcast and looking directly at me. 'The only problem is, I cannot provide the bait,' I concluded. 'Can you?'

His brown eyes were gleaming with a mixture of admiration and excitement. 'I'll simply have to, won't I, young lord? It may not work, but your reasoning is sound. It's worth a try.'

CHAPTER 9
Monday, 11 February 1521

Aisha Raschid had never visited the house of a stranger, or any seat of authority. The only person in the world aware of her inner rebellion against the rules imposed on her sex by religion had been her brother, Paichi Markar, in whom she had always confided. For instance, women were not permitted daily prayer or to visit the mosque whenever they had their bleeding, making it doubly a curse. She questioned whether these restrictions were indeed the teachings of the Prophet or whether they reflected the insecurities of males which had led men to place curtains around women's lives in the first instance.

Lacking a confidante after she left her brother, Aisha had adopted another male custom. She maintained a secret diary.

This afternoon, she took special care with her appearance, though she would be hidden by her *yashmak*. She glanced down at her maid, Sabrina, who was intent on pinning the silken underblouse to her silver pantaloons. Her glance travelled down to Sabrina's wide, homely face, the grey hair tied in a knot at the nape of her neck. Sabrina had always been like a mother to her.

'The Arabic word *Islam* means submission, obedience and commitment to the will of Allah so we can have peace within ourselves,' she observed to the bowed grey head. 'The path was pointed out by our Prophet because man had veered from it time and again, though it had also been revealed by the earlier prophets, Adam, Noah, Abraham, Isaac and Jacob, Moses and Jesus. Our Prophet, Muhammad, alone, inspired by Ishmael, committed the word of Allah into writing in the Holy Koran, but it did not take men long after his death to start interpreting the word according to their desires. And I believe that it is man and not the Prophet who has placed women in a position of subordination.'

'If you say so,' Sabrina mumbled unconcernedly through the pins in her mouth. 'Stop fidgeting, child.'

'Our Prophet said that man needs two things for his development,' Aisha continued. 'The wherewithal to maintain life – whatever each of us and the society in which we live requires for material fulfilment – and a knowledge of how each of us and our society should behave in order to maintain justice and peace in our lives. Surely, Sabrina, justice must extend to all human beings, including women. That is why I'm going on this mission today. I am the instrument of Allah to ensure that we receive justice and that we are able to continue fulfilling our material needs. For years now, we have been able to carry on our trade because we have the ships and the foreign connections which neither the Sinhala nor any of the native people of this region possess.'

'Our people have been sailors for countless years.' Sabrina looked up at her squarely. 'Even before they brought horses and silks to this land in exchange for its gold, precious gems and spices. That is where our power began.'

'Exactly,' Aisha continued. 'And we have given the world its first real civilization, the science of mathematics and astronomy, the Arabic script, the cultured arts. Here in Lanka, we even supply the Sinhala with food from abroad, because internal wars and the invading Cholas have made them dependent. We have governed the lives of all in Lanka because Allah gave us the material resources and the will to exploit them.' A grim note entered her voice. 'Then came the Portuguese. They are worse than the ravening Mongols of the east. Having taken over our influence in the entire ocean by sheer force, they are now here in Lanka. I am a Ghazni and a Ghuri. I can match the accursed of Allah in strength, ferocity and cruelty.'

Sabrina completed her pinning, helped Aisha don her silver overshirt, then the mustard brown robe of shiny Kashmiri silk, finally the hood and veil revealing only the dark, luminous eyes. 'Nothing will ever draw a veil over your spirit,' she observed quietly.

They travelled to the governor's mansion in two separate horsedrawn buggies. Abdul Raschid occupied the first buggy.

Aisha's, following, was curtained on all four sides, so that she and Sabrina travelled in darkness, except for an occasional peek through the curtains.

The staff of the governor's mansion was obviously puzzled by the presence of the two veiled women, for Aisha could discern them whispering to each other. She had asked Abdul to remain outside. A guard captain escorted them through a great ante-room furnished with black ebony couches into the centre court verandah, from which they entered a large audience chamber furnished with more black ebony couches, crimson-cushioned, on floors of white mountain crystal. The walls of the chamber were adorned with frescoes in the black, orange and red colours of the Sinhala artists, illuminated by a dozen twelve-tiered brass lamps, their lighted wicks like a hundred unwinking stars. Aisha took the couch at the rear end of the chamber, with Sabrina standing on her right.

The guards withdrew, leaving them alone. Aisha noted the ebony table at the far end of the room, with a single matching chair behind it. Within moments she heard the clack of sandalled feet and the guard captain reappeared. 'All rise and greet General Prince Maya Dunne, Commander-in-Chief of the armies of the Great King of Lanka.'

Aisha stood up. A tall, slim man walked towards the ebony table, followed by a slightly shorter man of like build. The first man reached the table, went round it, then turned to face the room. One brief glimpse of the clean-cut features and Aisha knew that this was the most handsome, noble-looking man she had ever seen. She sank low in salutation. As she rose she probed the general's face, the sides of his eyes, his mouth, his cheeks, his chin, for some sign of weakness. She found none.

The general took his seat at the desk. The young man standing behind was so like him they must be father and son.

'I understand that the person to whom my summons was issued is not present?' The general's voice was deep, its inflection sharp, commanding.

'Yes, lord,' Aisha replied, injecting submissiveness into her voice, playing the role of the timid Muslim woman.

'And are you his chief wife, madam?'

99

'I am, lord.'

'Why is the accused not present?'

'He didn't realize he was accused. He merely received a summons to attend an inquiry.'

A glint in the general's fine eyes and a slight relaxing of the sides of his mouth told her the shaft had gone home and he had received it with good humour. 'You are right, madam,' he confirmed. 'Will you then state why the witness is not present?'

'My husband, Abdul Raschid, has come to the mansion with me, but decided to remain outside because he has been very sick since last night and deemed it best not to spread any infectious disease.'

'You are aware of the incidents at the port today and are prepared to speak on your husband's behalf?'

'Yes, lord.'

'You may proceed.'

'When the foreign ships arrived, one of the guard captains, named Majid, disobeyed my husband's instructions because he desired to raise a revolt against us, for more pay. He assembled about five hundred guards at the waterfront and fired arrows at the *parangi* visitors, who killed many of them in retaliation and destroyed our valuable property.' She allowed a controlled sob to escape her. 'We have punished many of the guilty, lord, but we helpless people have suffered untold loss.'

A short laugh from the general told her she had overshot the mark with her talk of helplessness. 'You are hardly helpless, madam, with over five hundred fully armed mercenaries whom you euphemistically call security guards. Perhaps you are unaware of this?' A sarcastic note had entered his voice.

'That is possible, lord, for after all I am only a woman and in *purdah*. I do not see much beyond this veil, but I believe that anyone, however strong, who is the victim of far superior force can be helpless.' She kept her eyes downcast, yet the silence told her that the observation had gone home. 'My husband got to the scene only after the event, lord. I am witness to that. He was in the port only after you had stopped the disturbance and left. Since he might have an infectious disease, he talked to no one, merely observed what had happened and came straight home, angry but unable to do anything because the damage had already been done.'

'He gave no instructions while at the port?'

'No, lord. There was no one to whom he could issue instructions, and he told me he felt he should leave the situation in the hands of the port authorities.'

'Why is that?'

'Because the arrival of the *parangi* made the situation a political one. My husband is but a trader. If he is a rich one, then he pays more to the government in duties, taxes and levies and can only look to the Great King for protection and . . . er . . . compensation for the acts of foreign invaders.'

That amused smile touched the corners of the general's mouth again, but he deliberately avoided her complaint. 'What has your husband done about this . . . ah . . . security guard captain, Majid, who raised the standard of . . . er . . . revolt?'

She forced a heavy sigh. 'Alas, he was killed by the fire of the *parangi*, lord. And all his chief rebels with him. It is the will of Allah who has punished them for their misdeeds. Since they did not die for Islam, they will even now be in the infidel's hell.'

'You are obviously a religious lady. Is it not unusual for you to attend any public event, especially an inquiry of this sort?'

'Our religion teaches us to do our duty, lord. I am but the humble servant of my lord, the One God, and of my master in this life, my husband Abdul Raschid, who is not guilty of any wrongdoing.'

'I appreciate anyone who does their duty in the face of odds,' the general responded gravely. She could not tell whether he were serious or toying with her. 'Well, I think we have gone as far as we can tonight. You are right to deduce that the situation in the port is political.' A grim note entered his voice. 'The lives taken and the damage caused were occasioned by men in your husband's employ. Regardless of whether they were demonstrating against him or acting contrary to his wishes, he has to accept the ultimate responsibility for their actions.' The tone of the general's voice permitted no protest. 'Far from receiving compensation therefore, he will pay for any damage caused to the port facilities and the life and property of others. Let this be

101

a lesson to him, however, to disband his security force and pay the government what it costs him to maintain it, so he can have better protection.'

He paused; his expression tightened. 'I am closing this inquiry now and waiving the right to shut down your trading operations, on one condition. Are you prepared to accept it?'

Her chest tightened. 'What is it, lord?'

'That you give the Great King your unqualified and ready support on demand in future against all his enemies.'

Relief flooded her. 'I can swear to that, lord.' It was only after the words came out that she realized that she had walked into the general's trap and betrayed the fact that it was she who made the decisions.

Monday, 11 February 1521

Fernao had been thrilled when his father directed him to accompany the delegation that would attend General Prince Maya Dunne at the governor's mansion. The admiral and his entourage had donned formal clothes of white satin, embellished with gold facings, for the occasion.

Captain Oliveira headed the group of officers, which was met at the main wharf by coaches and a cavalry escort. 'The general knew that we would not travel without our own armed bodyguard,' Admiral de Albergaria observed grimly, noting the number of coaches drawn up. He was taking with him all the escort agreed to, fifty fully-armed *degradado* commanded by a burly sergeant. 'I remember Vasco da Gama's first visit to the Zamorin too well to repeat his performance.' He was referring, Fernao knew, to Vasco da Gama's near-detention by the Zamorin of Calicut.

At the governor's mansion they were cordially received. The admiral requested permission to post Portuguese sentries around the perimeter of the building, with a reserve of twenty men in the courtyard and ten inside the mansion. They then partook of refreshments in the dining hall, including a variety of Sinhala curries, fruit, curds, honey and sweetmeats, accompanied by the local palm wine. On orders from the admiral, the

Portuguese ate and drank only whatever their hosts enjoyed. Fernao found his hosts courteous, hospitable and refined, without any of the arrogance and vulgarity of the Indian ruling class.

Finally, they assembled in the audience chamber, ready to commence their discussions. Fernao was excited by the historic occasion. What an event to write about some day!

The lights of the great multi-wicked brass lamps made for a glittering scene. Like the rest of the mansion, the chamber was elegant and comfortable, cool with ocean breezes, a pleasant relief from the heat of the day at the wharf and especially on board the flagship. A long, black ebony table occupied the centre of the room, with three matching chairs covered by rose-pink cushions on each side and a more ornamental chair at the head. The oldest man of the Sinhala group, the brother of the Great King, occupied the head chair, with Admiral de Albergaria on his right, the Sinhala general on his left and their host, Prince Maitri, in front of him. Captain Oliveira, a lean sinewy senior captain named Gaspar da Costa and Fernao stood at the back of the admiral's chair. Behind the general stood the only other person in the room, the young man with whom Fernao's eyes had locked challengingly in the harbour that afternoon, Prince Tikiri. He would act as interpreter.

Prince Wijayo rapped the table lightly for attention. 'We can n-now get d-down to business. Admiral de Albergaria, having welcomed you f-formally and we hope hospitably to our shores, on behalf of the Great King, we are now c-commanded to inquire as to the n-nature of your visit and your f-future intentions.'

All eyes were fixed on the admiral, who signalled to Fernao. The Sinhala seemed puzzled as he stepped forward and handed a scroll to his father then stood respectfully behind him again.

'We have arrived in your country in pursuance of this document, my lords,' the admiral declared. 'It is the treaty executed in the year 1505 by and between your Great King and our Captain, now Admiral, Lorenzo de Almeida, on behalf of the King Emperor of Portugal when part of our fleet visited your port of Galle. Your Great King faithfully delivered the four

103

hundred *bahars* of cinnamon promised under this treaty and the annual er . . . gifts, while my Emperor has afforded your trading ships freedom of the seas. Only one more of the terms of the treaty remains to be fulfilled, the erection by us of a factory in the port of Colombo for the mutual benefit of our countries.'

Prince Wijayo looked blankly at each of his colleagues. The general's expression had not changed, while Prince Maitri remained relaxed, non-committal. Prince Tikiri was tense with suppressed anger.

'Our Great King is unaware of that portion of the document,' General Maya Dunne began. 'Is it in your language?'

'Yes, my lord, but as you can see it bears the signature and seal of your Great King, Parakrama Bahu IX, who had just ascended the throne at the time and continues to rule with the noble honorific "Dharma" attached to his name, by virtue of his piety. My Emperor and I trust that he is in good health and spirits.'

'He is, my lord admiral.' General Maya Dunne had recovered command. 'And we trust your own King Emperor is likewise in good health and spirits?'

'Indeed so, by the grace of God and the saints,' the admiral responded smoothly. 'You are not repudiating the treaty, are you, my lords? You will give us the *sesmaria*, land concessions?'

'Of course n-not,' Prince Wijayo replied. 'I m-mean of course we are not repudiating the treaty. Indeed, our concern is to extend it to our m-mutual advantage.'

'The advantage to you is obvious, my lords.' Having sensed that Prince Wijayo was the weakest of the four Sinhala present, the admiral was directing the full force of his personality on the old man. 'If we establish a factory in Colombo, it will give us a base of operations . . . er . . . trading operations in this part of the Indian Ocean to which we will more fully extend the protection of our war fleet, which I am sure you have heard can exercise considerable force.' He smiled to make the warning sound like an assurance and Fernao was pleased that his father was a diplomat as well as a fighter. 'We all had ample evidence this afternoon of the militancy of the Mouro.' A grim note had entered the admiral's voice. 'I tell you, my lords, this is an attitude we have found throughout the entire East Indies, from Basra to the Moluccas. The Mouro desire to resurrect the dead empire which they formerly ensured through brute force by a monopoly of trade. We Portuguese are a civilized people. It was our Admiral Vasco da Gama who first introduced a policy of fair prices for all local produce, nearly twenty years ago, to prevent exploitation by the Mouro traders, the sultans and the Zamorin. Fulfil the terms of our treaty and you will reap rich rewards.'

And if you do not, we shall blow your seaboard cities to hell, Fernao thought savagely, and was surprised at the ferocity of his reaction. What was happening to him?

'The offer of your p-protection on the high seas is m-most attractive,' Prince Wijayo observed.

'So long as it is confined to the high seas,' General Maya Dunne interjected.

'We have no desire to expand our territories, merely our trade,' the admiral responded blandly.

'A policy you have reportedly followed in Cochin, Cananor, Calicut and elsewhere,' the general retorted, but with a smile that robbed the words of offence.

'Whether it is for the benefit of the Great King of today, or whomever may be the Great King tomorrow, the advantages of our having a trading fort . . . er . . . post in Colombo are obvious.' Again the admiral's statement was directed to Prince Wijayo.

Wijayo is the man who may reap the benefits of our policy, Fernao thought with a fresh spurt of admiration. Since the Great King has no children, when he dies, Prince Wijayo will succeed to the throne. 'Any ruler, especially of an island kingdom, should welcome the protection of the naval might of Portugal in these waters at no more cost than fair trade, of which we do not even demand a monopoly,' he heard the admiral add, and thought, I must grow to be like him.

Prince Wijayo was apparently both impressed and gratified. 'I b-believe we can accede to your request,' he began, looking at his fellow Sinhala.

'As soon as the Great King has ratified it,' General Maya Dunne put in smoothly. 'And specific details of the terms and conditions of what is at present a broad agreement have been worked out.'

Fernao's total attention had been centred on the men around the table. Now he looked across the room for Prince Tikiri's reaction. The dark eyes flickered contemptuously away from Prince Wijayo.

'Which brings me to two more important points,' the admiral stated. 'I am here as the representative of the Viceroy of Goa, who acts for our King Emperor. I would deem it a courtesy to be granted an audience with your Great King, so that I can pay him my respects, convey the felicitations of my Viceroy and His Imperial Majesty and personally deliver to him certain gifts I have brought as tokens of our esteem.'

'The Great King would be d-delighted,' Prince Wijayo replied.

'It will, however, take some time to arrange,' General Maya Dunne intervened again smoothly.

'The second point relates to our countrymen, whom Captain Lorenzo de Almeida left behind in the port of Galle sixteen years ago, two Franciscan friars, Father Juan and Father Perez, and our trade representative, *a senhor* Duarte de Brito.' A smile touched the corners of the admiral's mouth and he brushed back his blond moustache with a wide forefinger. 'I also understand that Duarte de Brito now has a child, known as Julietta, though she is said to be a *mestico*, half breed. I fear they have been sadly neglected by us and have lived too many years in virtual exile, so I should like them to visit me on my flagship without delay.'

Fernao had watched Prince Tikiri as he translated back. Was there a quickening of his eyes at the mention of the name Julietta?

'How do you know whether they are even alive after all these years?' the general demanded with an amused expression.

The admiral was put off his stride for the first time. He cleared his throat. 'I assume they are, my lord,' he responded stiffly.

'And I am aware that communications have passed between some of them and your Viceroy,' the general stated bluntly. 'We shall certainly arrange for them to visit you. They have been honoured guests of the Great King all these years.'

106

Monday, 11 February 1521

Kodi watched the mansion from behind the dark shadow of the mock-orange hedge. It was brightly lit on both floors, with the exception of a few scattered squares of blackness that told of unoccupied rooms. Sinhala guards, carrying spears, swords at the waist, stood to attention at the entrance to the mansion and the courtyard and surrounding the building, all illuminated by hissing flares placed on sockets in the ground. Portuguese sentries, in their blue and red uniforms, wearing iron tunics and helmets, muskets at the ready, patrolled selected sectors of the courtyard, save for four who had fixed duty points at each corner. The coaches that had brought the party were drawn up so close by that the smell of leather, horse-dung and sweat hung heavy on the air. The animals stood placidly in their harnesses, occasionally stamping, snorting, grinding their bits.

Since he had never done this sort of thing before, except once in his youth when he was courting a higher caste girl in his village and risked being murdered by her kin to keep assignations, Kodi's heart was beating rapidly. Many times during the evening, he had regretted agreeing to do as Prince Tikiri had requested, but each time some sense of national duty and the hope of a singular achievement had pushed him relentlessly on.

Now here he was, with the most beautiful young girl in Mutu Vella, a hooded, cloaked figure by his side. Lila was a prostitute by profession, but of the most stunning proportions, tall and full-breasted, with a tiny waist and generous hips. The jasmine scent she was wearing combined with a more subtle skin fragrance to make even old Kodi have thoughts of possessing her. Her breath was perfumed with sweet *valmi* root and her large, dark eyes sparkled when she whispered, 'I have never taken a white man before. I wonder what it will be like. How much longer must we wait?' Strangely, she seemed unafraid.

'He will need to be quick, so don't expect a miracle,' Kodi whispered back. 'It's almost time now. Having been at sea these many days, perhaps not even lying with a woman for weeks, knowing that his officers are in there eating, drinking, having a good time, we only require enough time for him to realize that

107

there is no danger, so he can leave his post.'

Kodi eyed his target through the hedge. The tall, lusty looking *parangi*, his pitted skin ruddy in the flarelight, stood barely twenty-five yards away, his musket held at the ready. The sentries patrolling on either side of him converged. One made a remark in their language. The three men laughed, obviously quite relaxed now. They looked up at the clouded sky, devoid of a single star. The target sentry shrugged, the other two men walked away in opposite directions.

'Now', Kodi directed and backed away into the deeper shadows.

Lila gave a soft moan. The target sentry came alert, his body straightening. He turned swiftly in the direction of the sound. Lila moaned again, started hobbling slowly forward.

The sentry glanced swiftly to either side of him, then advanced towards the gap in the hedge. Lila sobbed once, pretended to stumble and fall, allowing her hood to become displaced. The *parangi* saw her and came up, to find Lila bent, holding her ankle. Musket in hand, he stood staring down at her.

Lila raised her face up to him and Kodi knew the sentry was lost, for even in the semi-gloom she was a creature of beauty. Glancing alertly through the gap now, the sentry knelt, placed his musket on the ground. Lila lifted a palm to his shoulder, pointed to her ankle and moaned softly again. The sentry went wild. He grabbed Lila and started raining kisses on her. She pretended to struggle at first but soon stopped resisting. She raised a warning hand and pointed to the greater darkness of the grove below.

The man was blinded with desire now. He sprang to his feet, lifted Lila in his arms as if she were but a cushion. She clung to him, her arms round his neck as he sped downhill with his precious burden.

A low female giggle from the dark grove told Kodi the play had begun. He stole forward, picked up the precious musket, inspected it carefully. He hefted it in his hands seeking the weight of each part and the balance. He peered carefully into the muzzle and ran sensitive fingers along the stock, the firing mechanism, the barrel. Finally, he knew how it worked and every part of it was committed to his memory.

I have learned the secret of the *parangi* firearm this night, while the *parangi* soldier probes the secret weapon of the Sinhala in the very grove where his cannon balls landed this afternoon, Kodi thought. He laid the musket exactly where he found it and melted into the shadow of the mock-orange bushes again.

A shriek from the grove, quickly stifled, brought him to a halt. Was it pain or delight? Kodi peered through the gloom towards the grove, but it was inky black. He shrugged mentally. Lila knew how to take care of herself. The *parangi* looked as if he had a huge organ and his lust in taking a woman probably made him thrust too hard. The cry was not repeated.

Kodi glanced through the hedge. No one seemed to have heard a sound. He had best leave. Lila regularly serviced the mansion guards at night, so she could find her way home alone.

CHAPTER 10
Monday, 11 February 1521

The courtyard of the mansion was finally quiet after the *parangi* left. The night was still except for the faint rustle of dark branches from a breeze not strong enough to move the heavy, burnished clouds overhead. A gloomy night in more senses than one.

My father and I strolled to the south-western boundary of the courtyard and paused to survey the scene below. The flares and lamps of the port glowed yellow, the Portuguese ships were dim ghosts of light on the vast darkness of the ocean.

'It's a sad day for the country,' my father observed, shaking his head. He sighed, then forced himself to brighten. 'But it's certainly been a long and eventful birthday for you, has it not?'

I was sorely tempted to tell him that it could be eventful for the country too, because Kodi had already slipped me word of the success of his mission, but I quickly decided that it must remain a secret until I could actually present my father with the fruit of my ingenuity. 'The most eventful day of my life, thanks to you, *tha*,' I replied instead. 'I need not tell you that I shall follow you to the uttermost ends of the earth.'

His sideways smile was impish. 'Let's not go that far; the ends of Lanka will suffice,' he said, then added quickly, 'But I do appreciate the expression of your devotion.' He turned towards me, his face sober. 'Now that you have entered a man's estate and have acquitted yourself honourably and with dignity today, I have made some decisions concerning your future. First, as to your patrimony. You shall be the feudal lord of the ten western villages of the Sita Waka Korle, deriving all their income and the service of their people. I shall have these villages administered on your behalf for the time being, but always remember that more important than the rights of an overlord are his feudal duties to his people.'

Overwhelmed by his generosity, I fought back my tears. 'You will remain in residence at the Jaya palace for the present,' he added quickly, 'and continue your studies in military strategy and the martial arts, but I now name you commander of the first cavalry squadron of the Great King's armies. The special assignment of this squadron henceforth will be to act as a reserve for port security, so it will have quarters both in the palace and in Mutu Vella, where I shall be arranging for a total of ten cavalry squadrons to be accommodated. Governor Prince Maitri Pala has agreed that your room in the mansion will always be available to you. If you show the promise I expect in your duties, I shall appoint you colonel of the entire cavalry regiment at the appropriate time.'

I glowed for a few moments, my eyes shining. Such heady stuff for a sixteen year old. Then apprehension struck. 'But, Sir,' I addressed him formally now, as befitted his rank. 'If I am promoted too fast, other officers will become jealous and dissatisfied. They will say I am being favoured. Forgive me, but should I not prove myself first?'

'Of course you are being favoured,' he retorted. 'But not only because you are my son.' A passionate note entered his voice. 'Young men such as you are rare and must be trained fast to lead our country, now that we are faced with the greatest threat in our history, the *parangi*, white man.'

From now on I would be spending less time in the palace. I had been conscious of Julietta all day, as if she were witnessing everything I did. Now suddenly the thought of her spun into sharp focus. Just when I had discovered her, I would be seeing less of her. She would be sleeping at this moment. Yet how wonderful it would have been if I could have woken her and given her my news. Her eyes would have shone, she would have clapped her hands, crying, 'Oh, Prince Tiki-tiki, I'm so proud of you.'

With his uncanny perception my father picked up my thoughts. 'Put all goals out of your mind from now on, except your duty to king and country,' he advised quietly. 'When the time comes, you will wed for the cause alone. There must be no woman in your life who cannot enrich that cause.'

111

Julietta would indeed enrich our cause, as my inspiration and help-mate if she were beside me, my heart cried imploringly, but all I saw outside was my father's face, now stern as my own reality.

Monday, 11 February 1521

The admiral's cabin, on the poop deck of the flagship, was small but well lit by shiny brass oil lanterns hanging from the low ceiling. It had built-in seats, cushioned in blue velvet, along the two sides and a bunk bed at the far end, before which the admiral now stood. The narrow table between the seats was riveted to the wooden deck, as was the writing desk and chair alongside the entrance door, at which Fernao was seated as directed by his father. The whole atmosphere of the cabin was one of warmth and cleanliness, created by waxed woodwork, highly polished brass and the framed etchings of ships on the panelled walls. The admiral's figure, still in white satin uniform, looked bigger than ever as he paced the confined space.

'You can never trust the *pretos*, blacks, or the *canarim*, people of the Indian coast,' the admiral declaimed. 'The only way to ensure their co-operation is to force it.'

Fernao idly wondered whether compliance could be called co-operation if it was enforced. While appreciating the privilege of this little personal talk, he was suddenly feeling very sleepy from the heavy meal and the palm wine served in the governor's mansion.

'That General Maya Dunne is the one person we have to watch,' the admiral continued. 'He is tough and I think he can be cunning.' He paused in his stride and faced Fernao. 'Which is why I asked you to step in here for a talk.' He paused, searching his son's face. 'We have sailed together for four years now. I hope they have been rewarding ones for you?' The question came out abruptly, as if the admiral were ashamed to intrude a personal note.

Fernao was surprised. 'Why yes, Sir. Yes indeed,' was all he could reply.

For a moment, the pale blue eyes searching Fernao's face had a haunted look. 'This comes hard for me, my son.' The strong voice had an unusual note of gentleness. 'I have to admit that I have been more of a mentor to you than the parent you may have needed, especially after your mother died, God bless her soul.' His voice toughened again and the old icy stare entered his eyes. 'It was necessary, however, to turn you into a true de Albergaria. As with all *fidalgos*, nobles, family has been more important for us than the individual. I therefore elected to be your leader rather than your parent or your friend, to command your respect instead of earning your love. And yet...' He scratched his blond beard, resumed his pacing, seemed to be speaking to himself. 'I feel much more than leadership towards you, feelings that have remained unexpressed.' He stopped, looking down at Fernao, almost a plea in his expression. 'Do you understand?'

Fernao did understand and was suddenly filled with a sense of futility. He had indeed grown up respecting his father, stifling every need, whether for a parent or the ambition to become a writer, in order to behave like a true de Albergaria. Be a de Albergaria! Be a *fidalgo*! Follow the code of the *cavaleiro*! It had all been dinned into his ears. Then he had been posted to the Indies and another world of the code had been opened to him, trade, conquest, bombardment, bloodlust. He had learned to accept all this as a world within his world. Now, when his father was hinting of love, the very instincts his father had bred in him prevented him from having the feelings of a son. He knew that his father's words should reach some part of his heart, but his father had caused that part to disappear through the years. So today they would both pay the price.

He remembered the nights he had lain in bed conjuring fantasies about rescuing his father from danger and being rewarded by love and gratitude. All that frustration and disappointment seemed to have led to this moment, with his father revealing the emptiness within him only to be met by an emptiness he had created himself. It was a display of weakness and sentimentality such as he had been taught to hold in scorn. 'I understand, Sir,' he responded aloud, then lied. 'I have always felt the same way.'

'Thank the good God for that!' his father exclaimed. He pondered a while. 'It is sad that we should understand each other only when the moment of parting is close at hand.' He shook his head. 'Well, that is always the price one has to pay for being what we are.'

Father and son stared at each other through the golden lamplight, with the same ice blue eyes, the same ice blue look. We are still strangers as people though so close to each other as fighting men, Fernao thought.

'By the way, now that you have grown up and we understand each other, you may call me, *o pai*, father, when we are alone.'

Suddenly, Fernao felt a spasm of disgust. Where were you when I really needed *o pai*, his spirit clamoured, when I was a little boy and wanted a father to hold me, to give me some tangible proof of love. Times, incidents flashed through his mind, the night he had a nightmare and had awoken screaming only to be reprimanded for cowardice, the day his little puppy had been killed by a horse's kick. Nonetheless, he maintained a warm, respectful exterior. 'I shall try and remember, s . . . er . . . *o pai*,' he responded softly. 'It is difficult after all these years.'

'Indeed!' The admiral cleared his throat. 'I shall be sailing for the Maldives very shortly,' he declared abruptly. 'I shall leave behind but two *nao*, the *Ascension* and the *Santa Maria*, to protect the factory we shall start building next week, by which time I expect to have the Great King's *sesmaria*. The site for the factory will be at the rocky inlet on the southern boundary of the port. What do you think of it?'

'Is it not too far removed from the port centre, sir?'

'A tactical location is of greater necessity than one convenient for commerce.' The admiral paused. 'Which brings me to another important matter. As of this moment, you cease to be a midshipman and are commissioned in His Imperial Majesty's Navy.' He strode to one of the seats, bent down, opened a locker and drew out a sword, belt and gold insignia of rank. 'Stand up, Fernao Soarez de Albergaria, officer and *cavaleiro*.'

His heart beating faster with pride, Fernao sprang sharply to attention.

'You are hereby appointed a lieutenant in the Navy of His

114

Imperial Majesty, Dom Manuel I of Portugal.' The admiral buckled the sword belt on him, then handed him the gold insignia. 'These insignia of your rank and that sword were given to me by my own father when I was first commissioned in the Navy. Wear them with pride, bear them with honour.'

Shame flooded Fernao at the coldness and disgust he had just felt. Surely where there was a common dignity there could be a common love. Could not the controlled love of a strong man be strength rather than weakness? Could not the admission of human need be the toughest of all assignments? His regret expressed itself in a curious hardening of the sides of his eyes. 'I shall serve my king and you, my admiral, with my life if need be,' he solemnly declared. 'On my oath and on my sacred honour.' Fernao meant every word and for the moment nothing else mattered.

'And you shall likewise serve Holy Church?'

'I shall indeed, Sir.'

'Good. Now sit down again, my... er... *o filho*, son, and listen to what I have to tell you.' He took a red silk handkerchief trimmed with white lace from his sleeve and blew his nose loudly in another rare admission of emotion, then took his seat beside the desk to unveil his plans. 'As I have already indicated, we shall build a fort, not a factory. It will enable us to dictate trade and to play whatever part is necessary in the politics of this country to produce the maximum benefits from that trade. As I see it, we should side with Prince Wijayo against General Maya Dunne and Prince Raigam. Prince Wijayo has the makings of a puppet. You shall remain in Colombo as aide-de-camp to Captain Oliveira, and my personal, unofficial envoy in Lanka.'

Fernao was stunned. He had never expected to be released from beneath his father's wing. Another gush of gratitude for his father swept through him. 'I shall endeavour to be worthy of your choice, Sir,' he declared.

'*O pai*,' his father requested, with a smile.

'*O pai*!' Fernao responded obediently. Suddenly, he thought of another father and son, General Prince Maya Dunne and Prince Tikiri. From the plans the admiral had unfolded, Fernao suddenly knew the cause of his feelings towards the young man.

115

Tuesday, 12 February 1521

My mind was bright, whirling with the events of the day. Clad only in a blue sarong, I lay awake for hours, staring at the night sky, tossing and turning on my yellow mat, which is all that covered the hard wooden bed, a discipline I had insisted on since boyhood in order to toughen my body and prepare it for military campaigns ahead. When I finally drifted away, my sleep was solid and heavy as a Portuguese warship.

I did not hear the crowing of cocks that announces the false dawn, but was awakened by a clamour of excited voices in the courtyard below. I wanted to turn over, shut out the sounds and sink back into the inviting depths of sleep, but a spark of consciousness intruded recollection of yesterday's momentous events. Remembering the *parangi* ships, the Moors' response, and Kodi's mission, I leapt out of bed, re-fastened my sarong around my waist and padded to the open window. What I saw in the dim grey light of dawn caused me to turn sharply, reach for my white *kurtha* and don it, slip on my black sandals and hasten downstairs.

A group of red-uniformed guards had formed a circle around a body. Two bare-chested gardeners, one of them old Sena, jabbered away to them, with cries of 'Aney!' and 'Apoi!' Tears were pouring down Sena's dark cheeks.

'We must inform the captain immediately,' one of the guards said.

I pushed my way through them. The guard recognized me. 'Make way for the prince,' he commanded.

She lay naked, face-down, her skin fair against the cold grey paving. It was the first time I had seen a fully naked woman. Even lifeless in death, the long black hair in disarray, her figure was magnificent. One of the guards pointed silently to her buttocks, smeared and clotted with blood. 'What fiend could have so brutalized her?'

'Aney! Apoi! That is not all,' Sena wailed. 'You should see her womanhood. This must be the work of some demon.'

'Surely he must be a devil. May the *devas* curse him,' the other gardener cried. 'You should see her face and neck. She

116

was savagely beaten and strangled to death.'

The grim truth began to dawn on me, like the lightening of the earth at that moment. Yet some wild hope made me demand, 'Who is this woman? Where did you find her?'

'Her name is Lila,' Sena replied, sobering before my stern gaze. 'We found her body when we went to start work beside the jak grove that you visited yesterday. She is a prostitute, Prince, who sometimes services our retainers. But even a beast did not deserve such a fate.' He began weeping again, wiping the snot from his nose with the back of his hand.

'Who did this?' I turned around. 'Does anyone know?' *I* knew. And my heart was numb and cold with the knowledge.

I met only puzzled eyes, some tear-filled. How many of those eyes once gazed on this woman's beauty with desire?

This full realization that I alone amongst all those present knew how this happened, that I alone had caused her gruesome mutilation and death tore me apart. I was near vomiting. I had to be alone. 'Cover the body and report this to your guard captain,' I hoarsely directed. 'He will institute an inquiry.'

Back in my bedroom I stood by the window and stared down at the courtyard. The corpse lay, shapeless now, beneath a brown blanket. I could never tell anyone what had happened and bring the animal to normal justice. This was a dread secret shared by a metal worker and a prince, one a symbol of the material, the other of the spiritual, both responsible for the crime. But I never dreamed that this would happen, a part of my mind pleaded in excuse. Give me the wilful wrong-doer any time, another part of that mind declaimed, rather than the thinking man who acts without sufficient forethought. What right did I have to cause Lila's death? Could I justify it by the results for my country? No, no, a thousand times no, my heart cried.

At that moment I faced up to the cruel reality of what lay ahead, shorn of all the glamour with which I had vested it, hellish conflict, bloodletting, wounding, maiming, killing, all for a cause. Nothing would be the same for me any more. My life as I had known it had ended with that corpse beneath the blanket. Yet the guilt would remain with me for ever.

My gaze shifted to the harbour. The Portuguese warships were huge dark blobs upon pale waters. In one of those ships the creature who did this gruesome deed probably lay sleeping peacefully, satiated, fulfilled. The curse of the gods upon you, I silently cried.

Foul *parangi*, I have been told that you are deviates, a crueller race than the Tartar hordes of Mahmud of Ghazni or the Mongols of Tamur and Genghis Khan who ravaged the Indian continent. You rape and mutilate human beings. You have laid the mark of the beast on the sacred soil of my native land. Your minds are as diseased as your skins.

Foul *parangi*, I swear by the *devas* to shed the last drop of my blood to avenge this pitiful corpse, to kill you as you have killed, to dishonour you as you have dishonoured this poor woman, to drive you from my motherland however long it takes.

Shaken by the intensity of my feelings, trembling, cold with sweat, I remembered Julietta. Chill as the tombs was my hatred of her at this moment, for she too had *parangi* blood in her veins.

By choice, I had never held a woman to me. The first fully naked woman I had ever seen was a twisted, brutalized corpse for which I was responsible. Would I ever be able to take a woman without remembering?

Like a man drowning in seas run amok, clutching at frothing water, I grasped an inspiration. Kodi must surely have seen the *parangi* guard, even in the uncertain light. There were not that many of them in the mansion. If I could somehow identify the man, some day I could have more than his liver. Even the faint prospect of vengeance streaked my misery with savage joy.

CHAPTER 11
Friday, 15 February 1521

Prince Tikiri had been strangely cold and withdrawn ever since he returned from his mission in Colombo. Julietta was hurt and bewildered. For the first time in years, she felt that she did not have anyone in the world. Even Kukka, the brown and white puppy he had given her, now grown up, was sick in his kennel.

Concerned only with love, I sailed on the clouds of romance with Tiki-tiki and I believed we loved each other that magic afternoon, she thought, as she sat staring miserably at her reflection in the dressing table mirror of her bedroom in the Jaya palace. The next afternoon, he returned to the palace and I have suddenly crashed to the earth. Tiki-tiki has been avoiding me for three days. Why? Could he have regretted his confession of love? No, that was impossible. Could his father have forbidden him to have anything to do with me? Possible, but then he would have told me about it, or even rebelled. She knew Tiki-tiki. What could have happened?

She had heard from her father that Tiki-tiki had been appointed a squadron commander in the king's cavalry and had been given a patrimony of ten villages. Was the prince now so important that he had no time for a *mestico*, half-breed? Surely he was not like that. Had he decided to be practical since he had entered man's estate? After all, in his position, he could never marry her. She understood this, had expected nothing from him but his love and to be a part of his life, though he had become her whole life. Now it was the fourth morning since that magic day. She would somehow have to make the opportunity to talk to him.

Her thoughts were interrupted by an urgent knocking on the door. Since she had just finished dressing for school, she rose from her settee, went to the door and opened it. Her father stood at the entrance, his normally tired-looking face flushed with excitement, an open scroll in his hand. 'I hope I am not disturbing you, Juli?'

'No, *o pai*. I was about to leave for school.'

He flourished the scroll before her with a laugh. 'We are going to be with our own again at last.'

'What do you mean, *o pai*?'

'We have received an invitation to visit the flagship of Admiral Lopo Soarez de Albergaria tomorrow.' His hand was trembling with joy. 'All of us, Juli, you, Father Juan, Father Perez and I. Isn't it wonderful? The admiral will make a separate cabin available to you, so we can stay on board for a few days. And do you know what? There are some Portuguese ladies from Goa with the fleet. They are to become *morador*, settlers, in Colombo. So we shall at last have a white Christian society here. And who knows, some day we may even sail away to our beloved Portugal, leaving this heathen prison for ever.'

She had never guessed how strongly her *fidalgo* father had felt about his enforced exile in Lanka. It instantly brought to mind a question. Am I white, father, she wondered. What do I know of 'a white Christian society'? I know no other land than Lanka, no other place than the Jaya palace with its fixed routines relieved by an occasional *perahera*, procession, or celebrations like the Sinhala New Year and the Buddhist *Wesak*. The thought of leaving her sanctuary and her beloved Tiki-tiki for ever made her stomach grow weak. 'C-can we . . . er . . . accept such an invitation without the Great King's permission?'

Her father slapped the scroll with the back of his hand. He seemed a new man, more vigorous than she had ever known him. 'It says right here "With the gracious approval of His Majesty, the Great King Dharma Parakrama Bahu IX, Emperor of Lanka." Fancy that, Juli, Emperor of Lanka. What man could resist such a title? Our people certainly know the art of diplomacy. No, no it's all arranged.' He shook the scroll. 'The admiral is even throwing a formal dinner party with music and dancing on his flagship tomorrow night. It's life again.'

Her heart sank. For her, it was death – the death of her entire past and her hopes. Suddenly her life was turning topsy-turvy. She would really have to talk to Tiki-tiki today. Then years

120

of obedience came to the fore. 'I am glad for you, *o pai*,' she said. 'I shall wear my new blue dress to the dinner and we will all be happy again.'

For the first time ever, he opened his arms to her. As he held her close, she breathed his body smell and felt the beating of his heart. It gave her a strange knowledge of their blood tie and his humanity. She found comfort in it.

Friday, 15 February 1521

Desperation lent Julietta courage. Prince Tikiri had absented himself from the classes of Father Juan and Father Perez, but he still attended those of the Buddhist *bhikku* and the Muslim *imam*. The latter ended at noon that day. Once again he had avoided her gaze throughout the session and was about to hurry away the moment the class was dismissed, but she anticipated his move and reached the verandah before him. She turned to face him, blocking his path.

'How nice to be able to speak to you again, Prince Tikiri,' she said. 'My, you have become so important that we poor commoners don't even get a passing glance from you nowadays.' What was that look in his dark brown eyes? Surely it could not have been hatred.

He flushed beneath his tan, fingered the high collar of his white tunic as if loosening it. 'No, no, it's nothing like that. Only that my father has given me many important duties to perform.' He glanced towards the garden like a trapped animal. 'Now I really must run. I'm late already.'

'Then I'll run with you.' She saw the flash of something different in his expression, but could not identify it, only felt it make her heart go out to him. At that moment, some deep woman's instinct told her that Tiki-tiki needed her more than ever. 'Here, hold my slate. I'll show you who can run faster.'

His gaze softened. He glanced quickly over his shoulder at the other pupils emerging from the classroom, then took the slate. 'All right, you win. I'll walk you home.'

Her heart leapt. She noticed Father Juan standing at the door of the teachers' room. He nodded slightly in approval, making her feel like a betrayer.

They walked in silence, the sunlight warm on their heads. 'Do you know that my father and I are going to visit the fleet tomorrow, Tiki-tiki?'

'So I had heard.' He sounded indifferent.

They were by the hibiscus hedge now. She stopped, laid a hand on his arm, gently restraining him. 'Do you remember this place, Tiki-tiki? Or did it mean nothing to you?' Her voice broke; she could not restrain her tears.

He looked at her with a sort of wonder, like a blind man seeing light for the first time. 'Why are you crying, Juli? Please don't cry.'

'Why do people cry, except when they are heartbroken? Oh Tiki-tiki, please don't play with me. I love you. I want nothing from you except to be a part of your life. I know I can never be your wife, or even your mistress, but I just want to feel close to you even when we are separated. Like the day you went to Colombo. My heart was singing and yours sang with mine. I need to be something to you, however tiny, and to give you my all.'

He stood looking down at her, the black eyebrows furrowed. She could sense a tremendous struggle going on inside him. 'You owe me nothing, Tiki-tiki. No one owes me anything.' She sniffed, reached for the lace handkerchief in her cuff and wiped away her tears. 'After all, I am only Julietta. Less than the dust. When your people despised me, you uplifted me, gave me a place in the sun, a feeling of being whatever *you* are, even a Sinhala. Dare I say that today?' Some reserves of desperation gave her the strength to hold his gaze.

'You are not less than the dust, Juli.' A note of bitterness entered his voice. 'You are a great *parangi*.'

Some inkling of the truth dawned on her. 'Me, a *parangi*? You must be joking. Why, to them I am just a *mestico*, a half-breed. Oh Prince, if I am anything at all, I am where I was born and raised, where I have lived and moved and had my being. You alone can make me what I long to be, a Sinhala in your heart. That is all I want.'

122

Something in him broke then. A sob escaped him, not from his throat, his chest, or any physical part of him, but from his soul. He stared at her with a pitiful expression. Woman-like, she knew that something awful had smitten him. She reached out and grasped his arm. He came unresisting as she drew him behind the hibiscus hedge. She looked around, for his sake, not for hers. There was no one to be seen. She held him in her arms.

He stood stiff, resisting, but only for a few moments. Then with a groan he clasped her to him so fiercely that she gasped. She turned her face up to him and their lips met. It was the sweetest thing that had ever happened to her, for she could feel his life force and hers merging through every part of their beings. This time, he did not fumble. His eyes were closed and he just held her as if he would never let her go.

He moved his lips away to kiss her wet cheeks. 'I thought I had lost you, Julietta,' he whispered brokenly.

'How, beloved Tiki-tiki?' she whispered back, kissing his chin. 'I never left you.'

He sighed, drew away. 'It's a long story.'

'Listen, my darling Tiki-tiki. I love you so much that I know when something is wrong with you.' She touched his face with a gentle hand. 'Something *is* wrong, isn't it? Dreadfully wrong?'

He stared at her dumbly for a few moments, his face racked with such pain that her heart cried out silently. He nodded.

'Tell me about it.'

'I can't speak of it.'

'Do I mean so little to you that you cannot share your grief with me?'

'It's not that. It's just that it is such a secret, so shameful.'

Suddenly she felt a hundred years old, the mother of the earth. 'I want only to share your shame, Tiki-tiki. Give the glory to others.'

He looked at her in wonder. 'You are the only human being who has cried for me. Those precious tears.' He laid a tender finger on her cheek, as if to take up a jewel and possess it for ever. 'And now you give me someone with whom I can share my shame?'

123

'Yes. And do you know what that means?'

He shook his head, smiling wryly now.

'You will never be alone again.'

His eyes misted, but he was not of the breed that weeps, she knew. 'Sit down, Julietta, and I will tell you.'

Sitting beside her on the green grass by the red-flowering hibiscus, he shared the dread secret about Lila with her.

When he had finished, she wept for him, the tears pouring down her cheeks. 'Oh my poor Tiki-tiki, how you have suffered.'

'Do you see why no one else must ever know?'

'Of course.'

'You promise you will not tell anyone.'

'I promise. But you must promise me something too.'

'What is that?'

'You must stop blaming yourself. You could never have dreamed that the poor woman would suffer such a fate. If you had even guessed you would never have risked it.'

He was silent then, fiercely contemplative. 'I think that is one of my greatest problems,' he finally declared in melancholy tones. 'If I had intentionally to make Lila or anyone suffer such a fate for the sake of my country, I would have to do it.' For an instant his gaze was piteous, almost that of a lost soul, then it hardened with resolve. 'That is my destiny, Julietta, and I cannot shun it.'

Friday, 15 February 1521

Julietta had hoped to avoid Father Juan after school was over for the day, but he called at her house and asked her to return to the schoolroom with him.

Seated on her settle, she felt like a trapped animal. Angry grey clouds scudding in from the west had obscured the sky. Birds were twittering and scolding in the branches outside, as if resentful that the earth was darkening ahead of time. The distant moo of a cow intruded upon the voices of some of her classmates, at play when they should have returned home. The air felt thick, near stifling her. She closed her eyes.

'Well, my child, you certainly had a nice long talk with your prince, did you not?' Father Juan stood before her, smoothing his white cassock with his palms. She suddenly realized that he had cruel, grasping hands, the white fingers long and skeletal. She instinctively looked up at his eyes to find them glittering.

She nodded. 'Yes, Father.'

He looked around to see whether anyone was within earshot. Suddenly the whole place seemed deserted to her.

He drew up a stool and sat down facing her, his palms on his knees. His eyes held hers again in that hypnotic stare he had given her four days before. 'Now tell Holy Church all about it,' he commanded.

Father Juan listened in silence, his gaze unwaveringly on her while she obediently told him all the events Prince Tikiri had recounted. She omitted only the secret she had promised never to divulge, regarding Kodi, the musket and Lila. Not even a priest could make her break that trust, she told herself fiercely, even if he damned her to eternal hell.

When she had finished, he questioned her closely. She answered him with frankness.

'Is that all you have to tell me, child of the Blessed Virgin?' he finally demanded.

'Yes, Father.' She was very firm in her response.

He stared at her thoughtfully, the black pupils of those yellow eyes like needlepoints that could pierce her very soul. She stared back at him, defiantly almost. Suddenly, his mouth twisted in an amused smile. 'Are you looking forward to visiting the warships tomorrow?' he inquired.

She was startled, then relaxed because the inquisition was over. 'Why, yes, Father.'

'To being with our own people, in the atmosphere of Europe and Portugal again?'

'I have never known that atmosphere, Father.'

'Oh yes! My poor child, nor you have.' He paused. 'Well, you will enjoy it. We may all be away several days. Father Perez and I will have to minister to many of our people on the warships, to help the servants of God who have accompanied them. It will be too long before we can minister personally to our own flock.' He sighed, scratched his dark beard reflectively. His look and voice gentled, but there was steel beneath both. 'You had best come to me for confessional after vespers this evening, Julietta.'

She knew then that Father Juan was convinced that she was holding back important information.

Friday, 15 February 1521

I felt curiously relieved after sharing my secret with Julietta. Her whole attitude had left me elated with the knowledge that she loved me truly, more determined than ever to make her my wife some day. Yet I had not revealed my hatred of all *parangi* to her, my thoughts of vengeance, or the plans whirling around my head like sparkler wheels. I did not tell of my visit to Kodi at his factory in Mutu Vella on the morning of the discovery of Lila's body either, or of Kodi's grief and guilt. He had been able to give me a fair description of the *parangi* beast, right down to the pock-marked face and a tell-tale scar running along his right cheek from eyebrow to chin, and had even drawn a picture of the man for me.

As I walked away from Julietta, following a sad leavetaking because we were to be parted on the morrow, I recalled my conversation three days earlier with Kodi.

'The best way in which I can avenge Lila's murder, lord, is to manufacture the musket as soon as possible,' he had stated quietly. 'As you know, my factory is loaded with work, especially from ships in the harbour. I shall hand all of it over to my son and my assistants and concentrate on producing the instrument of our vengeance.'

His words had helped me in my torment. There is no better salve for the tortured wounds of guilt and helplessness than the prospect of revenge. 'How soon, Kodi?' I had inquired.

'Three, perhaps four days. Since I shall be working on this secretly, I shall send a messenger to you at the Jaya palace as soon as I have tested the weapon. He'll carry a blank *ola* leaf that says, "This is for your horoscope, Prince." I pray you then to come to my house, for it would not be advisable for me to bring the weapon to the palace or for you to visit the factory. Many forces would be hostile . . . '

I was ecstatic. Kodi was many jumps ahead of me. 'But how can you actually make it work?' I demanded.

He smiled his gentle smile. 'It's no good only for display, lord. Having heard about these weapons before, I deduced how the weapon is fired last night. The gun is loaded from the muzzle, with iron pellets that must be rammed in. It has a flash pan for gunpowder and a fuse that can be lit which touches the gunpowder by the pulling of a trigger. The mechanism will not be too difficult to produce. It is the barrel and stock, putting the whole together and preventing a flash from getting to the pan of gunpowder that requires care and knowledge. But if a *parangi* craftsman can accomplish it, why not a Sinhala?' His smile had turned to a grin.

'What is gunpowder?'

'It is the black powder we use in our fireworks. The Chinese people are reported to have had it for hundreds and hundreds of years but have considered it barbaric to use it for death and destruction. Since my factory produces fireworks for our festivals, I have the gunpowder readily available. I shall put it into the musket in the same way that I make our rockets and see what happens.'

'You mean you will test it too?'

'Yes, lord, but secretly so no man shall know.'

'Won't it be dangerous?'

He shrugged his bony shoulders. 'There is danger everywhere.' A note of bitterness entered his voice. 'As Lila discovered in her safe profession.'

I appreciated Kodi's quiet heroism enough not to embarrass him by praising it. 'Send me word then,' I finally bade him. 'And I shall leave all else aside and come to you immediately.'

I spent the whole day in a daze that was Julietta, despite my sadness that she would be gone from the palace the next morning.

Saturday, 16 February 1521

To my surprise, three hours after the *parangi* left in their coach, Kodi's messenger, a neatly dressed, clean-cut young man, waited on me in the palace. Introducing himself as Palitha, the master craftsman's oldest son, he offered me Kodi's promised *ola*. My first reaction was one of relief that Kodi had come through his weapon-testing unscathed. Then excitement such as I have never before experienced flooded me.

I directed my chief attendant to see to it that Palitha was fed, my horse, Rama, was saddled and a quick meal was brought. I bathed, changed into a blue tunic and pantaloons and rode off within the hour, for the first time in my life without permission from anyone, leaving word for my father that I had gone to Colombo in connection with my new appointment there and would be back before nightfall. It gave me a glorious feeling of independence to be able to leave like that, the boyhood years suddenly seemed like imprisonment!

Kodi lived in a modest cottage on a little promontory at the northern end of the harbour, which had been used exclusively by the fishing boats of the Sinhala for centuries. He must have been a very rich man with all the business he commanded, but, sadly, it was not advisable in our society for people of lower castes to flaunt their wealth. Fronting the quietly lapping waters of the bay, the house was built of *kabook*, the local bricks cut from pebbled earth, plastered over with white lime. Its red Calicut-tile roof was shaded by a giant green tamarind tree at its rear, facing the quiet lane leading to it.

Not a soul was in sight when I dismounted at the entrance gates, stroked Rama's sweating flank and smiled at the sideways roll of his eyes. I walked him into the compound and tethered him to a slender *murunga* tree. Neat beds of green onions, red chillies and purple brinjal occupied the whole of the left side of the compound, with guava, papaya and mango trees on the other side. As I rounded the side of the house, coconut palms, their roots partially eroded by tides, leaned over the sparkling noon waters before me. An idyllic scene, the refuge of a man who had worked honestly and diligently all his life.

Kodi, dressed in white, his silver hair hanging loose to his shoulders from his noon bath, awaited me on the front verandah. As he rose from his obeisance, he beamed at me from ear to ear, his brown eyes sparkling. 'Your timing is excellent, lord,' he stated. 'The neighbours are all enjoying their afternoon nap, my son hasn't returned from the palace and my wife and daughter went to visit relatives who live nearby, so I am alone. Will you deign to be seated?' He indicated one of four straight-backed ebony chairs placed against the verandah wall.

Only the dictates of breeding made me accept the seat, because my mind was clamouring to see the finished product. Cut out the formality and show me the musket, show me quickly, I wanted to shout. Knowing my eagerness, he hastened into the dark interior of the house. I looked around swiftly to see whether anyone was about. Only the splash of a wavelet and the querulous grumble of a mynah disturbed the silence.

Then Kodi stood before me, holding up his creation in gnarled hands. My breath caught. I sat still, turned to stone. He had silver-plated the barrel and polished the dark *nadun*-wood stock. The weapon gleamed, a work of art, a thing of beauty.

'Hold it, lord.' Kodi's whisper held some of the awe owed to divinity.

I rose slowly to my feet. He placed the musket in my hands. It was heavy, but I held it lightly, reverentially at first. Then a longing to seize it swept through me. As my grip tightened, the feel of its power in my grasp vibrated through my entire being, bringing back the memory of the cannon ball I had held five days ago, shaking me to the depths.

I laughed aloud in ecstasy, madness too. I placed the gun to my chest as I had observed the *parangi* soldiers do and pointed it in the direction in which their warships must lie. 'This is the beginning of the end for you, foul *parangi*,' I whispered.

Tears were streaming down Kodi's dark cheeks. A surge of gratitude towards him produced inspiration. 'All such weapons made by the Sinhala, large or small, shall henceforth be known as Kodi-thuwakku guns, so your name shall be remembered throughout history.'

He broke into sobs. 'Forgive me, lord, but I am much moved.'

129

He sniffed, went to the edge of the verandah and blew his nose. 'Let me compose myself and bring you the powder and shot to show you how the gun works.'

I held up my hand, struck by a tremendous thought. 'You manufacture great pipes and anchors of iron for ships. You make wheels and giant rivets. Can you enlarge this weapon to produce a cannon? That would be the more fitting weapon with which to avenge poor Lila.'

He stared at me through his tears, in shock. 'Why, lord, I had not thought of it.' He paused reflecting, involuntarily wiped a dark cheek with his hand. 'Of course, lord. Yes, yes, of course. The principle is the same, the barrel and the shot would be bigger and we would need a strong base against the shock. I fired the musket late last night when I was alone in the factory, holding it against my chest and was nearly knocked over.'

I laughed gleefully. 'You will live to see the victory your hands have wrought!' I exclaimed. 'The three-day miracle, it shall be called.'

He grinned sheepishly and looked down. 'I have a confession to make, young lord,' he said. 'No one on this earth could have produced that musket in three days. Two years ago, a fellow craftsman from Goa, named Sidi, visited me. He had been commissioned by a rich Mouro to manufacture one of these weapons. It was an impossible task for him, so he thought I might be able to accomplish it.' He lifted his eyes to mine and smiled his gentle, apologetic smile. 'It would appear that I have some small reputation for craftsmanship in this part of the world. But all Sidi had was a diagram, which he gave me. After he left, I worked secretly on several prototypes of the weapon, but without success. The problem was to make the moulds for the metal parts. I finally solved this and did produce those parts, but putting the whole together so the weapon could be fired presented a real problem. When I saw the *parangi* musket, touched it, felt its jointing, everything fell into place and I was able to put it together quickly. There, now you know the truth. I am not as clever as you thought me to be and it was you who helped make the miracle possible.'

'And Lila,' I added softly.

He nodded, the tears springing back to his eyes.

'Now please tell me what this work of art cost you. That includes your labour during the whole of the past year. I shall pay you ten times your cost.'

He straightened his bent back proudly. 'Forgive me, young lord, I appreciate your offer, but it is insulting. The gun is my humble gift to the Sinhala nation. Also, I have a more practical reward in the name you have bestowed on my family.' Again, that gentle smile. 'I am an ancestor already!'

It was my turn to feel prickly-eyed. 'Forgive me, Kodithuwakku, *mahatmaya*, Sir, I meant no insult, but an unintentional slight is worse than a deliberate one.' I paused, thinking. 'I know that when I take this weapon to my father, he will want to start manufacturing it on a massive scale immediately. Can we set up the necessary factories?'

'Certainly. If you will permit me, I shall let my son, Palitha, in on the secret once you give me the word to proceed. He can then concentrate on this work wherever you need him while I carry on with my usual business.'

'Do you think Palitha can carry on merely by your explaining the details to him?'

'He is his father's son,' Kodi replied.

CHAPTER 12
Saturday, 16 February 1521

With the tacit agreement of her husband, Aisha Raschid had assumed control. She had spent the past four days carefully gathering information about the *parangi*, through her spies in the port, and about the plans of the Sinhala from paid informers in the governor's mansion and the Jaya palace.

She had the dead buried, paid compensation to their dependents and commenced repairs to the damaged warehouses. She assessed losses and ordered the resumption of trading as if the *parangi* did not exist, bolstering the morale of Moor and Sinhala employee alike. She found herself in her element. I have the Ghazni blood in my veins, she thought.

On the day following the confrontation with her husband's men, groups of *parangi* had come ashore in organized relays, obviously for exercise. They had walked the wharves and the waterfront, always under watchful sentries and the threat of the ships' cannon. On the second morning, a group of *parangi* had actually marched to the marketplace just outside the southern end of the port to negotiate for fresh meat and produce in exchange for gold *cruzados*, which they seemed to spend freely. They rented wagons and carried vast quantities of their purchases to the ships. The next day they established land headquarters in a tent at the base of the main wharf. Seeming more relaxed thereafter, they wandered freely about the port. Some of the men even visited the marketplace and others went to the town in search of women.

The time was right. That afternoon, she sent a respectful request to her husband to wait on her in her private chamber. He arrived looking as worried as he had seemed since the day the *parangi* arrived. Catching sight of his flabby face as she straightened up from her salutation, she noted the sagging cheeks more sharply than usual. A man is like his sexual organs, she thought, flaunted when virile, depending on a woman when it grows limp. What happens when even a woman's power can no longer make it rise?

The divan creaked under Abdul Raschid's weight. He was sweating as usual, tugging at the collar of his pink tunic shirt and pulling down on the front of the dark brown waistcoat. He absently reached out for a piece of yellow *muskat* from the gold sweetmeat salver on the brass stand beside his divan. Aisha hated his discussing anything of importance while munching food, like a fat bull chewing the cud and trying to moo at the same time.

'You desired speech with me, wife of mine,' her husband said smacking thick, wet lips. 'I came immediately.'

'Yes, husband. The time has come for us to have a frank talk.'

He nodded, continuing to munch.

'The events of the past three days have created a crisis situation,' Aisha proceeded.

'That is certainly true.'

'Have I not done all that is necessary to safeguard our operation and keep our trade going?'

'You have been of enormous assistance to me and I thank you for it. You have been a devoted wife and helpmate.'

She could have exploded at his condescension. Though she held herself in check, she knew she could not afford to ignore it. 'Since you are the real leader, doing all the work, I have decided to revert to being nothing but your devoted first wife.'

His jaw dropped, revealing pieces of yellow *muskat* mingled with saliva behind his white teeth. He looked so comical in his surprise that Aisha could have laughed aloud.

'Ah...ah...er...you don't have to do that,' he began. 'I appreciate your continued help.' Then surprisingly he found his strength. 'But I'll handle things alone if that's what you prefer.'

She felt rebuffed. Her voice suddenly became cold and hard as marble. 'Let us start all over again.' She moved forward to look down on him. 'I asked, have I not done all that is necessary to safeguard our operation and keep our trade going?' Her voice rose. '*I...I...I...* Did you hear me?'

'Don't you dare raise your voice to me, woman.'

133

'Listen,' she hissed. 'You are nothing without me, because my brother is the king of commerce and you are his subject. Do you want to end up a corpse in the harbour?'

He was silent, not intimidated but obviously shocked by the new woman he was seeing.

'Did you hear me?' she demanded.

'How could I help but hear you.'

'Do I speak the truth, or falsehood?'

He shook his head, stared at her, his small brown eyes inscrutable. He ran a palm over the sweat on his bald head. He looked down. 'You speak the truth,' he conceded, but he was obviously not beaten.

It came hard for you, but may all victories be as easy for me, Aisha thought. 'Then listen to me.'

'I'm listening.' He continued staring at the marble floor as if his mind were elsewhere.

'The time for channelling everything through you has ended. The world need not know it, for you are my husband and I will not debase you in the eyes of men but shall continue to do you all honour. Your position, however, is such that you can no longer command obedience with a flick of the fingers, as a labourer with his wife merely because he is a male. You have to earn it. Remember that, my husband. Since it is I who now deal with those we face on the military and political level as I did that evening in the governor's mansion, I alone shall determine our political and military policies. I am not asking you, I am telling you, husband of mine.'

He raised his head suddenly, a surprising strength in his gaze. 'I am but a trader, descended of traders,' he asserted. 'I am good at my job.' A fierce note entered his voice. 'Let no one, not even you, deny it.' He held her eyes with a challenge that stimulated her. 'If you do, then you can carry on by yourself from now on without me, for I shall divorce you.'

He held up a flabby hand in command as she started to explode with fury. 'Hear me out, Aisha,' he continued. 'I know that divorce will mean the end of a rich, comfortable life for me, but you see, I have faced up to that since the *parangi* came, when suddenly all the security I had built through the years was

134

about to be destroyed. I would rather be a poor trader in peace than a rich one in conflict.' There was a strange new dignity to him and his high-pitched voice was firm. 'You come from generations of warriors, Aisha. You are different. I see now that you would thrive on conflict. Your blood calls on you to lead, to reach for the stars. As for me, I merely want to live as well as I can. So grant me the honour of admitting my worth in the one thing I do well and we shall have some substance for the future. Otherwise, you will have made me nothing and I will have nothing to offer you.'

She knew he was not bluffing and stared at him with a new respect. Somewhere deep beneath her abdomen something stirred, amazing her. For the first time in her life, she became conscious of the depth of craving within her for this strength from a man, some man, any man of true quality. Glorying in her own strength, she now found the mercy her ancestors had extended to the valiant whom they could command. 'You are the best in your profession, husband of mine,' she conceded, bowing low.

A smile touched his lips. 'I thank you, wife of mine. I now accept your demands on two conditions.'

'And those are?' She was ready to smash him down again.

'The first, you never shame me before others.'

'I have already promised that.'

'The second, you recognize that we need each other, in our home and at work. We shall be partners. Each commanding our own spheres of operation but consulting each other on all major decisions. I alone shall be the one to tell the world of your new responsibilities, as if it were my decision.'

'Accepted.'

He chuckled, his smile almost boyish. 'I am no longer frightened or worried,' he declared. 'We will make a good team.'

'We will indeed. Now, our first mission must be to establish trading relations direct with the *parangi*. They will buy heavily, pay in gold *cruzados* and ensure us a magnificent volume.'

He stared at her in amazement. 'But . . . ' he began, then a slow smile creased his face. 'What wisdom,' he declared. 'Follow the leopard for the kill.'

135

Saturday, 16 February 1521

Fernao had received Abdul Raschid's message with surprise. Why select me, he wondered. Why not my father, the admiral, or Captain Oliveira? He quickly realized that his father would never have visited the home of a trader, however eminent, and that Captain Oliveira could not leave his command post.

One of the hangers-on had identified the messenger, he seemed no more than about fourteen, as the son of Abdul and Aisha Raschid. 'Bring as strong a guard as you feel may be necessary for your protection,' the message had concluded. 'For you must make it seem that you are coming here only to hold inquiry into the attack upon your troops when you first landed. No man must suspect that we are discussing the future. In further token of our trustworthiness, we are sending you our most precious possession, our only son, Ali, hostage against your safe return. Do not, we pray you again, divulge the true purpose of your mission to anyone save your captain and your father, the admiral, for wagging tongues can loosen teeth and none can eat without teeth!'

Fernao's fellow countrymen had arrived shortly before noon from the Jaya palace and were even now his father's guests on the flagship. He had been with the marketing detail, buying produce since early morning, so he had not seen them. But he had overheard one of the officers say that the girl in the party was quite beautiful. He had no great curiosity about them, however, because he had been filled with a sense of mission since his father had promoted him and given him specific duties.

It was just past the noon-hour when he knocked on the solid teakwood gates of the Raschids' house in the quarter which the natives called Slave Island. He glanced at the slim, erect figure dressed in blue standing beside him. An attractive youth, with fair skin, dark hair and feminine features. Only some lurking expression in the large black eyes warned of inner ferocity. He had decided to bring the boy with him rather than leave him at headquarters where he might run the risk of attempted molestation by some of the sex-starved perverts from the ships.

A crowd had followed them, was now increasing, murmuring

questions as the gates creaked open. Saluting guards stood on both sides of a paved walkway bordered by flower beds blossoming orange, yellow and red. The smell of hot grass came from green lawns, tree-shaded, that sloped down to the silver waters of the lake, across which the noise of the city reached him faintly. With its flat roof, the house was typically Moorish, painted pink, built like a fortress.

Bidding the boy accompany him, Fernao stalked to the front door, followed by his escort of thirty men, muskets at the ready. He halted halfway and directed his men to take up positions around the house.

The door opened before he reached it. Two huge Nubian guards, arms folded across bare chests, stood before him, bowing low.

This was the moment. Fernao's heart began to thud against his ribs. 'Come with me,' he bade the boy and walked inside, his hand ready to go for his sword at the slightest sign of foul play.

To his surprise, the anteroom he entered was bright with sunshine from the adjoining verandah which opened out to a splendid courtyard. He heard the splash of a water cascade and the trilling of birds as he was led across the courtyard into a large reception chamber.

Here, the incense of Arabi, glowing on brass burners, gave the chamber an exotic feel and accorded well with the ornate ebony furniture inlaid with mother-of-pearl lining the walls, the huge red and green Persian carpet on the marble floor, the two great elephant tusks mounted on ebony stands beneath the archway and the priceless ornaments on their marble pedestals.

A tall, obese man, dressed in white with the inevitable brown waistcoat, came forward. He had a flabby face, surmounted by a bald head and spiked by two small eyes. He bowed, salaaming, hand to stomach, mouth and head. '*Salaam aleikum*! I am Abdul Raschid,' he said. 'Welcome to my humble abode, lord. My home is your home.'

Fernao was surprised at the man's fluent Portuguese. He saluted in return. '*Aleikum salaam!*'

'And this is my chief wife, Aisha.' Abdul Raschid indicated the tall veiled figure dressed in a brown robe, standing in front of a gold-cushioned divan.

The woman bowed low and Fernao saluted again. 'I am returning your son,' he stated.

An expression of surprise crossed Abdul Raschid's face, while the woman's interest obviously quickened. Fernao knew immediately that he had done the right thing in bringing the boy.

'But he is your hostage, lord,' Abdul protested.

'No longer,' Fernao stated, feeling somewhat proud of himself. 'I decided to trust you.' He noted approval in the dark eyes behind the veil. This is the one I have to deal with, he decided, not the man, for Mouro women seldom, if ever, attend such meetings. 'The boy may retire, I presume, since you will want our discussions to be private, even from him.'

Abdul Raschid smiled agreement. 'You may leave, my son,' he directed. 'Remember you have your homework to do for the *imam.*'

'Pray sit down, lord.' Raschid indicated a tall ebony chair. He clapped his hands twice while Fernao took his seat, and one of the huge guards appeared on the instant. 'We are not to be disturbed or overheard,' Raschid commanded.

'Yes, lord.' The guard bowed and withdrew. Husband and wife sat side by side on their divan.

'I want to make certain things clear before we begin our discussion,' Fernao stated. 'I have shown you my trust by returning your son to you, but I want no misunderstanding.' He smiled grimly, deliberately couched his words in the past tense. 'If anything had happened to me, my men would have torn your house apart. If anything had happened to them, my father, the admiral would have pounded your entire city to bits. So I want you to know that I returned your son to you freely, as the act of a nobleman, an officer and a gentleman of the Army of His Imperial Majesty the King of Portugal.'

'We cannot claim such distinguished representation, lord.' It was the woman who responded, speaking for the first time. Fernao found her voice golden, mellow, even though somewhat muffled by her veil. 'We are but humble traders. Yet we too

138

have our own code of honour, dictated by the laws of hospitality.'

Fernao accepted the gentle rebuke, it was no less, with a slight nod of his head. I am learning, he thought. I must remember never to be pompous. 'The other circumstance you must understand is that I am only here to listen to you,' he continued. 'Discussion may be all right, but I can neither negotiate nor conclude any agreements.'

'We understand,' the woman responded, her black eyes so inscrutable that Fernao wished she would remove her damned veil.

'Would you like some refreshment, lord?' Abdul Raschid intervened. 'Pomegranate juice would be very cooling in this heat.'

'No, thank you.'

'Some *nannar* perhaps? Have you ever tried it, the extract of the *sarsparilla* root? Very good for the blood.

'I've heard of it, but no thank you. I've just had luncheon.' It was not true, but Fernao had already decided beforehand not to take any refreshment in case it was poisoned. 'May we start our official business now?'

'Forgive us, lord, for detaining you with our offers of hospitality,' Aisha spoke once again in gentle reproof. 'Let us indeed come to the point. Your fleet is here to extend your trade interests in Lanka. It is obvious that you will establish your objectives by force, if necessary. We Mouro have fought you on the Indian Ocean for over twenty years now. Here in Lanka, our predecessors established a monopoly of trade two hundred years ago. The people needed rice and sugar from Bengal, rice from the Coromandel, sandalwood and spices from the East Indies, cloth from Gujerat, silver, copper, coral and quicksilver from the Middle East. We Mouro supplied it. In return, the natives provided cinnamon from their wet forests for the world, coconuts and areca nuts for Malabar, elephants for the Coromandel and Bengal, masts, planks and yards for Ormuz. When my husband and I came here, twelve years ago, we discovered that it would be more profitable to channel the entire cinnamon trade of all the Indian Ocean countries through the headquarters of my brother, Paichi Markar, in Calicut. Lanka's cinnamon, being the finest in the world, has commanded the best prices, but it has also had to face competition. By monopoly trading, however, we eliminated competition and now command our own prices.'

Fernao had been listening intently. The woman had spoken the truth, as he knew it. 'Pray continue,' he said.

'The Mouro are necessary for Lanka,' Aisha stated flatly. 'Without us and our vast fleets of trading ships, the people here would starve.'

'I am aware that you have dominated Lanka more effectively through trade, madam, than you could have done militarily.' He saw the black eyes flash and could have bitten his tongue off. Merely listen, you fool, he told himself, and do not talk or make smart remarks to show how clever you are. 'But that is what we are all here for, isn't it?' he added, hoping to rob his words of offence. Again he sensed her smile. Was she playing with him?

'Since you admit your presence here is solely to enrich yourselves, we have a proposition to make,' Aisha continued. 'You are hungry for more cinnamon and spices. We can provide them. Twenty years ago, your Pedro Alvares Cabral shipped four hundred *quintal* of cinnamon from Cannanore alone, but still your total shipments averaged only five hundred *quintal* annually and you paid premium prices to achieve this. You may be receiving gifts of cinnamon from our Great King, but as you pointed out just now, it is we Mouro who dominate the sources of supply and you cannot seize those by force of arms.' She was openly smiling now.

Touché, Fernao thought. What a woman! But I have been learning from her and it is my turn to be enigmatic.

'I am going to be frank with you, lord. We buy a *quintal* of cinnamon here for one *cruzado* and sell it in Calicut at three *cruzados*. This includes the costs of storage and shipping, but as you can see, the profit is excellent. We will always have cheap sources of supply that will never be available to you, not only because the Sinhala are already in debt to us but also because they have discovered you to be free with your gold.' Her gaze was now intent. 'I propose that we act as your buying agent in

140

Lanka. We will purchase as much cinnamon as you desire, payment in advance, for the factory you intend building in the port, and supply it to you at one and a half *cruzados* a *quintal*. You could sell this at Diu for ten *cruzados* a quintal or at Ormuz for twenty, but we have four requests to make.'

'Why should we pay in advance?'

'We have to pay our suppliers, to whom we extend credit for their production work. Your orders will be large and, frankly, we must have some security.'

'What if you take our money and don't give us the goods?' He could feel her scorn at his crudeness.

'You can tear our house apart and pound our entire city to bits.' She was quoting him, somewhat maliciously. 'Now, as to the four requests.'

How diplomatic, Fernao thought. Neither of these people will refer to 'conditions', only to 'requests'.

'The first is that you confine your sale of our cinnamon to Lisbon and Europe, which you have the ships to reach while we do not, and where you can command sixty *cruzados* and more a *quintal*. The second is that your fleet affords safe passage to ships flying my brother's flag between Lanka, Calicut, Ormuz and Diu.' She held up a hand beneath the robe. 'Not anywhere else.' She paused. 'The third is that our operation here acts as your exclusive buying agent. The presence of bidders would only drive up the price,' she added quickly. 'Our fourth request is that you give us your protection in the port of Colombo.'

Fernao's head was reeling with the immensity of the woman's concept, but he maintained an outward appearance of calm. What a coup it would represent for them all if it could be made to work. There had been rumours before they set sail from Goa that the Viceroy might be replaced by Admiral Vasco da Gama himself because trade results had been so poor these past years in comparison with the vast expense of maintaining and safeguarding operations. Viceroy Soarez would surely jump at an arrangement which would enrich the royal coffers with no great outlay, and help him retain his job! '*Magnifico!*' He could not help exclaiming aloud.

'Your country alone can convey goods to Europe by sea on a

large scale.' Aisha pressed her advantage shrewdly. 'The other powers, and especially your Venetian and Netherlands rivals, make use of caravans along the more expensive overland route. At some stage, however, the Spanish, the French, the Dutch and the English, will follow your sea route and compete with you. What better for your country than to be firmly entrenched in trade, as we Mouro have been, before they arrive?' She fell silent, her downcast gaze confirming that she had no more to say.

He thought swiftly, felt the grip of power-hunger within him. 'I shall convey your proposals to my father immediately. He has the authority to approve them, pending ratification by the Viceroy.'

They discussed details of Aisha's proposals, timing, quantities, the first shipment.

'You are a very clever young man,' Aisha concluded. 'I would like to be frank with you. Our hope is that being the bearer of this unique concept will make the lord admiral decide to leave you here in charge of the trading operations, young as you are. We will be available to guide you.'

And to stab me in the back because of my youth, Fernao thought. He already knew that the Mouro paid only a half-*cruzado* locally for a *quintal* of cinnamon, not one *cruzado* as the woman had stated, and that their selling price in Calicut was almost five *cruzados*, not three. The old saying was: Never trust a Mouro when your back is turned, but especially face to face!

CHAPTER 13
Saturday, 16 February 1521

Kodi had made a beautiful satinwood case for the musket, the ramrod, some musket pellets and the fuse. He wrapped it with cloth so that it would look like any large package and I could carry it across my saddle.

Having resisted the urge to gallop all the way back to Jaya, I reached the palace in the late afternoon. Guards and attendants alike must have been shocked to see a prince ride on horseback carrying a package like a tradesman! I handed Rama to a waiting groom and the package to an attendant, bidding him follow me.

I made directly for my father's quarters, which adjoined the Great King's to the right of the centre courtyard. These consisted of a wide anteroom from which doors led to his study and bedroom, both of which had windows opening out to the spacious gardens beyond. The floors were of white mountain crystal, the furniture black ebony, the gold Buddha statues on pedestals glowed in the evening light.

The attendant left the package on the centre table and departed. My father was seated at his desk facing the open window, which framed sunlit treetops, green beneath a cloudless blue sky. The chatter of a magpie, the shrilling of a mynah bird and the occasional cawing of a crow were the usual prelude to the approach of night.

'Well, young man, where have you been all day?' my father inquired, smiling.

My moment of triumph had arrived. 'Obtaining what my commanding general needs to drive the *parangi* away.'

'Oh!' His black eyebrows shot up, then that amused smile crossed his face. He obviously thought it was a boy talking big. 'And what do you have to report to your commanding general?'

'I would rather show it to him . . .' It was my turn to smile now. 'I wish at the same time to give my *tha* a return present for his unique generosity to me on my sixteenth birthday. Will you please follow me?'

He decided to humour me, stood up and stretched. His shadow fell on me as I led the way to the anteroom. He watched curiously while I removed the cloth wrapping from the package. 'I hope you haven't been squandering your new wealth on presents for me,' he volunteered.

'This cost nothing, *tha*,' I responded, then realized that it had cost a human life. I lifted the clasp, opened the lid and reverently raised the heavy musket from its red velvet bed.

His gasp was my reward, for he never displayed any emotion. I turned and presented the musket to him, watching his fine black eyes widen with surprise at the long silver barrel, shining in the golden light of the room. He stared at the weapon, speechless with fascination, making no move to take it. 'Where did you get this?' he demanded in a whisper. 'Did you have it stolen?'

'I had it made. It is my present to you and our gift to the nation.'

'Who made it?'

'Kodi, the master craftsman.'

'But how, how?' The normally urbane man was still astounded. I would treasure these moments all my life.

'Hold it first, *tha*, then I'll tell you the story.'

He reached for it then, his hands trembling slightly, his eyes beginning to glitter. He grasped it in his hands. 'Ha! It's real!' he exclaimed excitedly. In one smooth motion, he placed the stock firmly against his chest. 'Ha! Praise be to the *devas*.'

I told him how I had come by the musket, excluding only the name of the decoy lady because I did not want to spoil those moments for him by linking the enterprise with Lila's death, of which he was aware. 'You will give me the order to start manufacturing these immediately?' I inquired when I had finished.

'Of course!' His eyes were moist on me. 'Thank you, *putha*. Thank you, thank you, thank you.' He shook his head, held the musket out again. 'Will this thing work? Has it been tested?'

'Yes, to both your questions, *tha*.'

144

He examined the weapon more closely. 'Here's where it is loaded, here's where the fuse goes and here's the pan for the gunpowder.' He looked up suddenly. 'What about ammunition, the ramrod, the fuse, the gunpowder?'

'All in here.' I patted the wooden case. 'Kodi provided it all. I have told him that for this service, he is henceforth an ancestor with the family name Kodi-thuwakku.'

'A princely bequest.' He took a step forward to peer into the case, pondered awhile. 'I long to fire this thing. Have you tried it?'

'No. I wanted you to be the first Sinhala, other than the craftsman, to fire a gun.'

He clapped me on the shoulder, nearly dropped the weapon. 'Whoa! Careful now, Maya Dunne!' he exclaimed, childlike. 'I should love to fire it in the garden right now, but that would not be wise!' His face jerked towards me, his expression alert. 'Does anyone know you have this?'

'No. Only Kodi. He will tell his son, Palitha, if you decide to go ahead with largescale manufacture of the weapon. I brought the package over from Colombo myself.' I grinned. 'Everyone was shocked to see a prince carrying a package. The palace will hum with gossip about it.'

'We'll invent an excuse, that it was a present you wished to deliver to me personally, new weapons, battle-axe, sword, anything. No one will question what it is since I am leaving for Sita Waka at dawn tomorrow. The Great King has decided to give the Portuguese admiral an audience, which I do not wish to attend. I shall try the weapon out in private at Sita Waka.' He paused, his look kindly. 'You should be present too, but it will not look good for us to leave together, so you can depart on Friday saying you are going to spend the weekend at home. I want you, however, to go to Mutu Vella after dinner tonight – yes, this very night, that's how urgent it is. Get to Kodi and Palitha. Have Palitha prepare to go independently to Sita Waka, taking along whatever equipment is needed for the factory. We shall establish it there, not in Colombo. We shall fire our weapon on Sunday, together, you and I.' Then he added softly, 'Henceforth always together, son.'

'I am honoured, Sir,' I replied. 'I shall carry out your wishes to the letter.' A thought struck me. 'We are going to need more than the equipment to produce muskets.'

'What d'you mean?'

'Kodi believes he can use the same technique to produce cannon.'

'Dear *devas*!' He was speechless for a moment. 'Fabulous, fabulous.' He brandished the musket. 'Power, that's what it means. Real power at last.'

I understood his feelings so well.

He placed the base of the musket against his thigh, the barrel extending towards the ceiling. 'Briefly, the admiral will have his audience at noon tomorrow. Your grandfather, Prince Wijayo, and your uncle, Prince Bhuvaneka, have persuaded the Great King to accept a treaty of alliance and mutual protection with the *parangi*. They are allowing the leopard into the goat enclosure. Your uncle, Prince Raigam, and I do not wish to be associated with this policy, because the *parangi* want the land not to build a factory, but a fort, which they will man with a regiment of seven hundred men and spare cannon they have brought with them. All this for trade? Bah!'

My own black outrage was suddenly beamed by a wild hope. 'Sir, I crave a boon.'

He paused, turned to look at me, simmering down, a puzzled smile breaking across his face. 'A boon? That's a strange word for a prince to use.'

'Perhaps I am a suppliant in this, Sir, because of the news you have given me.'

He glanced at the musket shining in its case. 'Fire away!' he directed me ironically.

'When the *parangi* disembark their regiment, could you please request them, say as a gesture of courtesy, to include the same guard that accompanied the admiral and his entourage to the governor's residence? I believe there were fifty men.'

'Why?'

'Please do not ask me for the moment, Sir, but grant me this boon.'

He scratched his chin reflectively, was about to frame another

146

question, but set it aside in his usual decisive manner. 'I will ensure it through my father, Prince Wijayo, who will soon become the favourite of the *parangi*.'

Saturday, 16 February 1521

The night is ideal for my father's dinner party, Fernao thought as he stood on the bridge watching the great copper globe of a full moon rising like a witch's warning above the dark tree line beyond the city lights to the east. Overhead, the spangles of countless stars on a deep blue sky spanned the Milky Way. A light westerly breeze caused the red, green and blue lanterns that had been strung across the main deck of the flagship to cast swaying mosaics of colour on the long dining table, complete with silver, china and sparkling glassware, that had been set up on the deck.

Surveying the scene from the bridge, where he waited for the admiral to emerge from the stateroom, Fernao noted that the chief supply officer had placed pink frangipani, white jasmine and orange marigold flowers in an elongated cross on the snow-white linen tablecloth. A uniformed seaman already stood behind each of the twenty settles around the table. The meal would be excellent if the odours of roast chicken and spices drifting from the far cook's galley were any indication. He wondered how the men felt about the delicious smells from a feast they would not share.

A small band, consisting of two fiddlers, a flautist, a drummer and a tambourine player, occupying stools on the aft deck, were tuning up. They looked cool in their white satin uniforms, the puffed pantaloons held up by broad maroon sashes.

His father's guests were to include Captain Oliveira, the two Franciscan friars from the Great King's palace, *a senhor* Duarte de Brito and his daughter, the fleet physician and six senior officers who had brought their wives with them from Goa to take up residence in Colombo. The admiral had gone out of his way to try to make the occasion memorable, so that the exiles could savour a cuisine and culture they had not enjoyed for years.

Fernao had returned directly from the Raschids' house to the flagship, where he reported the discussions to his father. When he completed his report, the admiral had sat lost in silent thought for several minutes. Fernao knew that his father already had all the information necessary, from his own sources, to assess the Mouro's proposals fully, without the need for consultation with experts. Finally, a slow smile had dawned on the admiral's rugged face and he had scratched the side of his great nose as he was wont to do when pleased. 'You have done well, Lieutenant de Albergaria,' he had said. 'This looks like a splendid opportunity. I shall formally announce my decision tomorrow morning, but I accept the Mouro's proposals and conditions. I shall not haggle with them over prices, for that is no way to start a joint venture. You, lieutenant, shall receive due mention in my despatches to His Excellency the Viceroy and His Majesty the King. Under the circumstances, I hereby appoint you, in addition to your military duties, to act as the factor of our government in these trade operations. Though you may be very young for the job, you are a student of commerce in this region and you know the Sinhala and Arabic languages. Besides, *a senhor* de Brito can help you.' A smile had parted his blond moustache from the beard. 'Of course I shall be accused by some of driving the family coach, but that's what families are for after all and our coach is a distinguished one! This could be a splendid opportunity for you to gain new experience and much wealth, since factors are permitted to retain a small percentage of all trade they generate as an inducement to greater endeavour. See that you make the most of the opportunity. Our ancestors may turn in their graves to see a de Albergaria become a trader.' He had shrugged his massive shoulders. 'But after all, even our emperor is a trader nowadays!'

Fernao's eyes had been on the companionway from which the guests would emerge. Now the officer of the day stepped through the entrance. The band struck up a haunting Iberian melody, violins quivering rich, flute piping in a pattern of sparkling raindrops above the drum beat. The guests emerged, led by the two friars in their white cassocks. When they all stood on deck, the colours of the bulky uniforms of the officers and the long dresses and jewels of the ladies made a glittering display. In accordance with the latest fashion, the ladies' dresses were tight at the waist, full at the hips, giving grace to the carriage, the frilled collars adding poise to the head.

Fernao's eyes drifted to the last of the guests. His first impression was of a striking blue dress of the sort worn by princesses in Portugal. Then he noted the slender figure, graceful as a swan. His eyes sought the face. Its beauty captured his attention. He wished he were a painter, not a writer, so that he could reproduce that face on canvas, its exquisite bones, its delicate colouring, the contrast of fair skin with dark auburn hair. What colour would her large eyes be?

Yet his viewing was detached, almost professional. His experience of women was limited, by his own choice. He had never been taken in by a pretty face or an attractive figure. Being young, handsome and the son of an admiral, many were the inviting looks he received while in port. Most Portuguese mamas thought him a good catch and almost literally threw their daughters in his way. On occasion, even married women had cast suggestive glances. He avoided casual alliances simply because he held women in the same esteem in which he had held his dead mother. He did not think of sex, so never needed it.

As if by instinct, the girl raised her eyes to meet his gaze. Their glances locked for a second. A thrill ran through Fernao. She was familiar, somehow reminded him of his beautiful mother. He sensed a kind of puzzlement in her expression at the mutual recognition before she modestly looked away, leaving him entranced at what had been his first moment of silent communion with a woman, an exquisite moment. This must be Julietta de Brito. Suddenly, he was glad to have been chosen, as the youngest officer, to be her escort at dinner.

Duty called. He turned around, walked to the door of the admiral's stateroom and rapped on it. The admiral, a magnificent figure in white satin and burgundy, had been awaiting the signal that would tell him his guests had arrived.

Fernao followed his father down to the main deck and stood behind him. As the officer of the day formally presented each guest, Fernao walked down the line, impatiently awaiting the moment when his eyes would meet Julietta's again.

She curtseyed low as she was presented to his father. Fernao could not remember when he had seen such grace. How could someone who had lived in a different culture all her life curtsey so naturally when most women floundered, joggled or exaggerated the greeting? Then he stood before her, ready with his smile of recognition while he was introduced as her escort. She greeted him with bent head and did not look directly at him even when she placed her right hand lightly on his left wrist so that he could lead her to her place. Clearly she had been taught all the manners and graces of the European courts, but he was vaguely disappointed.

The band struck up a livelier tune, the violins scraping away, the tambourine jangling. The wine glasses were filled with a golden Madeira, the only wine the ships carried. The admiral rose to his feet, his guests with him, and gave the toast of His Imperial Majesty, Dom Manuel, King of Portugal. Fernao noted that Julietta took but a sip from her glass. It was probably the first wine she had ever drunk.

The planned succession of courses began with a white fish indigenous of the Indian waters called seer, lightly grilled with a hint of saffron and the tang of lime.

'I don't suppose you've tasted Madeira before?' Fernao ventured, when Julietta took another sip from her glass.

'No I have not, Sir,' she responded, looking down at her plate.

Was she avoiding his eyes? If so, why? She seemed taciturn. Could it be that, bred in an Asian court, she had no conversation and he would endure a dull evening?

He tried some of the fish. Delicately spiced, the flesh was firm, the flavour milky. Suddenly he remembered a piece of advice given him by a wise old servitor. If you want to be interesting to people, you must be interested in them. 'Your dress is so beautiful, *a senhora*,' he remarked. 'It reminds me of a painting I once saw of a dress worn by the Princess Isabella.'

Her head turned quickly in his direction. 'My father has a copy,' she responded. 'The *duenna* of the Jaya court had my

150

dress made from the picture.'

'That's truly remarkable. Do you like looking at paintings?'

'Oh yes. I . . . I,' she stopped short, blushing then.

Your blush mantles your cheeks like the sinking sun in a clouded west, he thought. Aloud, he quietly urged, 'Go on, please. You what?'

She looked down. 'I have wanted to imitate those styles.'

His interest quickened. 'You paint?'

'I try to.'

'I've wished at times that I could paint, when I've seen something beautiful, but what I really wanted to be once was a writer.'

'Why once? Why not now, Sir?' She blushed at her earnestness. 'I don't mean to be forward, but why don't you become a writer, if that is what you want to be?'

'A good question.' He pondered it. She was making him think. 'I suppose it's because of my family obligations and the pattern my life has taken since I came out east four years ago. There is no opportunity here for a writer.'

'Forgive me, Sir, but don't you think that the opportunity to write exists everywhere so long as you have parchment, stylus and ink? You don't have to print and circulate a book to be satisfied.'

He stared at her, a forkful of fish halfway to his mouth. He lowered the fork. 'You know, you're right,' he conceded.

'I hope I have not offended you with my frankness.'

'You never could, for it seems we are both frustrated artists.' He paused, thinking again. 'You have made me realize that I have not been completely honest with myself,' he resumed slowly. 'I have been making an excuse of my naval career for not producing anything creative, maintaining an extensive diary as a sop to my sense of guilt!'

'I would like to read something you have written, not from your diary of course.'

'And I would like to see one of your paintings.'

Unaccountably, his statement seemed to send her into herself again. She became thoughtful and he ate in silence a while before venturing to draw her out again. 'You have lived all your life with the Sinhala people. What do you think of them?'

'I regard myself as a Sinhala, Sir.'

He was taken aback. 'But . . . ' he began and stopped abruptly.

' . . . you are of Portuguese blood,' she completed his sentence, then glanced squarely at him, her expression suddenly hard. 'Actually, I'm of mixed blood, a *mestico*, I'll have you know. My mother was a Sinhala.'

Moved by a sudden access of tenderness and compassion, he held her look. It must have registered with her, because some of her defensiveness abated and she glanced away quickly. 'I don't know what you mean by mixed blood,' he observed gently. 'I always thought that blood was blood and the king's blood just as red as that of a peasant. I knew about your mother. "Birth does not the Brahmin make",' he quoted from the Buddha.

Her eyebrows rose with interest, her expression softened. 'You know of Lord Buddha's teachings?'

'I have read them.'

'But you are a Catholic and are not supposed to read about other religions.'

'What about you?'

'I grew up in the palace of a Buddhist king. The Buddhists are a very tolerant people, but one cannot avoid the rules of the palace school.'

'Yet the Buddhist king has not allowed our friars to work wholeheartedly towards converting his people to our faith.'

She puckered her forehead. 'That is a political necessity,' she pronounced. 'Just as being a Catholic is in Portugal.'

'Unfortunately, all politicians use religion to further their temporal aims. I have to agree though that the Buddhists are more tolerant than us Christians.' He paused. 'But you are not drinking your wine.'

'Perhaps it is because I may not have a tolerance for it!' She dimpled, but obediently took another sip of Madeira and he thrilled to her compliance. Their attendants removed the fish plates and substituted clean platters.

'Some of the food reminds me of home,' he remarked.

'You have a home in Goa?'

152

'No, I live on the flagship. I meant my home in Portugal.'

'Is your mother in Portugal?'

'No, my mother died when I was a boy.'

'Oh, I didn't know. I'm sorry.'

'Why should you be, *a senhora*, when you never even knew a mother?'

'That is why I can be sorry.'

'Oh.' He held her glance. She looked away quickly, but he felt as if a bond had been established between them.

The waiters served their chicken. 'Stringy, I'm afraid,' Fernao pronounced, and was delighted to hear Julietta giggle.

'It reminds me of some of the ladies of our Court,' Julietta observed with a straight face. 'They are either very fat or very scrawny.'

'The palace farm has every variety of animal,' he observed. 'From fat sows to scrawny chickens.'

'Ah, but also snakes and jackals.'

They laughed aloud together and it was only the glances the other diners cast in their direction that reminded Fernao that he had barely spoken a word to the plump matron sitting on his other side. The young woman was bubbly with Madeira, so he had no difficulty initiating a string of banalities about the events of the last few days, the weather and the sort of accommodation that would be available in Colombo for married personnel. But he found himself waiting impatiently for each moment when he could turn in the other direction, speak to Julietta, observe her beautiful profile and the sparkling aquamarine of her eyes. He found himself talking to her as if she were an old friend and realized how much he had been starved, without realizing it, for the companionship of an intelligent, cultured girl.

Finally, dinner was over. The band struck up a *kaffringha*, dance. The admiral took the floor with Captain Oliveira's wife. He danced stiffly, like a ramrod, but with military grace.

'Have you learned how to dance?' Fernao inquired of Julietta, wondering how she could have done so in an alien country where men and women barely had social contact.

'Yes,' she replied. 'My father taught me. He said it would be necessary for me some day.'

153

'He was right. The necessity has arisen tonight. Will you do me the honour, *a senhora?*'

'Oh no,' she began, then, caught up by his excitement, she rose eagerly to her feet.

The moon was mystic high in the blue heavens, the music was magical. Julietta was a natural dancer. Fernao was entranced.

CHAPTER 14
Saturday, 16 February 1521

Impatient to get to Kodi and have him start on his assignment first thing in the morning, I summoned six cavalrymen from my squadron and rode at their head for Colombo immediately after dinner. A full moon shone silver on the placid waters of the moat. Those long dark figures immobile on the shore were the crocodiles, a silent menace beneath a brilliant starlit sky.

I thought of Julietta and wondered what she was doing, experiencing a stab of jealousy, dark as the groves through which we rode, at the thought of her with dozens of young men of her own kind. She had been protected in the palace, not the least by our customs, but I had been told that the *parangi* women were so free with men that they even danced together. I reassured myself with my knowledge of Julietta. She was open and charming with all people, but there was a reserve to her that a few men in the Court, including princes and nobles, had discovered. She loved me and would hold herself for me alone. Far from being wanton enough to dance with any man, she would never dance to anyone's tune in life but mine!

We rode through the sleeping suburbs of Colombo city, followed by the barking of dogs. The city itself was still alive, especially in the streets of the tradesmen, the inns and the taverns. Hearing the clatter of our cantering horses' hooves, people hastily made way for us, except for a pair of drunks, teetering in our path. We slowed to a trot to swerve past them. One, a short jolly fellow, raised the inevitable finger, bidding me stop and have a drink. I laughed, called back my regrets over my shoulder. My men, too well disciplined to comment, rode silently on either side of the shouting men.

I headed for the port area in Mutu Vella, knowing that Kodi would be working late at his factory to catch up on arrears caused by his concentration on manufacturing the musket. We slowed to a posting trot as soon as we entered the orderly rows of warehouses, now lying in darkness. Six guards ran towards us, swords gleaming in the silver moonlight between the buildings. 'We are the Great King's men!' my aide called out to them. They must have recognized our uniforms, for they saluted and allowed us to pass.

Kodi's factory was no more than a former wooden warehouse, running parallel to a dock used for careening ships. Beyond it lay the pebbly shore, gently stroked by the white lace of journey's end for the ocean's wavelets from restless waters shot with silver moonbeams. There were no guards here, but I glimpsed the lamps of the *parangi* ships between the buildings. The flagship had coloured lights strung over the deck, a pretty sight. My breath caught. Julietta would be on board. She was so near and yet so far away, separated from me not only by space but by my purpose that could brook no personal needs. Yet when that purpose was done, my destiny fulfilled, I would reach for personal happiness with the woman I loved, as my hero King Abhaya Gamini once did. After all, he was only twenty-four when his campaign ended and he married his Raji.

The factory door was open, spilling yellow lantern light through the dark shadow of the building. I signalled my men to halt, slid off Rama and, throwing the reins over his neck, strode into the building. It was long and narrow, lined with workbenches, metal equipment and tools gleaming in the lantern light. One of the many great kilns at the far end blazed red as a Hindu hell.

I looked around for Kodi. There was no sign of him. I heard a commotion outside. Kodi had gone out and was returning. I turned to find Palitha instead, flanked by two of my men. He was dishevelled, wild-eyed, his hair hanging loose.

From the depths of the factory building, I heard the groaning of a man in mortal agony.

Saturday, 16 February 1521

Word of Prince Kumara's arrival from Kandy had been sent ahead by fast messenger, so quarters had been assigned to him in the Jaya palace. He and his escort of ten riders – the sub-kingdom did not have any proper cavalry – had been delayed on the second day of their journey by a flash-flooded river, so they arrived after the dinner hour that night. The wagon containing presents from the prince's father, King Wira, to the Great King would follow in two days, after which he would seek a formal audience. Meanwhile, he had been impatient to get to the scene of the action.

He was conducted by an attendant to his quarters, which to his delight adjoined those of Prince Bhuvaneka and Prince Wijayo. On his last visit two years earlier, he had been allotted one of the smaller suites, consisting only of an anteroom and bedroom, in the section reserved for young, unimportant princes. This time, even his attendant was obviously a more senior man, trim, small, alert, a white turban on his black hair. Either I have acquired added importance in the Court or I have new friends, the prince thought cynically. 'Have a message sent to Prince Wijayo that I shall be calling on him within the hour,' he directed the attendant.

The prince bathed, changed, ate. Then, having received an affirmative response, he hastened to Prince Wijayo's quarters.

'Well, grandson, I hope you l-like your new quarters,' Prince Wijayo commented when they were alone in the study, seated across the great ebony desk.

'Certainly, grandfather. They are literally far removed from those I had two years ago.' He slapped at a mosquito's hum and grinned.

'You now have f-friends in C-court,' the old man responded, pushing back his settle and stretching long legs. 'I arranged that p-personally, I'll h-have you know.' He shot Prince Kumara a surprisingly sharp glance from beneath shaggy white brows. 'I'm g-glad you m-made it here today, because . . .' he paused, obviously to change direction. 'It is the right time of the year and a beautiful night.' He grunted and stood up. 'Shall we take a short walk in the garden? It's cooler outside.'

As he rose to his feet, Prince Kumara felt a thrill go through him. A walk outside, especially at this time of night, was an invitation to important news, definitely to secrecy. 'Certainly, grandfather.'

157

Only the splash of a fountain, sparkling silver in the moonlight, and the sounds of night, croaking bullfrogs underlaid by the ceaseless creak of crickets, disturbed the stillness of the garden. Prince Wijayo contented himself with a series of satisfied grunts at the scent of the queen-of-the-night with pauses to stretch, giving the impression of a casual walk on the green lawns, until they were some distance away from the lights in the open windows. He glanced around to ensure that there was no one around. 'It would not be g-good for anyone to see me d-doing more than taking a walk with my favourite grandson.'

'I understand, grandfather.'

'You know of the arrival of the *p-parangi*?'

'Yes.'

'The d-divisions that always existed b-between my son, Prince Maya Dunne, and me have f-finally surfaced with this event,' Prince Wijayo observed. 'Your uncle, P-prince B-Bhuvaneka and I are united in our views, with which the G-great K-king agrees. After all, we must be loyal to the G-great K-king regardless and support his p-policies in every way.'

'Certainly.'

'The G-great K-king welcomes the arrival of the *p-parangi*. He feels that they will g-give him military support against our real enemies, the Mouro.' He paused to clear his throat and spit. 'Ahem! They have of course started t-trading with the Moors, b-but after all, that's what they're here for and we c-cannot grudge them that.'

'My father too agrees that we must have peace with the *parangi*,' Prince Kumara intervened, reassuringly. 'As a matter of fact, that is one reason why he sent me down here promptly on receiving news of the *parangi* ships.'

'G-good. Now here's the position.'

They had reached the dark trees that bordered the outer wall of the palace, so they paused by common consent. Prince Kumara listened intently while Prince Wijayo briefed him on the events of the past days. 'So you see, the *p-parangi* admiral will have his audience with the G-great K-king t-tomorrow,' he concluded. 'I want you to be p-presented to the admiral.' His gaze was intent. 'I take it that you will also want to visit the admiral p-personally?'

'My father and I had so hoped.'

'I shall arrange for that. Tell your f-father he will be in my debt for that.'

'Yes, grandfather.' Inside, Prince Kumara felt only hard contempt for this weak old prince who had to resort to trading like a dry-fish vendor to establish his position, but he injected a solemn note into his voice. 'You may also be sure of our loyalty and allegiance when you become the Great King, as the *devas* assuredly intend.'

A light breeze fluttering his white hair, the old man peered more closely at him, then looked anxiously around at the shadows of the night. 'I have a new p-plan for ruling the c-country,' he declared. 'All this talk of a unified kingdom is the chattering of monkeys. If your father gives me his unqualified support, I shall appoint him an independent k-king of the *K-kande uda rata*, hill country kingdom, which will include the sub-sub-kingdoms of Pera, Gampola and Hangura. We can have such a k-king in Lanka, so long as he gives allegiance to the G-great K-king. It is called ud-d-ud-d-decentralization.'

'My father will be pleased at your graciousness. We might even hasten . . . ' He hesitated deliberately, inviting the question.

It came sharply. 'Yes?'

Prince Kumara laughed deprecatingly. 'You know what I mean, grandfather. It is best not to speak it aloud.'

He was rewarded by a knowing glance.

'You see, the G-great K-king is my brother, so it would be a sin for me . . . ' It was Prince Wijayo's turn to hesitate. 'Even to think of succeeding him,' he ended lamely. 'B-besides, it would be d-disloyal.'

Prince Kumara decided to take this old bull by the horns. 'I think you and I understand each other, grandfather,' he stated firmly. He looked around casually to ensure absolute privacy. 'You must know that my father and I are for you completely. We will do everything possible to help you in your goals.'

The old eyes gleamed in the semi-darkness. 'And I shall do everything p-possible to help you, P-prince, especially while you are here. I think we now have an alliance.'

'Without a word signed because it would not be timely.'

'You have a nice turn of speech, grandson.'

'So my father was good enough to say just two days ago.'

Saturday, 16 February 1521

Julietta lay on her bunk in the cabin she shared with the other two ladies, staring at the darkness. The flagship was silent except for the occasional creak of timbers and the slap of gentle swells against its side. The dinner party was a thing of the past, but she would never forget it as long as she lived. It had been the single most exciting event of her life, as exciting in its own way as those moments when she and her Prince Tiki-tiki had confessed their love for each other. She had been made to feel like a princess, not a *mestico*, all evening.

She could not deny that Fernao de Albergaria had made it possible and had proved himself a wonderful companion. She was in love with a prince. Why did he not make her feel a princess? Was it something innate in Prince Tikiri, his background and upbringing, or her own sense of shame from living in a palace and a society where rank and caste, birth and creed were deemed important and created segregation?

'Ours is a society in which nobility of character and brave deeds count as much as rank,' the admiral had stated in a brief speech toasting the King Emperor of Portugal again at the end of the dinner. 'It is the avowed policy of His Imperial Majesty for his subjects to marry local people, so that new societies loyal to His Majesty, to our country and to our Church can be created in these outposts of his Empire.'

Fernao had privately explained that the princes and nobles of Portugal were conscious of their rank back at home, but in the Indies, it was more the office a man held that counted, and all the Portuguese, their foreign wives and their children, were a single community bound by ties of culture and language, religion and common loyalty.

As she thought about it now, she told herself that she loved Prince Tikiri and would always be as faithful to him as the

160

heroines in storybooks had been to their lovers. But tonight she faced a serious problem. How could she be a slave to the prince's customs and traditions after having discovered her own true heritage?

She pictured Fernao in her mind's eye. The tall, slim figure in the elegant white uniform, the lean, sensitive face with those pale but brilliant blue eyes that could mist with compassion though they held the potential for being chill as clear cold skies. They had been most vivid when Fernao and she had finally stood by the ship's rail, gazing at an ocean sighing gently beneath the sparkle of moonbeams and restless swells.

'I feel like a new person,' she had quietly confessed. 'I am flattered that you should have danced mostly with me all evening.'

'I alternated my duty dances with each of the other ladies between dancing with you. I too feel a new person somehow.' He had turned to her, his eyes melting. That was when she had looked away. She was not for Fernao de Albergaria.

'You and the lieutenant make a fine couple.' She recalled the admiral's remark while he had danced with her. 'He is a fine young man with a great future.' He had paused, a strange expression of haughtiness in his cold blue eyes. 'A de Albergaria first and last.'

The remark had puzzled Julietta at the time. She now wondered again what the admiral had meant. It must be something good because he had been especially cordial to her when he finally rose to signify that the party was over, before retiring to his stateroom.

Father Juan and Father Perez had beamed their approval all evening, but Father Juan had managed to whisper to her, 'Don't forget your duty to Holy Church and neglect Prince Tikiri.' She hated the friar at that moment, then begged the Blessed Virgin for forgiveness and resolved to recite twelve Hail Marys in restitution.

She suddenly realized that Prince Tikiri – all evening she had been thinking of him as Prince Tikiri, not Tiki-tiki – would be furious if he knew that his girl had danced in public, especially with another man. Sinhala of all classes regarded dancing as the

161

privilege of lower castes. To entertain was the birthright of those lower orders, whose duty it was to make public displays. To be entertained was the privilege of birth, which carried with it the duty of public restraint.

The undercurrent of guilt that had lain within her during the magic calm of the past hours now rose to the surface, left her curiously drained. She got up from her bunk, knelt down and prayed to the Blessed Virgin for guidance.

Saturday, 16 February 1521

I had never seen anything so gruesome in my life, not even Lila's corpse. Kodi was sprawled on the paved floor, the upper part of him in the lantern light, the rest in the shadow of a workbench. His right eye was a mass of charred black and red flesh, his left was flickering, his face was streaked with blood and sweat, his white *dhoti* soaked with blood and urine. His right hand lay on the floor, the fingers smashed, lifeless. Beaten and tortured, he groaned in agony each time he drifted into consciousness.

'Father!' The cry was Palitha's. Frantic, he knelt on the further side of the old man.

I heard a sound as of air escaping from a pierced drum. I realized it came from me. I knelt too, reached out tenderly to touch the ravaged face. I wished I could place his head on my lap. 'Get a physician,' I commanded one of my shocked cavalrymen. 'Immediately!'

'Yes, Prince.' He raced away.

'Leave us.' Some instinct made me command the other guard.

'Prince!' His voice a bare whisper, Kodi's single eye was focused in my direction, not at his son. 'They ... they ... wanted the musket.' His voice faded away, the single eye closed in agony, his breathing became laboured, rasping through his chest.

'Who, Kodi, who?' I fought back the tears, not through pride, for I would gladly have shed them in abundance for this poor, decent man's racked body, but because I would not give them to the fiends who mutilated Kodi. 'Who did it?'

162

Somehow my deadly quiet urgency must have penetrated his layers of pain. 'G...g...*goondas*,' he whispered, his nostrils flaring with the effort. 'Two m...m...masked *goondas*. Mouro...I think.' He paused, struggling for breath.

Palitha gave a great groan, turned an anguished face in my direction. 'It must be the same men who ransacked our house. I went out for dinner because *amma* and my sister are away and returned to find it almost wrecked.' His face broke up, tears started streaming down his cheeks. 'Look what they have done to my poor father. They beat him up, smashed his hand, then put out his eye, trying to find out the secret of the gun.'

'They didn't get it from me, they never would have.' The words uttered softly, weakly, were nonetheless crystal clear.

I gazed down at Kodi in amazement. His single eye was wide open, staring at me, the face contorted into a smile, grotesque, but still a smile.

'It shall belong only to the Sinhala,' Kodi stated, still clearly. 'Palitha, it is now up to you. Sorry I could not tell...tell... you...'

His breathing rasped harshly in his chest, started to rattle. The open eye widened, lost its focus, the jaw dropped, the nostrils flared in a desperate reaching for breath. With a great gasp, Kodi half-rose, then slumped back, his head thudding on the floor. One final rattle and the head flopped lifelessly sideways, accompanied by Palitha's cry.

The Sinhala legacy of a *parangi* musket had taken its second toll. I stared down at the death mask of the metal-worker hero and an icy calm gripped me. Palitha's wailing receded into the distance.

I have grown up, I thought. There is no room even for pity in the world I have entered. Kodi is dead. Palitha must and shall carry on his work. That call of my country is all I care about, save for vengeance.

Whoever did this foul deed knew what they were looking for. How? Besides me, only Kodi, Palitha, my father and I were aware of the secret. Could one of Kodi's workers have discovered what he was doing and betrayed him? Kodi had been so certain of total secrecy that this was unlikely.

163

Who? Who? Who? The question kept spinning in my mind like a top, its nail piercing my brain, gouging . . . until something opened up.

One other person had been aware of what Kodi was doing. Julietta!

What possible connection could there be between her and Mouro *goondas*? I had told Julietta about the plan to manufacture the musket yesterday, so she was unaware that the weapon had actually been made. She left this morning on her visit to the Portuguese fleet . . . the Portuguese fleet . . . the Portuguese fleet. The top gouging my brain swivelled and flopped to a halt.

I had to review the sequence of events, but now it was my head that was spinning.

Julietta went to the flagship today, so she may have told her hosts about it or accidentally let something slip. So far, so good, but what connection could the *parangi* have with the Mouro?

Dear *devas*, the young *parangi* lieutenant visited Abdul Raschid's home only this afternoon.

Stunned, suddenly drained of all energy, I stared down at Kodi's lifeless body.

I did this to you. Could Julietta have done it to both of us?

My heart shrieked soundlessly, in mortal doubt, my mind bereft of the power to think. Only my instincts cried out, Never, never, never. Julietta would *never, never*, intentionally or unintentionally, betray me or the Sinhala. Why just the other day she told me she was nothing else but Sinhala. Only tonight, as I saw the flagship decked with coloured lights, I told myself that my real destiny was not to rule the country but to unify it, so that when that task was done, I could ask Julietta to be my wife. But who else could have betrayed the secret?

Utter desolation filled me as I realized that I had to set aside the foolish, romantic dreams of youth before the demands of manhood. Yet love and hope kept intruding doubts on my suspicions.

There was no way in which Julietta could have passed information to the *parangi*. She was never close enough to her father to share any secret with him. The only person she confided in was her housekeeper, a Sinhala with no *parangi* connections. Julietta knew no other *parangi* except Father Perez and Father Juan.

Wait a second, some remote corner of·my brain commanded. Supposing she told one of the friars? But why would she? Something nagged, something I knew was there, if only I could reach it.

What? What? A story I had heard tell, a remark. Yes, that was it, not a remark but a chance statement Father Juan had made almost a year ago, when he was telling us about the merits of the Inquisition in Portugal, that friars used what he referred to as the confessional, to obtain truth from Catholics and were only entitled to betray them for the greater glory of God.

Julietta frequently attended confessional with Father Juan. Why, she had done so only last evening. She must have told him about Kodi's project then. He would immediately have reported it to the *parangi* admiral because it was not in the interests of the Catholic Church and the Portuguese government for the Sinhala to have firearms. Father Juan had not been his old sweet self since the *parangi* fleet arrived. I remembered how keen he had been for me to share all I knew with him that first day.

Never trust a fanatic of any religion, my father had once warned. I had seen the fanatical gleam in Father Juan's yellow eyes just a few days ago. In a flash, I knew that the friars would attempt to impose their religion and their government on my people, using every method in their power.

Desolate, bitter, I realized that I should never entrust secrets to Julietta again. If nothing else, it could place too great a burden on her. Then, the stark knowledge hit me that I should sever all connection with Julietta if I was not to risk betraying my country and my people. Oh God of my Julietta, I wish I were dead instead of poor Kodi sprawled before me.

A fierce desire for vengeance seized me. Two dead people, both tortured to death. They had to be avenged.

Having spent all night trying, without result, to track down the trail of the murderers and then making arrangements for the disposal of Kodi's body, I got to the palace too late to talk to my

165

father. He had left for Sita Waka before dawn. One of my problems was that I could not divulge the real reason for Kodi's murder to anyone but my father. Meanwhile, I arranged for Kodi's son, Palitha, to be protected before he secretly left for Sita Waka with all the equipment necessary to commence manufacturing muskets, even though Kodi had been murdered before he could instruct Palitha in the technique and method. If only I had instructed him to communicate with Palitha straightaway, instead of waiting for my father's approval. If only . . . if only . . .

That very night, the most terrible 'if only' was added to the list. One of my father's contacts, a courtier, contacted me. I learned from him of a conversation Julietta had had with Father Juan the day before she left for the flagship, when she had agreed to tell him all she learned from me. My dreams of romance, my hopes for a happy personal life were shattered. I was left in a dark void. Only it was not void, but tore me with anguish.

All through that night I lay awake, struggling to hate Julietta. In the cold dawn, the light had gone out of my sun. I would walk alone in the dark from now on, but far from hating Julietta, I still loved her.

CHAPTER 15
Monday, 18 February 1521

The embassy conveying the Great King's agreement, written in Portuguese on *ola*, to grant 'Admiral Lopo Soarez de Albergaria, his staff and entourage' an audience at noon the following Saturday had just departed. The admiral had received the men on the main deck, so they could be properly impressed by the soldiers drawn up in two ranks and the brave display of senior sea captains in their white and gold uniforms. Now he returned to the poop deck, stood by the rail and watched the receding barge, carrying the embassy across the brown waters, glistening in morning sunlight, back to the main wharf.

Standing behind him, Fernao observed that work in the port was definitely back to normal. Carts and wagons transporting produce were trundling in or out, bare-chested labourers, their bodies already glistening with sweat, were loading and unloading wagons or boats. Their cries of 'Hodi!' ... 'Hell-ay! ... ' reached him above the clatter and thud of the soldiers on deck dispersing to their other duties. Even the smells of the flagship, a mixture of tar, gun-oil and cooking, seemed to be ready for the day's duties.

'The Great King is obviously eager to see us,' the admiral remarked. 'A slightly different reception from that received by Vasco da Gama from the Zamorin of Calicut twenty-three years ago and the excuses proffered by the Middle Eastern potentates to our various missions since. Da Gama's encounter in 1498 led to our first contact with this country, you will recall. The Zamorin impounded our ships and demanded that we seize a Sinhala vessel, heading from Colombo to Ormuz in the Persian Gulf carrying a load of cinnamon, precious gems and five trained elephants, as a condition of their release. In a sense, it was a service to Portugal for that seizure opened our eyes to the potential of Sinhala trade.' There was a glint of humour as well as satisfaction in his eyes.

The Great King probably wants the audience done with so that he can sleep in peace without the threat of our great *nao* in his principal port, Fernao thought. A fort is merely an enclave, but a flotilla can carry death and destruction anywhere along his coastline. 'It's possible that some of the acceleration was supplied by Prince Wijayo,' he volunteered aloud.

'Indeed. That old fox not only fears us, but also hopes that we will give him the means to enter the farmyard.' He half turned towards Fernao, his smile widening. 'And why not, lieutenant? A grateful, compliant ruler would suit us very well. The message he has sent us, requesting a private interview, smacks of intrigue. The man is either plotting to take over the succession or, at the very least, planning for it. I intend observing his conduct during tomorrow's audience. If he supports our plans, as I am certain he will, I shall arrange to see him privately before I depart these shores.'

'All very intriguing, Sir,' Fernao suggested, his eyes crinkling. 'The Great King, by report, is not the kind of ruler who can be influenced, but Prince Wijayo could probably be manipulated. You are absolutely right, if I may say so, to cultivate him. He offers us the prospect of more than normal fair trade.' A savage inspiration seized him, made him wonder at himself even as he uttered the words. 'We might even encourage him to hasten the realization of his ambitions. Better a new, murderous puppet in our hands than the independent *dharmista*, as they call the Great King.'

The admiral's great head jerked around, the eyes seeming to bore into Fernao, sending a stab of apprehension through him. Had he overshot the mark? He returned his father's stare levelly. The blond head turned back towards the shore. The admiral reflected a few moments, during which Fernao's heart beat faster. The massive body then turned slowly around to face Fernao, the look in the ice-blue eyes an acknowledgement that Fernao had come of age.

The admiral nodded approvingly. 'Indeed.' He paused. 'Something tells me you are going to do very well in this part of the world.'

168

Saturday, 23 February 1521

The days had passed by so quickly, with all he had to do, preparing for the new trading operations, that Fernao barely saw Julietta. Besides, the entire group of the Jaya palace were invited on board the other *nao*, and only returned to the flagship to sleep. Yet he thought frequently about Julietta and wished they could make time to talk. He recognized a change taking place within him. The pursuit of power and the actual power afforded by his new responsibilities were giving him more decisiveness as a person. The first time he thought of subtly exercising power to compel Julietta to respond to him, he dimly glimpsed a warning sign that the attitudes of official life were already seeping into his personal desires, and that this might not be good in the long run, but he simply had neither the time nor the inclination to dwell on its implications. Life, moving fast, was heady, exciting.

The Great King had sent three white carriages drawn by black Scindhis to convey the admiral's embassy to the palace, with open horse-drawn wagons for the escort. These were lined up at the base of the main wharf by dawn on the Saturday morning, the horses restive, the coachmen smart in their red tunics and white pantaloons, though their brown feet were bare.

The admiral had selected his delegation to impress the Great King. Apart from Fernao, he had detailed Captain Oliveira and six of the best built and handsomest captains from the flotilla, besides Father Juan as interpreter and an escort of fifty armed musketeers commanded by a lieutenant. Dressed in ceremonial white uniforms, the delegation made a brave display when it boarded .the coaches three hours before noon. Fernao and Father Juan rode with the admiral in the leading coach, Fernao on his left, the white-cassocked friar on his right.

'Certainly seems like an auspicious day,' the admiral remarked as they rattled away from the wharf to the clip-clop, clip-clop of hooves. He glanced appreciatively at the silver sunlight, sniffed the scent of cinnamon in the cool air, then settled back against the red and gold cushions, still erect.

You'll *make* it auspicious, Fernao thought, glancing sideways at his father's imperious, craggy face. He straightened his own shoulders to sit up, very erect, as befitted his role.

The gangs of bare-chested labourers and their white-clad overseers who paused to watch the passage of the 'procession' were friendlier today, but Fernao still picked up a resentful glance here and there.

Once clear of the city, they made good progress along the Jaya highway, Father Juan indicating points of interest. Fernao knew what to expect for he had received precise reports from the two friars and *o senhor* de Brito about the palace and its protocols, the city of Jaya and the area around. But still he found the lush green countryside, the orderly, clean people they passed, many of them smiling and calling out '*Ayu-bowan!*' in the traditional greeting, most pleasing. He was glad to find that the poverty of India was absent here.

Strangely, Father Juan never once commented on one of the most beautiful features of the ride, the bell-shaped *dagobas*, glistening white, their gleaming metal spires thrusting towards the cloudless blue skies.

They came to the city moat. Father Juan pointed out the long, still shapes of the crocodiles. It was the first time Fernao had seen these reptiles at such close quarters. He could not restrain a shudder at their size and latent power.

'They make the moat as dangerous as shark-infested waters,' the admiral remarked grimly. 'Unfortunately for the Great King, our modern weapons render their presence abortive.'

Trumpets blared and drums began throbbing as they approached the entrance to the palace. Drummers, trumpeters, dancers in flounced pantaloons and magnificent head-dresses formed up to greet them. Fronting the palace, a guard of mounted cavalry in red and white uniforms was drawn up on either side of the great courtyard. The crowd of dignitaries were gorgeously dressed in silken *dhotis*, held up by broad gold belts with gem-encrusted daggers. Their white cambric shirts had ruffles and jewelled buttons down the front, their waistcoats were of black, red, dark blue or dark green velvet, heavily brocaded with gold and silver, the sleeves puffed. They wore jewelled shoes, curving upwards at the front and three-cornered hats, also brocaded, rather like crowns because of their tiny gold spires. They were led by Prince Wijayo, who towered over them, and a portly man, obviously another prince of some importance, with a shiny round face, a protuberant moustache and small eyes. General Prince Maya Dunne, his son and Prince Raigam were conspicuous by their absence.

Fernao had seen more impressive, highly ornamented buildings in India, but the audience hall, built, he understood, in accordance with traditional Sinhala architecture, had a classical chaste elegance all its own. A great moonstone carved in granite with figures of birds, animals and fruit in each of the three arcs formed the apron, from which broad granite steps, the balustrades graced at intervals by pots containing masses of creamy coconut flowers, led to the verandah of the hall, a tall building open on three sides with a peaked roof supported by great, soaring teakwood columns.

The drumming, music and dancing stopped abruptly, leaving a sudden silence. 'Welcome to the c-court of His Majesty, D-Dharma P-Parakrama Bahu IX, Lord of the Island of Lanka and all its K-kingdoms,' Prince Wijayo greeted them as soon as the entire delegation had alighted and the musketeer escort, as previously ordered by the admiral, had formed two ranks facing the hall. He waved a graceful hand at the portly prince standing next to him. 'I would also like to t-take this opportunity of p-presenting to you my oldest s-son, n-next in the line of s-succession, after me, P-Prince B-Bhuvaneka Bahu.'

Fernao noted Prince Bhuvaneka's weak chin and that sense of manipulative power swept through him again. Here is a man who will indeed make a puppet, he thought.

After an exchange of pleasantries, Prince Wijayo led the delegation up the steps and into the crowded audience hall, gleaming and glittering with the national dress of the princes, noblemen and gentlemen-at-arms. The hum of conversation died down when they entered and a few hundred pairs of eyes were turned in their direction as they walked down the aisle. The entire hall was illuminated with lighted candles in great silver candlesticks and multi-tiered brass lamps, their wicks fluttering.

171

The most impressive dignitary was the Great King himself. Dressed like the princes and noblemen, but in cloth of gold, seated on the golden throne of Lanka encrusted with gems, wearing his golden crown, sceptre in hand, King Dharma Parakrama was indeed a regal figure of immense dignity. His face reminded Fernao of carvings of the Buddha he had seen in India. On either side of him, six giant Sinhala dressed in white stood straight and still, bearing huge lighted candles on intricately carved silver candlestands.

Ornamented chairs of ebony, carved and cushioned in red, had been placed on either side of the platform to face the throne, three on each side. Having knelt to the Great King and kissed his hand, the admiral, Father Juan and Captain Oliveira sat on the Great King's right. The rest of the delegation had remained with the princes and nobles in the front of the hall. Prince Wijayo, Prince Bhuvaneka and a nobleman who was the king's interpreter took the chairs on his left. Fernao stood beside his father.

Refreshments were served by red-uniformed attendants while small talk went on – a variety of juices, including melon in gold goblets and coconut water, both tinctured with lime, Sinhala sweetmeats on gold platters – as a prelude to the discussions which would be followed by the Great King's luncheon.

Fernao noticed that the Great King did not partake of the refreshments. They had been warned that, like the *bhikkus*, he did not take anything but water after the noon hour.

When the attendants had withdrawn, others appeared bearing golden bowls, with red and white temple-flower petals floating on clear water and snowy white napkins for the washing of hands.

Finally, when all the attendants had departed, a hush settled on the hall.

'You requested audience with us, Lord Admiral,' the Great King stated. 'While we are pleased to receive you at any time because of the love and esteem we bear for your King Emperor and your people, we have been informed that you desire some assistance from us in the execution of your trading objectives in this region. How may we help you?'

Fernao could not help a feeling of pleasure that for once he had met a ruler who could come directly to the point. He listened watchfully, eager to learn, as his father went over their intentions and desires in furtherance of the treaty of 1505.

The Great King also listened attentively and in silence to Father Juan's translation. The admiral ended by nodding to Fernao to produce their copy of the original treaty.

As Fernao stepped forward, the Great King held up his hand. 'We need no more than your word, Admiral,' he declared, smiling graciously at Fernao in case he felt rebuffed. Fernao felt a twinge of conscience for his thought of the previous day contemplating the ruler's death. 'We shall certainly grant you a *sesmaria* for the property you have selected. The one problem that presents itself is that the treaty of 1505, which we have studied, makes provision for the erection of a factory, for processing cinnamon, not a fort.' The glance of the fine, black eyes was questioning.

'You are right, Your Majesty,' the admiral declared. 'But we have found in our operations elsewhere in the Indies and in the Middle East that this sort of enclave saves the rulers a great deal of trouble protecting our establishments, because we can then, with the sovereign lord's approval, protect them ourselves at no cost to the sovereign.' He paused, eyed the Great King with proud eyes. 'Once we are permitted to be in such a position, we can also provide military support to the sovereign lord against his enemies.'

An amused twinkle appeared in the Great King's eyes. 'We are a *dharmista* ruler, Excellency,' he stated. 'We have neither enemies nor any who would desire to dispossess us.'

Fernao glanced at Prince Wijayo, noted the enigmatic glance he exchanged, ever so briefly, with Prince Bhuvaneka. These two have different ideas, he thought.

'In that event, we can also offer Your Majesty's ships the freedom of the seas,' the admiral volunteered shrewdly.

'Now that has its attractions,' the Great King responded in pleasant tones.

It took but a few minutes of discussion for the Great King to agree to the admiral's request. The whole audience had obviously been pre-planned, right down to an offer of the Great King to send an annual gift of one hundred and fifty measures of the finest quality cinnamon to the King Emperor of Portugal. Coming on the heels of the agreement which they would now sign with Abdul Raschid to act as their broker, the entire mission to Colombo could be pronounced an outstanding success.

'My King Emperor will be most gratified,' the admiral ended euphemistically.

The Great King nodded to his own interpreter, who hastened from the hall but returned in a few moments carrying a scroll bound with red silk ribbon. He opened it with a flourish, displayed the Great King's seal. To Fernao's amazement, he read out the terms of the agreement! For once, Admiral de Albergaria seemed stupefied, then a slow smile spread across his craggy face. 'Touché!' he seemed to say.

The interpreter handed the scroll to Fernao.

'Your Majesty, I have one more fraternal request from my King Emperor,' the admiral stated.

The Great King's hairless eyebrows lifted. 'Please feel free to state it, Lord Admiral.'

'His Imperial Majesty is as deeply concerned with matters spiritual as you are, Sire. He would appreciate your royal approval for the establishment of a centre and cathedral in Colombo by the Order of our St Francis, to which Father Juan and Father Perez belong. Being aware that you are a devout follower of the Doctrine of the Buddha, which advocates tolerance towards all religions, he hopes that you will permit the members of this Order to minister to your people and to teach them the Catholic religion as freely as your *bhikkus* spread your doctrine.'

The Great King's expression changed, a hint of iron entered the bland voice. 'We would personally have no objection to approving such a request,' he said flatly. 'But we doubt that the Buddhist people of this country, and especially the *bhikkus* and their leaders, are prepared for it. Great resentment would result.' He pondered awhile. 'We are, however, much disposed to please our royal brother, your King Emperor. For the present

174

therefore we shall agree to the Order of Saint Francis establishing its centre and preaching in the city of Colombo alone, which has a more heterogeneous population.'

'My sovereign will be delighted and grateful,' the admiral responded. 'As will the Holy Father and every sovereign in Europe. They will recognize that you are indeed an enlightened monarch.'

Fernao could not help but notice how Father Juan's eyes gleamed with excitement. He wondered at the Great King's hidden sigh.

Saturday, 23 February 1521

When they returned from the Jaya palace, replete from the Great King's luncheon, Fernao found that a table covered with white linen, with settles around it, had been installed on the main deck of the flagship to receive Prince Kumara of Kandy, for whom the Crown Prince Wijayo had arranged a meeting with the admiral that same evening.

When Prince Kumara was piped on board with his entourage, Fernao noted his flawless, golden skin, brown eyes, shiny black hair and fine features with admiration, for this was one of the most attractive, magnetic personalities he had encountered in the Indies. Though very young for such an important mission, the prince appeared quite self-confident, almost cocky. Looking more closely, Fernao noticed that the eyes were translucent, like two clear stones, and totally devoid of expression.

Greetings over, they sat around the table in the golden light of the westering sun, the admiral at the head, Prince Kumara at his right, Father Juan to his left to act as interpreter.

'My uncle, Prince Wijayo, has assured me that I can talk freely at this meeting, with no fear of reports to any other party?' Prince Kumara started the meeting almost abruptly, his look questioning.

The admiral nodded his agreement. 'Certainly, Prince.'

Unexpectedly, the prince came directly to the point. 'In that event, I am directed by my father, King Wira of Kandy, to invite you, Lord Admiral, to maintain a permanent embassy in our capital city. We will place a suitable residence at the disposal of your representative and his staff, provide them with servants, food and all the wherewithal for maintaining a luxurious standard of living. We will also pay them all necessary stipends, in accordance with their rank. So it will not cost your government one single *tola*.'

'What do we get out of this?' the admiral demanded, rising to the occasion with equal bluntness.

Prince Kumara produced a small parchment scroll from inside his tunic. 'Something that would take you long to work out.' He tapped the table gently with the scroll. 'This is a map of the island of Lanka prepared by a Mouro trader. It shows where the principal ports of the island are located. It...er... happened to fall into my father's hands.'

Your father probably had the man murdered to obtain it, Fernao conjectured.

'Are there other major ports besides Colombo and Galle?'

'Oh yes.'

'Such as?'

A cunning gleam flashed across the pale eyes, so fleeting it was barely noticeable. 'Those I shall reveal to the Lord Admiral when I have his promise that he will establish an embassy in Kandy.'

The admiral was obviously taken aback. 'What good would such an embassy do your father?' he demanded, changing tack. 'Besides, the Great King might not like it. He might even deny us access to your capital through his territory.'

The prince grinned, displaying perfect white teeth. 'Your last statement first, Lord Admiral. This map,' he tapped the scroll lightly on the table again, 'depicts two different routes to our capital from two of those other ports, one from the east, the other from the west. The Great King does not have physical control over that territory. He need not even know that your embassy is intended until it arrives, by which time it will be under my father's protection.' He paused. 'As to what good it would do my father; first, it would give him great prestige. Second, the very existence of this kind of alliance would enable him to enlist the aid of the sub-sub-kings of the hill country to

176

establish a common rule, which could then be extended over the entire island ... er ... in alliance with you and your King Emperor.'

'With your father as the Great King, I presume?'

'Naturally.'

'Where would Prince Wijayo and Prince Bhuvaneka fit in?'

'They would be permitted to retain their lands.'

'But aren't they your allies today and in the line of succession? I mean, it was Prince Wijayo who made your interview with me possible.'

Prince Kumara shrugged. 'Human beings are like clouds, merging and parting. That is life.' He paused, awaiting the admiral's response. Perceiving only silence, he nonetheless proceeded smoothly. 'I know that you have made amicable arrangements with the Great King, but if my father becomes Great King with your assistance, he will give you a monopoly of the export trade of Lanka and join you in driving out the Mouro. Think how much more effective you have been in India whenever you joined forces with powerful native princes. Besides, my father would give you approval to establish forts at every important harbour in the country. You could then buy directly from the suppliers without having to go through Mouro middlemen thus vastly increasing your profits.'

The prince has obviously done his homework, Fernao reflected with grudging admiration. He is as conscientious as he is utterly without morals.

'I am listening, Prince,' the admiral responded. 'You become more interesting by the minute.'

'Forgive me, Lord Admiral, but I think you mean that you become more interested by the minute,' the prince responded with an impudent grin. 'Do we have an agreement?'

'First the map,' the admiral demanded, holding out his hand.

'First your word.' The pale eyes of the prince flashed cold.

The admiral threw back his head and laughed aloud. 'I am inclined to your proposals, but would have to act according to the situation from time to time. Surely you know that?'

The prince shrugged again, handed over the scroll. 'I too will need to act according to the situation created by you from time

177

to time,' he stated. He looked deliberately at Father Juan. 'You can see that I am a soul in need of saving, Father,' he asserted. 'I would like to extend a cordial invitation to you and your fellow priests to visit our capital ... er ... as part of the admiral's embassy, of course, to expound your religion to my father, to our Court and to me. We will make suitable accommodation available to you and give you every opportunity to preach your gospel freely to our people. I shall personally donate the money needed to build a church in Kandy.' He grinned wolfishly. 'Most Buddhists repent their sins. They would find the concept of forgiveness and salvation through repentance, without having to undertake the tiresome process of labouring along a Noble Eightfold Path, most attractive.'

Fernao did not know whether to be impressed or disgusted; then he noticed Father Juan's face. It had come alive, the pale yellow eyes gleaming, the jaw tight beneath the dark beard, the look of the religious fanatic offered grace.

The prince's gaze reverted to the admiral. 'After all, your priests have left their homes and their native land so far away and come to a strange country just to preach the gospel.' His tone was casual. 'How noble! They are here in the great tradition of all missionaries, of both your religion and of the Buddhist doctrine. I consider it churlish that such devoted, selfless priests have not been extended the opportunity to spread their gospel during their many years of exile.' He paused, his look became more pointed. 'Indeed, I am personally so impressed with their zeal and devotion and so convinced of the power of your God that it might take very little to convert me.'

Sunday, 24 February 1521

Fifty miles east of Jaya, a day and a night away on a good horse, at the base of the central highlands of Lanka, our mansion in Sita Waka is the centre of our extensive family holdings. Set in spacious grounds, with green lawns and large beds of burgundy-leaved cannas, it is a gracious two-story granite structure with a roof of red, half-round country tiles, built around a great centre courtyard with a balcony running above all four sides. It was in its usual immaculate condition when I arrived late that Saturday evening, with flares flaming and hissing along the entrance roadway and golden light flowing from every window.

As I handed Rama to the grooms, my father, dressed like me in white pantaloons and tunic, emerged on to the front verandah to greet me. Three family retainers in their white uniforms with broad red sashes at the waist clustered behind him. I smiled at each in turn, especially my favourite, their chief, Nanda, tall and stately as an aristocrat, his long silver hair tied in a knot at the nape of his neck and held tight on top of the head by a curved tortoiseshell comb. I then followed my father into his study. This was a small chamber adjoining the spacious hall at the front of the mansion. Many-tiered brass lamps, their multiwicks glowing like offerings before a shrine, shed a golden glow within the room. The floor was completely covered by a matting of closely woven strips of creamy bamboo on which a large Pahlava rug of maroon and green had been placed. The desk and chair and the settees, covered with red velvet cushions, were of brown *nadun*-wood. On the right of the desk was the inevitable alabaster stand on which was placed a golden statue of Lord Buddha in the traditional lotus pose, with two tiny clay lamps before it and incense holders wafting the scent of camphor into the room. The walls were lined with shelves containing *olas* bound with ivory or ebony slats. The austere elegance of the whole reflected my father's character and personality.

We sat beside each other on a settee and disposed of the formalities. He briefed me fully on Admiral de Albergaria's audience with the Great King, about which he had already received a detailed report. I had the impression that he was glad to have someone with whom he could finally share his goals.

'You must be tired from your journey,' he finally stated. 'A bath and change of clothing are indicated, followed by dinner.' He paused, his expression serious. 'I sense, however, that something is bothering you, Prince.'

179

Amazed at his sensitivity, I could not deny him, and blurted out the facts of Kodi's death. He listened in silence, his dark eyes flashing in anger at first then softening with compassion as he recognized my anguish and sense of guilt. 'I tried everything possible within the limits of my powers to track down the murderers, but it is as if they never existed,' I ended, frustration in my voice.

'H'mm.' He stared thoughtfully into space. 'Have you any idea as to who could have instigated it?'

'It could only be the *parangi*,' I asserted vehemently.

'How could they possibly have known what Kodi was working on?'

I nearly choked on the question. I could not possibly tell him the truth of my suspicions. It made me feel so betrayed, so isolated, so alone, that I avoided an answer and burst forth crying, 'Vengeance, *tha*, I demand vengeance. I beg you to help me avenge this foul deed.'

'Against whom will we wreak vengeance?' he demanded soberly. 'Besides, if you and I go on a mad quest for vengeance, people will wonder why we seek to avenge the murder of a master craftsman. You *must* realize that we should do absolutely nothing. Kodi has given the Sinhala the modern weapons we need.' His voice vibrated with unwonted passion. 'He gave of his brain, his tortured body and his life for our cause. Let us not diminish his nobility. Let *him* be the avenger through our producing his instrument of vengeance for the Sinhala people.'

I saw the wisdom of his words, but impatience struggled against that vision. He noted it and added, 'Palitha is on his way here already. His secret factory awaits him, with kilns and furnaces, at our place on the Kitul rock hill. It is quite remote, as you know. He can set up his machinery and equipment there and also test-fire his muskets in complete privacy. It will all be done in the guise of a fireworks factory, so no one will be suspicious.'

'The only problem is that Kodi could not give Palitha detailed instructions before he died.' I could not keep the misery from my voice. 'Palitha will have to start afresh . . . and he is not Kodi.'

'At least he has Kodi's prototype to work with.' He rapped his

180

thigh with a clenched fist. 'Time. How much time do we have? It will not be long before the *parangi* attempt to dominate our affairs.'

Sunday, 24 February 1521

The request from Prince Wijayo had been channelled through Father Juan, who, having received the message privately while conducting Sunday Mass in the small church at Jaya that very morning, delivered it personally to Fernao's father on board the flagship. The prince would deem it an honour if he were permitted to visit the flagship that evening. He had never seen a naval fighting ship before and would appreciate the opportunity.

Fernao, who was in his father's cabin at the time, had been surprised, but the admiral seemed to have anticipated some such move, though he had meant to initiate it himself.

Fernao was fascinated by the ensuing conversation.

'Rather precipitate, wouldn't you say?' the admiral had observed, a knowing glint in his eyes.

'The prince probably desires to avail himself of the opportunity of a ... er ... visit, before you leave our shores,' the friar responded, smiling broadly. 'For more reasons than one.'

'We are certainly attracting all the power-seekers.'

'Except the strongest of them, General Prince Maya Dunne.'

The admiral had scratched his massive jaw. 'That one and his whelp will give us a lot of trouble,' he asserted.

'Would you like me to be present so I can act as interpreter, admiral? My Sunday tasks are done.'

'I rather think not, Father. As you say, Prince Wijayo's visit is for more reasons than one. Even though the prince selected you to deliver the message, your presence might prove to be inhibiting because of your years of association with the Jaya palace. Lieutenant de Albergaria is a competent interpreter and, being also my son, might open Prince Wijayo to greater confidences.'

'A wise thought.'

To the surprise of everyone except the admiral, when Prince

181

Wijayo arrived, he was accompanied by his oldest son, Prince Bhuvaneka. 'The plot thickens,' he muttered to Fernao as they awaited the visitors on the poop deck.

The inspection done, refreshments were served on the main deck. Fernao noted that Prince Wijayo was not exactly averse to the Madeira wine, which he claimed never to have tasted before. Gradually, by a process of manipulation, the prince contrived to get himself, Prince Bhuvaneka, Fernao and his father alone on the foredeck.

The port was hushed as Fernao gazed towards the city in which lights were beginning to glow. Cawing crows were winging their way back to the treelines or circling them. Dusk, creeping in from the east, had started to overtake a sun preparing to bed in flaming reds and oranges behind them.

Prince Wijayo stood beside the twin-culverin, his white hair fluttered by a land breeze that brought the cloying smell of copra. 'Ah! Now we c-can t-talk in p-private,' he observed, Fernao translating. 'There is no p-privacy anywhere in the world except for p-peasants and pheasants.' He grinned, seeking approval of his wit.

'You may indeed talk freely here,' the admiral encouraged him, his ice-blue eyes sweeping the deserted foredeck. He took in the sailors lounging around the main deck and the soldiers standing beside the ship's rail, gazing hungrily towards the city, where their comrades who had shore-leave would even now be enjoying themselves at the taverns and brothels. 'We are quite alone.'

'My s-son will explain my p-proposal to you,' Prince Wijayo stated, nodding towards the portly Prince Bhuvaneka.

'My father desires me to tell you that he welcomes your presence in Lanka wholeheartedly,' Prince Bhuvaneka began in a high, naturally hoarse voice. 'As you have probably guessed, it is he who arranged for your audience with the Great King and prepared the *sesmaria* exactly as you desired it. You will undoubtedly have noticed the absence of Prince Maya Dunne, his son Prince Tikiri and Prince Raigam from that event. You can expect no support, only opposition, from them. Also, you know that it is my father who organized the meeting you had

182

yesterday with Prince Kumara of the Kandy sub-kingdom.'

'I am indeed gratified by the loyal support and courteous welcome that Prince Wijayo and you have extended to me and to the men under my command. The Viceroy and my King Emperor will undoubtedly share my gratitude.'

'Ah, gratitude!' Prince Bhuvaneka raised a pudgy brown finger for emphasis. 'A most commendable emotion, but only to the extent that it breeds mutual support.' He paused, his small eyes directly on the Admiral, their message clear. 'My father and I would also like to bring to your notice that we share a willingness to permit your Holy Church and its friars to preach your religion and make conversions. We both believe that the Buddhist *bhikkus* and clergy have too much of a hold on the people and therefore too big a say in the government.'

'You may be sure that any ruler who co-operates with Holy Church and its emissaries will have special support from my own government,' the admiral responded. 'We do indeed have the impression, with due deference to the Great King, that it would be to the benefit of your remarkable nation to be free of so much religious influence in your administration as soon as possible.' He sighed heavily. His craggy face softened but his eyes were bleak in the gathering dusk. He gripped the ship's rail and stared in the direction of Jaya.

Prince Wijayo's voice cut through the silence. 'We shall see what we c-can d-do to hasten that liberation,' he said.

183

PART TWO

The Making
of the Kings

CHAPTER 16
Saturday, 12 March 1524

Standing beside Julietta on the western rampart wall, Fernao turned away from the rose-grey and silver afterglow of the sunset to survey the completed fort. Behind him, breakers crashed, hissed, foamed white lace upon the rampart wall that rose sheer from the ocean, sent up damp spray smelling of seaweed. Across the fort the dark waters of Colombo harbour glinted restlessly, two great *nao* warships dominating all the vessels.

So much had happened since his father's flagship, *Santa Caterina*, had sailed into that harbour three years before and yet it had been a time of peaceful trade and progress. The admiral had departed four weeks later, his mission successfully accomplished, and returned to Goa after sailing round the island and visiting the Maldives. Work on the fort had, however, commenced the Monday after the *sesmaria*, land grant, was made by the Great King Dharma Parakrama Bahu. With the driving force of Captain Oliveira behind it, the fort had been completed in two years. Built in the shape of a triangle, it was now fully manned. A wide channel had been cut at the base of the headland, connecting the ocean and the lake near the shore with the harbour. This channel, being on the city side, served as a moat, complete with a drawbridge. Sheer rampart walls, crenellated for defence, were built up flush from the harbour on the northwest and the ocean to the south. The rampart wall on the third side was built away from the moat, leaving a small *maidan* in front for better defence. With the ocean to the west and south, the lake, the moat to the east and the harbour spreading north and northwest at its feet, the fort was protected by water on all three sides. Its solid block walls, with ground oyster shells and coral for binding, permitting several hundred defenders to stand side by side to fire their muskets at an attacking enemy, were reinforced at regular intervals by the long snouts of cannon thrusting through embrasures. Circular watchtowers, glowing with lamplight and dark with the shadows of sentries, dominated the three points of the triangle. A central tower, at the base of which the headquarters were located, rose three stories tall at the centre, its lighted windows telling of men at work. The factory, storage rooms, officers' quarters, men's barracks and armouries were spread on all three sides beneath the shelter of the battlements.

Fernao felt a great warmth at observing the men lounging about the parade ground, hearing the tinkling of a guitar, and the voices of the dark figures sitting around a campfire raised in a rousing Algarve chorus. He had helped create this small township out of a barren headland. Looking back, he recalled other events of the past three years.

Within five months of their arrival, the Great King had died under mysterious circumstances. Crown Prince Wijayo had succeeded him and, to add to the resulting political uncertainty, the old man had made a young princess of extraordinary beauty, from a powerful Sinhala clan known as the Kiri Vella – the name of their area – his queen. Fortunately, the queen already had a young son named Prince Deva Raja from her previous marriage, so it was unlikely that she would seek an heir through her new husband and alter the succession. When Prince Wijayo died, he would therefore be succeeded by his oldest son, Prince Bhuvaneka, who was himself loyal to the Portuguese.

Fernao's thoughts were interrupted by a sigh. Surprised, he turned to Julietta. 'Why the sigh?' he inquired.

She stared at the waters beneath her, long white fingers gently placed upon the edge of the rampart, the wind whipping her auburn hair. 'I don't know, Fernao. I suppose I was thinking of our cottage in the palace, missing its velvet feel at dusk, the sound of birds preparing for the night, the scent of wild jasmine.'

Fernao was really concerned. He had been courting Julietta for three years now. While they had become close friends, he could see no signs of her opening up to any closer intimacy.

'But that sounds ungrateful,' Julietta hastened to add. 'You have all been so terribly kind, helping us to find a place in the city until the fort was completed and then allotting us permanent quarters within its walls. Believe me, I'm most thankful. And I do appreciate our regular evening walks on the ramparts. To prove it I have done a painting of the fort at dusk as a present for your birthday tomorrow.'

The gesture touched him so much he set aside his concern. They had exchanged formal birthday and Christmas presents, but this was the first time in his life that anyone had given him a gift of self-expression. 'I couldn't ask for anything better. Thank you, Julietta.'

'On the contrary, it is my pleasure, Fernao. You are the only friend I have in the world.'

He cringed at the word 'friend'. If Julietta was to be his friend, he wanted it as part of something far deeper, for he had fallen in love with her along the way and had only been held back from declaring his love by that wall he sensed within her. 'I wish so much that this fort were good and sufficient for you,' he blurted out. 'You too are the only friend I have and I want you to be contented. Everyone must have the feeling of home, even if it is in a prison cell, or a ship's bunk. Wanting something you can't have means discontent.'

'Oh please forgive me, Fernao. I am very contented and I do indeed regard our quarters in the fort as my home, but I suppose I'm not one to forget past ties easily.'

'I'm glad, Julietta.' He looked at her deeply, giving her his message with glowing eyes. Receiving no more than an affectionate response, he turned his head back towards the darkening horizon. 'I want you to know that I am selfishly thankful to the Blessed Virgin for keeping you single.' He paused, then decided to take the plunge. 'I know there is something deep within you that is sad and ... and ... er ... even lonely. I wish I could touch that part of you, because ... because ... ' He lapsed into silence.

He heard her breath catch. Knowing he had hit the truth, he swung between the temptation to press on and the need to be unselfish. What finally decided him was a flash of awareness that he should handle her with care. But at that instant, he realized with a kind of wonder that he wanted to share everything with her, his whole life. He would be twenty-one tomorrow. More than anything in the world, he desired to marry her, to impregnate her with his seed and have her bear his children. He thought of that flat stomach round and taut with his children. Feelings he had held in check came tumbling out of dark recesses within him. He noted the curve of her breast, the tiny waist, the flaring hips. He thought of her naked on her back, legs spread, ready for him to enter her, and his penis hardened with desire for her so much it was a pain against his codpiece.

Suddenly, the way seemed clear. There were two kinds of love, he reasoned. One kind flared mutually on an instant, twin sparks merging into a single flame. The other kind came from slow flames that grew out of mutual affection, respect and common bonds. It was hard for him, the romantic, to accept this latter type of love, but he had no option. If he married Julietta, he could wait, however impatiently, for her either to discover her love or to learn to love him from within the ties of marriage. He simply could not face the risk of losing her to someone else.

The reasoning brought a surge of desire for power, this time emotional power, within him. He knew what he must do. But it had to be done wisely, with cunning even, and subtle pressure. As a plan formed in his mind, he justified it by assuring himself that he would make the end, Julietta's ultimate happiness, justify the means.

Long moments passed while they stared at the ocean in silence, lost in their separate thoughts. Are we looking at the past, the present or the future, Fernao wondered. Whatever the answer, it is in the dark. He felt a sense of gloom whose origin he knew to be the uncertainty of the future because of the despatch that had arrived from Goa the previous week.

'I hope I have been good for you.' The words had come quietly from Julietta. 'I sometimes wonder whether I am being fair to you, monopolizing your attention. I mean, there are other young ladies . . . ' She paused.

Fernao turned towards her on the instant. 'Oh yes, like plump, juicy Maria or Tricky Teresa.' He laughed low. 'No, no. There could not possibly have been anyone else but you,' his voice deepened, 'the fairest of all.'

'Oh Fernao.' She seemed both pleased and embarrassed, but the tone of her voice discouraged further compliments.

The men's voices became muted in a haunting lovesong. So many of them down there, far from their country, devoid of love unless they took a native woman. Though sometimes hurt that he could not reach into her, how fortunate he was to have the most beautiful young lady in the Estado da India as his companion. The distant sounds of the city intruded, the reedy notes of Sinhala pipes above an insistent drumming, a reminder that in one of its streets a few minutes of loving could be bought. Yes indeed, he was fortunate.

He decided to touch a chord. 'There's something I'd like to discuss with you, something I would never mention to anyone else,' he stated. 'Since our King Dom Manuel died almost three years ago, the new King, Dom Joao III, has not proved himself businesslike or capable. As you know, he sent Admiral Vasco da Gama back to Goa last year to replace the Viceroy, in an attempt to mend his fortunes. This has made things impossible for my *o pai* too, because da Gama is authoritarian and determined to increase profits in every way possible. He believes that the Portuguese Treasury has been drained by vast commitments of men, ships and material in the East Indies, from the Cape of Good Hope to Sumatra without adequate returns. My father and I believe that we can only recover the investment by retaining a powerful military presence wherever we trade. One way in which Admiral Vasco da Gama is seeking to restore the fortunes of our Treasury is by putting each station on a strict profit and loss basis. If you cannot increase your income, reduce your expenses, he says.'

'Is that going to affect you, Fernao? I thought we were making a handsome profit out of the Colombo operation.'

'Unfortunately, handsome is not enough because of our high capital costs and overheads. We had a despatch from Admiral Vasco da Gama on the supply ship that arrived from Goa last week. He is bringing to bear on his new mission in the Indies the same ruthlessness and drive that enabled him to discover the sea route to India twenty-seven years ago, plus a vast knowledge of shipping and trade. He wants an end to the fair-play policy that has made my work as factor such a joy to me these past three years, if that is what it takes to turn a greater profit. Thank the good Lord, I had these years in which to learn from your father, from the Raschids and from every possible source, for I face the greatest problem of my life as a factor.'

'Oh Fernao, I hope you have at least set aside some of the money you have made from your trade commissions these past three years.'

'Trust a woman to be practical first. And I do appreciate your concern, Julietta. Yes, I have made enough money these past three years to live modestly the rest of my life without ever falling back on the de Albergaria fortunes.' He smiled wryly. 'Or perhaps the lack of them.'

'You have loved your work, haven't you?'

'Indeed. I have learnt so much about men and business. I feel more productive than I could ever have done as a naval officer, not the least because I can see the prosperity I have helped bring to the Sinhala, the Mouro and my own people. Now suddenly it is all in jeopardy.'

'What does the Viceroy demand?'

'Either show a profit of one hundred per cent of cost, including amortization of our original capital outlay, within the next two years, or close the fort down and keep it going merely as a trading factory.'

'Oh, Fernao, how awful for you. I'm so sorry.'

She laid a gentle hand on his arm, the first time she had ever touched him. It sent a thrill through him. He looked at the slim fingers, white against his dark sleeve, then instinctively placed his hand over hers. She was cool to the touch. Some magic passed between them. He did not know what it was, simply that it was there, before he withdrew his hand, and rejoiced.

'Thank you Julietta,' he said softly. 'Your concern means a great deal to me.' He paused, decided to test her. 'This new directive places the burden of a choice on me. Do I continue as

191

a factor, or return to a full-time naval career?' He watched closely for her reaction, felt a throb of elation from the look of apprehension that crossed her face at the possibility that a return to his naval career would mean his leaving the country. 'Fortunately or unfortunately, however, another complication has arisen.'

'What is that?' Was it unshed tears that caused the sudden brightness in her eyes?

'For over a year now the Great King Wijayo has been investigating the guaranteed prices we are paying the Mouro for cinnamon. He has discovered that our regular purchases have produced such a greatly increased supply of cinnamon that the Mouro are beating down the prices of the producers. They buy more than they need to fulfil our orders, stockpile and create artificial excesses, which enable them to claim that they are over-stocked and to obtain supplies at distress rates.'

'How dreadful of them.'

'Certainly, but those are the methods of business. The Great King summoned me for a discussion last evening. He desired me to cut out the Mouro completely and deal exclusively with him as the supplier, so we could both make much more money. I asked him to defer any action until I could, as a matter of honour, give the Mouro adequate notice. With the Viceroy's new directive, I had the most unpleasant duty today of informing the Raschids that I would have to give them notice of termination of our contract as soon as the Great King sent me a formal offer.'

'Dear sweet Jesu, what was his reaction?'

'He had been aware of the Great King's investigation, but I've told you the way in which these two operate, the man whines and the woman is watchfully silent. Finally, Aisha Raschid inquired as to whether we would continue trading with them if they dropped their prices substantially. I had to respond that, under the Viceroy's orders, once I received a formal offer from the Great King I could not allow them to make a single *cruzado* on any deal.'

'What did she say?'

'Nothing, except to repeat, "Once you receive a formal offer from the Great King," as if that might give them some respite.'

'Did you see any significance in that?'

'The way she said it, I thought she was pondering the possibility that the Great King might be removed from the realm of formal offers! It sent a chill through me.'

'Oh Fernao. You don't think she would have him killed?'

'Anything is possible in politics and trade. After all, it would be poetic justice, for the Great King probably got rid of his predecessor.'

She looked down at the fort, her eyes slowly sweeping over every feature of it, possibly comparing its peace with the gruesome possibility of murder. 'If you don't produce the required profit, will all this come to nothing?' she inquired softly.

Something broke loose within him. 'Do you know what building the fort involved, Julietta?' he inquired, his voice rising passionately. 'The ceaseless, back-breaking labour of men, day and night, in rain and sunshine, cold and unbearable heat. I have seen them toiling through sickness, some dying in the process. What did they do it for, except to create a temporary haven, a home? Now, with a snap of his fingers, the world's greatest explorer can turn it into an empty shell, stone and mortar, devoid of life and vitality.' A wave crashed against the black rocks below, sending up salt spray to lick their faces.

'I know how you feel, Fernao.' Her eyes were luminous, her voice trembled. 'Believe me, I share your feelings because I too am a part of your creation, though a far lesser part, for it is my home too now. But may we not be misreading the Viceroy's intentions? Could his threat be merely to put pressure on you all to produce more profits?'

'How much profit will be enough, is the question.'

'He said one hundred per cent of the cost. Perhaps he would be satisfied with fifty per cent.'

'When a man sets a certain measure of profit as his goal, it does something to him. All he can see thereafter is that figure, a percentage; then, if he realizes it, he will want more and more, because he has become consumed with his own longing, like some creature that feeds off its own body to satisfy its hunger.

Perhaps I should empathize with that and proceed ruthlessly, but I have a different concept in mind. I hate to see fair trade end and contracts dishonoured. Certainly the Raschids have had more than their fair share of profits, but they set up the business at a time when we had no other source and they have been good for us. It's simply not right.'

'People have goals, Fernao, which need not consume them.'

'A man may have a goal, but not a country, Julietta. A country is people and people need something more than the profits of rulers. They require a distribution of wealth for the benefit of all.' He paused and turned to look at the gleaming blackness of the ocean, feeling a sudden release from having spoken to her. 'I shall do my duty by my Viceroy, my King and my country regardless.'

From his great frustration, he was sorely tempted to declare his love for her, to tell her he had just decided to ask her father for her hand in marriage, but some instinct held him back, told him it had to be accomplished in more subtle ways.

Wednesday, 16 March 1524

Four nights later, in Kandy, Prince Kumara awoke from a light sleep feeling delightfully relaxed. He sat up in bed and stretched. The sounds of night reached him through the open window, the croak of a bullfrog, the creak of crickets from the High Forest, the jungle hillside that rose above the city of Kandy. Hearing the whine of a mosquito, he looked for it in the soft lamplight, smacked at it with both hands and missed.

The sound awoke Manel, naked beside him. She opened her eyes and looked at him sleepily. 'Is it that hour again, lord?'

'Unfortunately, yes.'

'I wish you would spend a whole night with me some time. I always hate it when you leave.'

He clucked impatiently. 'We made our deal,' he declared, 'didn't we? You give me sex, home-cooked meals and fidelity. I provide you with sex, a nice home to cook in and infidelity.' He laughed at his own wit. 'After all, it's you who elected to be a courtesan, long before I met you, and I'm giving you far more

194

than you got from Lord Pilima, a married man with six children.'

'I know, lord,' Manel replied submissively. 'But you have been so good to me that I think about you all the time. Besides, with the other men I practised a profession, but you I have come to need.'

'I'm flattered. At least I've made an honest woman of you.' He chuckled. 'You can no longer fool around with other men.'

'Do not despise me because I am a courtesan, lord. I am a human being, with feelings like any other.' She placed her hands behind her head. 'And after all, if I sold my services before, I was no different from many wives who sell their bodies, even their minds and their *atman*, to men for a marriage ceremony and the respectability it gives them. Unlike many a wife, I at least have never given my body to any man I hated. As for you, I simply worship you.' She reached under the sheet, caressed the inside of his thighs and tickled his organ.

He felt a strange tenderness at her words. He had boasted about infidelity to her to sound manly and modern. In point of fact, she satisfied him so totally that he had stopped having sex with other women.

'I want to tell you something, Manel,' he said, leaning over her. 'I was thirteen when I had my first woman. She was an older palace attendant who needed it, so she was very wet, but she had never borne children, so she was also delightfully tight. It was I who crawled to her mat, but she ended up practically raping me. The sensation of moving in and out of her was so fantastic that from then on, I went after it with a will. That sensation became all I needed from a woman.'

He paused, took in the black hair framing the olive complexioned face with broad cheekbones, the taut skin giving her a classic beauty. He looked deep into her large, brown eyes. They were almond-shaped, flecked with black and limpid as a doe's. 'I never had much more from a woman anyhow,' he continued. 'Even my mother never gave me real affection. Perhaps it's because I sought no more and had no more to give than the taking, but part of it had to be that she was Prince Maya Dunne's half-sister and they are a cold, proud bunch.' He

195

relaxed, leaned back against the cushions.

Manel remained silent, motionless.

'I have my ambitions and my plans,' Prince Kumara continued. 'There is no part in them for a woman. Oh, I suppose I shall be married some day, but I have no burning urge to beget heirs and hand down legacies. There is nothing I can do about what takes place after I'm gone. Look at the mess made by the children of parents who have died leaving them position, rank, money. A man or a woman can only be as they are and as circumstances will permit and try to be what they want to be. I count myself lucky not to have had a single child from my escapades all these years. Perhaps it is because I don't have any seed!' He chuckled, then grew serious. 'But I want you to know this. You have been unfailingly kind to me, always been here for me. Your cooking has been a joy after the palace meals. You are the greatest lover in the world. You drain me so much that I have no desire left for any other woman.' He looked at her, nodding. 'So there you are, a confession of weakness from the most cynical, amoral man in the world.'

'Lord, don't you know that it is not weakness, but strength? And don't you realize that I have at this moment derived even more strength from your strength?'

He stared at her in amazement, thinking. 'Maybe you're right,' he finally volunteered. 'But right, or wrong, it's the truth.' Then with a return to his normal self: 'Though I'd rather lie than tell the truth!'

'Lord, I also want you to know that you are not without seed.'

'What?' He sat up, startled. 'How can you say that?'

'Because I have the proof of it, right here.' She patted her still flat stomach.

'You mean ... ?'

'Yes, lord. I am bearing your child.'

'Oh *devas*!' He pulled away from her. 'Just when I thought that everything was going right between us.'

She sat up abruptly, stared at him through the tears that had begun to well in her eyes. 'You need have no fear of the baby, or of me, lord. I would never do anything to hurt or harm you. I would rather die. Oh, I know you are selfish and cynical, that you have no faith in anything, or anyone, but as you say, you

196

have made an honest woman of me and for that I shall be eternally grateful. Having been your mistress, if anything were to happen to you, I would rather gather wood, or do housework than give myself to anyone else.'

'You ... you say that, when all I have given you is total unfeeling?'

'Everything is relative, lord. They say that in dry lands, a drop of water is precious.'

Feelings such as he had never experienced before were flooding Prince Kumara. For the first time that he could remember, he felt muddled, confused. 'You are one of the most dreadful things that can happen to a bad man,' he finally declared gently. 'A good woman.' He became his decisive self again. 'You needn't worry. I shall look after you and the baby.' He smiled at her with his eyes, something he had never been able to do before. 'After all, you have proved my manhood and I should behave like a man! Just keep on giving me more sex and home-cooked meals. And this baby. I must go now.' He leaned forward, kissed her lightly and swung out of bed.

She burst into tears, sobbing away every sorrow she had ever known and held back. He let her cry on while he got dressed. She was still weeping, but tears of joy, when he left the house, feeling strangely moved.

The three-bedroom cottage he had bought for Manel was located on the street immediately to the north of the palace. It was conveniently situated for his visits, which he made openly since it was permissible for him to have a mistress once he came of age. Now he walked quickly to the palace along the flare-lit street. It was deserted, but the thoughts kept whirling through his mind like the wind that was whipping up whorls of dust on the street.

To his surprise, the guard captain at the entrance gates informed him that King Wira desired his presence immediately in the dining chamber. The Kandy palace was built around a huge central courtyard, and had a separate building behind for the females with its own central courtyard. All of it was connected by well-lit verandahs, from which every room could be reached.

The prince's father was seated, as usual, on gold cushions at the far end of the dining chamber. He made obeisance and entered. The room was brightly lit with many-tiered brass lamps on which countless wicks flickered with small golden flames.

'Where the fuck have you been?' King Wira demanded irritably.

'Doing precisely what you so elegantly express, with my mistress, lord.' He hated coarseness so much that the past three years had seen him treating his father with an increasing degree of insolence on such occasions.

'Ah, our court jester!' King Wira remarked, his heavy pectorals shaking with laughter, as usual, at his own dry joke. He simmered down. 'Well, there isn't much to laugh about,' he grumbled. 'The news is bad.' He reached for a parchment scroll beside him.

Prince Kumara was instantly alert. 'Tell me about it, Sire.' He always treated his father formally when official business was at hand.

'As you know, the *parangi* have been a source of disappointment to us. Their admiral spent only three weeks in the country after you visited him. He despatched the two friars, Father Juan and Father Perez, to us through the Mantota harbour in the north, along with a platoon of thirty musketeers, but no diplomatic mission, no armed reinforcements. We have fulfilled our part of the bargain, but I ask you again for the umpteenth time, did the man promise to help us take over the entire country or did he not?'

'And I repeat for the umpteenth time, Sire, that he did not. I submit that we must be patient, but having fulfilled our part of the bargain, right down to my being ready for conversion to the Catholic religion at any time, it is perhaps time we took the initiative. Let us swing into action with our army against the sub-sub-kingdoms of Pera, Gampola and Hangura. When the *parangi* see our success, they may be more disposed to support us in our move to take over the Jaya kingdom. Till then, they will continue coddling the Great King.'

'What Great King? That Wijayo is only a shitty fart! Remember his great boasts of a new policy, under which I was to be appointed king of the entire *uda rata*, hill-country? Well, it was

198

just a bunch of his foul wind.'

'But he has three sons.'

'Bah! Bhuvaneka too is a windbag and Raigam is stupid. Only my brother-in-law, Maya Dunne, is to be feared, but his strength lies in Sita Waka, far away from Jaya.' He paused, absently scratched his bare chest with his left hand, his pig eyes distressed. 'But all that is over.' He shook the scroll before him. 'This is a written response to the oral message I secretly sent Captain Oliveira through the friars' agents. It is signed by the admiral's son, Fernao de Albergaria, and it gives us our answer directly. They received orders from their new Viceroy three days ago that may make it necessary for them to send their soldiers back to Goa, leaving only a token force in Colombo to maintain their factory in the fort.'

'What?' Prince Kumara felt as if the world had been pulled down over his head. 'Please give me that, Sire.' He seized the scroll, held it up to the light of one of the brass lamps and read. The blood drained from his face. 'Santa Maria,' he whispered, the phrase he had learned from Father Juan automatically escaping him. 'The *parangi* pigs have betrayed us.' He hesitated. 'Please forgive me, Sire, I must think.' Years of training made him back away from his father's presence. When he reached the door he turned around and stood on the verandah staring into the dark courtyard.

What to do now? How to achieve his object? He looked up at the sky for inspiration. It was puddled with heavy white clouds. He looked at the fountain, idly wondering why it was not splashing. The reek of some dead animal smote his nostrils. I must think clearly and decisively, he told himself, concentrating without tension on the problem.

The fountain would not splash without water, which only a human agency could supply. The obvious lesson was, be self-sufficient. For three years now, they had waited for other human agencies to support them, the *parangi*, the friars, the Great King. That was a mistake. What he had told his father just now was even more correct in the light of the message from the *parangi*. Strike with what was available, going for the weakest first. Before that, prepare the political climate with alliances. He

199

grinned into the darkness before rejoining his father.

King Wira looked at him alertly. 'Well, have you found a solution?'

'What solution, Sire? We are where we have always been, so we need not act in haste as before. Let the *parangi* depart. There are many ways of catching fish.'

'Such as?'

'Such as nothing.' He paused for effect. 'It occurred to me just now that I have always been very fond of my uncle, General Prince Maya Dunne. We are well aware of his problems and strength. Since we cannot make a foreign alliance, let us consider making a domestic one so that we have fewer enemies to contend with when we do march against the sub-sub-kingdoms. Prince Maya Dunne and Prince Raigam will not be disposed to pull the Great King's *kos-atta*, jak-seeds, out of the fire for him. If we can keep them neutral with a few *parangi* muskets, we can wrest for ourselves what the Great King promised and failed to deliver.'

CHAPTER 17
Wednesday, 16 March 1524

That same night, in her bedroom in the Jaya palace, Queen Anula, now the wife of the Great King Wijayo, faced the first stage of her plan.

Prince Wijayo, as he had been then, had first met her three years before when he was visiting relatives at her village, known as Kiri Vella, white sands. She had been the widowed Princess Anula at the time, her husband having died under mysterious circumstances. She could seldom restrain a secret smile at the recollection. Her husband had been a prince only by title, not by disposition. An overbearing bully, he had often assaulted her and the circumstances of his death were certainly not a mystery to her. Unfortunately, the lover for whom she had poisoned him proved unfaithful, so he too died under mysterious circumstances. I have been aptly named, she sometimes thought, remembering that other Queen Anula who had ruled the country centuries before by disposing of nine husbands and several lovers in succession. Unlike that Queen Anula, whose consuming sexual desire had resulted in an untimely death, she regarded sex merely as an instrument for the achievement of her goals.

Prince Wijayo, who was both lustful and lusty, made no pretence about his desire from the moment he set eyes on her. And why not? Though she had borne a son, Prince Deva, who was then four years old, she had been only twenty at the time and was an acknowledged beauty in the classical Sinhala tradition: flawless dark complexion, oval face, large black eyes, luxuriant black hair that fell all the way to a waist that was trim as a virgin's in spite of her childbearing. Though only of average height, her breasts were large and her limbs full and rounded. More than all else, she knew that she exuded a sexual magnetism that drew the attention of most men.

She had rejected the old man's stammered pleas – she hated his stammer – foiled his advances and refused his offers of marriage, while still encouraging him with deep looks, an occasional caress in her voice and phrases of double meaning. Disillusioned with men, she had decided to fire her arrow at the best target. Prince Wijayo could become that if he outlived the Great King but she had no desire whatever to give herself to the old fool unless he succeeded to the Jaya throne.

When several months later he did become the Great King she finally accepted his suit with seeming reluctance and married him, but her aim had not been a position in life but the wielding of supreme power, directly if possible, otherwise from behind the scenes.

Once he married her, however, King Wijayo had demonstrated a surprising strength, foiling her attempts. Now, over two years later, she had decided that her only recourse was to manoeuvre her way into power. Since the old goat, as she thought of her husband, was not as malleable as she had expected, she had finally decided on her best course of action that very morning and would implement it immediately, but a step at a time.

Tonight was the night. Though she squirmed at the prospect of getting his organ erect, caressing the great frame with its wrinkled skin and sagging member, she was determined to use her lovemaking skills to complete the first step. He had a tremendous compulsion to give her orgasms and she had a tremendous ability to climax or shut off at will. She would let him prove his manhood and demand that he prove his love.

She wore a white nightdress of sheerest silk, a present from the *parangi* Captain Oliveira. It revealed the contours of her dark skin to perfection, the nipples thrusting, the pubis an enticing dark patch between the full limbs. She wore a makeup that gave her skin a rosy glow and black *kohl* made her lashes long, her eyes limpid. Her hair was loose, gleaming with perfumed oil, a jasmine scent which blended into the odours of incense. The great canopied bed had sheets and cushions of pink silk, a colour that never failed to inflame the old goat. As soon as she heard the familiar knock on the door, she opened

202

it. King Wijayo stood at the entrance, dressed in blue pantaloons and a white *kurtha*. She struck a sinuous pose. A gasp escaped him. Lust entered his eyes. 'T-two years n-now and you look more seductive than ever,' he declared. He smelled of arrack, which he drank copiously to fortify himself for his sexual exertions.

She moved aside for him to enter, closed the door behind him and turned to face the room. 'You are not only a king, you are a magnificent animal,' she said softly, shaking her head in disbelief. 'Your virility makes my blood pound.'

'You m-mean that?'

'Why else would I say it, Lord?'

'Of course.' He drank in her body, his rheumy eyes lustful, stroking his white beard the while. 'We wish you c-could have known us t-twenty years ago. We would have m-made you scream for m-mercy then.'

'Spare me, lord. You make me scream for mercy now. There is only so much a poor woman can take from a stud.' She made her voice turn fierce. 'That's what you are, a cocksman and a stud.'

'You d-don't m-mind helping the c-cock on its way.'

The old theme, she thought with disgust. Aloud she said, 'I love it. You give me a sense of power. And once it is up, how stunning it is. I am indeed a lucky woman.' Actually, his organ was lean and stringy. 'Oh, I can't keep my hands off you tonight.' She made for him, started fondling his genitals.

In a few seconds, they were undressed and naked in bed, he flat on his back, she kneeling above him. She took her time and began to drive him wild with light kisses and caresses all over his body. Finally, she coaxed his organ erect. Then he pulled her down with brute force and laid her on her back. He mounted her and prepared to make entry.

The time was right. She crossed her legs. 'Lord, before you drive me to exhaustion, there is something very important I have to tell you.'

'Later, later, woman.' He was panting now. His breath had the smell of old age, mixed with the arrack.

'Lord, I want it to be perfect for both of us,' she whispered,

203

her eyes lustrous with feigned longing. 'If I don't tell you about it now, I'm sure to forget.' She flared her nostrils, knowing it excited him. 'Once you get me all worked up, I forget everything else and when I come and come and come,' she caressed her own breasts in gentle sweeps, touching the nipples with the tips of her forefingers, 'as I know I will tonight, because I'm so excited, I don't even have the life to think. You do understand, don't you, lord?'

'Yes, yes, but let's g-get your news over with so we can m-make you c-come and c-come and c-come.'

She noticed his organ beginning to go limp again, reached out to fondle it. 'Your three sons are plotting to assassinate you,' she stated almost casually.

'What?' His eyes bulged, his jaw dropped. Kneeling, he was poised over her like a fish on a line. 'What d-did you say, woman?'

She looked up at him with tender eyes. 'Knowing how much Prince Deva and I love you, your three sons are planning to assassinate you, I said.' She went at his organ, trying to stimulate it, but it had gone completely limp This is like trying to milk a cow that has gone dry, she thought, squeezing and releasing as she had seen peasant women do with an udder.

'Huh!' He pulled away and lay down beside her, staring at the pink canopy. 'Why would they want to d-do that?' he finally inquired. 'And how do you know?'

'May I have your word that you will not probe them, lord?'

'Yes, yes,' he replied testily.

'I shall not divulge all of them, lord. It would not be in your best interests. But they include your courtiers, Lord Eka and Lord Kandura, who were approached, though so covertly that it cannot hold up as evidence, and others who, believe me, are unimpeachable. As to why your sons want to kill you, surely the reason is obvious. They want to rule. Did they not kill King Dharma Parakrama?'

'No!' The word escaped him involuntarily and it filled her with fierce satisfaction to know that her suspicions that it was he who had arranged for the death of the late Great King were correct. 'I mean, they could not p-possibly have d-done something like that.' Alert now, he pondered awhile. 'We too had heard of this plot from our own sources. What d-do you think we should d-do?'

So the men she had bribed to carry the same false news to the old goat had earned their money. 'I have a simple solution, lord.'

He directed a sharp glance at her. 'What is that?'

'Is it not obvious? They want to kill you because the carrot of succession dangles before them. Remove it, Sire.'

'You m-mean k-kill my sons?' He did not sound the least bit shocked at the possibility.

'That would be too grave a step...at least for the moment, lord. My solution is far simpler. Remove Prince Bhuvaneka's right to the succession.'

'How?'

'By formally adopting your son, our son, Prince Deva Raja.'

'What? We could not possibly do that.' He sat up. 'Yet why not? It is our right.' A smile slowly spread across his face. He nodded, thinking deeply. 'Perfect; just perfect. We abort their plans and punish them at the same time. You are beyond price, Anula.'

'I have my price, lord.'

Suspicion crossed his face, tensing it. 'What is it?'

'You must make me come and come and come.'

His expression relaxed. He reached over and began fondling her breast. 'We shall pay you for your services,' he declared. 'Tonight, you are our whore.'

She pretended to groan at his touch. 'Anything for you, lord,' she gasped. 'You drive me wild.'

'We demand the most superb sex you have ever given us, tonight. Your payment, on our sacred honour, shall be an instrument of formal adoption of Prince Deva Raja as our son, which we shall execute tomorrow morning.' A chuckle escaped him. 'We should love to see the faces of our three sons, especially B-Bhuvaneka, when they hear the n-news. Serve the b-bastards right.' How ironic, his own sons bastards!

She reached for his penis again, her heart so full of triumph that she determined to give him the best ever, not as a gift of

205

gratitude, an emotion she did not believe in, but from the sheer joy of her success.

Thursday, 17 March 1524

My father's intelligence system in Jaya and Colombo was superb. It even included a gardener who had been taught Portuguese. It was through this spy network that we learnt about the visits of Prince Kumara and the then Prince Wijayo and Prince Bhuvaneka to Admiral de Albergaria's flagship that Sunday in 1521, and as a result we had suspected that the Great King's death had been planned. This time our news sources were, however, beaten by Prince Bhuvaneka.

The prince had lived in the Jaya palace from as far back as I could remember, while my father, being the youngest of the three brothers, had preferred to look after our family holdings in Sita Waka, while Prince Raigam did likewise in the Korle region that bore his name.

Prince Bhuvaneka was therefore one of the first to receive the stunning news of King Wijayo's formal adoption of his stepson, the seven-year-old Prince Deva Raja. Filled with consternation, weak man that he was, he threw caution to the winds and rode post-haste to his one source of strength, my father in Sita Waka. He reached our mansion the following morning, 17 March by the Christian calendar, looking thoroughly shaken as we sat in my father's study to hear his news.

'A most dreadful situation,' he began, as soon as we were seated. 'I mean how could a father do it to his own children, however crazed he may be over a woman or besotted by drink.' His fierce moustache was positively bristling, the plump cheeks quivering with emotion.

My father glanced briefly out at the high-grilled window where a sparrow had settled on the sill and begun twittering excitedly against the background of a clear blue sky. 'Such a beautiful morning for news of great moment,' he remarked light-heartedly, obviously wanting to soothe his brother. 'But tell me, what has our father done?'

'You can be so calm, when...' Prince Bhuvaneka paused.

'Oh, you don't know, do you. The love-crazed madman has formally adopted his stepson, Prince Deva Raja, as his own son and heir.' The sparrow flew away with a fluttering of wings.

'What?' Even my father's usual calm was shattered. 'Say that again.'

Prince Bhuvaneka repeated his news, more slowly this time, savouring my father's shock.

'By the *devas*, this is outrageous. It cannot be tolerated!' My father echoed my own outrage.

'Absolutely not!' Prince Bhuvaneka responded. 'But what shall we do about it?'

My father drew a deep breath, composed himself. He tapped his desk rapidly with a forefinger, as he was wont to do when thinking. Finally, he smiled with his white teeth, not with his eyes. 'You know, Bhuvaneka, this is perhaps as good a time as any for me to tell you that you have only got what you deserved.'

'Wha-what do you mean?'

My father looked stern now. 'You plotted with our father for the succession. Some say the two of you even organized the death of our uncle. Now our father has gone his own way. You are the only one who will suffer from his action. Why come to me?' I had never seen him look so hard, the chiselled face so set.

Prince Bhuvaneka's jaw dropped. 'But ... but ... ' he began, then a cunning gleam entered the small eyes. 'You are the Army Commander so it is up to you to uphold our sacred traditions,' he declared. He essayed a smile. 'Besides, you are wrong to imagine that I plotted for the succession.' Your denial came too late, I thought. 'It was always my intention that, whenever I succeeded to the throne, each of us brothers should be kings of our own right, you in Sita Waka, our brother in Raigam and me in Jaya.'

There was contempt in my father's eyes, but breeding probably held him back from a harsh rejoinder. 'Is that what you still intend?' he inquired calmly.

'Absolutely. My honour on it.'

'I would have you understand me, Prince,' my father

207

responded firmly. 'I will not help you in this situation because I hope for some reward. You well know that I am for a unified Lanka, but such unity can only be effective with a strong ruler. If we have to divide the country to make it strong again, so be it.' His deep voice grew solemn. 'But the news you have brought is serious only because it offends our sacred traditions, not because it hurts any of us personally as our father's children or his possible heirs. Behind the violation of the principle, however, is a man who has shown himself unfit to rule, a man who was once a man indeed but who is now being manipulated by a clever young woman.'

'You are completely correct. My sp . . . friends in the palace assure me of this. Although our father is firm in certain things, his wife leads him – shall we say by the nose and not refer to a more accurate part of his anatomy? This move shows that she is clever and dangerous.'

'Which is precisely why we should do nothing for the present.' My father nodded.

'Do nothing? What on earth do you mean?'

'If we act now, the people will believe that we are moved by personal pique and are pursuing our own ambitions. We need a good, solid, national or moral issue for our move, one which will outrage the people as well.'

'Such as what?'

My father's dark eyes glinted grimly. 'You may be sure that this move is the first phase of a plan. You have been removed as a successor. Isn't it obvious that this is because Queen Anula desires to wield power from behind the throne? How will the move help her unless her son succeeds to the throne . . . '

'While he is young enough to be a puppet,' Prince Bhuvaneka interrupted excitedly. 'Which means she may turn her attention to the Great King's demise next.'

'Precisely. Or perhaps to our demise, as an intermediate step. Remember, there is talk that she is not averse to killing for her own ends. If we move now, we would be falling into a trap that may have been set for us. While this may well be an overestimation of Queen Anula's cunning, we cannot afford to take a risk. Let us therefore go about our business calmly, accepting this outrageous act with seeming grace. Sooner or later, the next step will be taken. Let us give her room to walk, so she can fall into her own trap.'

Thursday, 17 March 1524

It had to be the will of Allah. Five days after she and her husband had been informed by Lieutenant de Albergaria of the drastic change in trading policy that was impending because of the Great King Wijayo's greed, Aisha Raschid learned that she had an ally in Queen Anula.

Having answered the *muezzin's* call to evening prayer, she retired to the chamber from which she directed her side of the business. The great oil lamps were unlit, the room illuminated only by a single taper on a silver sconce. She awaited the coming of night with a mixture of eagerness and apprehension covered by her normal studied calm. Like an exciting woman behind the *yashmak*, she thought coldly.

It was dark outside. Aisha rose, knelt to give her husband salutation, then focused her attention on the two men who accompanied him. They worked for her, but she had never met them before. They were both dressed like Sinhala traders in coloured *dhotis* and white *kurthas*. One was tall, gaunt and dark, with a cleanshaven hatchet face, a hooked nose and a squint, all of which gave him an eerie appearance in the uncertain light. The other man was short and stout. His broad face, fair complexion and black moustache made him look like a jolly trader. Yet both men carried themselves with more dignity and self-assurance than the average trader who visited the Raschid mansion.

Her husband dropped his voice to introduce the tall man as Lord Kandura and the shorter one as Lord Eka. They acknowledged her salutation with dignity.

'I have posted guards outside, so you have absolute secrecy here,' Raschid assured the men. He gave a self-conscious giggle. 'My wife and I have found her chamber a most wonderful place for ... er ... confidential discussions. Please be seated, my lords.

209

Aisha, the two lords are very wise gentlemen, for they supped with me but ate and drank whatever I did, after I had partaken of it.' He giggled again. 'Of course, with my appetite, they had an excellent variety of choice!'

Apparently casual, the visitors looked around, selected a divan facing the entrace and sat down side by side.

'If the lords would like sweetmeats, they are there.' Aisha nodded her veiled head towards a silver stand beside the divan. 'We ship the Turkish delight all the way from the Arabi country.' As she sank on to the divan facing them, beside her husband, she noticed that he already had his mouth full.

'We have been unaccustomed to such luxuries in our Court for some time,' Lord Eka volunteered, with a sigh. He had a dry metallic voice, Aisha noticed, and delivered each word in a flat monotone. 'Which is an indication that the royal treasury is being handled with care.'

'Surely the Great Kings of Lanka have not become poor?' Aisha's inquiry was a statement.

'No. The late king was austere by conviction. He left a fabulous personal treasury when he died. Our present king is austere because his interests lie elsewhere.'

An awkward silence fell. It was obvious to Aisha that the two courtiers would not take the initiative, so she decided on a bold approach. 'As you know, lords, my husband and I have been grateful that you have accepted our humble presents from time to time.' Actually, the presents had not been humble. They consisted of great bribes of money, jewellery and costly gifts from abroad, which had kept the two courtiers on her payroll ever since she had learned of Lord Kandura's regular gambling losses and Lord Eka's expensive mistresses. In exchange, the two courtiers, who were bosom friends, had kept her supplied with information. It had delighted her to learn that they were also trusted henchmen of Queen Anula. 'I hope that these poor gifts have helped alleviate somewhat the austerities of your Court.'

'Indubitably,' Lord Eka replied, his teeth white in a smile beneath the black moustache. 'They have helped in a modest way.' Lord Kandura merely stared, Aisha could not determine at what, because of his squint.

'We are old acquaintances, my lords, so let me be frank,' Aisha said. 'We have just learned through you that the young queen is greatly troubled about her future and that of her son. She could even be in some danger now that the young prince has been formally adopted and named the Great King's heir.'

'The queen's concern is understandable,' Lord Eka responded. 'The three sons of the Great King are all ambitious men.' He sighed ponderously. 'It is sad that they have no filial piety nor loyalty.'

'The Great King is over seventy years old, while the queen is but twenty-three and the boy prince seven. Her enemies may try to kill her and her son before the Great King dies and leaves her in a position of power.'

'We cannot let that happen,' Lord Eka leaned forward, speaking softly.

'There is only one solution. First, anyone who opposes the Great King's wishes must be destroyed . . . and the sooner the better.' Aisha had spoken with deadly quiet. The words were out. The two men could turn her in.

To her relief, Lord Eka gave a short, grim laugh. 'You are absolutely right,' he declared. He glanced briefly at his silent companion, who merely squinted at the taper flame without moving a muscle of his face or body.

'Are there men brave enough in this kingdom, loyal enough to risk death for their Great King and the rightful succession?'

'Yes. At least two.'

Now they understood one another and she could talk openly, Aisha suddenly felt free of that tightness in her chest. 'Such men should be given great rewards for their fidelity and devotion,' she declared. 'My husband and I, as loyal residents of this country and grateful subjects of the Great King, will pay handsomely in advance so we can share in the noble objective. Is that acceptable, my lords?'

'Perfectly,' Lord Eka answered. 'I speak for Lord Kandura as well. We have already discussed this with each other and, of course, with the queen.'

Aisha was elated. She would co-operate with Queen Anula in the elimination of the three brothers, after which it would be a short step to collaboration in removing the impediment of their trading future, the Great King himself. Why, the two events might even be made to coincide. That idea appealed to her sense of timing. 'Surely the queen will reward you suitably too, with fiefdoms and official positions, when her son ascends the throne.'

'So she has promised us, but naturally our own actions are guided purely by patriotism and devotion to our country.'

'Of course.' Aisha was willing to keep up the pretence of nobility if that was what the two lords desired. 'Which brings me to the other reason for this meeting,' she stated smoothly. 'The longer the queen and her son have to wait for the succession, the greater the danger that it may never take place. Anything can happen. And of course the more delay, the more the receipt of benefits by loyal subjects will be postponed. So you may want to consider yet another duty higher than that towards any individual.'

Lord Kandura made his presence heard for the first time. He coughed, then moved the focus of his gaze.

Lord Eka's black eyes had widened, but he displayed no other emotion. 'The thought had never even entered our minds,' he stated. 'After all, the Great King is very old...'

'His family are all long-lived,' Aisha interjected coldly. Then she revealed the iron. 'I realize that he may wear himself out servicing his young wife, that she might even help him on his way, but it could be a great risk, a job half done. Your one security and hope of final reward will be to make way for Prince Deva Raja to become the Great King sooner rather than later. You need his mother as Regent.' Aisha's glance at the men for their reaction was piercing.

Lord Kandura spoke for the first time. 'The lady is right.' He had a crackly voice. 'I've gambled often and lost. I'd like to gamble and win for once.'

Friday, 18 March 1524

In her chamber in the Jaya palace the following night, Queen Anula faced King Wijayo as soon as he entered without any attempt at sexual wiles. 'As you know, lord, Prince Bhuvaneka

212

went to Sita Waka immediately after learning that you had adopted our son. My contacts inform me that the two princes plan to assassinate you, our son and me.' She forced tears to her eyes. 'How could sons plot against their own father? What monsters they must be to want to kill someone as good as you. They are your own flesh and blood, lord, but forgive me, they are no more than parricides. What mother nursed them with her milk?' Her eyes widened with terror. 'If they can be thus to you, what will they not do to me? Help me and help my fatherless boy, we to whom you have extended your divine protection. We have only you. I'm so afraid.' Her face broke up and she hid it with her hands.

'Have no f-fear,' the king bade her grandly, taking her in his arms. The smell of alcohol on his breath robbed his words of some of their effectiveness. 'We t-too have learned of this p-plot.' She knew that he had learned of this through her own sources. He moved her hands away from her face and looked at her with deep intensity.

Suddenly, for the first time, she saw the latent strength and stubbornness of this man she had so frequently despised. Finding the nobility of his breed, the dignity of his office, she marvelled, knew a moment's pause before her ambition shoved her forward. 'I can look to you then for protection, Sire?'

'Of course.' He was enjoying the role.

'I may be of some help, Sire,' she ventured.

'How?'

'Lord Kandura and Lord Eka are both courtiers of great loyalty to you. They hinted that they would be willing to deal with your three sons if you so directed them.'

He was quick on the uptake, betraying no sign of his age. 'You mean that they d-desire the assurance of those p-permanent rewards that we can extend to them?' he inquired sharply.

She gazed at him, wordless.

'We c-can see that,' he mused. 'We c-can see that.' He lifted his head with sudden decision. 'N-none of our three sons is fit to rule this c-country,' he stated flatly. 'Buvaneka is weak, Raigam is secretive and Maya Dunne is a hot-head, over

213

ambitious. Yet we d-do not wish to be directly responsible for reprisals against these would-be p-parricides. If you arrange for their d-disposal, you will not only have earned our gratitude but even our respect as a lady of strength, ability and resourcefulness. As a t-token of that gratitude, we give you our solemn oath, b-before the K-Kataragama g-god, that if you accomplish this m-mission and remove these m-monsters f-from the f-face of the earth, we shall appoint you Queen Regent of this c-country, second only t-to ourself.'

CHAPTER 18

My father and I were in his study the morning we received the shocking news at Sita Waka. My father and Prince Raigam were to be summoned to the palace for a conference by the Great King. There all three princes would be assassinated in their respective quarters by persons unknown!

'The queen has revealed her hand, as you forecast, Sire,' I told my father. 'It has not taken her long.'

'People of blind ambition rush blindly to fulfil those ambitions,' he responded grimly. 'And as I also forecast, our deaths will be followed by the final phase of the queen's plan.' He pondered awhile. 'Summon your two uncles and Prince Vidiye to a secret meeting at our residence in Horana the day after tomorrow, late at night.'

Tuesday, 22 March 1524

Horana is a small village about forty miles south and west of our mansion. It was central for all parties involved and far removed from cities and townships. The three princes, my father and I had already met there once for a general discussion after Prince Bhuvaneka's visit to Sita Waka. Prince Vidiye had common cause with us because he too was in the line of succession to the throne. Though far removed, he would still have been ahead of Prince Deva Raja under normal circumstances.

Built in a dark grove of jak and breadfruit trees, the residence was isolated by vast stretches of jungle. It was a safe meeting place, particularly at the hour of midnight, which gave us all several hours of darkness in which to reach it unobserved.

As we sat around the dark brown *nadun* wood table in the hall, the musty smell of a closed room was overpowering. Under tapers throwing a fitful light the scene suddenly seemed unreal to me, for we were indeed no more than conspirators. But what choice did we have?

We first compared notes in an attempt to get to the truth of the stories we had received from our various contacts. They all coincided: there could be no mistake about the assassination plan. A chill silence fell on the room, disturbed only by the *thuk...thuk...thuk* of a lizard and the riffling of a breeze through the tiles.

'What do you propose?' Prince Bhuvaneka finally inquired. 'It seems to me that our only course is to ignore the summonses, throw down the gauntlet and create civil war.'

'I say we gather all forces loyal to us and attack Jaya,' Prince Vidiye volunteered, his large dark eyes rolling from Prince Bhuvaneka to my father.

'That would take too long,' Prince Raigam intervened.

'Our only course is a quick preemptive strike which will force our father, the Great King, to abdicate,' my father declared, his chiselled features stern.

'But how, is the question; we do not have the necessary forces,' Prince Bhuvaneka interposed.

'I believe I have a solution,' I declared quietly.

All eyes were suddenly focused in my direction. 'I did not consult you about this, Sir, because I worked out my plan only as I rode here this evening,' I apologized to my father, and was grateful for his encouraging nod. 'The key is my cavalry regiment.' I went on to outline my plan. 'It is the only way we can ensure the secrecy essential for the preemptive strike you propose.'

I finally looked around at the others. My chief reward was a glint of appreciation in my father's eyes. We discussed details for over an hour, but what finally emerged was my original plan. I glowed at the sober praise of the other men, but was sick at heart because the action to be taken was against my grandfather, however ghoulish his intentions, and the legitimate sovereign of our country. It was indeed a sad day for Lanka, sadder than the day the *parangi* arrived, for this time we were tearing ourselves apart.

We stared at one another bleakly. This was a moment in

history and we were writing it. What would the historians say about it in the *Chula Vamsa*, our record of modern times?

'What happens afterwards?' Prince Raigam finally inquired.

'A triumvirate, as the old Romans would say,' Prince Bhuvaneka asserted. 'We have already assured Maya Dunne of this. He, you and I will rule as the Great Kings together, or subdivide the country into our three kingdoms. You have my solemn oath on it.'

It was finally decided unanimously that this would be the solution until the Council of Nobles made a final ruling as to the succession. But there was no satisfaction in our minds as we filed out into the dark night.

Friday, 25 March 1524

As we awaited the moment for the attack, the smell of sweat and damp leather was heavy in my nostrils, and I sensed that the horses were as restive as the men. Even my normally calm black Rama kept laying back his ears and grinding on his bit. The animals must catch our tension and feel the oppressiveness of pre-dawn air, strangled by burnished white clouds that threatened rain, eerie from vivid flashes of lightning in the west followed by the rumble of distant thunder. We were to advance at dawn, one hour from now. My first battle. Sinhala against Sinhala, what a sad event.

When I played in this dark grove of jak, coconut and cashew trees outside the south gate of the Jaya capital as a boy, I never dreamed that three years later I would one day be leading a crack cavalry regiment of a thousand men in an assault on it.

Thinking of the past brought Julietta to my mind. I had not been able to get over my love for her, even though she had fitted so readily into the *parangi* scene, including their parties and dancing, foreign to our Sinhala culture. Word was that she and Lieutenant Fernao de Albergaria would be married. So what? I had my own destiny to fulfil.

Why then do my eyes prickle with tears at the thought of her? Why does my heart clamour to find her in the Jaya palace again today on the green lawn behind the hibiscus hedge? My love for

217

her would never die. My mind still cried out, why did you do it, Julietta, why did you do it to me?

The memory of Lila and Kodi intruded. Shortly after Admiral de Albergaria departed, I had identified the *parangi* fiend who brutalized and murdered Lila. I saw him swaggering about the streets of Colombo with his fellow *degradados*. He was even on guard duty on one of my official visits to the port. Each time the blood would rush to my head and I had to fight the unprincely urge to leap on him and tear out his throat with my bare hands. Instead, I noted him well and bided my time.

My thoughts were interrupted by the whinny of a horse, and I glanced over my shoulder. My cavalry bodyguards were making way for a rider pushing through. Even in the gloom, there was no mistaking my father's erect seat.

He nudged his horse alongside. 'Everything ready, Prince?'

'Yes, Sir.'

'I've just had some interesting news from Kandy. One of our people there has discovered that a messenger is on his way from my . . . er . . . brother-in-law, King Wira, inviting me to visit.'

'What?' I could hardly believe my ears. 'They betray the Sinhala cause, ally themselves with the *parangi* and the Catholic friars and now want to court you? They must need your support for a serious move.'

'That's my guess too. Since their greatest hopes were pinned on the *parangi*, there must be a serious rift.'

'Surely you will not accept the invitation, Sir?'

'Of course not, but I may take them up on the offer of amity in case we need them some day. There is nothing like disillusionment to encourage help against a common enemy.' His smile was white in the semi-gloom.

'At least King Wira will stop bragging if his alliance with the *parangi* has ended,' I said. 'And of course the conversion of Prince Kumara, which has been as imminent for the past two years as the wedding of an unattractive older sister, will probably never take place.'

My father turned sober. 'Now to the business at hand. Report your state of readiness.'

'The three cavalry detachments of one hundred each, under

Prince Bhuvaneka, Prince Raigam and Prince Vidiye, are in position outside the North, South and East Gates. My own two companies for the first assault through the main gates and the two reserve companies which will follow and open the gates for the other three are awaiting the order to move. I have allotted six musketeers each to the four assault forces. They will only be used if our main plan misses fire.' Yes indeed, we had been able to manufacture muskets and would be using them, if necessary, today for the first time. Technical problems and the fact that Palitha was no Kodi had made production difficult, so we had only twenty-four of the weapons.

He smiled at my turn of speech. 'Good. You have done a superb job of training your regiment and moving them here secretly, Prince.' He paused. 'Don't judge your grandfather too harshly. He is crazed by love and desire. When a man is young, he can attract the attention of a woman, perhaps inspire love, through the call of flesh to flesh. When he grows old, he has only his wealth, his position, power and influence,. Throughout history, whenever a powerful old man has been attracted to an ambitious young woman, what he has had to give her in exchange for her favours has frequently led to his downfall. Your grandfather cannot escape the laws of cause and effect. He has sought to bestow on his queen what was not his to give, so he must pay the price.'

These were sobering thoughts. We both fell silent awhile. The lightning and thunder had ceased so the storm must have passed along the ocean. That pale glow in the east, above the dark outline of treetops, heralded daybreak. The first roosters began crowing at the false dawn and dew started to drip from the branches.

'Do you know why I'm coming with you?' my father inquired abruptly.

'Because I am leading the main assault force, Sir.'

'Wrong, Prince. Three years ago, on your sixteenth birthday, I promised you that we would ride to battle together. Soon? you asked. I replied, very soon. It has taken much longer than I thought and . . .' his voice had a tremor in it, he cleared his throat and stared into space, 'a different direction. Instead of riding together to unite the country, we are on a divisive mission. But it is necessary to eradicate evil.' He sighed, then exploded. 'Your grandfather has permitted the *parangi* free entry everywhere to the detriment of the Sinhala Buddhists. Our poor are exploited, our Doctrine is slighted by coerced conversions to the Catholic religion. Even our ancient Sinhala court is slowly becoming a shoddy imitation of the West. All the Great King wants is a safe seat on the golden throne until his death. Our nation has been betrayed. We are here to save it.'

'Ahey! Ahey!' The cavalrymen behind me had heard my father's words and respectfully echoed their solidarity with the cause.

'*Narki vissay, gettath ussay*,' someone said quietly. 'The sexual-poison in an old man is taller than a house.'

He was speaking of my father's father and neither General Prince Maya Dunne nor I could turn to defend our family honour. Sad, sad, sad!

Friday, 25 March 1524

Her talk with Fernao had left Julietta confused about her feelings. During the three years she had known him, he had seemed strong, considerate and refined, with never a care in the world except for his less fortunate fellow human beings. Though there were times when he expressed himself passionately, she never associated him with day-to-day worries. He was a de Albergaria, the son of the admiral commanding the East Indies Fleet and a young man with a promising future. Now suddenly, having discovered that he faced really serious problems, she found herself feeling protective. Wanting to help him, she realized that such emotions sprang from the part of her she had closed off against other men because of her love for Prince Tikiri.

She loved Prince Tikiri with all her heart. Though he had hurt her so bitterly by rejecting her, she could never love or give herself to any other man. She liked Fernao immensely, enjoyed his company, depended on him, respected him. What then did she feel for him? Was it love of a different kind? Could a woman love two men at the same time? She could tell that Fernao loved her. Was it fair to continue their friendship just because she needed a friend? What were her alternatives? She shuddered at the answer ... none!

She tossed and turned in bed night after night, in the days following that conversation, with no result. Meanwhile, Fernao had made no further attempt to draw as close to her during their walks on the ramparts, but had been his usual friendly self.

Tonight, lying in bed in the quarters allotted to her father in the fort, she was nagged by some fear she could not identify. Did it mean another sleepless night? At this rate, she would soon have black rings under her eyes and Fernao might not even find her attractive any more! Although the thick rampart walls against which the quarters had been built ensured coolness, they also meant that hardly any breeze came through. Her room was small and opened out into an inner courtyard where the air could get very close. She was so restless in bed that her housekeeper, Menika, who had insisted upon sleeping on a mat in the room after their move to the fort in order to protect her against the large numbers of single men it contained, sleepily asked what was wrong.

Julietta finally drifted off into the deep stupor of slumber that follows a restless night, only to waken with a start. Through the gloom, the sand clock on her dressing table showed a little over an hour before dawn. Her mind was bright and alert even before she identified what had woken her. It was fear in the pit of her stomach and the fear was linked with Prince Tikiri. He was in danger. She had never discovered why he had ignored and avoided her since she left the palace. It had hurt her deeply but there was no longer any way in which she could find out what had happened. Could he have become jealous of her relationship with Fernao? Was he disgusted by the reports he must have received these past years about her conduct in the Portuguese community, which was perfectly well-bred by Western standards but immodest according to Sinhala culture?

Whatever the causes, she had tried to forget Prince Tikiri, hate him even, but she simply could not. He was the man she loved. What did she feel for Fernao then?

Suddenly, it was all unbearable. She simply had to talk to someone. She sat up in bed, tossed her long hair from her face. 'Menika!' she called.

The old woman was up on the instant. 'What is it, daughter? What? What?'

'Please light the lamp. The darkness is stifling me.'

Murmuring words of reassurance, Menika fumbled for flint and tinder on the table. She struck it, caught the spark in a cloth wick soaked in oil and lit the brass lantern. She was revealed in a sleeveless bodice and waistcloth, her brown skin wrinkled, large eyes brimming with concern. She came up to Julietta's bedside. 'What's wrong, daughter? Are you sick?'

Julietta shook her head. 'No, I simply want to talk to you, Menika. I realize it's selfish of me to disturb your sleep, but I need you. Please sit down.'

Menika squatted on her haunches with the natural grace of all Sinhala village women. She smelled of night clothes. 'What is bothering my *chuti*, little one?'

'Your little one must be growing up,' Julietta responded with a smile, then grew serious. 'I just woke up with a strong premonition that Prince Tikiri is in danger.'

'Prince Tikiri? And why must you be thinking about Prince Tikiri after all these years when you have been going out with another nice young man?'

'I am still in love with Prince Tikiri.'

'Madness. You have hardly set eyes on the prince for over three years and you say you are still in love with him?'

'Are you surprised?'

'No.' A look of infinite kindness entered Menika's eyes. 'No, little paddy bird, I am not surprised. Having known you since you were born, getting on seventeen years now, there is not much about you that escapes me even though you may not speak of it.'

'Oh, Menika!' Julietta reached out and touched the wrinkled brown cheek. 'You are indeed my mother, better than any mother could have been to me. Your look is so full of compassion at times. Tell me, why is it that I have never seen such a look on the faces of the Portuguese?'

'That is part of the Sinhala heritage. It comes from our religion, I think, which is that of Lord Buddha, the All-Compassionate One. Our people can be just as cruel as any other race, but we have a tradition of compassion.'

'Tell me what I should do about my premonition, Menika.'

'There is nothing you can do. That is the lot of women, to suffer at the danger of those they love and not be able to do anything about it. If you accept that lot and if you realize that all is *kharma/vipaka*, cause and effect, something no one can really change, you will at least be easier in your mind. Though we are sentient beings, we are helpless before the laws of cause and effect.'

'But I am a Christian, Menika. I believe in God, in the Lord Jesus Christ and the Virgin Mary.'

'Then pray to them for aid. Ask them to help you bear your fears and to protect your loved one from harm.'

Julietta felt easier. 'You are right. When I am afraid, I sometimes forget to pray, and when I do pray, it is not properly.' Julietta stared at the shadow of the lamp's frame on the opposite wall. The muted crash of breakers against the rampart intruded into her consciousness.

'What *kolang*, silliness, this is about your loving Prince Tikiri,' Menika broke in quietly. 'He is not for you, so you should forget him. Even if he had loved you, there would have been no future in it, only trouble.'

'I know,' Julietta whispered. 'But when you love someone, it is there, inside you all the time, possessing the best part of you and preventing you from giving it to anyone else.'

To Julietta's surprise, Menika's eyes misted. 'I know what you mean.' Her voice broke.

So Menika too had once loved and lost. 'What happened?'

Menika wiped away a tear, sniffed and rubbed her nose with the back of her fingers. 'Oh, it was a long time ago, in our village. He was the son of the village headman, a beautiful man, with golden skin, dark eyes and shiny black hair. Unfortunately, he was of the *goviya*, farmer, caste which regards itself as the highest and my family were of the lower jewellers' caste.' The tears were welling in eyes that stared inward at the past.

223

Her own problems forgotten, Julietta slowly rose from the bed, knelt beside Menika. She placed an arm around the bony shoulders. 'Tell me all, Menika, please tell me.'

'There's not much to tell.' Deep sobs were racking Menika's body now, like those of a hurt child. 'We eloped, but his father discovered where we had gone and came with his relatives to the little hut on the mountaintop that my Banda had bought for us. It was at dawn after our first night together.' She was staring into space now, seeing it all. 'The father swung at me with a sword, but Banda leapt forward, took the blow on his head and fell bleeding. He died on the spot.'

'Oh dear God and the Blessed Virgin.'

'I wish they had killed me too. But they were so appalled by what they had done that they took Banda's body and departed leaving me as if I had never existed.' She shrugged, fell silent, stared into space. 'I didn't even have the right to bury him.'

'What did you do then?' Julietta was so horrorstricken, she could barely frame the words.

'I don't remember. I honestly don't remember anything that happened for a long time afterwards, except wanting to die. Then Banda came to me, one dark night; it may have been in a dream, but it was very real. He told me to eat, to clean myself up and live. I asked him what I had to live for and he replied, For me and the one to come. I said, But you have gone for ever. He smiled that sweet, white smile of his and said, What we knew was for ever, because no one can take that away from us. One night? I asked. And he responded with questions, Did you want a lifetime? If so, did you not, on that single night, have my entire lifetime as dictated by my *kharma*? What is a lifetime? Then he was gone and I awoke to the empty darkness, shivering. I somehow found the strength to do as he asked me, but I determined never to leave our home. So I carried on alone as we had planned, growing vegetables and fruit, with a few hens and a cow.'

'How long did you live there?'

'Until it was time to deliver my baby.'

'Oh Menika, you have a child?'

Menika shook her head slowly and gave a deep sigh. 'No,

even that was not in my *kharma*. The baby was stillborn. And when I returned home from the village midwife, I found that Banda's father had seized the property since it belonged to his son.'

'Oh, the cruel, cruel fiend.'

'No, my golden child. He was merely being himself and he did me the greatest favour of all. He taught me the truth of what Banda had told me in my dream. Men could take his life, and my possessions, life could take my baby, but no one could take what Banda and I had known.'

'But how did you live afterwards? Did you go back to your parents?'

'No, they had disowned me for the shame I had brought on them. Besides, they were afraid of Banda's father and I did not want to cause them embarrassment or harm.'

'How did you manage to live, I mean food, shelter ... '

'When one is not afraid of honest labour, it is always possible to earn a living. If I had been of the *goviya* caste, I would have been too proud to do anything else but toil in the fields. Being young, pretty and of lowly caste, I did various menial jobs and finally hired myself as a domestic in the mansion of the district overlord. To cut a long story short, I was so good at my work that I ended up in the palace.'

'Being young and pretty, did you not find a man whom you could love and marry?'

Menika smiled then through the tears, a slow, sad smile. She shook her head. 'I knew that part of my life for ever on the mountaintop.'

'One night?' Julietta demanded, incredulous.

'One lifetime. After I had known Banda, there could be no more, no one else. Besides, if I had gone with another man, that would have been yet another lifetime. Since no one can have two lifetimes, I would have had to lose the first, the most precious of all.'

Dumbfounded, Julietta could only stare at Menika in silence. Then both her arms swept round the frail old body and she held Menika tight, crooning to her, something she had never done before to anyone, except her dolls. What a wonderful,

225

unique person, this Menika. So much grief, so much idealism and she had never even suspected it all these years, taking from Menika without ever really giving. Now from this serving lady she had learned a new dimension of love and the heights of virtue. 'I love you, Menika,' she whispered, her throat aching, her chest tight.

Menika clung to her, broke down sobbing.

Compassion does not belong to any one person or race, Julietta thought. It just is, if you set aside selfishness, self-protection and let it flow. 'All these years you have lived without your man and your baby, for others?'

Menika gently disengaged herself. She wiped her cheeks, her eyes with the edge of her cloth. Her expression resumed its normal firmness. 'I have lived all these years with my man,' she stated flatly. 'I have wanted no other.'

'But physical need, Menika, the desire to hold and to be held.'

'Do you have it, my golden girl?' Menika shook her head. 'It's all in the mind except with those who have the *vissay*, poison sex-yen in their *prana*. If you don't tell yourself that you need it, you don't really need it until it comes. As for a baby, if I lost one, I was given another.' She reached out a gentle hand and touched Julietta's cheek. 'Such a beautiful baby too, the fairest in the land.' She laughed lightly. 'Mine and no other's. You were not always easy, but oh, you were always worthwhile.'

Kneeling, they fell into each other's arms, laughing and crying. 'You were so stern at times!' Julietta exclaimed.

'When you needed it.'

'I know, I know.'

Finally Menika gripped Julietta by the shoulders, pushed her back the better to be able to see her face. 'Now I'm going to be stern again,' she declared. 'You have a fine young man courting you, why don't you marry each other?'

'He has never asked me, and I have hoped that he would not. After all, I love Prince Tikiri and you of all people should understand that.'

'What is this love you are talking about?' Menika demanded sternly. 'You and Master Fernao see each other every day; he is your escort at parties, you dance together, you are husband and wife in everything except in name and in bed.'

Julietta blushed. 'Is that how it seems?'

'That is how it is. You like each other, you respect each other, you enjoy each other's company, you are both tolerant and thinking people. You love each other as family, but are not prepared to admit it. Listen, little paddy bird, we have arranged marriages in Lanka, as you know. Not all of them work, but the majority result in deep love. Let the romance of Prince Tikiri rule your heart, as mine has been ruled these thirty years and more, but let affection and regard, which never came to me, rule your life.'

'You can say that?'

'Of course, because I had Banda and you have never known the prince.' Menika hesitated. 'I'll tell you a secret. You think of me as romantic and true to a dream. I am all of that, but I also know that if Banda and I had lived a long life together,' she laughed without mirth, 'or even a short life, our love might have ended. Open yourself to this estimable young man and let him decide whether he can love all of you, then he will open himself up for you to decide whether you love all of him. Give yourself a chance.'

Julietta shook her head violently, then her whole body began to tremble. She gazed piteously at Menika, silently begging for help to break loose from the chains with which she had bound herself. Oh, the aching, aching pain, the agony of giving up something to which she had clung all these years, her lifeline since childhood after she became an outcast through Mala's harsh words.

But Menika merely looked at her with compassion, made no move to help her.

Julietta began shaking more violently, as with the ague, her teeth chattering. Oh Mother of Mercy, help me, she silently prayed. The sweat began trickling down her face and body.

Finally, it eased and with it came a growing sense of peace. She stopped shaking, her trembling ceased. She looked directly at Menika, barely seeing her.

'What will you do?' Menika inquired, in a gentle voice.

'I do not love Master Fernao in that way.' The words seemed

227

to come from outside her. 'I can't possibly marry anyone else while I love Prince Tikiri.'

CHAPTER 19
Friday, 25 March 1524

When that first glimmering of dawn appeared over the tree line to the east of the city, my heart started to beat faster with excitement. Waiting for the action to commence, even with my father calm beside me, had been a time of mixed emotions. Fear was ever-present, heavy in my entrails, fear of death, fear of being maimed, perhaps for life, fear of the first moment when I would use my sword to slay a fellow human being, a Sinhala at that, fear of the uncontrolled anger and hatred I would generate for a cause and in order to preserve my own life. Yet anticipation had also been light in my head, the certainty of invincibility had never ceased to be a steady reality in spite of the doubts that cast their ever-present shadows.

I glanced at my tiny sand-timer.

The waiting was over. A curious calm instantly settled over me, as if the responding parts of me were suspended somewhere outside and only an inflexible, deadly purpose remained within. I knew at that moment, with startling clarity, that this was the real me, a man destined to be in battle all his life and therefore blessed with the aura of invincibility of which I had been so certain. It was a curious, indescribable sensation.

I glanced at my father, received his nod. I half-turned in the saddle to command attention, raised my hand then pointed it through the trees to the broad highway. I relaxed, sat deeper in the saddle, squeezed gently with my legs and eased my hands on the reins. Well trained to my aids, Rama automatically moved forward. I was soon in perfect balance with his motion.

'The *devas* guard you,' my father called out softly.

Captain Wickram, my square-faced aide, brought his bay alongside. Behind were the twenty men of the advance guard I had selected to give the appearance of my normal escort, my six musketeers well-hidden in their centre, muskets pointing upwards to look like lances. We broke into the comparative light of a fallow field, made for the broad highway over brown soil tufted with yellow paddy stalks. Once on the highway, we urged our horses to a fast trot, hooves clattering on the cobbles. Before long, the massive walls of the city loomed ahead, the moat twin glimmers through the lightening darkness.

My stomach tightened. Would we be given the open entry into the city that had always been available to me, or would there be some suspicion because of the early hour? With a great clattering of hooves, we rode over the causeway to the moment of discovery. I noted the silent shapes of the crocodiles. Two suddenly came alive and slither-splashed into the shadowy waters. I'm glad I'm not there, I thought, but would I really rather be here?

I glanced up and saw guards peering over the battlements. It was light enough for them to identify me. I raised my hand, steadied Rama to a walk then brought him to a halt, my men in perfect unison behind.

'Who goes there!' one of the guards called out. 'Is that you, Prince Tikiri?'

I recognized the voice of Captain Tilak, a guard commander. 'Yes indeed, Captain,' I shouted back.

'What brings you at this early hour? Not an emergency, I hope.'

'No, no! Merely a summons from the Great King to attend him bright and early,' I lied, hating myself for it.

'We had no word of it, but you're welcome any time, Prince,' he responded, then turned around. 'Joti, Hema, open up for the prince!'

The great teakwood gates, weatherworn, ribbed with iron, creaked open. We rode slowly through the yawning entrance beneath the granite archway. The city beyond was barely awake as yet. We paused at the paved courtyard for vendors, deserted at this hour. Captain Tilak, a burly, black-haired Sinhala, walked down the rampart steps to greet me.

My men swung into action exactly as they had practised on a mock-up of the fort laid out with rope in the swamps north of the river mouth in Colombo. The six musketeers dismounted and levelled their weapons at the duty sentries; ten of the cavalrymen leapt off their horses, drew their swords and secured the wheels that opened and closed the gates. The remaining cavalrymen fanned out and started to gallop along the north and south streets skirting the ramparts to open up the other gates for the groups led by Prince Bhuvaneka and Prince Raigam.

'What is this, Prince?' Captain Tilak demanded, fear and anger in his dark eyes.

'We are taking over the government,' I stated very quietly.

He drew his sword, came on guard. 'Over my dead body, Prince, for I am sworn to protect the Great King.' He laughed unaccountably, then paused at the thunder of hooves.

The main body of our cavalry squadrons, my father leading them, was galloping in column towards the open gates.

Captain Tilak's jaw dropped, but only for a moment. 'It is to the death then,' he cried.

My blood was suddenly hot. A mad desire to run him down, stamp aside anyone and everyone who stood in my way, seized me, but some deeper instinct savagely controlled me. 'You are a brave man, Captain Tilak.' I had to shout to make myself heard above the din of fast-approaching hooves. 'We need Sinhala like you for our cause. We mean the Great King no harm. He is my father's father and we are not a family of parricides. But the time has come to win back our security and self-respect. See, my father, General Prince Maya Dunne, approaches. Prince Bhuvaneka, Prince Raigam and Prince Vidiye have by now taken the other three gates. Get your men and ride with us to liberate Lanka.'

Captain Tilak hesitated, his eyes flitting from me to the approaching column, then back to me. Finally, he lowered his sword. 'All right, Prince,' he smiled. 'I am with you.'

'Good man. You shall be rewarded. Assemble your men quickly in the courtyard. We must hasten to the city.'

I turned Rama in the direction of the approaching cavalry. The pounding of hooves beat into my bloodstream. I do not know whether it was instinct or Captain Wickram's warning cry that made me clap my heels into Rama's flanks. The gallant

231

steed took off like a bolt from a crossbow as Captain Tilak's sword seared down my thigh. One moment of streaking pain, then comprehension of the attack dawned on me. Rage and blood-lust such as I have never before experienced consumed me; a red mist swam before my eyes. I drew my sword, raced Rama round in a clattering circle. I saw Captain Tilak standing alone, on guard, his teeth white in a gritted smile. As I approached him, he raised his sword aloft. I parried his great slash with my sword, circled his weapon, reversed and swung back in one smooth motion. The sword bit flesh, jarred up my arm as it met bone, was nearly wrested from my grasp. I circled again and saw Captain Tilak sprawled on the ground, red blood dripping from the gash in his neck.

At the sight of his now pathetic figure, the blood-lust suddenly left me. I reined Rama to look down on my dead opponent. A brave, dashing figure one moment, helpless in death the next. He did not have to die. Or did he? My first killing. Or was it murder? I suddenly felt cold, became aware of a great silence. The lead of the cavalry column was halted under the archway. My father sat his horse motionless at their head, pity for me in his glance.

'Give Captain Tilak a hero's burial,' I curtly directed no one in particular. 'My wound can wait.'

As we had practised, we galloped through the city. It was beginning to come alive, milk vendors half-asleep driving their carts, the odd working man walking purposefully, two vegetable women, dressed alike in blue cloths and white jackets, baskets on their heads, swinging gracefully towards the entrance courtyard. Bleary-eyed men and women, excited children charged to their front gates, as we thundered past their homes.

The palace loomed ahead. A great, white relief flooded me when I saw the yawning entrance gates of the capitol. We did have loyal supporters in the palace then. Suddenly a question intruded. I raised my hand, giving the signal to stop.

'What is it, Prince?' My father inquired.

'It could be a trap, Sir.'

His eyes widened. 'So it could, Prince. So it could. Good thinking.'

What to do next? 'If it is a trap, I must spring it,' I declared.

'No, Prince,' my father commanded sharply. 'Not you.'

'It has to be me, Sir. I am leading the advance guard.'

Without waiting for his approval, I clip-clopped Rama towards the open gates.

Friday, 24 March 1524

Aisha was about to perform her ablutions in anticipation of the morning prayers when the eunuch sought leave to see her. She received him at the entrance to her chamber. He looked heavy and black in the glow of the lamps that had been lit against the coming of daylight. He is running to fat, Aisha thought. All eunuchs get flat-footed and flabby in their old age. 'Why did you wish to see me?' she demanded.

'News of the utmost urgency, lady, from Bala, one of our spies in the port governor's mansion.' He had a soft, high voice.

'Quickly then, please. I'm about to say my morning prayers.' She could not restrain a tremor of apprehension, since events of such dire consequence were at hand.

'Prince Tikiri and his entire cavalry regiment have vanished.'

The man always had a flair for drama.

'Gone? Where?'

'We don't know, lady.'

'What d'you mean you don't know? A thousand men don't simply vanish into the darkness.'

'They were in camp last night. Bala awoke during the first watch after midnight, went outside for a call of nature and noticed that the camp had no sentries. He checked and found it deserted, except for camp-followers.'

'Were the horses gone?'

'Yes, lady.'

'That means they are off on an exercise or a military operation. If it was an exercise, why the secrecy? So it has to be a military operation.' The tremor turned into fear, but she remained outwardly calm. Today was the day set by Lord Eka and Lord Kandura to assassinate the three princes. Had they got wind of the plot? Her own position, indeed her whole life, could be in jeopardy if the assassination attempts failed. Her mind started to race, her heart began beating faster. With a supreme effort, she regained her normal stern control. The situation required immediate action, so this was one of those rare occasions when she cursed the fact that she was a woman.

'Summon my husband here immediately,' she directed the eunuch. She heard the *muezzin's* call to prayer, faint in the distance.

'Allah is the Greatest ...

'Come to prayer ...

'Come to virtue ... '

No Muslim within earshot could ignore the summons, but today was different. She would offer action to Allah, instead of prayer. She hoped that He would understand.

She waited impatiently for Abdul Raschid to join her, her appearance totally calm.

'What emergency has to take priority over prayers?' Abdul demanded as he waddled in. 'Except that I know you are not one to create ghosts out of shadows, I should have ignored your request.'

Aisha's smile was chill. 'What I have to tell you is no shadow,' she asserted. She watched him closely as she gave him the eunuch's message and her evaluation of the situation.

Her husband's flabby face began slowly breaking up as the danger of their position dawned on him. He barely let her finish before he interrupted. 'If Lord Eka and Lord Kandura are captured, they are sure to betray us.'

'Precisely.'

'I warned you not to do this.'

Aisha eyed him with cold contempt. 'When?' she demanded icily. 'I seem to remember some active support from you, and it was you who gave the bribes.' A vivid desire to be cruel streaked through her. 'It's you they'll seize and torture, not a mere woman.'

He always seemed to find some reserves of dignity when he was pushed against the wall. 'If that is the will of Allah, so be it.' He drew erect, the flesh of his face firm again.

'Allah can be made to favour us,' she retorted.

234

'How?'

She told him.

'But whom should I implicate as the plotters?' he finally inquired, smiling now.

Aisha's eyebrows lifted. 'Who else but those cold-blooded murderers, Lord Eka and Lord Kandura? Tell the truth, husband.'

'About Queen Anula too?'

'No, best leave her and her little son out of it for the present. After all, our own quarrel is with the Great King, not with the Queen or the three princes. We shall need the Queen for the real action if this one has failed.'

Friday, 25 March 1524

Fernao was amazed when Aisha Raschid was announced. A woman, any woman, leave alone a Muslim in *purdah*, in a fort at this early hour could only mean a crisis. He received her in his office, a small room with high slits for windows on the ground floor of the headquarters tower. It was almost cold when he entered, but the heady scent of Aisha Raschid's attar-of-roses perfume cleansed its musty air.

'*Ola, a senhora* Raschid,' Fernao greeted her. 'Pray be seated.'

Her veiled female servant left the room as Aisha resumed her seat on a settle opposite his long brown *nadun* wood table. He took his usual chair, leaned forward with his elbows on the table and waited, knowing from experience that if he asked questions he would receive only chit-chat.

'You must wonder what brings a respectable Muslim woman to your fort at this early hour,' Aisha stated. 'Rather than keep you in suspense, I shall come straight to the point. Prince Tikiri and his entire cavalry regiment disappeared from their Mutu Vella camp last night.'

Fernao's heart began to pound. He listened intently, without once interrupting, while Aisha recounted the facts, organized to keep herself and her husband in the clear, and her suspicions.

'So you believe that the Great King summoned the three princes, his sons, to attend the Jaya palace this morning so they

235

could be assassinated by Lord Eka's and Lord Kandura's men?' There was an incredulous note in his voice.

'I not only believe it, I know,' Aisha asserted. 'If I were you, lord, I would want to safeguard my trading position. These political events make your Viceroy's request, that you send the *terco*, regiment, away, impractical.' He could sense her smile beneath the *yashmak*. 'From our own point of view, of course, this means that you should not contemplate any changes to your present trading pattern, because you never know whom you will be dealing with in Jaya!'

'Events are moving fast,' Fernao observed aloud. 'What you say makes good sense, but of course the final decision will have to be made by Captain Oliveira.' How fortunate that last night the captain had put the entire garrison into a twenty-four-hour state of readiness, as an exercise. 'Supposing we send our soldiers to Jaya this morning, complete with cannon to save the Great King if he is indeed in danger?'

He noted the tiniest widening of her eyes. So you would not like that, he thought dispassionately.

'That would be a mistake,' she replied quietly. 'After all, it may well be too late.' She shook her head and sighed. 'If the Great King is doomed, why waste your forces to save him? It would be better to support his named successor so that the Sinhala feel you are upholding his will and their traditions. As you know, lord, it is Sinhala tradition for the king to name his successor. Even his court jester may be so named.'

Fernao knew that this was not strictly true. It might be Mouro, but it was certainly not Arya custom. Still, he did not wish to debate the point. 'So what you are saying is that we should go in with force after the Great King is ... er ... disposed of and establish a puppet ruler in his place?'

'You are very clever, lord.'

'Why should that not be one of the three princes?' He paused, struck by a thought. 'Or even Prince Tikiri?' He knew the suggestion was absurd but he was testing for the woman's reaction.

Her laugh rippled through the room. 'Forgive me, lord, but

236

that would not be practical. Prince Tikiri would be no one's puppet.'

'Would he battle his father and uncles for the crown?'

'He is reported to be more interested in the task than in any prizes.'

'I want you to know that if sufficient men and resources had been mine, I would have ridden to the Great King's rescue,' Fernao declared, finally tired of all the plotting and fencing. 'As a Christian and a good Catholic, I believe in right and wrong. Attempts at assassination are fundamentally wrong.'

'You are not here as Lord Fernao,' she admonished. 'The power you wield belongs to someone else and you must only use it as they would have you. That is a matter of honour as well as of right and wrong.'

He stared at her in astonishment. 'You may have a point there,' he finally conceded. 'But meanwhile, we may be losing precious time, so I must ask you please to excuse me.' He rose to his feet.

Aisha rose with him and fixed him with a compelling glance. 'Allah's will be done,' she finally stated. She gave him grave salutation and turned towards the door, then paused as if struck by a sudden thought. When she spoke, it seemed as if it were to the closed door. 'I beg you not to trust Prince Tikiri,' she advised in a low voice. 'He hates you unto death.'

'Why? He barely knows me.'

'You stole his woman.'

CHAPTER 20
Friday, 25 March 1524

Easy in the saddle, but with my heart thudding against my ribs, my body tense, I mince-gaited Rama towards the open entrance of the capitol. He seemed nervous too, kept pricking up and laying back his ears. I could not see into the dark window slits of the sentry towers, so my eyes were fixed on the yawning gap of the entrance. Suddenly, absurdly, it seemed to me like the gap of a fallen front tooth in an assassin's mouth, the dark avenue of trees beyond, his throat. Prickles rose on the base of my neck. Would my father's contacts who were supposed to open the gates to us, be our betrayers, the agents of the Great King?

Excited voices were raised behind me. I heard shouts. Intent on my mission, I ignored them.

'Wait, Prince!' My father's urgent voice whipped into my tight consciousness.

I relaxed the reins and Rama came to a stop. I half turned in the saddle, became aware of movement in the centre of my men's ranks. I wheeled Rama quickly around and watched the cavalry column parting to allow my squadron commander, Captain Jagat, to push his chestnut hurriedly through. The captain's rugged face was tense with excitement, sweat pouring down his face. To my surprise, he was carrying a little boy perched on the saddle before him. In a trice, I recognized the dusky skin, curly black hair and small features of Prince Deva Raja, the adopted son of the Great King. What on earth could the little crown prince, the Great King's named heir, be doing here at this hour?

Suspicion smeared my mind like sewer waters on white sand. My father had already turned round to face the newcomers. I urged Rama forward and repositioned myself beside him.

Neatly dressed in blue tunic and pantaloons, the little boy was all smiles, his black eyes sparkling. Captain Jagat drew rein and saluted. 'I'm so relieved I got through in time,' he stated, panting from his exertions. 'Prince Deva Raja has news of life and death.'

'Where on earth did he come from?' my father demanded. 'Why aren't you in the palace, Prince?'

Prince Deva Raja spoke up. 'My royal mother sent me away in the night.' He had a thin, piping voice, not cultured as that of a prince should be even at this early age. 'I *don't like* my mother.' He was mentally stamping his foot.

'Where did she send you?'

'To the home of my friend, Anura.'

'And who is Anura?'

'The son of a lord in my father's court.'

Your 'father', I could not help thinking, in surly fashion, wondering how my own father was reacting to the claim.

Rama pawed the ground impatiently and I brought him under control, but I was also beginning to grow impatient at my father's questions. We were allowing ourselves to be diverted from the timing of our attack. My father must know that too, but here he was coaxing a little boy as if his being outside the court was of some supreme importance.

'What are you doing away from your friend's house?' my father inquired gently.

'I sneaked out to watch the fun.'

'What fun?'

'The battle that is to take place.'

'What battle?'

'The battle at this gate.'

'Who said that a battle would take place here?'

'My father, the Great King.'

'To whom did he say it?'

'To his commander, when he gave orders for the guards to fight.'

'Fight whom?'

'You and my cousin, Prince Tikiri.' He pointed a finger at me, then stuck it into his nose. Even at that dire moment, I wished someone had taught the prince his manners. 'And my mother

239

told me that when you were both killed it would be easier for me to become the Great King some day.' He puffed his little chest with pride.

'What about the other two princes, my brothers?' My father was still gentle, but like a seasoned runner who does not pause in his stride.

'Oh, they too will be killed today, when they arrive.'

I heard the hiss of indrawn breath and realized that it came from some of my men who were within earshot.

'Where are the guards waiting to kill us?' my father quietly probed.

'You are a silly uncle!' Prince Deva Raja pointed again. 'Where else but behind the gate?'

I now understood my father's patience. He turned his head. 'The crown prince has just saved your life,' he declared, a semi-humorous smile creasing the sides of his mouth. 'You have been spared for greater things despite your impetuosity.' I accepted the rebuke with a bowed head. It was my father who had saved my life.

'Why don't you go in and fight, so I can watch?' The little boy's tone was petulant.

I ignored him. 'What now?' I demanded of my father. 'We mustn't miss our timing.'

'Are the guards waiting only at the gate?' My father had swung back to face Prince Deva Raja.

The little boy had started sucking his thumb. He nodded, his eyes widening.

'Do you know exactly where they are waiting?'

'Yes. In the courtyard.'

'Why are they not on the rampart walls?'

'Where they would be seen? They have to pretend it's an accident.'

My father thought awhile, then grunted as he frequently does when he has made a major decision. He wheeled his bay around to face the fort, a devil-may-care smile on his face. 'They are waiting for us, Prince. So we go in, just you and I.'

I was appalled. I believed myself brave but this was madness.

My father sensed my thoughts. 'After all, we can hardly deny a crown prince his entertainment.'

240

Friday, 25 March 1524

Queen Anula had not slept a wink the whole night. True to his word, the Great King had appointed her Queen Regent the previous morning, but the momentous events she had set in motion lay ahead. When she poisoned her first husband and her lover, she had depended on no one but herself. Her present plan involved so many other people and circumstances that she felt uneasy, though she never once wavered in her determination.

Once again, she had serviced the Great King right royally during the night, but he had been too right royally drunk and was obviously too right royally apprehensive deep inside for the task to be easy. When she finally accomplished it, he had quickly passed into a stupor. Barely an hour later, an urgent knocking at her door brought the news from a guard loyal to her, whom Prince Maya Dunne had taken into his confidence, of the impending assault. She had awoken the Great King and summoned Lords Eka and Kandura. Unaware of the princes' entire plan, they adopted a new strategy in two phases. In the first, Prince Maya Dunne and Prince Tikiri would be ambushed as soon as they entered the west gate of the capitol. In the second, the other two princes would be killed when they arrived at noon in answer to the Great King's original summons. Only she, the Mouro couple, Lord Eka, Lord Kandura and the assassin, Jalma, knew of the third phase of the operation!

When the planning session was over and Queen Anula had sent her young son away to safety, the Great King had promptly gone back to sleep. She hated him for it. Meanwhile, the flashes of lightning and the distant rumble of thunder made her jumpy.

She heard the faint crowing of a cockerel, glanced through the high-grilled window and noticed that the sky had lightened, though it was still overcast by lowering white clouds.

Drunk or sober, the Great King always awoke at this time as if there were a sandclock in his brain. A snore and a slurp ended in a sharp grunt. He sat up with a start, his great, wrinkled body erect, a dribble of sleep saliva on his grey beard. 'What? What?' The inevitable questions. Queen Anula steeled herself for the equally inevitable 'Ho! We gave you a good t-time last night, d-did we not?'

241

'You really screwed me, lord. You left me exhausted.' Wishing that her husband would go away, she sat up too, clasped his head and kissed it. 'M'mm . . . uh! You are the greatest, O great, Great King.'

He smiled smugly, then recollection entered his faded eyes. 'Not long to go n-now,' he declared. 'We wonder if our p-plan will work.'

Queen Anula swung shapely dark legs out of bed, stood up and stifled a yawn. 'Everything will go according to plan, Sire,' she asserted with a confidence she did not feel. 'You will be rid of the two monsters who pose the greatest threat to your rule within the hour and by noon your kingdom will be totally secure.'

'We wish we could share your confidence,' he grumbled. 'We should have g-got Prince Maya D-Dunne at the main city g-gate, as we suggested. Once you allow the jackal into the f-farmyard, it's easier for him to g-get at the chicken coops.'

'I would hardly describe myself as a chicken if I were you,' the Queen asserted drily.

'You are sure that Prince Tikiri's cavalry regiment will not attack when the father and son are killed?'

'What will they have left to fight for? Besides, once those two are killed, it will be easy to pick off each row of the cavalry column under the archway if they dare to enter.'

The Great King scratched his white head reflectively. 'We rather liked Prince Tikiri.' He sighed. 'Well, it's t-too late now to change our p-plans.' He glanced out of the window. 'Damn that Maya D-Dunne. To think that I had such a *p-pereythaya*, accursed spirit, for a son. He was always d-difficult, even as a child.'

'You will be rid of him soon, Sire.'

Friday, 25 March 1524

Aisha's last words had jolted Fernao like a violent fist in the stomach, and the jolt had shaken loose the truth. After the Mouro woman departed he sent a messenger to summon

Captain Oliveira, then stood at the entrance to his room in a kind of stupor.

'You have taken his woman . . . you have taken his woman . . . you have taken his woman!' The words kept ringing in his head until he wanted to clap his hands to his ears to shut out the sounds. But they came from inside so that his only defence was a clamouring counterpoint: 'No, Julietta is mine . . . no, Julietta is mine . . . no, Julietta is mine.' He wanted to rush to the ramparts, replace the dawn with a sunset, turn back the clock to yesterday. Instead, he quietly closed the door of his little office and sat behind his desk, fighting to regain control.

The vivid flashes of lightning and the rumble of distant thunder were a fitting accompaniment to his first overwhelming fit of jealousy and possessiveness. Then reason finally intervened. If Julietta was Prince Tikiri's woman, how had they kept contact with each other these past years? No, the Raschid woman must have lied to make him jealous, and to pit him against Prince Tikiri so he would intervene. How would such intervention benefit the Raschids? Only if it resulted in the removal of the Great King. What of Julietta? Could it be that she secretly loved the prince? A hopeless love through the years? The thought inflamed Fernao. Then he recalled the flicker of interest in Prince Tikiri's eyes when Julietta's name had come up during that first conference on the Mutu Vella hill . . . and the instinctive rivalry between him and the prince the very first time their eyes met. And Julietta's inner withdrawal.

Reasoning it all out he became convinced that his only recourse was to marry Julietta at any cost. He would never, never let her belong to anyone else. 'No man takes what is mine with impunity.' The de Albergaria motto kept hammering in his head. He had just turned twenty-one. He had already waited too long. Why had he waited this long? It was not because of Julietta's reticence alone.

The vision of *a mae*, his mother, rose in answer. He saw her face, vivid in beauty, the long, dark hair, the rosy skin, the exquisite bones, the sparkling aquamarine eyes brimming with love. He heard the tenderness in her voice as she called him *mey pequeno bebe*, my small baby or *mey amar*, my love, and

243

felt the comfort of her body. The images were so real they brought tears to his eyes. Then, Julietta's face suddenly began to alternate with his mother's, so alike that they seemed the same person, shuttered on and off. The images jarred loose the ancient grief he had stifled because a de Albergaria never demonstrated feelings or responses. A sob escaped him. Placing his elbows on the table, his head in his hands, his shoulders shaking, the dry sobs he had stifled years ago when he saw his mother on her bier for the last time broke loose, but even today the tears would not flow.

A waxen face, a stiff figure in a shroud, suddenly impersonal, the dead cheek cold to my lips, the once warm skin, parchment. Where is my a mae? Who is this imposter lying on a bier? What would her breasts feel like if I laid my head on them? I must shut out this ghoulish, obscene creature from my vision, from my whole life, if I am ever to be happy again. I must for ever resist the feelings I had for a mae because they are a monster that turned to rend me.

So he had remembered his mother's physical image, but shut out the love. So he had held back from the pursuit of Julietta. Now, all that was over. His dry weeping subsided, left him completely drained, as if his entire being had been closed up in a barrel and shaken silently as a physician shakes a medicine mixture. He reached inside his tunic, took out a handkerchief. Staring into space, he wiped his sweaty face.

He had been right all along. Love was indeed anguish and betrayal, at least by the enemy Death who cheats two people who love each other unless their love first becomes a cheat. He hated Prince Tikiri, with a passion that came from the depths of his being.

At that moment, a single peremptory knock sounded on the door of the room. He knew that knock. He leapt to his feet and was not surprised when the door creaked open and Captain Oliveira stood framed at the entrance, his big, burly figure almost filling it. He was dressed for battle, leather thigh greaves above flaring, black breeches and armour covering the white slashed doublet. His bald head shone in the lampglow as he stepped into the room. 'You sent for me, lieutenant?' The sharp

244

blue eyes did not seem surprised or upset at being summoned so early in the morning.

Fernao saluted. He was connecting Captain Oliveira's obvious preparedness to move with the so-called exercise and the twenty-four-hour state of readiness. Suddenly, he was convinced that Captain Oliveira had known of the princes' plans. How? Through whom? He set the questions aside to reply. 'Yes, Sir. Thank you for coming. But I have just received some urgent news.'

'Sit down and give it to me.' Captain Oliveira straddled the settle opposite the desk.

'I have just had a visit from Aisha Raschid, Captain.'

'This morning?' The thin eyebrows shot up again, the burly frame tightened. 'What did she want? A lusty young Portuguese to screw her ... uh ... right royally?'

Fernao knew his captain well enough to realize that the frivolity was a cloak that hid his feelings. 'Not this time, Sir. I'm certain that the lady, being in *purdah*, would expect to perform such rites with her privates in private.'

'Cheeky bugger, aren't you?' The captain relaxed again. 'Well, I'll let that pass. What do the Frenchies say, nobles oblige ladies with the chivalrous malady.' He deliberately mispronounced the French, but there was a note of awe in his voice as he named the dread disease Cristoforo Colombo had brought back from the New World. 'Why the blue tits don't you get on with your story?'

Fernao recounted all that Aisha Raschid had told him, and when he had done, the captain stretched his legs, clasped his palms behind his head and stared at the wooden ceiling. Fernao became aware of his high body odour. The crash of waves against the ramparts, interspersed with vivid flashes of lightning, intruded upon the sudden stillness of the room. 'It seems as if the Great King may be kicked out,' he stated. 'We must make sure that only someone favourably inclined to us and our trading rights sits on that throne in Jaya.' He grinned. 'Good thing we're ready to march.'

In a moment of insight, Fernao stared at his superior, who was now smiling broadly. A couple of unexplained absences alone from the fort, a word here, a suggestion there, flashed across his mind. This martinet who had seemed so much on the surface in all things, concerned only with military matters, had been quietly negotiating alone and behind everyone's back with Prince Bhuvaneka, the weakest link in the chain of succession, the ambitious man they could manipulate most easily. Incredible. One never knew!

Captain Oliveira, still smiling broadly, echoed his own conclusion. 'You never know, do you?' He sprang to his feet. 'Have two troops of artillery with their cannon and two companies of infantry assemble immediately. We march on the Jaya capital.'

CHAPTER 21

Friday, 25 March 1524

Realizing that my father was serious, my throat suddenly ran dry. Not to be outdone, however, my answering smile was careless.

'Have the six musketeers advance on foot immediately behind us to back us up,' my father commanded Captain Jagat. 'We must act quickly so as not to upset the timing of Prince Tikiri's plan.'

'A fight, a fight, I'm going to see the fight at last.' Prince Deva Raja was clapping his hands. I could have kicked his little behind.

The musketeers dismounted and ran forward, their weapons gleaming dully. 'Advance ahead of us almost to the end of the archway,' my father commanded them. 'Leave space for the prince and me to ride through, then get your muskets ready to fire. Follow us once we ride past you.' He turned his head alertly at a commotion behind us.

Rama pricked up his ears and I swivelled him around. Our men were glancing backwards at a roar of voices. A crowd of men was approaching, chanting slogans.

I caught the words 'Kill them!' Kill whom? Our tight-packed column? My stomach tightened. My cavalrymen were tense. Could we be opposed by enemy at the front and the rear? Could the Great King have outsmarted us?

Suddenly I identified a slogan. 'Maya Dunne *jayawewa!*' *Jayawewa!* May he triumph, the traditional Sinhala cry of support. The crowd was for us!

My father's fine dark eyes glinted in a sudden smile. 'It is the people of Jaya,' he observed, a rare emotion in his deep voice. 'They are Sinhala Buddhist patriots, joining our ranks uninvited.'

The roar of voices was almost deafening now. Then voices arose to hush the clamour. The roar subsided. Soon a great stillness hung upon the air, disturbed only by the harsh cawing of crows circling above and the scrape of hooves as my father's mount turned to face the newcomers.

'The Great King plans to murder our three princes!' a voice bellowed. 'We, the Sinhala Buddhists of the city of Jaya, will not permit it. We want a ruler who will preserve the purity of our race, defend our language, our customs and our Doctrine. Make way there, soldiers, for this is no longer your fight but that of the people.'

My cavalrymen parted like mud before the ploughshare as the people pushed through, led by a bare-chested giant of a Sinhala, weaponless. His long black hair hung loose to the shoulders, his broad olive-skinned face was set in pleasant lines, the large dark eyes gentle. He was followed by a great crowd of Sinhala, most of them bare-chested also. They carried an assortment of weapons, swords, spears, knives, hatchets, scythes, axes, but they all had two things in common: fury and purpose.

The giant stopped in front of my father, lifted a gaze to him that I could only count as noble.

'Who are you?' my father quietly inquired.

'I am Dharma,' the man replied, his voice deep and resonant.

'Are you the leader of these people?'

'For their present purpose, yes.'

My father's eyebrows rose. 'You are not one of their regular leaders?'

'No, Prince. I normally take no part in the affairs of men. But I learned yesterday that the Great King had planned to kill you and your two brothers. That is totally against all Sinhala *charlithraya*, traditions, so I summoned the people last night to be ready to march on the palace at dawn today.' His teeth were very white and even when he smiled.

'How did you learn of the plot to kill us?'

'How did you, lord?' Dharma was laughing now; neither he nor my father could betray their sources.

A puzzled expression crossed my father's face. 'What do you do normally?' he demanded.

'I am a scholar. Men might even call me a philosopher.'

'A philosopher leading men to violence?' My father echoed my bewilderment.

248

'Certainly, Prince. What better quest for a philosopher than a cause? And what better effect for a just cause than violence to establish it?'

'But you are personally unarmed.'

'Violence is more than physical action, lord. It is a state of mind. Each of us here acts according to his *kharma*.'

It takes a Sinhala to be spouting philosophy before a violent fight, I reflected. But I was impatient for action and anxious to safeguard my timing for the assaults from the other three gates. My first major military plan had to mesh and work.

My father made up his mind. 'All right, Dharma, what do you propose?'

'Your life and that of your son are more precious than mine,' Dharma began.

'I doubt it,' my father interrupted with quiet sincerity. 'I certainly doubt it. But please proceed.'

Dharma acknowledged the tribute with a nod of his great head. 'Will you let us, the people, handle this our way?'

My father eyed him questioningly. 'Only on condition that the Great King is not harmed.'

'You have my assurance on that, lord.'

'Very well then.' My father backed his mount and I followed suit. 'Captain Jagat, return Prince Deva Raja to his friends.'

Captain Jagat handed the bellowing prince to one of his troopers. 'I want to see the fight,' the boy screamed.

Dharma turned to the huge crowd he had brought with him. 'Shout your slogans when I raise my hands!' he commanded. 'Till then, I want absolute silence.' He certainly had a grip on the men. He cupped his hands and turned towards the entrance. 'You loyal Sinhala guards, stop skulking and come to the ramparts!' he shouted. 'Listen to the voice of the people.'

I watched, fascinated, as a murmur of voices arose from the ramparts and was followed by calls and shouts. A round black head appeared above the left rampart wall, then another, followed by one on the right. Soon the walls were crowded with heads of various shapes and sizes, peering over the top without offering us a target. The sight was somewhat comical after all the tension; they looked like a bunch of turtles ready to withdraw their heads at the slightest sign of action.

249

'They have no heart for their purpose,' my father commented drily.

'Nor they have,' Dharma agreed, then raised his voice to a shout. 'We are coming in now, the two princes with us. Lay down your arms, comrades, for if you offer the slightest resistance, the people will tear you limb from limb.' He stood there tall and proud, arms akimbo, gazing fearlessly at the defenders.

'This is General Ratna, commander of the palace guards regiment.' The voice came booming out of the right sentry tower. 'The princes and the people are welcome. We will offer no resistance, but we are soldiers of the Sinhala army, not defeated mercenaries, so we shall not lay down our weapons but shall join you as brothers in arms.'

'Bravely spoken, General,' Dharma responded. He turned to face us. 'I shall go in first with the people following. Please be good enough to let us take the lead on this occasion, Prince, so that history may say that this was a victory of the people.'

My father nodded, bright-eyed. We backed our horses to make more room. Dharma raised his hands and the chanting started again, rose, swelled to a crescendo . . . 'Maya Dunne, *jayawewa*! . . . Maya Dunne, *jayawewa* . . . Maya Dunne, *jayawewa*!'

Through a mist in my own eyes, I noticed that my father's had also misted. Hundreds of smiling faces were lifted towards us as the people drew close. My father raised his hands high above his head, palms together. Dharma pointed towards the entrance and started marching forward. The crowd seethed after him, shouting, hands reaching to us in greeting. Someone took up the old marching song of the Sinhala '*Anthara, Veithura* . . .' Another raised the ancient Lion Flag on a standard. Waving above the roar of the crowd, the proud golden lion rampant on a scarlet field swept past us into the dark archway.

Finally the pressure of the crowd eased. My father lowered his hands, grasped his reins. 'Come, Prince.' He eased his bay into the thinning crowd, smiling back at the grinning faces.

We rode beneath the gloom of the great granite archway and into the sunlight beyond. The familiar avenue of trees stretched

250

before me, but it was now packed with people marching relentlessly on the palace.

Dharma appeared, pushing his way back. He came up on my father's right as we reined in our mounts. The great man reached out to my father's stirrup, touched the sandalled foot, then raised his hand to his lips in a gesture of humble submission. 'The *devas* guard you, Prince.'

My father was obviously as surprised as I was. 'Where are you going?' he inquired.

'Back to my meditation.' Dharma smiled, his black eyes gentle. 'My task is done. Now it is up to the people and to you.' He paused, his face suddenly grave. 'I beg you to ensure that this tree of victory I have helped you plant today bears good fruit. You are known to be a true Sinhala patriot, to treasure our race, our language, our customs and our religion above your life. You are a prince who believes in honour and feels for the people of our country. If you fail us, I shall be the first to rise against you.'

Eye to eye, they stared at each other through the morning sunlight but there was no challenge in Dharma's gaze, only a plea, nor was there pride in my father's, merely a promise. They nodded in acknowledgement, two men tall above the milling crowds. Dharma raised his hands to his forehead, the palms together, in our traditional greeting. My father responded. To my surprise, his hands were at the forehead level he would use for a superior. My eyes suddenly prickled.

Dharma walked away, whence he had come.

Friday, 25 March 1524

When the Great King came striding into her chamber, shoes clacking over the floors of white mountain crystal, Queen Anula did not have to glance at his face to know that something was seriously amiss. The white and gold room furnished in creamy satinwood was her own private place and she had established that clearly from the start of their marriage, though with the appearance of humble submission.

As she rose from making obeisance to him, she observed that

251

his heavy, wrinkled face was drawn, but the white hair and beard were neatly combed and he was gorgeously turned out in a white silk *dhoti* and lace-fronted shirt, a red velvet waistcoat held at the neck with a gold clasp. His shoes were of gold cloth, his belt was jewelled. A slurping, snoring, old man had been turned into magnificence by clothes and a barber. No, it was neither the barber nor the clothes that had effected the transformation. An innate, regal dignity had re-emerged at a time of crisis.

'B-bad news!' the king exclaimed. He paused, listening. 'Can you not hear them?'

Now she heard the distant roaring and fear clutched at her. 'What is it, lord?'

'The p-people of Jaya have risen against us. They have surrounded the p-palace b-building and are d-demanding that we give ourselves up.'

She stared at him wild-eyed. 'What about your guards, General Ratna?' The truth hit her. 'You said your guards were loyal,' she screamed hysterically. 'Where are they? What has happened?'

'They were n-not loyal,' he replied simply. 'We were m-mistaken.'

'What about Lord Eka and Lord Kandura?'

'Lord Eka cannot be f-found. Lord K-kandura is in our audience chamber, helpless.'

She calmed down, trying to think clearly. 'The *parangi*!' She declared. 'The *parangi* promised to protect us.'

'We cannot get a m-messenger through. And if we d-did, it would be too late.'

'What d'you mean too late?' She held back a violent urge to swear at him.

He straightened to his full height, towering over her. 'Anula, listen to me,' he commanded gently, dropping the royal plural. 'As I told you, the palace is surrounded by the people of Jaya who have risen in support of my son, Maya Dunne.' Strangely, he was not stammering any more. 'You can hear them chanting "Maya Dunne, *jayawewa*." If you listen closely, you will discern an occasional Wijayo *bungawewa*, meaning may Wijayo be

252

destroyed. It has taken their action for me to realize the error of my ways, but I see it all very clearly now and I do not blame them or my son, only myself.' He paused, looking down at her with love in his eyes.

At that moment, she hated him as she had never hated anyone before.

'You and I had two good years together,' King Wijayo continued. 'They have brought us more happiness than many people know in a lifetime. Let us go out together, face the mob with dignity and offer them our voluntary exile. We can live in peace in my country mansion, where you and our son will never know want. Together, always together as man and wife, if never more king and queen.'

She stared at him incredulously. Could he be in his right mind? Did he not even suspect the truth? In her eyes, he was already stripped of his kingship and all that remained was just another wrinkled old man unable to grasp the reality of his age. 'You fool!' she hissed up at him. 'You poor, doddering, silly old fool.' She shook her head in disbelief.

He stared at her as if she had struck him in the face.

'Don't you know that you are nothing without a crown to distinguish you?' she pressed on. 'What would I do stuck in your cobweb of a family mansion, alone with you? Why, if that were what I wanted, I could choose any lord in the realm.' Her voice rose to a shriek. 'You are no longer the Great King in name, not even in shame. Get out!'

He continued staring at her, like a great wounded animal, but she felt not a trace of pity for him, only bitterness, contempt and a desire to escape from the danger surrounding her. She cared about nothing else. Even her son could be looked to later.

'I shall find my own salvation,' she screamed. 'Get out of here, you sonofabitch, and don't drag me down with you.'

The Great King's eyes brimmed with tears, but he held them back with strange strength.

'We regret we d-did not understand your t-true feelings,' he observed, very quietly. His stammer and his dignity had returned. He paused, eyeing her with sudden coldness. 'You are, however, still addressing the Great K-king of Lanka.

Remember to d-do so with respect. Otherwise, our last act as sovereign will b-be to have you executed.' He held her respect by sheer majesty before turning on his heel and striding out of the chamber.

Friday, 25 March 1524

Unable to sleep after her talk with Menika, Julietta had performed her ablutions early. Now Menika helped her don a frilly pink morning dress. It had a V-neck, wasp-waist and full skirt, which her looking-glass told her showed off her slender figure to perfection. She was touching up her eyes with *kohl* when she heard the trumpets sound. She paused, startled. Her heart started beating faster.

Menika caught her tension. 'The sound of trouble, little Missy?' she inquired solicitously.

'Yes. That was assembly for an emergency alert.' Julietta laid down the *kohl* stick and walked through the door of the bedchamber into the small living room. She raised the little latch of the peep-hole and stared outside.

The barely risen sun cast the long shadow of the central tower across the parade ground. A westerly breeze was sending the lowering white clouds scudding across the sky, leaving patches of blue in their wake. Dressed in red tunics and white pantaloons, men were pouring out of their quarters into the barrack square, where their commanders were barking out orders. Musketeers wearing leather bandoliers raced for the armoury. Gunners started rolling out the big cannon with a thunderous squeaking, clanking and thudding. Their mates wheeled out barrows containing cannon balls to the assembly point, where wagoners were hitching up horses. It was a scene of well-ordered rush, each part of the play enacted separately to be moulded into the tight single scene that would be the marching column.

She noted the tough looking faces of the men. A bearded giant with hair flaming red beneath his metal helmet was actually laughing with delight at the prospect of action at last. She could almost see the vivid blue eyes of a slender, blond gunnery officer startling against the tanned skin, as he directed his men to bring their cannon into position.

She saw Fernao emerge from the tower into the silver grey light of the parade ground. His slim, tall body in the white uniform was accented by leather body armour and thigh-greaves. Though so young, he carried himself with authority. As she distinguished the fine, sensitive features beneath the incongruous iron helmet, she knew he was riding out to danger. Supposing he never came back? The thought stabbed through her. Suddenly her anxiety for Prince Tikiri faded into the background to be replaced by fear for Fernao trembling in her stomach.

She made up her mind instantly. She simply had to wish Fernao godspeed. She called for Menika. 'Tell my *o pai* I shall be back shortly.'

Menika smiled her approval. 'May your heart find life,' she murmured. 'Here, don't forget your handkerchief.' She proffered the white lace handkerchief scented with jasmine, then opened the brown teakwood front door for Julietta.

'Thank you, *a mae*.' Tucking the handkerchief inside the cuff of her dress, Julietta stepped into the pale morning sunlight.

He must have had the same thought, for he turned towards her quarters and their eyes met almost as she took her first step.

Captain Oliveira strode up to Fernao, who said something to him. They both glanced in Julietta's direction. She smiled at Fernao and nodded, signalling that she wished to speak to him. He turned his head to excuse himself, then came striding towards her with that springy step, rising on the balls of his feet, she had always admired.

'You have ten minutes in which to say goodbye!' Captain Oliveira called out, loud enough for her to hear.

She stood in the sunlight, awaiting Fernao. She was still in love with Prince Tikiri, her romantic dream, but she could no longer ignore the fact that Fernao had her deepest affection.

Then he stood tall before her, his sensitive face serious, the ice-blue eyes searching. She sensed a wound in him since last night. Was it the thought of impending action? Unable to hold his glance, she blushed, dropped her eyes.

255

'You are fairer than the morning sunlight,' he said softly.

She did not know how to answer him in this vein. 'You are going into battle, Fernao?'

'We are marching out, possibly to battle.'

'May the Blessed Virgin guard you. I had to see you before you go. Was it shameless of me? I don't care. Where are you going?'

'To Jaya.'

Her pulses quickened. 'What has happened?'

His gaze suddenly changed from an outpouring of love to watchfulness. 'General Prince Maya Dunne and his son, Prince Tikiri, are probably attacking the palace at this very moment to overthrow the Great King and seize power.' He smiled grimly, seemed to be watching her more intently now. 'We want to be on the scene to protect our interests.'

'Aren't you going to protect whatever is right, Fernao?'

'There's a difference between who is right and what is right,' he countered. 'It would seem that the Sinhala are unable to determine which of them is right, so we shall have to act in our own best interests.'

Suddenly emotional about the whole situation, she merely gazed at him wide-eyed.

'Are you afraid that we might kill your lover?' he demanded, sudden harshness in his normally gentle voice.

'What lover? I don't have a lover.'

His mouth twisted into a bitter smile. 'What about Prince Tikiri?'

For the first time with Fernao Julietta felt defensive. 'Prince Tikiri was never my lover.'

'That's not what people say. It would appear that I have been foolishly wasting my time with another man's sweetheart.'

Hurt brought with it a gust of anger. 'How dare you say such things? What d'you take me for, a slut? I won't stand for it.'

She saw his pain deep in his eyes before he made to turn away and leave and in a flash she knew that his hurt concerned her more than her own. 'I'm sorry, Fernao,' she called. 'Please don't leave like that. Prince Tikiri was never my lover, nor was I ever his sweetheart. I don't know what people have been saying, but he was my girlhood companion and yes, I fell in love with him because he was the one person who stood by me when I was an outcast in the palace. You could never fully understand that because you are of royal birth and no one holds you less than the dust.'

Fernao had paused. She noted his blank reaction with dismay, but plunged on. 'Since he is a solitary person, Prince Tikiri may have loved me too. We certainly declared our love for each other one day three years ago, but we never met again. It was as if he had suddenly disowned me. I don't mind admitting that it hurt, oh yes, it hurt.'

His face began to relax. He probed her eyes for truth. Finally, he nodded silently. 'Why did you keep seeing me if you loved the prince?' he demanded hoarsely.

'Why did you come to see me just now if you thought I loved him, Fernao?'

He stared at her, stunned by the question. 'I guess ... I guess ... ' he floundered.

'So do I, Fernao. So do I. Prince Tikiri befriended the hurt child in me, but you befriended the woman. I want you to know that before you leave.'

'I do love you, Julietta.' His eyes were melting, tender, vulnerable.

A hand flew to her mouth. At that moment, she wished she could tell him that she loved him too, but all that she could bring out in a whisper to cover the inadequacy was, 'I'm so glad, Fernao ... so glad.'

'Time's almost up, Lieutenant!' It was Captain Oliveira's voice bringing them back to reality.

On an impulse, Julietta fished out her white lace handkerchief from her cuff. 'And here is my favour, Sir knight. Wear it when you ride to battle.'

His breath caught. 'Proudly,' he declared and tucked the handkerchief into the neck of his doublet.

Had the gesture been a mistake? If so, it was too late now. 'Come back safe, Fernao. May God, Jesus, the Virgin Mary and the saints guard you.'

'And you, my Julietta.' He stood to attention, saluted. 'Your

257

knight begs his lady's leave to depart and slay dragons.'

She knew that light-heartedness was the only way now. Fernao had set the example. 'You have our leave, most noble knight.'

She watched his slim figure turn and thought: God preserve my Tiki-tiki too, for he is not dragon, but a gentle prince. Was I wrong to give my favour to another man? She half-regretted the impulsive act.

CHAPTER 22
Friday, 25 March 1524

As we rode in, the red roofs of the palace buildings, splashed by sunlight, appeared through the branches of trees. We could see the people more clearly now, surging along the long avenue towards the palace and across the green parklands. They were dressed in blues and greens, reds and whites, some of them bare-chested. I could not help a momentary qualm, wondering whether we were right to allow these popular forces to be unleashed, especially without a leader. After all, this was mob violence, however noble the cause.

As my father and I trotted side by side along the avenue leading to the palace beneath a mosaic of sunlight and shadow from the overhanging branches of the *na* trees, I recalled the day it all began just over three years ago, right here from the Jaya palace. My grandfather rode with us then.

The roaring of the crowd increased, but it seemed to be spreading lengthwise along the boundary walls. My father was the first to observe what was happening. 'Dear *devas*, they are looting the Treasury and the barns!' He drew his sword and spurred his bay forward.

The clatter of hooves ensured us clear passage, and a quick glance through the trees showed the crowd spreading closer to the Treasury. 'Quick, men, through the gardens!' I shouted to my escort. 'Stop the looting at all costs.' My heart beating louder, I dug my heels into Rama's flanks.

The Royal Treasury, barns and storehouses were in a separate compound adjoining the palace building. Some of our former champions had already begun to stream back from their adventure, most of them laden with loot, jewellery, coins, packages which they laughingly displayed to their comrades. One of the looters, a lean, tough-looking Sinhala with a scar running down his face, shouted to an approaching friend, 'Must give these to the old lady and hurry back for more!' At his words the other man began to scuttle across the grass towards the Treasury. 'Go and take, *machan*. There is plenty for all of us,' the looter shouted gleefully after him.

I realized then that the criminals and vagabonds of Jaya, intent on their own foul purposes, had deliberately mingled with Dharma's patriots.

The great wooden entrance gates of the palace loomed ahead of the flying hooves of my father's horse. I noticed with relief that they were still closed. A crowd milled around them shouting slogans. With Dharma gone, no man among them had the courage to violate the royal precincts.

Ahead of me, my father had ground his steed to a halt. He stood on his stirrups and raised a hand for silence. The leaders of the crowd started to hush the mass of men. Within seconds an eerie silence filled the air, broken by the grumbling of mynah birds and the thuds and crashes of buildings under attack.

'Hear me, Sinhala patriots!' my father cried. 'Your work is done, your object nobly achieved. Thanks to your help, there is no resistance left that we cannot cope with. My two brothers, Prince Bhuvaneka and Prince Raigam, and my nephew, Prince Vidiye, will be here any moment now. We shall decide on a succession fit for the Sinhala people. Order your comrades to cease their looting, return to your homes and await word which we shall spread by beat of tom-tom tonight. Go now in peace and may the *devas* guard you all.'

A stooped old man, the skin of his bare chest wrinkled, stepped forward. He turned to face the crowd, his white hair fluttered by a sudden breeze. 'We are patriots, my comrades,' he quavered. 'Not looters. Let us do as the Lord Prince bids us and stop those robbers, for otherwise history will recall this heroic event not as an act of liberation but as Wijayo *ba kolla*, the spoiling of Wijayo.'

'Your troops and the decent folk here can handle the looting,' my father stated to me. 'Let us enter the palace and face what we must do.' I could see that he had no stomach for the job either, for he added, 'A patriot is like a surgeon wielding a knife to cut

260

his own limb to save the rest of his body from decay.'

I would never forget those words.

A sudden thunder of hooves from both directions announced the arrival of my two uncles and Prince Vidiye, who rode up fast, a superb horseman in perfect balance with his mount, his great frame well placed in his saddle. His enormous eyes were sparkling with excitement.

I was selected to demand entrance and I urged Rama gently forward, turned at the gates and rapped on them with the hilt of my sword. 'Open up!' I cried.

The gates creaked slowly open. The Great King's three sons, Prince Bhuvaneka in the centre, Prince Raigam on his right, my father on his left, rode slowly through, Prince Vidiye and I following.

It was a solemn moment, another moment in history. We clip-clopped past saluting guards and bowing attendants. We entered the great paved courtyard which in its short span of years had never seen men bent on such a purpose.

Grooms rushed up and held our horses' heads. As we dismounted, the chief attendant, dressed in white, approached and made obeisance.

'The Great King awaits you in the audience hall, my lords prince,' he stated. 'He is pleased to grant you audience.'

So my grandfather is attempting to placate us, I reflected fiercely, as we made our way to the audience hall. Under no circumstances can we let him remain on the throne. He has betrayed the country, threatened our traditional line of succession and plotted to have his three sons assassinated. They would have left their blood within these walls today if his plan had succeeded. All this for a young woman with whom he has become infatuated! He is a cancer that must be removed from the body politic. I imagined how he would plead and was filled with disgust.

The palace verandahs, usually so full of life even at this early hour, were deserted. Clearly the sycophantic courtiers, noble-men and princes were keeping to their quarters, awaiting the right person to whom they could pay homage.

The great double doors of the audience hall were open, its

261

flares and tapers lit. Through a gap between my father and Prince Bhuvaneka, I noticed that the hall too was deserted. Then my eyes focused on the platform. The Great King, dressed in white *dhoti* and red waistcoat, was seated on his throne, the golden crown on his head, the royal sceptre in his right hand. Standing behind the king and to his right was the tall, ungainly figure of a man dressed in blue whom I recognized as Lord Kandura, the arch plotter and assassin to be. At least the Great King has one fitting companion, I thought angrily.

As we all sank into instinctive obeisance, I reflected grimly on the customs ingrained in our Sinhala race. Even our executioners make obeisance to a condemned man before chopping off his head. Decent people obey law, custom and tradition, so they extend proper respect and good manners to the guilty even while punishing them.

We approached the platform and paused. I received my first shock. Instead of a begging, pleading grandfather, I found a Great King seated calmly on his throne, the left leg slightly bent, the right leg partly extended, in total majesty. I knew a moment of awe.

My eyes flickered to Lord Kandura. He stood stiffly to attention, looking straight ahead, I could not tell at whom or what because of his squint.

Silence reigned in the chamber save for the hiss of flares, the resin particularly acrid to my nostrils. No one could speak until the Great King granted permission, so we stood there before the once doddering old man who had been transformed into a proud monarch, awaiting his command.

He made full use of the silence to impress his regal presence upon us before he spoke.

'Being guilty of many crimes in your eyes, P-princes, we shall n-not commit the ultimate sin of repetition.' His voice was deep and strong. Never having seen him thus before, I felt a pang for what might have been. 'We know which of our actions you have f-found most abhorrent. We acknowledge and regret most of them. You are in the p-position of judges today. What p-penalty do you seek to impose on us?'

'We are humble subjects who have no power to impose

penalties on their sovereign lord,' Prince Bhuvaneka observed. 'We three are also children who may not seek reprisals against a parent. We beg you, having judged yourself, to impose the punishment on yourself, as the only competent authority to do so in this realm.'

The Great King smiled sadly. 'Ever the c-cunning one, p-prince Bhuvaneka,' he observed. A sigh escaped him, but he was still smiling. 'We hereby abdicate our throne, appointing you as our successor.' He shook his head slowly and, having just abdicated the royal plural, reverted to the singular. 'I would have p-preferred that you killed me rather than leave me to f-face a life of shame and regret.'

'You, your queen and her son, may remain in your quarters as long as you desire, until you have made other suitable arrangements,' Prince Bhuvaneka continued. 'As to the succession, we shall let the Council of Nobles decide how and by whom Lanka shall be ruled in future.' He turned to Prince Raigam. 'Anything you wish to add, Prince?'

'No.'

'You, Prince Maya Dunne?'

My father stepped forward. 'There is one other person here who cannot escape our judgement and sentence.' He flung a hand towards the silent figure standing behind the throne. 'You, Lord Kandura, are accused of being the instrument of the Great King and his queen to assassinate us. Are you guilty or not guilty?'

'Guilty, my lord,' Lord Kandura replied in a deep, dry voice, still staring somewhere ahead.

'What of Lord Eka?'

'He is guilty too.'

'Where is he?'

'He fled the palace this morning without telling me, lord.'

'You realize that you face the extreme penalty in view of your confession of guilt?' My father's voice was sharp.

'Certainly, lord. I gambled and lost again. I hope it will be for the last time.'

'We might defer sentencing this man until later,' my father suggested. 'He may give us useful information.' He glanced at the Great King. 'What arrangements do you propose for Her Majesty, the former queen, Sir?'

A cynical chuckle escaped King Wijayo. 'As you well know, the queen was always capable of making her own arrangements. When I last spoke to her, she assured me she would look after her own safety. At present all I know is that she has vanished.'

'We shall track her down and bring her back to you.' My father's voice faltered as the truth dawned on him. For my part, I felt sick at the thought of my grandfather being used and abandoned by a scheming woman.

'I doubt that you will find her, Prince. I very much doubt that she will re-emerge where you would have the power to apprehend her. As for me, I pray you not to inflict upon me the sentence of a living death by restoring her to me, for that is what it would be if I clasped that viper to my bosom again.' So saying he placed the royal sceptre on its stool and slowly removed the glittering crown.

Friday, 25 March 1524

Aisha Raschid was surprised when her husband announced his presence in her chamber so soon after his journey to the Jaya palace. He was seated on his favourite divan, sweating profusely but chomping away at a sweetmeat, when she entered and knelt to him. She sat opposite him in silence and waited for him to speak.

'Well, wife, I have returned from Jaya with my mission accomplished,' he stated grandly.

'Tell me all.'

He quickly brought her up to date with the events that had taken place in Jaya that morning. 'And I passed the *parangi* detachments heading for the capital on my way back, so I knew you had as usual fulfilled your own task admirably.'

She had listened to the story with growing apprehension. 'Did you get through to Prince Maya Dunne to warn him?' she demanded.

'No.' Abdul spread out his palms. 'It was too late. I know you don't have a great deal of respect for my character in an emergency, but at least give me credit for brains.' His calm was a challenge.

'Yes, I do know that you have brains,' she replied, surprised at her own meekness.

'I realized that our best course of action was to appear uninvolved.' Abdul Raschid stated. 'After all, I had to remember our principal object.'

'To do away with the Great King,' she replied slowly.

'Exactly. So I steered clear of the palace.'

She looked at her husband with an unusual respect. 'You are wonderful,' she declared sincerely.

'Thank you.' Her praise seemed to give him a new dignity. 'Oh, by the way, Prince Maya Dunne has twenty-four musketeers, armed with *parangi* muskets.'

She blanched. 'Muskets? Were they stolen from the *parangi* fort?'

'No such luck, wife. They were secretly manufactured in Sita Waka.' He nodded at her consternation. 'Our *goondas* must have bungled the job when they killed the metal-worker, Kodi.'

'But how?'

'As you know, the *goondas* were not supposed to kill Kodi, merely to confirm the information that our spies had brought us about his secret experiment, by torture if necessary, but they did their job too well and fled when Prince Tikiri and his escort suddenly rode up that night. Then Kodi's son sold the business immediately afterwards, and left Mutu Vella; we thought he acted out of despair at his father's brutal death. Well, we were wrong.'

Light dawned on Aisha. 'You mean, the son already knew the secret of manufacturing a musket from his father and went to Sita Waka to set up a factory?'

'Yes, Prince Maya Dunne must have set it up in some fastness in the mountains.'

'We must improve our spy system in Sita Waka.'

'I have already set that in motion.'

If Sinhala and *parangi* battled each other, there was still hope. She had done her work and Abdul his to prevent the disintegration of their trading empire. A surge of feeling at their unity of purpose and of gratitude for her husband suddenly swept through Aisha. He was fat and ungainly, crude and nervous, but he was indeed her husband, the father of her son. They had known many years of success and failure, elation and tribulation together. They rose or fell as a family. Today, Abdul had acted with wisdom, courage and resolve, not the least to protect her and the boy. Had she been as dutiful to him? The answer was no. She had allowed contempt for him and her domineering spirit to rule her womanhood.

The iron that had lain in Aisha's heart for years began to melt, sweeping the veils from her eyes. Abdul's glance connected with hers, recognized what was happening, softened instinctively. She thought of twin channels that had missed meeting each other for years being joined by the will of Allah. For the first time in her married life, she felt inside her womanhood the sparkle of desiring to draw her husband's manhood within her, as a symbol of a sweet, new communion.

CHAPTER 23
Friday, 25 March 1524

Held back by the slow-trundling wagons despite the need for speed, it had taken over three hours for the Portuguese column to cover the seven miles to the outskirts of the walled city of Jaya. By then, the sun was beating mercilessly down from a burnt blue sky devoid of any cloud. With the warmest season in Colombo, April, close at hand, the heat was almost unbearable. Fernao, riding a grey Arabi charger side by side with Captain Oliveira astride a bay at the head of the column, had been grateful for every patch of shade along the highway.

Yet the discomfort was diminished for Fernao because of his excitement that Julietta had given him her favour, the jasmine-scented handkerchief. He thought of a dozen romantic things he could have said to her besides, 'you are fairer than the morning air'.

All along the route, people, mostly women and children, the men being at work, had rushed out of their brick and tile homes to stare at the column. Most of them could not have seen a cannon, a musket, or so many white people in iron helmets in their entire lives.

Captain Oliveira had obviously been thinking about the future of their fort. 'This puts our Viceroy on the spot,' he declared. 'He must decide whether trade with Lanka is valuable or not. All this shit about one hundred per cent profit goes out with the buckets. If he wants to stay here and fuck, he'd better have an erect prick! I'll send him a despatch by the caravel which leaves on Saturday.'

'I'm sure you'll make the Viceroy see sense,' Fernao grinned. He raised his voice to be heard above the marching song some of the men behind had started. 'Pity you can't include some of your more . . . er . . . forceful language in it, Captain.'

'Fuck you!' Captain Oliveira grinned back. He pondered a few moments. 'Speaking of which, I'd like to know how your little farewell with *a senhora* Julietta went this morning? She's a lovely lady. Why the hell don't you marry her? Are you scared of your father? Remember she's of marriageable age and your attentions to her could spoil her prospects. Maybe your problem is that you can't get it up, but if you play fast and loose with that little lady, I'll have your balls.'

Fernao felt a spurt of anger. How dare this commoner speak to him about his private life, but discipline made him check the hot reply that rose to his lips. Then he was suddenly glad he had refrained, for after all the captain had done no more than express genuine concern for Julietta, the girl he loved.

'I appreciate your concern,' Fernao turned his head and nodded. '*A senhora* Julietta and I have been merely friends.' He paused, reluctant to unbare himself to anyone. 'Our first real exchange was when she gave me her favour this morning.' He touched the scented handkerchief.

'What the hell took you so long?' Captain Oliveira shook his head. 'You young people, I'll never understand you.' He paused, then added gruffly, 'Don't need to either, without any children of my own. By all the saints, I'd have driven 'em if I'd had 'em. All this business of platonic friendship is bullshit. I mean, it shouldn't take you three years to know you love a woman. Why . . . ' He broke off abruptly, changed tack again. 'So you told each other, I love you, this morning?'

'Yes, something like that.' Fernao stared straight ahead.

'Something like that! What do you youngsters tell each other nowadays? You stare soulfully into each other's eyes and say, "Something like that"? Incredible!'

They rode on in silence for a few moments. 'Well, I'm glad I gave you those great moments today,' Captain Oliveira finally stated. 'Like playing Cupid or something. Fancy Oliveira giving you the ten most important minutes of your life. The good God's instrument, or a marriage broker, or . . . ' his guffaw rang through the sunlit air . . . 'something like that!' He shot a quick glance at Fernao. 'Which raises the question, when are you getting married? You do intend getting married, don't you?'

'We didn't speak about marriage. The marriage broker, or the

268

good God's instrument or something like that, yelled that my time was up.'

'Son of a cannonball!' The captain laughed again. He glanced sharply in front. The leader of the scouts, a young sergeant, was trotting back towards them, 'Journey's end,' he stated.

'Journey's beginning,' Fernao replied softly. In more ways than one, he thought, for today, Friday the twenty-fifth of March 1524, marks the beginning of a new life for me. He reached up and touched Julietta's handkerchief again. I love you, Julietta, he said in his mind for the hundredth time that morning. I shall slay dragons for you on this mission. A surge of power swept through him. When I return, I shall marry you, whatever it takes.

Friday, 25 March 1524

In the Jaya palace, I was delayed in attending the conference immediately following the Great King's abdication by violent stomach pains that forced me to visit the privy in my quarters. This mission accomplished, I hastened back to the audience hall.

'Prince! Prince!' The desperate cry struck me from the verandah leading to the Great King's suite, bringing me to a halt as the King's chief attendant came rushing out, his eyes wild, tears streaming down his wrinkled cheeks, his whole body shuddering when he made obeisance.

A chill feeling seized me. 'What is it?' I demanded sharply.

He rose to his feet, still trembling, forced the words out through his panting breath. 'The G-great K-king is dead,' he croaked.

'What? Dear *devas*, when, how? Where is he?'

Wordless again, swallowing, the man pointed. 'The study,' he whispered. His teeth began to chatter.

My guts churning, I rushed down the verandah, plunged through the open door of the suite, ran across the great ante-room and paused at the doorway of the study. The windows were open, letting in bright sunlight. I glimpsed green branches and the burnt blue of the sky, caught the whistle of a bird above the splash of the fountain. Then my eyes focused on the giant figure sprawled on the white mountain crystal floor.

He lay beside his ebony desk like any other man. The Great King, my grandfather, was obviously dead. He must have suffered a stroke. Could we have caused it? How would I ever know? Questions flashed through my mind as I strode across the room and knelt beside the body. What loneliness did he know at his last moments, what disillusionment, what despair? Did he die feeling abandoned by his wife, his children, his people and even me, his grandson?

Who said there was peace and dignity in death? The Great King was no longer a figure of majesty. He had played his grand final act on the stage of life for a few minutes and departed to become a curiously twisted heap, grey hair dishevelled, face contorted. Blood had escaped from his nose and mouth. His blank staring eyeballs were popping out of their sockets in a tortured stare. He smelt of stale sweat, old age and death. Gone was all his dignity.

I reached out a trembling hand to touch his head, then noticed his neck. It was torn, abraised, streaked with blood, the livid flesh purple and red, white ligaments bared at the voicebox.

The hideous truth dawned on me like a cold, cold morning in hell. The Great King had been garotted.

Friday, 25 March 1524

The lean, cleanshaven sergeant rode up to announce that the column had reached its objective. 'The gates of the city are just round the next bend, Sir, only about three hundred yards away, but my lead scouts have returned with some important news.'

'Yes?' Captain Oliveira snapped.

'They rode ahead and found the township in disarray. Pedro, who has learnt the Sinhala language, questioned the locals. Their reports were confused, but then by the grace of the Lord, along came a very self-important official, no less a person than the head of the local town council, who had most precise information. It appears that five princes, that is the three

270

brothers, Prince Tikiri and Prince Vidiye, are in the palace and have seized power from the Great King.'

Captain Oliveira jerked in surprise. 'How did they get in? Wasn't there a fight?'

'Apparently not, Sir. The people of the city joined them by the hundreds and the guards regiments not only betrayed the Great King by letting them through but even offered their support.' He gave them details of the bloodless victory.

'Any casualties?' Fernao demanded.

'Only two,' the sergeant responded grimly. 'A guards captain, who tried to attack Prince Tikiri, was slain by the prince.' He grinned slightly. 'And the King's Treasury was partially looted before the rebel forces intervened.'

Fernao had been listening with increasing concern. 'This puts a different complexion on our operation, does it not, Sir?' he inquired.

Captain Oliveira nodded. 'Certainly does,' he replied, thinking hard. 'Are the city gates open?' he demanded.

'No, Sir. They are closed and the battlements are manned. More importantly, however, the entry bridge is crammed with people, unarmed civilians who have heard of our approach and are seated shoulder to shoulder, ready to die rather than let us proceed. I expect they hope to repeat their victory of this morning.'

'Holy mother of Jesus,' Captain Oliveira swore, then his blue eyes turned icy. 'They are certainly not going to repeat their performance with us,' he ground out. 'A few cannon balls will make them change their minds. We kill anyone who stands in our way.'

As I shall kill that bastard, Prince Tikiri, Fernao thought, gripped by a sudden ferocious power-lust.

Friday, 25 March 1524

Still kneeling beside my murdered grandfather, I quickly directed the chief attendant to compose himself and summon the guard commander, my father and uncles. As he departed, I found myself able to think. Whoever did this foul deed must

271

have entered through the window. I rose to my feet and reached the sill in a few strides. Leaning out, I searched the private courtyard. It was walled on three sides. The fountain splashed merrily in the centre, the paved walkways were bare, the green lawn devoid of life. The lovebirds and canaries in their cages, meant to awaken the king to bird-songs at dawn, were poised on their perches as if awaiting a new dawn.

I vaulted over the windowsill. Totally alert, I drew my sword and painstakingly searched every inch of the courtyard, the branches above, the inside of great bushes and even behind the great flower-pots. Not a soul was present. How could an assassin have entered? With the palace guards disorganized, it would not have been too difficult for him to have leaped over the wall and lain in wait for the opportune moment when the Great King was alone.

By the time I returned to the room, the guard commander had arrived. I directed him to have the entire palace grounds searched, but I knew it was in vain.

The princes hurried in, my father leading. They rushed to the dead figure in silence, squatted around it. Only Prince Vidiye remained standing. 'Who could have done this?' he demanded, his enormous eyes penetrating.

I suddenly gathered from his look that he considered me a suspect. 'I don't know, cousin,' I replied, realizing with a shock that I was the only one among us who had been alone and without witnesses at the time of the murder. I looked Prince Vidiye squarely in the face. 'I went to the privy and was returning to the audience chamber when the chief attendant came out saying the Great King was dead.'

'You were gone a long time for a visit to the privy, Prince,' he retorted. 'Were you by chance suffering from political indigestion?'

Anger flared within me, but I curbed the hot words that rose to my lips. 'What are you implying, cousin?' I demanded, deadly quiet.

'Leave the young man alone,' my father intervened, rising to his feet. 'We have enough problems on our hands without tearing ourselves apart with base allegations.'

'Base allegations?' Prince Vidiye questioned hotly. He pointed to the corpse. 'A king lies there dead, foully murdered. Don't you see that we will all be suspect and it will be written in history even if we escape its odium today? I'm for a fair fight, uncle, but this sort of thing is not in my makeup.'

'Nor in ours either, nephew.' I marvelled at my father's iron self-control. 'You are right to say that we should keep open minds as to who committed or instigated this foul murder. Let us take up that question when we have looked after my father's dead body in a fitting manner.'

'And destroyed any evidence meanwhile?' Prince Vidiye's large, fierce eyes were like glowing coals now. 'I came here to help you in what seemed to be a righteous cause, uncle, to force the abdication of a king whose conduct had become abhorrent to the nation. I now wonder whether I have not been trapped into helping you fulfil your personal ambitions. No, wait.' He held up a hand to silence my father. 'Let me ask your son a few questions.' He turned to me. 'Will you answer them?'

'Certainly, cousin.'

'You went out into the courtyard just now and climbed back through the window just as we arrived, right?'

'Right.'

'Did you find any evidence?' He pointed a finger at me.

'No, cousin.' I looked at the rude finger with lifted brows.

He took the hint and dropped his hand. 'You certainly had enough time out there to search for and destroy any evidence you might have left behind.'

This time cold anger left me cool and scornful. 'Is that a question or a statement?'

'Never mind. What took you so long in the privy?'

'Since when has a long call of nature become a crime?'

'I'm going to suggest something that's neither regal, nor princely, nor civilized, but necessary. If we go to your privy now, will there be evidence in the bucket that you indeed needed to spend so much time there?'

I was appalled as much by Prince Vidiye's crudeness as by the fact that absence of such grisly evidence might indeed seal my guilt in his mind, but I kept calm. 'You can carry out any

273

inspection you like, cousin, but what will it prove?'

'Enough for me to be suspicious and wary. There's no need for the inspection. I know the answer already from your face. I take back what I said about your removing evidence from the courtyard.'

'Good.' My father and I snapped out the word together.

The taciturn Prince Raigam had ignored us and remained kneeling beside his father, but Prince Bhuvaneka now rose to his feet. 'I resent your wrangling in the presence of my father's dead body,' he declared. 'Let us forget these differences and have him looked to by the morticians and laid out in State in the audience hall as if he never ceased to be the Great King.'

'You're right,' my father agreed. 'Our conduct has been unseemly.'

'One final word,' Prince Vidiye declared. 'Whomever the Council of Nobles may finally select to be the Great King, my presence here today has been to ensure that our time-honoured Arya *charlithraya*, traditions, are followed.' He eyed my father with determination. 'If you attempt to seize power, Prince Maya Dunne, I shall oppose you with every resource available to me.'

Questions swirled in my mind. What possesses Prince Vidiye? Why is he so bitter? Is he standing up for a principle, or does he fear my father because of his own ambition?

I glanced at my father. Though he had drawn himself to his full height, he still had to look up to meet the fierce eyes of his giant nephew. 'You have said a great deal today, Prince Vidiye,' he remarked soberly. 'I assure you that if I want the succession I shall take it regardless of your resources. But I intend honouring the solemn agreements that all of us made when we planned the late Great King's overthrow.' He stared at his father's dead body and for a moment his features twisted. Composing himself on the instant, he turned to me. 'Come prince,' he directed, his voice disdainful. 'Suddenly this room smells worse than the place your cousin so crudely desired to inspect.'

274

CHAPTER 24
Friday, 25 March 1524

Accompanied by the sergeant and two mounted men as escorts, Fernao and Captain Oliveira halted at the edge of a grove facing the city of Jaya.

About three hundred yards from them, the cobbled highway became a causeway, with black crows soaring over dull green swampland stretching into the distance on either side. The causeway became a bridge spanning a wide moat shimmering silver in the bright sunlight and ending abruptly at wooden entrance gates ribbed with iron, shadowed by a great archway. The heads of defenders, in close array, dotted the earthwork ramparts. A teeming mass of men, most of them barechested, dressed in red, blue and green pantaloons or waistcloths, squatted on the causeway.

'We have two alternatives,' Captain Oliveira declared. 'We can force entry, using our cannon and muskets to pound that masturbating rabble off the highway and into the water, so the crocodiles can eat their balls. Or we can stay put and allow the fuckers to jack themselves off until they starve.' He leaned forward easily in the saddle and glanced at Fernao. 'What would you do, Lieutenant?'

Fernao was caught up in the blazing urge to crush all opposition. 'We came here with a purpose, we should execute it,' he ground out.

A quizzical smile crossed Captain Oliveira's face. 'So it has finally got to you too,' he observed.

'What, Captain?' Fernao inquired defiantly.

'The power bug.' The captain paused, looked towards the entrance gates. 'How do you propose breaking through?'

'With cannon and musket, as we did in Ormuz, Calicut and the Malaccas.'

'H'mm. That might be over-kill and it could start a bloody

275

war. Don't you think a demonstration of firepower is all we need at the moment? After all, our principal object is to ensure that someone compatible with our trade requirements sits on the fucking throne.'

'You are right, Sir,' Fernao agreed reluctantly.

'Very well then, the men shall deploy as if for an assault on the gates, in a box formation for all round defence in case we are attacked. The cooks detail shall provide us with a hot meal without delay. The supply officers shall send out foraging parties and prepare for a stay of several days if need be.' He nodded towards a small barn at the opposite end of the grove. 'Headquarters shall be located inside that building. Summon the company commanders and the gunnery officers there.'

'Aye, aye, Sir!' Fernao saluted and started to turn his grey away.

'Oh, and Lieutenant, immediately after the noon meal, you and I, accompanied by a detail of six mounted men, will proceed to the palace under a white flag of negotiation.'

Friday, 25 March 1524

My father and I, still simmering over Prince Vidiye's base accusations, had barely crossed the ante-room when the guard captain came racing in. His broad features were shiny with sweat, the black moustache bristling, his expression worried. He saluted. 'Lord, the *p-parangi* have arrived.' He was stammering with excitement.

'What *parangi*?' My father demanded.

'An entire company with twelve cannon,' the captain replied, more steady now. 'They are led by their commander and his aide, Lieutenant de Albergaria.'

My stomach tightened at the mention of the man who was reported to be Julietta's friend. Though I had cast all thoughts of a life with Julietta out of my mind, I still bitterly resented her having a relationship with another man. I had known the first day I set eyes on Lieutenant de Albergaria that his path and mine would cross in violent opposition. Had the time come to settle the unspoken issue?

276

'Where are the *parangi* at this moment?' my father inquired.

'Outside the west gate of the city. The people are reported to be squatting on the causeway to prevent their gaining entry.'

'Unarmed men won't stop the *parangi*,' my father retorted. 'They'll simply blast their way through. We must get word to the people to disperse.'

'What's happening here?' It was Prince Bhuvaneka's voice.

He stood at the entrance to the study, Prince Raigam beside him, Prince Vidiye towering behind.

'Did you say that *parangi* had arrived in strength?' Prince Bhuvaneka continued. I wondered at something indefinable in his expression. He seemed more eager than disturbed.

'Yes, lord,' the captain responded. 'An entire company is outside the city, complete with twelve cannon.'

'And did I also hear you say that the people are squatting on the causeway to deny them entry?'

'Yes, lord.' He saluted and left at Prince Bhuvaneka's signal.

Prince Bhuvaneka glanced at my father. 'You are right, Prince. The *parangi* will simply blast their way through. We must avoid such bloodshed at all costs. The people must be asked to disperse.'

'How?' My father demanded sharply.

'You shall at least try? Aren't you the people's hero?' Prince Bhuvaneka's expression was suddenly bitter.

'Did you say "shall", Prince?'

Sensing an imminent confrontation, I decided to intervene, though I was almost shaking with outrage. 'The captain said that the entire *parangi* regiment is at the west gate. How dare they march into our territory! Give me leave to take my cavalry through the north and south gates and attack them on both flanks.'

'No, Prince.' My father laid a hand on my arm. 'You will be decimated if you attack them. I share your anger, but we must deal with them some other way. Meanwhile, it would appear that we face another invasion here.' He turned to Prince Bhuvaneka. 'Did I hear you right, Prince?'

Prince Bhuvaneka raised his head defiantly. 'You certainly did, General Prince Maya Dunne. We used the word "shall" as

277

befits an order of the Great King.' He was even using the royal plural.

'Who the devil appointed you?'

Sick with disappointment, I knew the answer before Prince Bhuvaneka declaimed, no less, in the firmest tones I had ever heard him use, 'The Great King named us his successor before he abdicated. You heard him. He was right, because we are indeed the heir under the Arya code. We have a sacred duty to accept the office.'

'What about our prior agreement that caused the Great King to abdicate? And what about your oath on it and on our decision that the Council of Nobles should make a final determination as to the succession, as required by our *charlithraya*, sacred tradition?'

'We hereby revoke the order to summon the Council. It is totally unnecessary.'

Betrayed! My blood was running hot, anger sweeping over me in great waves. No wonder the Sinhala had so frequently been a prey to invaders, when they could be rent apart by the personal ambitions of their leaders.

'Your plan has failed, Prince Maya Dunne.' It was Prince Vidiye speaking out of turn. 'Is not your son's offer to take on the *parangi* force added proof of your ambition to dominate the country?'

My father's smile was contemptuous. 'Prince Tikiri's desire is evidence that he is a patriot.' He bowed to Prince Bhuvaneka, his expression suddenly inscrutable. 'Your wish is my command, Great King,' he declared evenly. 'Prince Tikiri and I shall execute it together.' He flicked a glance in Prince Raigam's direction. 'Would you care to join us, Prince?'

Prince Raigam looked up, eyed my father squarely. 'With pleasure,' he asserted in quiet tones. He turned to Prince Bhuvaneka, his gaze half-mocking. 'So long as the Great King gives me leave.'

King Bhuvaneka, as he had suddenly made himself, nodded. 'You have our leave.'

I reluctantly followed my father's example, made obeisance and backed away from the ante-room.

278

'Have our horses brought to the front courtyard,' my father directed a guard captain, who saluted and hurried away.

'The dirty, rotten bastard!' Prince Raigam muttered under his breath as we reached the open verandah leading to the front entrance of the palace.

'That's a reflection on our revered mother,' Prince Maya Dunne chided, pretending outrage. 'We should have expected cunning from Bhuvaneka.'

'Why don't we take over the palace?' I demanded hotly. We stopped our discussions to return the salutes of two palace guards and an attendant.

'Don't you see the truth?' Prince Maya Dunne inquired quietly. 'Our new Great King never intended a triumvirate, or three kingdoms, or that the succession should be left to the Council of Nobles to decide. I'm sure he has been in touch with the *parangi* all along and they are here to ensure his succession. If we take over the palace, the *parangi* will intervene on his behalf and we are not ready for that. We must accept what we cannot alter, but it need not be for long. It's a sad time for the country, but what is saddest of all is that this will not be the last occasion on which the *parangi* will interfere in our affairs.'

Friday, 25 March 1524

Less than a half hour later, having galloped in silence through a city that seemed to hold mainly women and children, their anxiety hanging in the air like a pall, we brought our horses to a halt at the barred entrance gates.

The barrel-chested General Ratna walked out of the guard-house and saluted. 'You are fully briefed as to the situation, General Prince Maya Dunne, Sir?' He inquired, saluting.

'Yes. We are here to disperse the people and negotiate with the *parangi*.'

'What would you like us to do, General?'

'Maintain your present positions. Prince Tikiri's entire cavalry regiment is available to support you if necessary.'

'Good.'

Orderlies rushed up to hold our horses' heads as we dismounted. The blood of Captain Tilak, whom I slew this morning, stained the grey cobblestones. My badges of valour, I reflected dismally, and for what?

My father pointed to the sentry tower. 'I shall address the people from there,' he stated.

We climbed the rampart steps. Prince Raigam, General Ratna and I remained outside while my father entered the tower. As I looked over the battlements, the stench of the moat hit me. It lay placid, shimmering below me, the crocodiles basking in the sunlight, great tree trunks washed ashore by a flood. Black crows rode on their backs, pecking at insects on the tough hide. As I watched, the great eyelid of one crocodile opened lazily. He seemed to be winking cynically at the struggles of humankind.

The mass of people squatting on the causeway reminded me of a great catch of fish, except that the excited hum of their voices conveyed their humanity. I suddenly felt an overwhelming sense of pride in these men and gratitude for their loyalty to a cause. At that moment, I realized that *they*, not the sacred soil, were Lanka.

'Citizens, this is General Prince Maya Dunne speaking.' The heads turned when his voice boomed out of the sentry tower, then the people rose to their feet and faced the tower in a display of respect. 'I regret to announce that the Great King Wijayo, my father, having voluntarily abdicated the throne, was foully murdered an hour later in the royal suite by an unknown assassin, while his sons were in conference in the audience chamber.' He cleared a husk in his throat, while I blessed his wisdom in separating us physically from the dreadful deed. 'In accordance with the expressed desire of the Great King at the time of his abdication, my brother, Prince Bhuvaneka, has become the Great King. I want you first to give your traditional blessing to the new king, Maha Raja Bhuvaneka, *jayawewa!*'

'*Jayawewa!*' At first, the word emerged only from a few amid the ranks, then others took it up and presently the air echoed and re-echoed with the cry, 'Maha Raja Bhuvaneka, *jayawewa* ... Maha Raja Bhuvaneka, *jayawewa.*'

I wondered what the *parangi* were thinking. My eyes followed the highway, came to rest on the ugly snouts of two great cannon, placed on either side of its first bend. I then distinguished the *parangi* soldiers in red and white uniforms, with leather cuirasses and iron helmets, lining the dark groves facing the city at the edge of the swamp, caught the occasional gleam of a musket barrel. Strangely, I knew no fear, merely seething anger and a fierce determination to rid my country of these intruders.

The shouting died down. 'We have sad duties to perform, citizens of Jaya,' my father resumed. 'For we must bury our dead. You have nobly stood in the path of the invading *parangi*, for which I thank you from the bottom of my heart. But the Great King has directed me to treat with them personally. So depart now, proud in the knowledge of all you have accomplished today for our country, our *charlithraya*, our sacred institutions and our blessed Doctrine.' He paused. He must have placed his mouth against one of the bowmen's slits, for his voice carried more softly, but very clearly with not a trace of booming. 'I shall send for you when I need you again . . . some day.'

'Maya Dunne, *jayawewa* . . . Maya Dunne, *jayawewa*.' This time, the ready cry from hundreds of throats in unison rent the heavens, caused a flight of marsh birds heading towards the city to wheel away, changing direction.

Friday, 25 March 1524

The noontide sun shone fiercely on the highway but lay shredded by overhanging branches on the long iron barrels of the two cannon straddling the grey cobbles. Fernao had been inspecting their placement on foot with Captain Oliveira and Lieutenant Nantes when they heard the voice booming from the ramparts. They rushed quickly along the sheltered side of the highway to where the grove of trees ended at the swamp. Standing under cover, they listened.

Having become even more proficient in the Sinhala language during the past three years, Fernao was able to understand what was being said. 'That was General Prince Maya Dunne speaking,' he finally explained. 'The situation in Jaya has changed drastically. The Great King Wijayo has been assassinated.'

'By whom?' the captain demanded, without surprise.

'They don't know.'

'What was all the shouting about?'

'The first lot was for the new king, Bhuvaneka.'

Captain Oliveira smiled broadly. 'So Prince Bhuvaneka has succeeded to the throne? Good. What was the second round of cheering for?'

'I couldn't hear the words that preceded it, but I rather think it was for Prince Maya Dunne.'

'The people seem more for him than for the new king?'

'So it would appear, Sir.'

'What else did the general say?'

'He asked the people to disperse quietly to their homes, since he had been authorized by the Great King to negotiate with us.'

Before Fernao could go on to give details of all he had heard, he was interrupted by a great scraping, followed by clanking and squeaking. The huge gates were slowly opening. The people began moving back through them, first in a trickle, then in a stream.

'The way is clear!' Fernao exclaimed excitedly. 'Let's charge in behind them and crash into the city. The defenders will never fire on their own people.'

'Uh-huh. What if it is a trap?' A sudden inspiration made the captain's blue eyes sparkle. 'Besides, we need a little more than pushing in behind those arse-holes. Remember what your father did three years ago, Lieutenant?' He turned to Lieutenant Nantes. 'The leaders of that bunch of rabble are now at their rear, right?'

'Right.'

'Leaders need balls right, right?'

'Right.'

'Give 'em some, Lieutenant. Let 'em have two balls, one from each of those guns.'

Lieutenant Nantes saluted. 'Aye, aye, Sir!' Grinning delightedly, he ran off, shouting to his gun crews.

282

Fernao's mind tightened with the urge to display his power, especially to his opponent, Prince Tikiri. 'Why not give the leaders a salvo up their rear ends from the muskets too, since they created this situation?' Somewhere deep inside him a despairing voice inquired, What of honour? But power-lust and jealousy crushed the question.

'Good idea,' Captain Oliveira stated. 'You're developing balls, Lieutenant. You'll be your father's son yet. Only one salvo though, from six muskets. Kill too many of them and we may yet have a bloody war on our hands.'

Fernao rushed off and gave the platoon commanders their orders, then returned to Captain Oliveira.

'Let's go and watch the fucking comedy,' the captain suggested.

Sweltering in the heat, they made their way through the grove of jak-trees to the spot from which they had surveyed the fort two hours earlier. This time, the fringe of the grove was lined with musketeers, grim-looking men in their red and white uniforms. Some were barely past their teens, others were veterans, but they all seemed tough and fierce.

A sergeant began barking out orders. 'Ready! Select your targets! Aim!'

Six muskets were levelled towards the entrance gates, pointing across the swamp like talons of doom. At the other end of the sunlit swamp, beside the shimmering moat, the host of Sinhala civilians was slowly diminishing. Fernao glanced backwards. Fire, Nantes, fire, before they all escape. He was feeling a curious suspension of his inner self from the event, conscious only of a grim desire for the firing to be effective. He peered back through the trees. 'Fire!'

The flashes from the two cannon were followed by their thunder. Reverberations rolled through the grove as if from the twin puffs of smoke and made Fernao's ears sing. The harsh cawing of crows and the shrilling of frightened birds taking off arose from above him.

Fernao turned his gaze towards the entrance gates. The two cannon balls had sent the rearmost people sprawling on the highway. He could imagine the targets literally battered to death. For a single instant the entire crowd turned back to look. The lean shapes of the crocodiles that had been basking peacefully in the sun streaked for the waters of the moat and splashed in. The truth must have dawned on the remaining Sinhala, for they turned in obvious panic, began stampeding towards the open gates, their screams and cries drifting across the swamp.

'That's all the self-fuckers needed,' Captain Oliveira observed with a laugh. 'I doubt we'll have any more of that kind of shit directed against us in future. The power of the people! Bah! Give me the power of weapons any time.'

'Fire!'

The rattle of the muskets streaked across the grove like a succession of snapping firecrackers. Smoke puffs splattered the tree-line. The smell of cordite assailed Fernao's nostrils.

Across the bridge, six men had dropped like nine-pins. The screams of the wounded and the anguished cries of those struggling to escape into the safety of the city mingled with the frenzied cawing of the crows.

Fernao found himself exulting.

CHAPTER 25
Friday, 25 March 1524

My father had emerged from the sentry tower and was watching the people streaming back through the entrance gates when the thunder of the cannon followed by the whistle of cannon balls reached our ears. I gazed over the ramparts, noted the twin puffs of smoke from the *parangi* cannon, heard the great thuds beneath me. I glanced down and was stricken by the sight. Two men, clad in white pantaloons, lay flattened on the causeway near the bridge, their backs shattered, a gory mess. Four others were sprawled untidily in front of the two corpses, three of them screaming in agony. A soldier beside me vomited. The people below turned in the direction of the *parangi*, realized what had happened. Panic-stricken, they rushed towards the entrance archway, pushing and shoving to get in.

'The *parangi* are attacking!' General Ratna shouted. 'Quick, close those gates.'

'No!' my father roared. 'Leave them open. Let the people in.' I marvelled at his composure. He saw Prince Raigam looking at him inquiringly. 'Have the wounded evacuated, Prince.' My uncle nodded, rushed to the open gates, bellowing orders. My father turned to General Ratna again. 'Have your bowmen on the battlements ready to fire...' He was interrupted by the spattering rattle of muskets.

I glanced across the swamp, noted a scatter of gunsmoke drifting from the twin groves a split second before hearing the shrieks below. The *parangi* volley was deadly. Five men lay dead, face-down on the causeway, splattered with red blood, torn pink flesh streaked by white ligaments. A sixth, also face-down, floated in the moat. As I watched, a long, evil snout glided swiftly forward. One snap of huge jaws on a lifeless leg and the dead body was dragged down to the murky depths. A great writhing and splashing told of an underwater struggle for the spoils.

Sick with horror, I heard the wounded screaming with pain. A bearded man coughed up a gout of blood. A golden skinned youngster clad in a blue sarong sat staring blankly at a shattered leg.

'You fiends, I'll have your livers some day,' I screamed, forgetting all princely deportment. I turned to my father, tears of frustration prickling my eyes. Do something, I silently implored him.

'Have the dead and wounded carried in,' my father called out to General Ratna. He dropped his voice to address me. 'Get the cavalry regiment out to Sita Waka immediately.'

I looked towards the city. Hundreds of men were in flight, a rushing stream of humanity. How could I leave now? 'Why *tha* ... er Sir?' I inquired, aghast. 'Let me remain here and fight these accursed barbarians.'

'There will be no fight,' he assured me.

'How can you say that?' I demanded passionately. I pointed a desperate hand at the havoc below.

'Steady, Prince,' he warned. 'If they intended attacking the fort, they would have blasted us with all their guns. What they have just done follows their old pattern. Remember what they did three years ago? A two-gun salute to demonstrate their power.' Unusually for him, a bitter smile streaked his fine features. 'They have heard my words, so they know their man is on the throne and want to warn us that we must keep it that way.'

'You mean ... '

He nodded. 'Isn't it obvious from your uncle's reaction before he sent us out here? Having confirmed that the decision as to the succession would be taken by the Council of Nobles, notwithstanding that our father named him the successor, he changed his tune as soon as he knew the *parangi* had arrived. Assured of their support, he gave us the fanfare of his kingship. He never intended a three-king rule, merely used it as bait. He has obviously been in touch with the *parangi* behind our backs for some time now. I wish I could have borne you into a more

286

honourable family.' He paused briefly, sad. 'Hurry now. We have no time to lose. Your cavalry and the twenty-four muskets are our most valuable asset for the future.'

In a flash, I saw his wisdom. 'Are you coming with us, Sir?' A strangled scream from below made us both look downwards. The golden-skinned youngster lay on his back, eyes to the heavens, dead. The crowd was thinning, the crush had ended.

'Not immediately,' my father replied. 'I have unfinished business here with the *parangi* on orders of the Great King.'

I faced him resolutely. 'I'll send Captain Jagat with the regiment, Sir. I intend remaining here with you.'

His body went taut. 'You are defying my orders?'

'Never, Sir. Merely carrying them out. Only these were the orders you gave me as a birthday present three years ago. Remember?' My voice softened, pleading now. 'Together, from now on, always together.'

His dark eyes melted. We were of the breed that only sentiment can touch, but even sentiment would not permit tears. 'You are right, Prince. Have Captain Jagat lead your regiment through the east gate without delay, then rejoin me at the entrance. We'll face the *parangi* together.'

'Yes, Sir.' I saluted and made for the stairs.

'And Prince.'

I paused to look at my father. His eyes were haunted. 'We will indeed be together in avenging the wanton deaths, this maiming of our people.' His voice was suddenly harsh as a kiln-grate. He looked over the rampart walls at the distant groves. 'I pray we will fulfil that purpose some day.'

Friday, 25 March 1524

As he watched the last of the Sinhala disappearing into the fort, Fernao eagerly anticipated the inevitable confrontation with General Prince Maya Dunne.

Before long, he glimpsed the outline of three figures emerging through the archway into the sunshine. Even at that distance, there was no mistaking the erect carriage and proud gait of the general. On his left, with a spurt of hatred, Fernao observed a leaner, slighter version of him, Prince Tikiri. The shorter, stockier man on the general's right was Prince Raigam. The three men walked unhurriedly forward, as if strolling towards some palace event.

'Son of a fucking cannon, the buggers have still got balls,' Captain Oliveira observed softly.

Fernao felt a flash of envy. 'Well, it's the general who has them,' he responded. 'And he will dare too much one day.'

'I wonder. I really wonder. His eyes are the most intelligent of any I've seen on a man.' The captain's sideways glance was mischievous. 'His son has inherited them. He too must have the intelligence and the balls . . . uh . . . whether you like it or not, Lieutenant.'

'Touché!' Fernao responded. The thrust had been well deserved, but he did not like it.

'Since they're obviously coming to talk to us, why don't we meet them halfway? Come with me. I'll need you as interpreter. Have the musketeers cover us against the enemy bowmen on the ramparts. If it proves to be a trap, tell Lieutenant Nantes to pound the buggers to hell. I'll wait for you at the highway.'

The captain turned and began making his way through the grove. Having relayed the orders to the company commanders and sent a message to Lieutenant Nantes, Fernao joined Captain Oliveira.

As they stepped onto the sunlit highway, Fernao's heart began to beat faster and his skin was chilled beneath his dripping sweat. He felt naked and exposed. It only needed a good bowman to kill both of them. Reprisals would give no satisfaction to dead men. They matched their pace to that of the three princes, Fernao concentrating on the general. The entire earth seemed hushed, awaiting the event, while a thousand men watched from the battlements and a hundred musketeers from the groves. The cry of a marsh bird was an eerie sound.

As if by mutual understanding, the two groups came to a halt within five paces of each other. The general stood erect but easy, his right hand at his side, the left lightly on the hilt of his sword. His two companions were similarly posed.

'Welcome to the fair city of Jaya once more, gentlemen,' the general said. To Fernao's surprise, he was speaking in excellent Portuguese. 'Had we received advance notice of your intended visit, we would have offered you a more fitting welcome.'

Now what exactly did he mean by that, Fernao wondered.

Captain Oliveira was equally at ease. 'Our visit had to be undertaken at short notice,' he responded. 'I can't say regrettably, because our purpose was to save you and your two brothers from assassination.'

You old fox, Fernao thought. I did not realize how clever you are.

The general's eyes twinkled. 'Commendable of you, Captain. My brothers and I are flattered and most grateful. But as you can see, we are very much alive and in command of the situation. Permit me to introduce you once again to my companions. Captain Oliveira and Lieutenant de Albergaria, this is my brother, Prince Raigam.' The general waved a graceful hand to his right and Prince Raigam bowed, palms together at chest level. 'And this is my son, Prince Tikiri.'

Fernao looked squarely at Prince Tikiri, noting that the dark eyes were smouldering with controlled rage. The prince merely bowed stiffly.

'Your rescue mission can hardly be described as peaceful.' Cold iron had entered General Prince Maya Dunne's voice. 'You have killed or wounded many innocent civilians.'

Captain Oliveira shrugged. 'The innocent always suffer when there is violence among their leaders. We wanted to disperse the rabble standing in the way of our rescuing you and the Great King.'

Fernao did not need to see the slight widening of the general's eyes, the pinpoints of fire in them and the stiffening of the other two princes to realize that Captain Oliveira had slipped.

'So you knew that Prince Bhuvaneka had become the Great King at the time you gave the order to fire,' the general observed softly. 'That means you must have heard me addressing the people just now.'

The captain reddened, hesitated. 'I heard someone speaking, but we were too far away for me to distinguish the words.

Besides, I don't understand your language.'

'Nor you do, Captain. Nor you do.' The general eyed Captain Oliveira thoughtfully.

The captain stiffened. 'We are not here for a debate, General,' he stated, his high, raspy voice hard. 'You have just witnessed another demonstration of our firepower. We have merely swept aside a mob who stood in our way. Since we first entered the waters of the Indian Ocean many years ago, we have seized whatever we desired by force of arms. All we desire of your country and your people is peaceful and profitable trade. That can only take place while there is no conflict in your kingdom. You say Prince Bhuvaneka is now the Great King. We approve the choice. Some rabble have been killed and wounded. That's a small enough price to pay for the people to know that the might of Portugal stands behind your Great King Bhuvaneka Bahu.' His cold blue eyes held a sharp, pointed warning. 'Let no man attempt to usurp his throne while he is under our protection.'

The general bowed slightly, an amused smile crossing his face. 'Your warning is well taken, Captain, and will be made known to the people.' He sighed deliberately. 'Unfortunately, Lanka is a country with mountain fastnesses and forests that cannot be negotiated by your cannon. Its population is over ten million.' His fine eyes flickered momentarily towards the groves. 'So it will take more than a regiment to subjugate our people.' He shook his head sadly. 'Even if the entire might of Portugal is carried across the oceans, you could not subjugate a nation.'

'Don't try us, General,' the captain countered. 'That's all I say, don't try us.'

'Why should we? I am here as the Great King's emissary to negotiate your return to Colombo. May I inquire when you intend doing that, or do you propose to remain outside the city in considerable discomfort as our guests for ever?'

'My men and I shall return to Colombo as soon as I have seen the Great King and received his personal assurances as to his safety.'

'Let us understand each other, Captain,' the general replied in

290

sombre tones. 'Your words have ended my mission as the Great King's representative. I shall convey them to him and he will undoubtedly grant you an audience. You will find him in good health and spirits, obviously grateful that your promises to him have been kept.' He raised a hand as the captain started to speak. 'We have a saying in this country: *Danna apate' boru mokada*. May I tell you what it means?'

The captain merely nodded.

'Between those of us who know each other, what need is there for deception?' He paused. 'Now, I shall address you as Prince Maya Dunne. The rights of succession to the Sinhala throne are well established under Arya traditions that go back thousands of years. It is equally a tradition of this country that a king shall only rule as long as he does so with justice and wisdom. You have dared to interfere in the affairs of my country. You have maimed and slaughtered helpless citizens.' His voice shook once with anger. 'Your actions today have been barbaric, unworthy of a Christian nation.'

General Prince Maya Dunne looks every inch a king, Fernao told himself. Has my captain backed the right man? 'I respect the military might of your country,' the general continued. 'But I am not intimidated by it. My brother, Prince Raigam, my son, Prince Tikiri, and I will defend the independence of our country and the rights of our people against all, be it the Great King or the Portuguese. And now, I bid you farewell. We shall surely meet again.' He glanced at each of his companions. 'Come, gentlemen.'

'You mother-fucking bastard, for that I'll have your balls some day,' Captain Oliveira grunted.

The general paused and half-turned to look at the captain with aristocratic disdain. 'You have the oddest tastes, Captain,' he remarked. 'I am flattered by your desire to add to your collection.' He strode away.

The difference between the two men suddenly made Fernao feel sick at his superior's crudeness. What am I doing here, he wondered. Dear God, dear sweet Jesus, dear Mother Mary, save me from evil. I am set on the course of my life. Can only violence and ruthlessness accomplish it?

291

Tuesday, 29 March 1524

On Tuesday afternoon, four days later, the Portuguese force returned to Colombo and entered the fort in pouring rain, unusual for that time of year. They had not had to camp out in the groves outside Jaya because the Great King had made a barracks available for the men and provided quarters in the palace for the officers. Embarrassment had been avoided because Prince Maya Dunne, Prince Raigam and Prince Tikiri had departed the same day and the discussions with the Great King had been amiable. He was content to let the present trading arrangements stand. 'One should not make unnecessary changes when other drastic changes are afoot,' he had asserted shrewdly.

As they stood in the square before dismissing the men, Fernao looked up at the skies for some break in the low grey clouds, but in vain. All he saw was a uniform pall stretching to all points of the compass. The raindrops seemed to spit in his eyes, splattering on his face with malicious glee. No walk on the ramparts for you this evening, they seemed to cry. Fernao wondered how he could speak to Julietta's father in private. Ancient dykes within him had been breached, the sea was rolling in. During the days away, he had worked out his plan of action to cause Julietta to marry him. A *senhor* Duarte de Brito was one of the instruments he would use.

'I'd like a moment with you in the office after we've dismissed the men.' Captain Oliveira interrupted his thoughts.

'Aye, aye, Sir!'

The men began running to their barracks with shouts, curses at the rain and ribald laughter. Horses snorted and neighed. The wagons and cannon squeaked, creaked and rattled as they were hauled into position.

Fernao and Captain Oliveira walked steadily through the rain, headed for the tower, through the smell of washed dust. Officers did not run. They had to be an example of fortitude and dignity to their troops.

The office was empty, but orderlies had lit the lanterns in their rooms in anticipation of their arrival, so the pungent odour of burnt oil greeted them. They removed their dripping capes, shook them and hung them on pegs in the little ante-room. They stamped their feet on the grey paving and wiped their faces with dry towels placed for them on a little side table. Fernao touched Julietta's handkerchief. It was soaked, though he had tried to protect it from the rain. The jasmine fragrance remained, but faintly.

'Shitty rain!' the captain remarked and Fernao winced at the horrible contrast of the words with his romantic thoughts.

They sat at Captain Oliveira's desk, opposite each other. 'The caravel leaves with the tide tomorrow, so I asked you to see me because I've got to get this despatch out to the Viceroy,' the captain explained. He ran the palm of a huge hand back and forth over his bald head as if drying it. 'I'd rather fight than write, as you know, and we've both got a stake in this. You do want to stay in Colombo, don't you?'

'Yes, Sir.'

'Well, I'll need you to give me facts and figures of what the fort is costing us and how we can turn a hundred per cent profit from trade. I've already sent for *a senhor* de Brito to join you.'

Fernao's heart leapt. This would afford him the perfect excuse to talk privately to Julietta's father. God seemed to be opening the way for him. 'We'll have the figures for you by tomorrow morning,' he said.

'Good man.'

'But how can we achieve one hundred per cent profit, Captain?'

The captain grinned triumphantly. 'From trade alone, impossible! But the Great King has promised me a subsidy if we maintain our forces here for his protection, which will bring the percentage up.'

Fernao gaped at him in admiration.

'I told the fucking pagan that we would soon be under orders to pull out. It didn't take him long to come up with whatever it would require for us to remain in strength. He fears his brother, Maya Dunne, whose balls I'm going to have some day.'

'It was smart of you to back Prince Bhuvaneka secretly, Captain, but tell me why you did so, when it would have

293

seemed more profitable for us to support King Wijayo who was prepared to give us direct trade, cutting out all middlemen and with reduced prices for the cinnamon?'

'Prince Wijayo would never have given us the money subsidy. Now we can continue trading through the Raschids as before. We must never put ourselves in the hands of a ruler for trade, because he can use it as a whip against us.'

'Such a policy will also help us wield the balance of power.'

'To that end, it's also time we used our good friars to spread the faith. We need to import some *pai dos Christados*, some fathers responsible for converts. One final word before you leave. We should try and do something about the Sinhalas' muskets. It will only be a matter of time before they have enough to be a real threat.'

Tuesday, 29 March 1524

A *Senhor* de Brito's eyes were inquiring when he entered Fernao's room.

'Please sit down.' Fernao indicated the settle opposite his desk. 'I must apologize for bringing you out at this time of the afternoon and in such inclement weather, *a senhor*, but it would seem that you and I are to have a sleepless night.' He grinned then went on to explain what was required.

The factor listened in silence, nodding his dark head frequently to indicate his understanding. 'I don't think we will need the whole night,' he declared, when Fernao had finished. 'A couple of hours should suffice.'

'How so?'

'I had anticipated some such contingency,' de Brito stated, shrugging bony shoulders almost apologetically. 'So I assembled all the statistics while you were away. We only need to collate them to provide the figures in support of our projections for the future. I suggest that we meet here again before dinner.'

'Marvellous. You really are exceptional.'

The factor shrugged again. 'Part of my duty is to anticipate the needs of any situation.'

'That's a good philosophy.' Fernao pushed back his settle, spread out his legs. 'I hope you will agree to apply it in our personal lives as well, *a senhor.*'

'I . . . I do not understand, Lieutenant.' A puzzled expression crossed the factor's lean, scholarly face.

Fernao looked at him levelly. 'Your daughter and I need your help in making our future.'

'My help? What help can I give either of you?'

'As you know, your daughter and I have been seeing each other exclusively for three years now. I love her and desire to marry her.'

'To marry her?' The sad, dark eyes widened. 'But, Lieutenant, if I may be frank, you are a de Albergaria and my daughter is a *mestico.*'

'I love your daughter, *a senhor*, a lady, a woman beyond compare. As I said, I desire to marry her, but I'm not sure that she is ready to marry me, as yet. Meanwhile, we are both getting older. Your daughter is seventeen. It is time she married and settled down.'

'You are right, but what would you have me do?'

'Order her to marry me, but without her guessing that you are doing so at my request. Once you have so directed her, when the time is right, you and I can set the date, taking her consent for granted even if she has not given it. I need this with all my heart.'

'She can be headstrong. She may not obey me.'

'She will not demur if you tell her it is your dearest wish and that you could only die in peace if you knew she was settled and secure.'

'What of your own father, Lieutenant?'

'Leave that to me, *a senhor.*'

Tuesday, 29 March 1524

It seemed yet another sign from God endorsing his plan when Father Juan entered the tower, his cape dripping, soon after *a senhor* Duarte de Brito left.

'Ah, Lieutenant,' the friar's voice really boomed in the

confined space. 'How lucky I am to find you here. Could you spare me a few minutes?'

'Certainly, Father.' Fernao indicated the settle that had just been vacated by the factor and resumed his own seat behind the desk, a safe distance away from the priest's gusts of bad breath. 'As a matter of fact, it is my own good fortune to have you here. Have you just arrived from Kandy?'

'This morning.'

'Nothing amiss, I hope.'

'No, I am preceding a visit that Prince Kumara will be making to Captain Oliveira in two days' time, before he goes on to the Jaya palace for the Great King's funeral.' The cruel mouth tightened. 'It should prove an interesting meeting. And of course I am also here to visit my flock in your parts.' A smile parted the beard and the yellow eyes gleamed. 'It is all well timed to coincide with the need for news of your . . . er . . . own visit to Jaya!'

Fernao nodded. Just like Holy Church and especially Father Juan to want to keep abreast of political events, capitalize on them and, where possible, interfere. 'Well, Father, we have had great success with the royal succession. Prince Bhuvaneka Bahu is now the Great King. He is well disposed to us and to Holy Church and . . . er . . . we are discovering that his cooperation can always be solicited.'

Father Juan nodded grave agreement, but there was a cynical glint in his eye. 'I knew he would have his price.'

Fernao proceeded to brief the friar as to the events of the past few days, in greater detail than he might otherwise have done because of what he had in mind.

'It seems as if we are well placed,' Father Juan remarked when Fernao had finished. He was thoughtful awhile, quietly rapped the desk with long skeletal fingers. 'We must devise a plan for expanding our Church in Jaya,' he declared.

'The timing is right.' Fernao gazed down awhile, as if in thought. A flurry of rain splattered on the roof of the tower. He flicked his eyes to meet those of the priest. 'Which brings me to the subject of timing in my personal life.' He paused. 'I need your help, Father.'

296

'How can I help you, my son?'

'I wish to marry Julietta de Brito.'

The yellow eyes widened. 'I knew you were becoming close friends, but marriage? What will your father say?'

'That's another problem, but a secondary one which I shall deal with separately and on my own. As you can guess, I love Julietta. My immediate problem is to get her to agree to marrying me.'

'Have you asked her?'

'No, but I sense that her feelings may be elsewhere. Yet she has so much affection, regard and concern for me that the basis for a . . . er . . . Christian marriage exists.'

Father Juan's smile broke slowly across his face. 'The love of childhood which we had hoped to ex . . . ' He paused abruptly. 'You want us to bring the authority of Holy Church to bear on the young lady?'

'Yes, Father.'

Father Juan eyed him thoughtfully, then made up his mind. 'For a Christian marriage? Why not, my son?'

CHAPTER 26
Tuesday, 29 March 1524

Disgusted by the turn of events in Jaya and Prince Bhuvaneka's betrayal of us, my father and I left for Sita Waka, accompanied by my cavalry regiment, a few hours after our confrontation with Captain Oliveira, while Prince Raigam and his escort returned to his own lands about fifty miles south of Colombo. No sooner did we reach Sita Waka the next afternoon than my father set in motion a hurricane of activity. During the next three days, what with catching up on his normal duties as the feudal overlord of the Sita Waka region, nobles arriving post haste for discussions, messengers galloping to and from distant regions, my father barely had time to see me, so I contented myself with training my cavalry for whatever lay ahead; although I knew that my father would confide in me when the time was right, I waited impatiently for him to reveal his plan.

Finally, on the fourth evening following our return, there was a sudden lull in the activity and my father invited me to sit with him on the spacious front lawn of our mansion for a 'chat'. As I sat opposite him, sipping pink melon juice from a silver goblet, I was excited at the knowledge that he would at last tell me what he had organized, for I knew he would not take Prince Bhuvaneka's actions meekly.

Slanting sunlight bathed the green forested mountaintops but the golden air of our valley, tinged with wild jasmine, held that first breath of darkness that is night's herald. Two mynah birds were shrilling at each other from the dark spreading branches of the giant banyan at the centre of the lawn, a prelude to the wilder concert to follow when all their comrades returned home to nest. It was said that this banyan tree was planted by the first of our ancestors to reside, though briefly, in Sita Waka. This was King Parakrama Bahu, who ruled the country from the former capital, Polon. He had planted this banyan tree and his seed during a visit to relations in the area when he was a young man, more than one hundred and seventy years ago. King Parakrama Bahu IX, King Wijayo, my father, my uncles and I were all descended from him.

This ancestor made himself the last king of a truly united Lanka, ending a superb military campaign as the Great King of the entire island, with no sub-kingdoms whatever, not even in the vulnerable north. During his thirty-two-year reign he erected great mansions at the revered *vihares*, temple residences, in Polon and Sigiri and renovated the *dagobas* at the first capital, Anu, including the exquisite Thuparama built by King Devanam Piya who first accepted the Buddha's doctrine in Lanka and the massive Ruwanveli Saya of King Abhaya Gamini. Originally built in the fourth century before Christ, Anu was known to all the civilized races, including the Greeks, Persians and Romans, for its wonderful buildings and its underground water and sewage system. But invaders from the barren wastes of South India began to move in. Although they got no further than the northern, north central and, occasionally, part of the eastern regions of Lanka, the pressure of their invasions caused the Sinhala to move their capital from Anu to Polon farther south. Eventually even that city proved too close to the Indian continent and the capital was moved again, to Jaya. The first King Parakrama Bahu also constructed eight major reservoirs and irrigation works to serve the people and ended up extending his dominions, by conquest, to Dambadiva in India.

My father was bequeathed the mansion and all the family holdings in Sita Waka by his uncle, King Dharma Parakrama Bahu IX. My father's older brother, Prince Raigam, was given all our maternal lands, known as Raigam *korle*, in the southwest region of the island. My father had extended the Sita Waka mansion and his grip on the region during his uncle's twenty-two-year reign by sheer force of personality, by his dedication to Sinhala Buddhist traditions and by efficient, compassionate administration. The *bhikkus* in particular had come to love him for his unswerving support of them and of the Doctrine.

I could not help but remember all this as my father and I talked, idly at first. An inner hauteur gave his face regality and he held his head so proudly that it enhanced his aristocratic appearance. Had I inherited some of this? What I had not, I would cultivate!

'This is Lanka,' my father broke one of our comfortable silences quietly, moved by the beauty and quietude of the evening. He breathed deeply, inhaling the scent of the jasmine. 'My favourite scent. Your mother loved it too.'

It was the first time he had referred to my mother that I could remember and his words touched me. I was very young when she died and, having been away in the Jaya palace some years by then, had never got close to her. Yet her death left a great emptiness, because I had loved her and found her a source of security and comfort many a time when I was very little. Even now, I could remember the feel of my head against her stomach whenever I ran to her in some misery, just for the solace of clasping my hands around her.

'Have you discovered the answer to the question I posed to you on your birthday three years ago?' My father suddenly changed the subject, his voice steady but his black eyes fixed on the distant mountaintops.

I was taken aback, because we had not discussed anything of a philosophic nature since that day and I did not even dream that he remembered.

'I have come to the conclusion that the religion or philosophy a man adopts is an extension of his character and he in turn becomes an extension of it.' I spoke slowly, trying to give my thoughts accurate expression. 'Cause and effect, each effect becoming a new cause. Man creates his own causes and therefore effects, but he is also governed by effects extraneous to him, which integrate with his thoughts, words and deeds. These rules for a man also apply to the group of individuals we call a nation. For instance, to answer your question more directly, the nature of the Indian people had the effect that it could not absorb Lord Buddha's Doctrine – one of the effects that became the cause for the Doctrine to die slowly in the land of the Doctrine's birth. When we can fathom the states of mind of the people who embrace various religions, we can almost predict how they will respond collectively in any given

300

situation. Our Buddhist ethic is unique. It gives the individual the responsibility for making himself such that he can respond to the various effects of people, life and circumstances in a way that will lead him to Enlightenment. Thus can all people be equal.'

'Do you realize that Lord Buddha alone gave woman true equality? Muhammad gave women an inferior place, the Hindus regard women as a lesser form of *kharmic* reincarnation so that wives must immolate themselves on the funeral pyres of their husbands, and the Christians speak of the Father, the Son and the Holy Ghost with no position in the Holy Trinity for women. If I were a woman, I'd be damned angry at that obvious example of male arrogance.'

'But what about the Blessed Virgin Mary?'

'A mere crumb from the male table, a necessary sop to women because the human race cannot comprehend a son without a mother to produce him. I understand that Christian women make more of the Blessed Virgin than men do, even seeking her intercession in their misery.'

'The revolt against the established order of the Catholic Church has in recent years been centred on a man named Martin Luther,' I stated, showing off my knowledge. 'Apparently, this Martin Luther was served with a Bill of Excommunication from the Church by the Pope and summoned to appear for trial before a Diet consisting of the Holy Roman Emperor, Charles V of Spain and princes of the German states. His statement at the Diet is so impressive that I committed it to memory. Would you like me to repeat it, sir?'

My father gazed at me quizzically. 'Certainly.'

I looked towards the mountains and reached within my memory. 'Since Your Majesty and your lordships desire a simple reply, I will answer without horns and without teeth. Unless I am convicted by Scripture and plain reason – I do not accept the authority of popes and councils, for they have contradicted each other – my conscience is captive to the word of God. I cannot and I will not recant anything, for to go against conscience is neither right nor safe. God help me. Here I stand. I cannot do otherwise.'

'What noble words,' my father declared. 'That man had the only excuse for opposing a sovereign ruler, conscience. What happened to him? Was he not seized and killed?'

'An attempt was made, but he was rescued by friends. His books were burned, yet I understand he continues to write from hiding.'

'The *parangi* are trying to establish the Catholic faith by force, coercion and discrimination in Calicut, Cannanore, Goa and Diu. It will be our turn next.'

'So you really think it will happen here in Lanka, sir?'

He nodded. 'They will also use every means to acquire wealth. Theirs is a materialistic world.'

'Wouldn't you rather say it is more acquisitive than our world, because all men have to be materialistic to some degree in order to survive.'

'You may be right. Then what is your conclusion?'

'I believe, sir, that being non-acquisitive, it is easier for people in our part of the world to pursue the truth. Lord Jesus said, "You shall know the truth and the truth shall set you free".'

My father smiled mischievously. 'Did he not also say something about the Devil quoting scriptures?'

Our laughter rang out in unison.

My father suddenly turned sober. 'Our country will be broken apart by the foreigner with his trade, his guns and his religion before it becomes whole again.'

The sound of drumming arose in the distance. The women of the village would be seated around the great circular *rabana*, its skin warmed by glowing coals beneath it, playing a *raban pada*, or tune ... *pitthala botth-thang* ... *pitthala botththang* ... *pang-paddikkang* ... As if in response, mynahs began screeching a full chorus from the giant banyan tree. The air was darkening under the threat of night, children's voices singing a *siyupada*, chant, reached us faintly from the servants' quarters of the mansion. Golden lamp glow shone through some windows. There was a peaceful eventide hush in every sound which was a part of the earth, of the ancient mountains around us, now etched purple dark against the rosy western sky, save for the red scars of the loggers' campfires on their breasts.

I felt a drumming within me, not of the distant *rabana* playing but of the spirit of my native land. I suddenly realized that all things, the silent trees, the screeching mynahs, the mystical mountains, had their own separate *prana*, yet we were a part of the greater *prana* of the earth. I had felt kinship with each of the parts of life in Lanka before, but this was the first time that I recognized the whole. It was a moving experience that reached into the core of my being, releasing such deep, deep love for all of it that tears reached out to my eyes.

Once again my father sensed my reaction. 'What does Lanka mean to you, Prince?' he inquired softly, his gaze gentle upon me.

For once I could not find words. I shrugged my shoulders, raised my palms and spread them out. 'This . . . all this!'

'What *is* Lanka to you?'

Again I shrugged, fighting back the tears. 'This . . . all this!'

'What do you have to give to Lanka?' His voice was low, intense.

'This . . . all this, back.' The words broke loose at last. 'To preserve all this in its godliness for our people and their children and their children's children.' I paused, became filled with purpose. 'I want to confess something to you, *tha*, and this is perhaps the best time to do it. I know that alliances are made through marriage, to strengthen military and political situations, but I want no part of them. They are a sign of weakness when one is waging a crusade, props that can tumble when they are most needed. So I have decided never to marry until all Lanka is united under Sinhala Buddhist rule.' I had been avoiding his gaze. 'I have not taken the vow of *brachmachariya*, but I crave your leave to live my life uncluttered by family responsibilities at least until the destiny of Lanka is fulfilled.' I could not tell him that my decision had in part been caused by my love for Julietta that had never died, despite her betrayal of me.

'Spoken like a man and a true Sinhala.'

His words crashed out like a fanfare of trumpets announcing my arrival in the hallowed courts of my country. 'Why?' I demanded hoarsely.

'Because you have realized that the living you has to sustain the whole with your own strength alone. Now you will not be afraid to die for that whole. Now, wherever you may be, wherever your dead body may lie, you will for ever be a part of this land, Lanka.'

We gazed at each other through the dusk in the deepest communion, nodded, looked away.

Fireflies had begun twinkling in the dark branches of the trees that lined the lawn. A mosquito whined past my face, but I ignored it.

'You may have wondered at the somewhat feverish activity of the past few days and guessed at its cause.' My father had obviously been leading up to this moment. I focused my attention on him, my eyes on his face which had become softened by the dusk. 'I did not want to mention any of it to you until I was sure of the support I needed. It seems that this support is now assured and the plan will unfold as arranged while we are in Jaya to attend my father's funeral next Monday.'

I listened in silence to his plan, marvelling at all he had accomplished in such a short space of time, proud of the support he had been promised in his fight for our principles. Yet, thought of the end results filled me with dismay at first, until he explained his reasoning.

'The physician sometimes has to break a fractured leg when it has been badly set, so it can become whole again,' he reasoned sombrely. When he finished speaking, a sigh escaped me, for the end result would be a Lanka fractured into three kingdoms.

Pitti-thala ... botth-thang ... pang padikkang ... pitti-thala botth-thang ... pang padikkang ... the drumming was very much in the background now.

CHAPTER 27
Tuesday, 29 March 1524

Prince Kumara was about to leave the Kandy palace that Tuesday evening for the home of his mistress when he was summoned to attend the King's audience chamber immediately. He was not surprised, for news of the assassination of the Great King Wijayo, the intervention by the *parangi*, the assumption of power by Prince Bhuvaneka and the obvious anger of Prince Maya Dunne and Prince Raigam meant a country in turmoil. He and his father, King Wira, had decided to postpone their military plans and the alliance with Prince Maya Dunne for the time being. Instead, King Wira had called up the Kandyan army reserves and sent reinforcements to the forts in the mountain passes. The city had seethed with activity, for barracks had to be provided for the troops and arms issued to them.

Prince Kumara himself could not see what all the fuss was about, since it was extremely unlikely that Prince Bhuvaneka or either of his brothers would attempt to invade the Kandyan fastnesses under such circumstances. Believing that King Wira needed to play with his toys, Prince Kumara went along with all the arrangements as if action were imminent.

The audience chamber was a small room adjoining the dining chamber. Its red-brick floor was covered by a locally woven rug of deep maroon and green. Gaudy tapestries of Jataka tales in yellow, crimson and black hung on the lime-plastered walls. The tamarind furniture included settles and a desk at the far end of the room, behind which his father now sat, the bulbous stomach a barrier between him and the desk.

'Ah, there you are!' King Wira exclaimed as soon as Prince Kumara entered and made obeisance.

The prince was about to make a smart rejoinder, when he noticed that they were not alone. The woman, dressed in pale blue bodice and skirt, sat on a settle to the right of the chamber and did not rise to greet him; she must be of higher rank. He glanced curiously at her face and was immediately struck by her sensuous beauty and sex appeal. More, there was something magnetic about the large, dark eyes that seemed to click into place with his gaze.

'This is our son and heir, Prince Kumara.' He barely heard the king's words. 'Prince, we want you to greet a cousin whom you have never met before. Pay your respects now to Queen Anula of the Kiri Vella branch of our family.'

So this was the woman for love of whom a Great King had been brought down. She seemed remarkably composed for one just widowed. When he straightened from his salutation, she raised her eyes again to his glittering gaze for an instant, this time with a sad half-smile, before lowering them quickly. To his amazement, that simple look gave him an instant erection.

'Our son seems to be tongue-tied, but please be assured that he is capable of intelligent speech from time to time,' King Wira commented drily, then belched. 'We have even taught him to read and write.'

Prince Kumara felt a flash of irritation. He did not relish being put down in front of this beautiful woman.

His father caught his reaction, smiled savagely. 'Well, let us to business, so the prince can hasten to the pleasures of the mistress to whom he has already lost his head and certainly his virginity!'

Prince Kumara knew an even greater flash of irritation this time. Then he saw his father's pig eyes on the queen and knew what the problem was. The old man was smitten by the young woman and was showing off to her.

'Queen Anula is a remarkable lady,' the king continued. 'She escaped from the Jaya palace in the nick of time, having disguised herself as a serving woman. She sneaked out through a wicket gate and mingled with the crowds who were looting the Royal Treasury.' He sniffed with the beginnings of a headcold, hawked and spat into a brass spittoon beside his desk. 'She located her son, Prince Deva Raja, and bribed a wagoner to get them both out of the area, disguising herself as a Mouro in *purdah*. Lucky for her, no one thought to check the boy for circumcision.' Prince Kumara found the reference odious, but his father was deadly serious and smug at his own cleverness. 'She knows even less of subsequent events than we do, except that her husband was foully murdered and Bhuvaneka is now the Great King.' A pompous note entered King Wira's reedy voice. 'We have extended our royal protection to Queen Anula. She will be safer here than in her native Kiri Vella, where her son will be sent with an escort tomorrow morning to be brought up by relatives.'

'We thank you again, lord,' the queen ventured tremulously. 'You are so...so strong, so decisive, so self-confident. A real man. We wish...We wish that our own lord, our late husband had been...' She paused, as if unwilling to say anything disloyal to the memory of King Wijayo.

The words jarred on Prince Kumara. The woman obviously knew how to handle men, for his father was basking in the praise like a fat water buffalo wallowing in mire. Suddenly he realized that she was exactly like himself. She must have sensed his thoughts for this time she turned dark eyes on him, melting while searching his depths. Was she serious or was she putting on that look, making him feel he was being caressed?

The king cleared his throat, glanced towards Prince Kumara. 'We sent for you, Prince, because the presence of Queen Anula in our court has added a new dimension to the political situation created by the three sons of her late husband – ungrateful, unfilial dogs to turn on a father!' He looked pointedly at his own son. 'We doubt that anyone will attempt to invade us, because our mountains and jungles are almost impenetrable.' The pig eyes reverted to the visitor.

Meeting Queen Anula was a strange experience for Prince Kumara. For the first time in his life, he found himself desiring to penetrate a woman, the human being, not merely her womanhood. 'You are more than a match for anyone, Sire.' He could sense the queen's inner amusement at his blatant flattery.

The king stroked his moustache with pleasure. 'I'll...' Having dropped the royal plural in a flush of self-importance, he quickly recovered. 'If any son-of-a-bitch dares to set foot in our territory, we'll teach him a lesson he'll never forget.'

Prince Kumara thought quickly. Was this the time to unveil the strategy he had conceived last night? He decided to proceed. 'If you will remember, you told me last night that we should consider making an alliance with the *parangi*. I would venture to suggest that you sent for me because you wished to give me orders to implement that excellent idea now that the queen is here, because the *parangi* are basically loyal. Since the Great King Wijayo, whom they supported, is dead, they will certainly want to ensure that his widow and the orphan child are not harmed.'

King Wira nodded sagely, his double chins wobbling with his jaw. 'You are smart to anticipate our orders.' He sighed, shot a glance at the queen, who appeared properly impressed. 'But then you have become so accustomed to our wisdom, Prince, that you have almost inherited it. You shall leave tomorrow for Jaya on a secret mission to negotiate with that man, Captain Oliveira. The declared purpose of your visit, will, however, be to act as our personal representative at the late Great King's funeral.'

'I shall follow in the wake of Father Juan, the friar.' He thought his use of the word 'wake' rather clever under the circumstances.

The king gaped for a moment, then caught on. 'Yes, yes. That was part of our plan. The *parangi* will be more inclined to support us if their friar asks them.'

'The friar has hoped for my conversion to their faith, lord, but as you know, it would be dangerous for me to become a Catholic without adequate *parangi* military protection. The friars have been very upset because so far we have thrown only a few beggars and townsmen their way. Perhaps the time has come for the *parangi* to provide me with the courage of my convictions!'

'You are a scheming bastard.' The words emerged from the king without thought, part admiration part watchfulness.

'Never a bastard, I trust, Sire.' Prince Kumara caught that flicker of amusement in the queen's eyes and thought, We are indeed two of a kind. 'If you will forgive my saying so, you are too lusty a man for there to be any doubt as to my paternity.'

The king laughed in spite of himself. He looked at the queen and jerked his head in Prince Kumara's direction. 'You see what I have to put up with.'

'He is his father's son, Sire,' the queen responded softly.

'Since I leave on my mission tomorrow and since the queen has become a vital link with the *parangi*, it is highly desirable that I hold converse with her,' Prince Kumara interjected smoothly. 'If you and her majesty would give me leave, Sire, I would like a private interview with her in her suite so I can be fully briefed.' He held up a hand as the king straightened in his chair, ready to object. 'This will take some time and your royal schedule must not be interrupted.' He smiled. 'We do not want the queen to think that ruling this kingdom is an easy matter, do we?'

King Wira glanced at the queen. 'Well ... er ... well ... What is your pleasure, madam?'

'We believe the prince, having inherited your sagacity, is right, Sire.' She kept her eyes lowered, briefly raised them to the king's with a glance that held promise, then stifled a sob. 'We cannot even be present at the funeral of our husband, to pay our last respects.' She composed herself with a seemingly noble effort. 'But enough of our own grief. We must set it aside since the prince leaves tomorrow and talk to him as he suggests.' She gave the king a demure glance. 'We shall of course always be available for ... er ... further converse with you.'

The king's small eyes gleamed with delight. 'Well put, madam,' he responded. 'You are indeed a person of royal conduct.'

'May we retire then, Sire?' She rose to her feet, half turned to face Prince Kumara. 'The *duenna* will chaperone the prince in my suite.'

I wonder how royally you will conduct yourself with this pig, my father, Prince Kumara wondered without acrimony. Having serviced a gaunt old king right royally for two years, such a beautiful woman should have no problems in this court. Yet he recalled that she had refused to marry King Wijayo until he became king. What condition would she impose before she

309

allowed herself to be conducted into the royal bedchamber of the Kandy palace? Certainly her position as a widowed queen was one of great strength, so sacrosanct that, by Arya tradition, she was inviolate; she would have to give only as much as she desired.

'Please give me leave to retire, lord,' he begged. 'Since time is short, I had best escort the queen to her suite.' He smiled and made obeisance to his father, pre-empting any denial of his request.

The queen had paused at the entrance. The king's nod was surly. *'Para balla,'* Prince Kumara barely heard him mutter, 'filthy dog!'

Tuesday, 29 March 1524

Julietta had seen the return of the regiment through the window of the foyer with pleasure. Fernao was her only friend. The wives of the officers, who now lived outside the fort, were only acquaintances with whom she had little in common. She had missed Fernao and their evening walks on the ramparts. Would he come over for her today despite the rain? Meanwhile, she thanked the Blessed Virgin for his safe return. Having received news daily of the events in Jaya from her father, she had already offered her thanks for Prince Tikiri's safety.

She recognized the light tap on her bedroom door. 'Come in!' she called.

The door opened and Menika stood framed at the entrance, her face inscrutable. 'Your father requires your presence in the parlour, missy,' she stated, then added in a lower voice, 'The *padili*, priest, is with him.'

Julietta was puzzled. She had expected Menika to announce Fernao. What was Father Juan doing here? She had always been rather scared of the priest, but he had left her alone these past three years when it became obvious that she had no contact with Prince Tikiri.

'Is Master Fernao with them?'

'No, missy.'

Julietta peered at her face in the looking glass, arranged a wayward tendril of dark auburn hair tidily into place before heading for the parlour. This was a largish room adjoining her father's study on the far side of the entry foyer. It was furnished with a white satinwood sofa, on which her father was seated, two satinwood chairs and two settles placed against the whitewashed walls. Blue cushions matched the large red, green and blue Indian rug on the grey flagstone floor.

Her father and the priest rose to greet her. Her father's lanky frame seemed somewhat rigid, the lean scholar's face tense. Father Juan on the other hand was very relaxed.

'Sit down, Julietta.' Her father indicated the vacant satinwood chair. He seemed so serious that Julietta felt a sudden qualm.

As soon as they were seated, her father came straight to the point. 'I have been seriously considering your future,' he declared abruptly. 'You are seventeen years old. You will soon be beyond marriageable age. It is time you were wed.'

She had never heard *o pai* speak so decisively or abruptly before, but that was not the reason her heart sank. She knew what was coming before her father uttered the next words. 'I think you ought to marry Lieutenant Fernao de Albergaria.'

'But, but...' She gazed helplessly at Father Juan for support, found him studiously looking away and floundered on. 'Fernao may not want to marry me,' she stated desperately.

'He does.'

There was no escape. She felt like a trapped animal. 'How do you know, *o pai*?' Then with a spurt of anger, 'Has he asked you?'

'That is immaterial.' Her father sounded positively stern. Why? 'The important thing is that he desires it and I, as your father, want you to marry him.'

Her heart began to flutter. She shot another glance at the priest, but he still avoided her gaze. 'The de Albergarias are of royal blood,' she pleaded. 'Fernao's father would surely disapprove of his son marrying a *mestico*.' Yes, she would even use that dreadful word against herself to avoid this trap.

'That has to be settled between father and son only after we have agreed on our side to the proposal.'

311

'But I don't want to marry Fernao,' she wailed, suddenly breaking down.

'Don't you like him?'

'Of course I do.'

'Respect him, honour him?'

'Yes, yes.'

'Then what else is there?'

'I do not love him in that way, *o pai.*'

'What do you know of the kind of love that makes a good marriage, Julietta?' The tense face softened before the next dreadful words were uttered. 'Besides, what alternative do you have? I shall not live for ever. Who will look after you when I'm gone? Can I die in peace knowing that you are alone, a beautiful young European girl in a heathen land?'

O, God, why do you do this to me? Tears sprang to Julietta's eyes.

'To be realistic,' she heard her father's urging through a haze, 'this is an ideal opportunity for you to marry a decent young man with a great future and settle down. You are a handsome couple. You will breed many fine children.'

Julietta shuddered at the reminder, of breeding children with a man she did not truly love.

'Lieutenant de Albergaria would do you great honour by marrying you,' her father insisted. 'He can take his pick of any of the eligible ladies in the Indies, or back home for that matter.'

'Then let him,' she retorted fiercely, in a sudden display of spirit. 'I am simply not available.' She dried her tears with her handkerchief.

'Do you want to hurt someone who has been so uniformly kind, devoted and true to you? Would you reject your dearest, your only friend?'

She was thrown into confusion again. I wish I were older and knew how to cope with this conflict, she thought. I wish I were independent and did not even have to face it.

'The two people in this world who have shown the most steadfast caring for you.' A sad note had entered her father's voice. 'And you do not care for our happiness. For what are you sacrificing us?'

312

'No, no, *o pai*. That simply isn't true. I'd do anything for you . . . and you know it.'

'Then what are we debating, my child?'

Her father sounded so tender and loving now that she burst into tears again. 'Fernao deserves better,' she sobbed. 'He deserves a wife who can love him truly.'

'You shall be that wife,' her father asserted, more gently than ever. 'You shall take your marriage vows and give him true love.' He paused. 'Let me tell you something. There are people who take the marriage vows yet betray their spouses. Along the long road of married life with all its pitfalls and sidetracks what is important is to be true to those vows regardless. That is what true love is about. And you are capable of it.'

Her sobs subsided, but only because she suddenly felt as if her heart had broken. She took the handkerchief from her sleeve again, blew her nose, wiped away the tears. 'Supposing I still refuse?' she inquired quietly.

'You will have disobeyed your parent and in so doing you will have disobeyed God.' Father Juan had intervened for the first time, his booming voice harsh.

'Suppose I enter a convent and become a religious?' she demanded desperately.

'Obedience and calling are essential requirements for a religious,' Father Juan intoned sternly. 'I could not permit you to join a holy order under such circumstances even if there were one available in the Indies.' He paused. 'I reminded you a long time ago that you had a mission to fulfil for Holy Church. The nature of that mission has changed. It is your duty to Holy Church and to your country to marry Lieutenant de Albergaria.'

'O Sweet Blessed Virgin Mary,' the plea emerged from Julietta without volition.

'When the Holy Ghost commanded the Blessed Virgin to give birth to Our Lord without impregnation, she knew she would have to bear the scorn of the ignorant, but without questioning she answered the call.' The words, remorselessly uttered, reinforced Father Juan's hold over her from the Jaya palace gardens three years before.

Some reserves of dignity made Julietta compose herself. She

had to play for time. That was it. She needed to know what Fernao really thought. She could see what he had to say during their walk this evening. She forced a wry smile. 'It seems as if I have no choice,' she declared lightly.

But her whole world had shattered.

CHAPTER 28
Tuesday, 29 March 1524

Alone with Queen Anula in the reception room of her quarters, Prince Kumara felt very cool and in control of himself. It was not customary for men to visit ladies alone, or even have access to the extensive female section of the palace. The portly *duenna* therefore remained at the far end of the adjacent ante-room, with the door slightly ajar, but with instructions from the queen to be out of earshot because affairs of state were to be discussed.

The last time Prince Kumara had visited this particular room had been years ago, when he was a boy and his mother had invited him in. Seeing the high forest through the red and yellow grilles of the window reminded him of the past.

The room was as he remembered it, red flagstone floor, small rugs of creamy coconut matting, two heavily carved ebony sofas with pink cushions facing each other against the white-plastered walls, with ebony settles on each of the remaining sides. The gold Buddha statue still adorned a small shelf covered with white linen at the far end of the room. Yellow temple flowers were scattered before it, two open clay lamps with lighted wicks, the twin flares erect and unwavering as sentries, on either side. Brass incense burners along the edge of the shelf, the joss sticks glowing red, filled the room with a sharp camphor scent. Incense keeps religion in and mosquitoes out, the prince reflected sardonically. The walls were decorated with crossed *sesath*, circular shields of dried *kenaf* leaves interlaced with tiny mica mirrors, long lacquered handles resting on the floor. Tiny golden flames from the wicks of the multi-tiered brass oil lamps placed on two sides of the room created a kind of magic if one stared at them long enough.

'You are so kind to be sympathetic to a poor widow in her tragedy,' the queen began, immediately they were seated. Her large luminous eyes were downcast, the light glow giving her face a tremulous beauty. 'It's been a time of chaos for me since I lost my husband. Everything feels unreal. I sometimes think it's a bad dream from which I shall wake to find the dear man beside me.' She sighed heavily. 'But I'm afraid I've no such luck. This is my *kharma* and I must accept it.' She raised a tear-jewelled gaze to him.

I will acknowledge the tragic effects of the last few days on your ambitions, Prince Kumara thought coolly, but I'll be hanged before I allow you to think you can put blinkers on my eyes as if I were some kind of donkey. You think you can fool a young man more easily than you did your late husband for two years and my father just now. I'm going to prove you wrong in the most downright manner possible. 'When one experiences such tragedies, madam, even the smallest set-back appears tragic,' he stated drily. 'We become unable to distinguish the good from the evil. Being cool and intelligent, during the past three days you must surely have been able to identify the real tragedies and be pleased at the good. For instance, you can be proud of the resourcefulness and courage you have displayed. As for your *kharma*.' He raised a deprecating hand, his smile deliberately cynical. 'I'm sure that you have always made your own *kharma* and will never be defeated by it.'

She stared at him wide-eyed, in seeming outrage, trying to probe his secret depths. 'Don't you believe in *kharma?*' she finally inquired, lamely.

'Not in the way that you used the word. I don't for a moment believe that some eternal, infinite, all-embracing fate decrees evil times to us as fitting punishments for our misdeeds. What Lord Buddha said was that our own actions have good and bad consequences for us and for others; they affect us by the qualities they breed within us.'

She looked down pensively. 'I wish that philosophy could afford me comfort in my grief, but I can't blame you for speaking thus. It is the privilege of the young.'

The implied rebuke irked him, but he kept his temper. His desire now was to reach and grasp the hidden depths of this woman so he could truly possess her. 'I do not think that the loss of your husband is a tragedy for you,' he asserted coldly. 'Your real concern is that you have lost your privileged position and all hope of seizing power through your son after his death.'

She looked up at him, genuinely shocked, but he responded with a mocking glance. 'You are shocked, madam, not at my temerity or the seeming brutality of my words, but because I, one of the young, as you put it, have probed your secret depths and have dared to state the truth though we hardly know each other.' He paused, his look gentled. 'I have done so because I believe we are two of a kind and it is important that we understand each other perfectly so we can work together for the achievement of our aims.' He deliberately spoke earnestly. 'Believe me, I feel for you in your tragic situation, but only because I can sympathize with you for having played for high stakes and lost.'

'You are kind to devote time, however little, and sympathy of whatever sort, to me.' Something roguish touched the sides of her eyes. 'Especially when it is time and energy you could be extending to your mistress, in the warmth of her arms.'

He laughed inwardly with delight. She had come out naturally for the first time, fighting instead of trying to manipulate. He glanced deliberately out of the window towards the carpet of green branches rising up the mountain, now touched by the first core of darkness. 'You are right,' he declared. 'Even the view from your room is the same as that from the cottage of my mistress. Strange how close you and she are to each other!'

Her face reflected total disbelief, a slender foot began tapping and was instantly stilled. 'Are you really a human being?' she inquired. 'Meeting you is like a part of my nightmare.'

'I assure you that meeting me can be the good part of your nightmare, madam. Everyone needs to find their other self in someone else so that they need not be alone. Husbands and lovers, concubines and mistresses notwithstanding, you and I have always been alone. Look on me therefore as the other you, one of the good consequences of your tragedies.'

Her red lips parted, revealing perfect white teeth in a kind of gasp. I'd like my cock in that mouth, he thought, but only when

317

we have reached perfect understanding and can react and respond to each other as a woman and a man, not as people who want to use each other. Yet he felt another erection.

'You said you were ready to be converted to the Catholic faith,' she reminded him, changing the subject. 'I can see its military advantages but will it not lose you the support of your people?'

'My people are Buddhists because that is what their fathers and forefathers have been. If one had power, one could convert them to any religion one chose, even the worship of pigs!'

'What about the moral issue . . . your beliefs?' She no longer seemed shocked either by his arrogance or his cynicism.

The question jolted him, but he remained impassive. 'I like the Catholic religion because I'm lazy,' he replied.

A quick hand uplifted from her lap, the forefinger pointed to the chin, betrayed her surprise. 'How so?' she inquired, genuinely curious.

'Buddhism gets us to Enlightenment, Nirvana, heaven, call it what you will, the long, laborious way. Let's face it, the Noble Eightfold Path is interminable and boring, extending through a multiplicity of births and rebirths, all of them suffering. The very thought of all that suffering, of the sum total of the energy and effort required, wearies me. The Catholic faith, on the other hand, offers me instant heaven.'

The smile now touched the sides of her mouth. He found the two little crinkles it made on either side quite adorable. She shook her head in wonder. 'Go on!' she urged.

'Actually, the Catholic concept is similar to the Muslim idea which derives from it,' he continued, stimulated by her obvious admiration. 'Except that a Muslim has to die for the religion to get to heaven instantly and I'm not quite ready for that . . . ' He gave a mock sigh. 'As a matter of fact, the Hindu belief is also extremely tiresome. Imagine having to be so good that you will return to the earth as rain! The whole journey upwards and back is tedious and . . . er wet!' He was showing off now.

'Ah, but I understand that the Catholic religion requires you to be forgiven your sins before you can get to heaven,' she countered, easy with him now. 'How will you manage that?'

318

'I have not the slightest objection to being forgiven my sins,' he declared airily. 'It presupposes my right to sin, which is terribly important to me.'

Her laugh rang out then, wholesome, free. She clapped her hands once. 'But you have to be sorry for your sins,' she insisted, her teeth white, eyes sparkling.

'That does create a problem,' he replied. 'For after all, my sins are my happiest moments in retrospect and I should not in good conscience repent them. So, being utterly devoid of conscience, I shall continue sinning on the grandest possible scale. Your mere peccadilloes, your shabby affairs, are disgusting, unworthy of repentance and as unforgivable as being a nonentity. I shall confess my sins for the vicarious delight of the poor, sex-starved friars, dutifully perform the penances of Our Fathers and Hail Marys they will inflict upon me and return to magnificent sinning, refreshed and strengthened by my purification and the knowledge of forgiveness ahead. After all, if we do not sin, God will have no work to do. I shall demand only one thing of Him. No Purgatory for me. I abhor halfway houses. It's instant Heaven for me or I may even refuse to sin, thus placing Him in a quandary.'

'I've never met anyone like you,' she burst out impulsively.

'Nor I anyone like you . . . which makes us two of a kind. We are lucky to have found each other. Two people who are completely and utterly selfish, totally devoid of morals and unswervingly opposed to concepts of any kind.' He made his eyes magnetic, held her gaze firmly but with a deliberate, controlled flood of tenderness. 'The magic is that being such *aware* people, so perceptive, we will not dare lie, cheat or pretend to each other. I don't mind admitting that I find you quite a treasure.'

A sob escaped her, jerking her slender neck. Genuine tears started rolling down her cheeks while she continued to look at him.

Long moments passed in silence. 'Madam,' he finally whispered. 'Most revered lady, I am now bridging the space that physically separates us with my eyes, my mind and my heart, so I hold you in my arms to comfort you, while you weep for all

319

you have not had and all you have been forced to be. This I can relate to, rather than the sham of your so-called tragedies.'

She nodded, still silent, still jerking out involuntary sobs. The tears continued to flowing unrestrained, her nostrils flaring and beginning to drip. These are the tears you taught yourself never to shed as a child, he reflected, because real sorrow meant weakness and weakness brought disappointment and hurt.

When the tears stopped rolling and her sobbing subsided, she continued staring at him, lost in some link between the past, the present and him. He rose to his feet, walked across the room plucking a handkerchief from the sleeve of his tunic. He stood tall before her and proffered the linen. She took it, now gazing upwards at him. She slowly wiped her cheeks, blew her nose and a rueful smile creased her mouth. 'Such heavy affairs of state, Prince,' she observed softly, as she returned the handkerchief. 'You have a beautiful face.'

He raised the linen gently to his lips. 'I hold the mark of your sorrow with reverence,' he declared. 'This handkerchief shall never go to the washerwoman.'

Her cheeks trembled, her shoulders sagged momentarily. Then she straightened, got a hold of herself. She adjusted a wayward strand of hair. 'Well, Prince, where do we go from here?' she inquired, her voice firm as of old. 'For the present, I offer you nothing but a watchful alliance.'

'Accepted,' he responded readily. 'It is all I offer you. When I return from my mission, we will make occasion for further converse. It strikes me that you can be a most powerful ally.' He smiled quizzically. 'What the three brother princes did to you will win you powerful sympathy from the *parangi*. They are a people who exploit you when you are fortunate but have a compulsion to extend a helping hand, as a sop to their consciences, when you suffer a terrible downfall. This derives from the Christian ethic, which is, after all, wholly dependent upon a leader being disgraced, tortured and crucified. So with my conversion and your recent crucifixion, we have two powerful moral forces with which to sway the *parangi*.'

'So young and yet so fiendishly clever and self-possessed,' he heard her say. 'You must be the incarnation of evil.'

320

'Without a doubt, madam. I am the male version, you are the female. We are what the slant-eyed races call Yin and Yang. When we become completely close to each other, without the slightest pretence, with no purpose other than each to bring joy to the other, we shall make a perfect match.' He paused deliberately. 'In every way. It will be a new experience for both of us.' He gave a short laugh. 'Why, it might even be worthwhile propagating our unique species.'

Tuesday, 29 March 1524

Fernao had planned his strategy to get Julietta to marry him almost as if it were a naval operation. First, he had softened her up by evoking her empathy with his official situation, then he had her father force a landing, while the big guns of Holy Church bombarded from a distance. Deciding that even more direct pressure was needed, he persuaded Captain Oliveira that same evening that he should go to Goa on the mail packet that was to leave Colombo the very next morning to present the trade projections personally to the Viceroy, Vasco da Gama, and persuade him not to reduce Portuguese military strength in Colombo. Fernao reasoned that while he was in Goa he would seek his father's approval to marry Julietta. He was certain that his father would agree. If he refused, Fernao would defy him and marry Julietta regardless. In either event, he would be able to present Julietta with a *fait accompli*.

Meanwhile, he would not even broach the subject to Julietta when he met her on the ramparts later that evening for their usual walk, but would casually mention his departure for Goa the next morning so that she could miss him again and be further softened to accept his proposal when he returned.

Part of Fernao was ashamed at his duplicity, and deep, deep down within him was a tiny alarm signal at allowing the power plays of his official life to seep into and govern his personal life. But loving Julietta, and wanting to marry her, he reasoned that he was doing it for her good and turned aside the thrusts of conscience and personal integrity.

He now stood beside Julietta on the rampart wall and

321

watched the grey-brown breakers lash against the black rocks. He had noted a certain reserve within her but he ignored it.

The rain had ceased, leaving behind its seething hush in damp air, beneath the roar of the waves, the strong odour of ocean.

As he had planned, he kept the conversation light, floating on the wings of his declared happiness at being with her again. He was rewarded by finding some of the tension slowly leaving her, but he remained wary, ready to steer the conversation away from marriage or Julietta's reactions to her discussions with her father and Father Juan, who had already given him a quick summary of what had transpired.

'I'm going to miss our walk tomorrow,' he finally declared, deciding that the time was right.

'Oh, why?'

He thrilled to the look of disappointment on her face. 'As a matter of fact, I won't be seeing you for a few weeks,' he added. 'I'm leaving on the mail packet tomorrow morning for crucial trade discussions with our Viceroy, Vasco da Gama, in Goa. You know what those are about.' He studied her face, saw her blink once, noted with joy the sag of her spirit. He had been right. She was softening up. 'It will also give me the opportunity to meet *o pai*, my father, again.' He smiled deliberately and gently at her, crinkling the sides of his eyes. 'He and I have much to talk about.'

His leavetaking at her front door was as before. He bowed over her hand, looked deep into her eyes and bade her goodbye.

'Godspeed, Fernao,' she said, her feelings obviously mixed. He sensed regret at his departure, gratitude for his restraint and an inner uncertainty. 'Come back home safely. I shall miss you.'

It was all working. Elated, he walked back to his quarters through the gloom of the night.

CHAPTER 29
Wednesday, 30 March 1524

She had given of herself fully and completely to her husband for the first time last night and she felt strangely relaxed and fulfilled this morning, her whole body seemed to float. Since Abdul was the only man she had ever known, the experience was completely new to her. Her altered attitude to him from the day the Great King was assassinated, had changed her husband. He was displaying new qualities of leadership in the business and tenderness in the home. Realizing that part of the blame for the past must have been due to her strong personality, she had begun treating Abdul as an equal. She quickly found that every step she took backwards drew him closer. Just last evening he had arrived with a present for her, the first he had given her since their marriage, an exquisite black pearl necklace, each pearl so perfectly graded in size that it must have taken years for the jeweller to obtain them from the pearl fishers in the northwest coast of the island.

They had dined alone last night, again for the first time ever. Suddenly, after dinner, she no longer saw Abdul as a great, obese creature, with small brown eyes and shiny cheeks, but as a tender man, the father of her son. It had released within her the flood-gates of long pent-up desires to give and receive physically.

As she sat on the divan in her reception chamber, following *zuhr*, the noon prayer, awaiting Abdul's arrival from the port, she luxuriated in the recall of their union last night. Responding to the needs she had at long last admitted to herself, Abdul had proved to be the perfect lover. She shivered at the recollection of his hands caressing her face, her breasts, her thighs, her ... she had never realized that he had such vibrant hands. Strange how a woman can be merely a stone, a receptacle, or a passionate mate to the same man, she mused. Those who shut themselves in can never evoke response from others. Women who resent the position of men in the world only create greater deprivation for themselves, more inferiority as human beings, by missing out on some of the most beautiful things of life.

The wonderful part of it was that she did not feel dominated or possessed by Abdul as a result of the sexual experience. On the contrary, she felt a new sense of power over him. This is the truest power of all, she reflected even as she heard Abdul's footsteps outside, interlaced with lighter steps that she identified as belonging to her son.

'News!' Abdul exclaimed before they were all seated. When he did not reach for his normal sweetmeat, Aisha was dimly aware that he had probably done so before as a kind of defensive gesture. 'The young de Albergaria sailed with the tide for Goa on the mail packet this pre-noon. It is said that he has gone to report directly to the Viceroy on events here and to obtain instructions for the future.'

Aisha knew a moment's alarm. 'What could that mean for us?' she inquired, then instinctively glanced at her son.

The young man returned her gaze calmly, but Aisha saw in his whole expression, in the slim relaxed figure dressed in white pantaloons and shirt and dark brown waistcoat, a reflection of her own iron personality. She felt twin thrills of alarm and pride. What have I bred? she wondered.

'Our son did us a great service early this morning,' Abdul said, a note of pride in his voice.

Stiffening, Aisha looked sharply at him. 'What was that?'

'It would appear that he has established his own little network of spies within the *parangi* fort,' Abdul explained. 'So he had word of Lieutenant de Albergaria's intended departure for Goa before we did. He visited the lieutenant and Captain Oliveira after morning prayers, discussed the trade situation with them and obtained their agreement that the lieutenant would strongly recommend to the Viceroy the continuance of our present trade arrangements regardless of what line the Great King may take, for another two years at least.'

Aisha's head swivelled towards Ali. 'How did you manage that, my son?' she inquired, her heart more full of pride at his achievement than at the results it could bring.

Ali spoke for the first time, his young voice as velvet smooth as ever. 'It was rather simple, revered mother,' he replied. There was strength too behind the soft voice that had but recently deepened into manhood. 'I saw Captain Oliveira first and offered him a handsome bribe for his support.' He spoke as if offering senior commanders bribes was an everyday occurrence.

'What kind of bribe? And wasn't that a terrible risk? I mean, he could have taken offence?'

'I didn't think there was a great risk and I used the technique I have learned from you and father. Discover a person's weakness and pander to it. Having seen you use money, women, position, favours, I reasoned that Captain Oliveira must have his own weakness and it was likely to be concern over his retirement some day. He is a married man with no children. For the past three years, he has had to depend on his pay as a naval captain, because no spoils have been taken in Lanka which he and his men can share. The recent orders of Admiral Vasco da Gama must have shaken him because they could leave him without a job. Naval captains who accept land assignments frequently end up without a ship. The day Captain Oliveira moved his troops to Jaya in support of Prince Bhuvaneka, I reasoned that there was complicity between the two of them and had my spies investigate. Their reports confirmed two secret meetings between Prince Bhuvaneka, as he was then, and the captain. I therefore became convinced that King Bhuvaneka had bribed the captain or promised him bribes for military support. Once a bribe-taker, always a bribe-taker.'

'What did you offer him?' Aisha demanded.

'A country estate of his choice in Portugal, to which he and his wife could retire to end their days in comfort.'

'Did the captain accept?'

'Of course.'

'And what of the young lieutenant? Surely he is not involved in all this?'

'No,' Ali responded. 'I reasoned that the lieutenant is not one to be bribed in that manner. But every man has his price.' Her son was not musing, merely stating facts as he had discovered them in his short life. 'Some people want money, others different things. The lieutenant desires marriage to this lady, Julietta, so his weakness, I reasoned, would be the need to take the lady for a wife and to have a happy life with her, preferably here.'

'Why here?' Aisha inquired sharply. 'He is a de Albergaria. He can go anywhere.'

'As a de Albergaria, yes. But I reasoned that this very fact would create some problems for him because of his marriage to a *mestico*, a half-breed, however good a lady she might be. I have no doubt that his father will oppose the marriage.'

I reasoned . . . I reasoned . . . I reasoned. How many times had Ali used these words? 'Everything is based on your reasoning!' Aisha exclaimed.

'What else is there, revered mother? And does it matter, if the reasoning is correct?'

'No, no, I suppose not.' This was a new role for Aisha, a defensive one. She did not know whether she was enjoying it or not, only that she did not mind playing it to this young son, the jewel of her heart. 'What did you offer the lieutenant?'

'I reasoned,' Ali's face, so like her own, the features almost feminine, broke into a mischievous grin, 'that the lieutenant's one hope lay in his job as a factor, which of course comes under the Viceroy, not under Admiral de Albergaria. The Viceroy is not of royal or noble birth. I spoke to the lieutenant separately. My technique had to lie in not seeming to intrude on his private affairs. You know how touchy nobles are about that sort of thing. So I presented his problem to him as my own.'

'How so?'

'I told him that I was in love with an infidel girl, a Sinhala of lowly estate, whom I wished to marry, but that you were both naturally against it. Would he intercede with you on my behalf?' He grinned again. 'From then on the conversation proceeded with complete sympathy and understanding between us. You know how it is with young lovers! He told me that one of the reasons for his mission to Goa was to ask his father's permission to marry the Lady Julietta. I naturally offered the

326

intercession of my powerful uncle, Paichi, who knows Admiral Vasco da Gama as well.'

'The lieutenant accepted the bribe?'

'Of course,' he replied again. And grinned. 'Nobles may never accept bribes, but they have a deep feeling of obligation for any understanding and help extended to them.'

'Will you contact your Uncle Paichi?' Aisha demanded.

'Of course not.'

'Isn't Ali amazing?' Abdul broke in. 'I'm really proud of our young son.'

'I too am proud of him.' Noting the youthful features, so innocently deceptive, Aisha was suddenly afraid for him too. Not much more than a boy, he was acting like a grown man. Her glance flickered to her husband. He nodded slowly, his double chin getting in the way as usual, the chubby cheeks lightly creasing in a slow, sad smile.

'How old are you, my son?' Aisha knew, but the question escaped her lips without thought, a product of her astonishment and dismay.

'You know my age in years, revered mother,' Ali answered gently. 'But I suppose I am as old as my father and you have made me.' He paused. 'Oh and by the way, we need have no fear of being betrayed by Lord Eka any longer. The Great King had Lord Kandura flogged to death today, but he refused to betray his accomplices and so we are completely in the clear.'

'You knew of the plot?' Aisha whispered, thankful at his news but stunned by his knowledge. Nothing had escaped the young man.

'Yes.'

'Why need we not fear betrayal by Lord Eka?' She already guessed the answer, but asked the question anyway with a kind of desperate hope that his reply would negate it.

'I had him traced to the Buddha *vihare* in which he had sought refuge and ... er ... had someone take care of him, in such a manner that the sanctuary of the temple was not violated.'

Saturday, 2 April 1524

My father and I, with our aides and cavalry escort, arrived at the Jaya palace two days before the funeral of my grandfather, the Great King Wijayo. It was a strange evening. Though there was no rain, lightning flashed vividly in the west, followed by the rumble of distant thunder. The heavy air smelled of burnt firecrackers. Notwithstanding the crowd of guests expected for the funeral, my father and I had been provided with our usual quarters, in adjoining suites, where a summons from the Great King, to attend him without delay, awaited us. We bathed, changed into fresh white tunics and pantaloons, wearing no ornaments as a mark of respect for the dead king, and hastened to the audience chamber.

The Great King Bhuvaneka sat at the ebony desk, looking wary in the golden taper-light. Prince Vidiye, his giant frame exuding hostility, the large eyes brooding, was already seated on the king's right; it was a breach of protocol, but my father and I took the vacant ebony settles to the king's left without comment.

The usual insincere platitudes as to health, relatives in Sita Waka, a pleasant journey and comfortable quarters over, the Great King cleared his throat, hawked and spat into a brass spittoon beside his desk. He fished out a red linen handkerchief from the sleeve of his white tunic and blew his nose. 'Before we get down to the matters we wish to discuss with you, we have an item of news,' he said. As his glance swept towards me, I instinctively prepared myself for a personal blow. 'Lieutenant de Albergaria sailed on the *parangi* mail packet this morning for Goa, where he will have policy discussions with the Viceroy.' He ran his tongue over his upper lip and eyed me deliberately, with malicious enjoyment. 'He also intends meeting his father, Admiral de Albergaria, on a family matter.'

He paused, savouring the moment, while I could only return his stare.

'The lieutenant will ask his father for permission to marry the *mestico* girl, Julietta de Brito.'

I could not tell whether the crash I heard was thunder

overhead or something that exploded inside my brain. I blacked out for a few seconds, came to again with a silent cry. No, no, Julietta is mine, she can never belong to another. Then suddenly an icy calm settled over me. What else could I expect after having ignored Julietta all these years?

'Marriage is often in the air at this time of year,' my father observed in flat tones calculated to bring me to my senses. 'My son and I thank you for giving us this romantic item of news, Sire.'

The Great King scowled, then cleared his throat as he came to the serious business of our meeting. 'Do you realize and acknowledge, General Prince Maya Dunne, that as the Great King we are also Commander-in-Chief of Lanka's army?'

'The Great King is certainly Commander-in-Chief of his armies,' my father replied, selecting his words with care.

King Bhuvaneka had perhaps not caught their implication, for he proceeded. 'You and your son arbitrarily removed the First Cavalry Regiment of Lanka to Sita Waka.' His voice hardened. 'We desire you to return the regiment to Jaya.'

'With or without its commander, Prince Tikiri?'

I was already shaking with silent fury, my reaction to the news about Julietta coldly thrust aside, for that could come later, when I was alone and able to endure its full blast upon my lacerated mind.

'We have rescinded Prince Tikiri's appointment. Prince Vidiye will take over command of the regiment.'

'You would make the new appointment without consulting your commanding general, Sire?'

'We ... er ... we have no need to consult anyone. We are the Great King.'

'Granted. But you have breached our *charlithraya* by your action, Sire, and have placed my own appointment as general in contempt. If you go ahead with the change, I shall have no alternative but to resign my command.' My father paused, his face tight at last but his fury still controlled. 'You well know the probable consequences of my resignation. I strongly suggest that you do not commence your reign with dissidence in the armed forces or by facing an inevitable struggle for power

329

'within them which I have kept in check these many years.'

The two men eyed each other across the space that separated them, my father relaxed again, the Great King alternatively apprehensive and blustery. Vivid flashes of lightning streaked across the open window and thunder crashed overhead. The first large drops of rain splattered on the roof. A gust of wind bent the taper lights and brought a sharper smoke scent to the nostrils.

'There is no need for such drastic action.' The Great King gave ground. 'We value your present leadership . . . er . . . and as you say, the time may be inopportune for a change in overall command.' He hesitated. 'What is your wish as to the command of the First Cavalry Regiment?'

'You know my wish, Sir. Prince Tikiri has spent three years training the regiment. It is our finest. He should remain in command of it.'

'And keep it as a private army?' Unable to contain himself any longer, Prince Vidiye was ignoring all rules of decorum.

My father half turned in his seat to face the prince. He was about to utter a reprimand, I know, but he obviously decided on another weapon. He turned back to the Great King, ignoring Prince Vidiye as if he had been a child who has spoken out of turn. I noted the look of hatred that crossed Prince Vidiye's heavy face before glancing back at the Great King for his response.

'Very well then,' the King declared, almost petulantly. 'Prince Tikiri may retain his command, but the regiment shall move back to Jaya.'

'When, Sire?' My father looked down, casually stretched his left leg out slightly, made himself more comfortable on the settle.

'As soon as possible.'

'Prince Tikiri, as the regimental commander, will decide when it is possible,' my father replied lightly, then proceeded without pause before the Great King could demur, raising his voice to be heard above the drumming of rain on the roof. 'Since that is out of the way, may I inquire what other matters you desire to discuss, Sire?'

330

'You have been manufacturing firearms in Sita Waka. This is war material and we desire its manufacture to be under our direct supervision.'

I should have known this was coming, but being inexperienced and unused to the subtleties of politics and military manoeuvring, I was nonetheless amazed.

'The nature of the production makes it as impossible for us to move the factory at present as it is for Portugal to manufacture the weapons locally,' my father responded.

'We should have the right to determine that,' the Great King retorted. His sore throat made him crack on the last words. You also have a sore head, I reflected angrily. I'd like to crack it for you! 'What do you think, Prince Vidiye?'

'You know my views, Sire.' Prince Vidiye's deep voice was tough, his tone blunt. 'Firearms represent power. We do not want anyone other than the Great King to wield such power.'

'Don't you think that such power will be wielded only on behalf of the Great King if he rules justly and wisely?' My father demanded, icy cold.

'If we decide upon investigation that the factory cannot be moved, we will arrange to assume control over it,' Prince Vidiye retorted.

'What "we" are you talking about, Prince?' my father demanded abruptly. 'The royal plural is the prerogative of the Great King alone. Are you already arrogating those powers to yourself?'

Prince Vidiye started up angrily from his seat but was restrained by the Great King's warning. 'Prince!'

'I beg your royal pardon, Sire,' Prince Vidiye muttered. 'But I find your commanding general most offensive.'

'My offensiveness to Prince Vidiye is only as great as his presumptuousness.' my father ground out. 'Let us defer a decision on this matter for a more auspicious moment, perhaps after our father's funeral, Sire, when you and I can discuss it in private.'

'Agreed.' The Great King seemed only too happy to concur.

By the time my father and I returned to his suite, my entire being was consumed by outrage, disgust, anger and yes,

331

apprehension. My father walked to the window of the study and watched the rain gusting and sweeping in the patches of lamplight falling from the building, the earth soaking up the deluge greedily.

When he turned towards me, my father had a peaceful smile. 'It's strange how hereditary traits sometimes reappear,' he stated sadly. 'Your grandfather married a younger woman, adopted her son and named him heir to the kingdom, betraying his nearest kin. Now his own son, having helped depose him for that reason, is also betraying his nearest kin.' He shook his head. '*Kharma/vipaka*, cause and effect. You and I have been on the defensive for a long time now, Prince. We had best regain the initiative before it's too late.'

CHAPTER 30
Sunday, 3 April 1524

Father Juan had insisted that he should go directly to the fort in Colombo and Prince Kumara had reluctantly complied. He would have preferred to wait until he had tested the mood of the palace and discovered at first hand what was taking place at Jaya before conducting any negotiations with the *parangi* captain. Besides, Colombo was seventy miles from Kandy and he was rather tired after starting his journey before dawn on Saturday morning and riding almost continuously, using relays of horses, for over thirty hours.

A heavy shower of rain when he was a few miles away on Sunday afternoon did not help. He was cold and soaked to the skin when he sat opposite Captain Oliveira in the fort. He studied the captain's burly figure, the broad features and sharp blue eyes beneath the bald head shining in the golden lamplight; then his nose tickled and he sneezed. Somehow he felt that it diminished his poise.

'I hope you have not caught a cold,' Father Juan sitting beside him observed, his yellow eyes belying his apparent solicitude.

Prince Kumara shook his head. 'I'll be all right as soon as I have a hot bath and get into dry clothes.' He hoped the friar had recognized his complaint.

'Well then, let's get down to business,' Captain Oliveira intervened. 'I had the opportunity of talking privately to Father Juan earlier and he tells me that you desire to be baptized and to convert to the Catholic faith. Is that right, Prince?'

The battle had commenced. Prince Kumara willed himself to be clearheaded. For the moment he merely nodded to allow the captain to reveal his hand. A gust of wind from outside brought a flurry of raindrops against the tower and made the brass lamps smoke.

'Is your desire to become a Catholic caused by religious or

political conviction?' the captain bluntly inquired.

These white foreigners, they have no manners, Prince Kumara thought with quiet scorn. He shrugged, wriggled unobtrusively as the wet of his clothes seeped to dry parts of his body. 'Are not convictions something between a man and the omniscient God?' His voice was gentle.

'That is one reason for the confessional,' Father Juan cut in smoothly. 'Through it, God's priests are able to reach the hidden depths of man. I insist that everyone goes to confession before baptism. With absolution of their sins they can enjoy the sacrament with a pure heart.'

Pork shit, Prince Kumara thought savagely. You use the confessional to discover men's secrets and exploit them. 'Convictions apart,' he said, 'both you and the captain here will undoubtedly recognize that adverse political consequences will follow my conversion. I shall need the protection of the Church once I've been baptized.'

'The best protection a Christian has is faith in Father and Son.'

Prince Kumara smiled. 'I realize that becoming a Christian is my real security, because it will save my immortal soul, but it is only while my soul manifests itself in this frail body that I can be of use to Holy Church in spreading the gospel. I expect the Church to recognize that and lend me its support. After all, is it not the combined policy of Church and State in your country to use every means in your power to convert the heathen?'

Father Juan and the captain exchanged glances. 'We do not desire to use force of arms to aid conversion,' the captain ventured.

'Is not the Inquisition supported by force of the king's arms?'

'And by the moral force of all true Catholics,' Father Juan retorted.

'True, but it is because the Church operates under the umbrella of the king's protection that it can fulfil this purpose of God. I shall need more tangible than moral support in our kingdom once I am baptized, not for myself but for Holy Church. Why, we might even initiate an Inquisition there.' Momentarily Prince Kumara reflected on the torture he could inflict on some of his enemies if that institution were indeed introduced to Kandy. He noted the glint of religious fervour in Father Juan's eyes, the narrow, bearded face glowing, and knew he had struck the right note. 'In my view,' he went on, 'the representatives of God and Holy Church in Lanka have been denied the support they have every right to expect. In consequence, Father Juan and Father Perez have been compelled to restrict God's work in this heathen country.' He made his voice low, fervent. 'Their twenty years of frustration must be rewarded. I would be God's instrument for ensuring that reward.'

'Yes, yes!' Father Juan hissed. The pent-up feelings of the years, the frustrations and disappointments broke loose. 'Captain Oliveira, I demand in the name of Holy Church that the *laissez-faire* attitude of the king's representatives in Lanka end forthwith.'

Captain Oliveira's fists clenched. Prince Kumara thought he would explode with a single word: Balls! But fear of the Church, obviously deep-grained in him, held the captain back. Instead, he inquired mildly, 'What would you have us do? We cannot interfere in the affairs of an independent sovereign state.'

'But you can make your presence felt, as you did six days ago at Jaya,' Prince Kumara retorted. 'We are not asking you to interfere in anyone's affairs,' he added, having deliberately used the word "we". 'Father Juan and I are merely requesting that, as the shepherd, you afford the Church and its flock protection.'

'Jesus is the only shepherd,' Captain Oliveira declared solemnly.

'Church and State are the successors of Jesus, as the shepherds of his flock,' Father Juan admonished sternly.

The captain sighed. 'What do you want?' he inquired.

'When I spoke to Admiral de Albergaria three years ago, I requested that you post a garrison in Kandy, for which we would pay,' Prince Kumara reminded him. 'Instead of complying with my request, the admiral sent us Father Juan and Father Perez with no support. They have been punching cushions for three years. Why don't you send a company of men and sufficient cannon to protect the Church in Kandy and give it the kind of support that would enable me to make high level

335

conversions?' He paused. 'Besides, the presence of your men would also demonstrate your loyalty to Queen Anula, who is in exile in our palace largely because of her late husband's loyalty to you. Surely it is a matter of pride and honour that you protect this lady.'

Captain Oliveira flushed. 'We look after our own,' he declared.

'Good, we seem to be in agreement, at least on the principle,' Prince Kumara concluded. 'I shall return here the day after the funeral to give you a report on the situation in Jaya. Meanwhile I must proceed to the palace before I catch my death of cold. I should not want to deprive Holy Church of her new ally,' he smiled.

Monday, 4 April 1524

Fast messengers on horseback had carried the news of the Great King Wijayo's death to all the towns in the country. From there the people were informed by beat of tom-tom, and the noble families had hastened to Jaya for the funeral.

The body of King Wijayo had lain in state in the audience hall of the palace for one week. Crowds lined up daily to file past his bier and offer their last homage, but they were much fewer and less tearful than those who had once filed past the nationally revered and beloved Great King, Dharma Parakrama Bahu IX.

One of the most respected and acknowledged leaders of the nobles was from the south. Twenty-eight-year-old Lord Wickrama Sinha was a tall, lean, swordblade of a man with an oval face, the unusually fair skin tight-drawn over thin Arya features. Bushy black eyebrows frowned above sparkling brown eyes, the left more heavily lidded than the right. Strangely for a man, he had the sweetest smile and a habitually kindly expression. His smile had fooled people at times; he was in fact fearless and ferocious as the cheetahs in his native jungles.

According to our *charlithraya*, a meeting of the Council of Nobles could be summoned either by the Great King acting alone or by a majority of the nobles acting in common. With the thirty nobles scattered about the country, obtaining majority approval from them at short notice was almost impossible, which the Great King Bhuvaneka had counted upon when he pre-empted the original plan to summon the Council of Nobles to decide on the succession after King Wijayo's death. But my father's determined efforts over the past week had given us hope and our opposition now coalesced in the Jaya palace. Between them my father and Lord Wickrama Sinha had contacted all thirty nobles, on the grounds that our immediate concern was only to preserve the right of the Council to determine the succession whenever there was any doubt. By early Monday morning, Lord Wickrama Sinha was able to present the Great King Bhuvaneka with a petition requesting his royal attendance at a meeting of the Council during the second watch that evening, after King Wijayo's cremation. Since twenty-three nobles signed the petition, the Great King had no option but to agree.

Any funeral is a sad event. I thought of my grandfather's huge frame a heap of ashes as we entered the audience hall. It was already brightly lit with tapers and lamps. Sitting in rows by order of rank, our white *dhotis*, frilled shirts and waistcoats lent added solemnity to the occasion. I noticed Prince Kumara, representing his father, King Wira of Kandy, sitting apart. The Great King entered and took his place on the Lion throne. Its wood shone, its gold gleamed, the nine precious gems sparkled in the light of the tapers affixed to silver stands held by the bare-chested *pandang karoyo*, six on either side of the king. Beneath the glittering golden crown, gem-studded, not even his lack-lustre looks and weak chin could diminish the Great King's majesty; a clown could be dignified by such regalia.

The Great King called the meeting to order. A bearer standing behind him rapped on the wooden platform with his long gold-mounted staff. The murmur of voices faded into silence.

'You are assembled here as the Council of Nobles of the illustrious kingdom of Lanka by virtue of a petition signed by more than one half of your number,' the Great King announced in his raspy voice. 'We ourselves, as your ruler, had deemed it

337

inopportune for the Council to meet at this particular time, when we are to commence a period of mourning for our late beloved King Wijayo, but we are here nonetheless in deference to your wishes.' His eyes sought out the chief signatory. 'You, Lord Wickrama Sinha, have headed the petition. Are you authorized to speak on behalf of your colleagues?'

Lord Wickrama Sinha rose to his feet. 'Yes, Sire.' His tone was decisive, his stance erect.

The Great King's glance swept through those present. 'Very well then, we take it that no one demurs?'

He was answered by silence, as was the custom when there was agreement. 'In that event, we demand you to state your reasons for this meeting.' He leaned back slightly on the throne.

'I am aware that sensitivity would have pointed to a later date for this meeting, Sire.' Lord Wickrama Sinha had a magnificent carrying voice that rang out through the hall. 'But such concerns must give way before the national interest. You have referred to a period of mourning. We are all followers of the True Doctrine, which precludes mourning merely because one *kharmic* manifestation has passed on to another. I am concerned lest this be an indication that you, our self-appointed sovereign, may be out of touch with the *Dhamma* and the traditions of the Sinhala people.'

They were bold words, which could have earned Lord Wickrama a sentence of death had they been uttered on any other occasion. The Great King's dark frown confirmed his anger at the challenge. 'Mourning is a mark of respect, my lords,' he asserted to the whole assembly, not deigning to address Lord Wickrama as an individual. 'As for our being self-appointed, we will ignore the churlish nature of the words as a reflection of Lord Wickrama Sinha's youth and remind him that it is the Arya tradition and our Sinhala *charlithraya* that appointed us, the oldest surviving son of the late Great King Wijayo, to succeed him. This custom and tradition, the late Great King himself endorsed when he abdicated in our favour. Lord Wickrama Sinha, your remarks are out of line. You shall withdraw them.'

The lord stiffened, drew himself to his full height. 'Pray

forgive me, Sire, but it is not my youth but the facts that will continue to speak even if I withdraw my words.' He paused, looking directly up at the Great King whom alone, as custom required, he could address. 'To take your last statement first, it is my understanding, and that of the other twenty-two nobles who signed the petition, that the Great King abdicated under rightful duress from you and his two other sons, having first confessed his guilt to offences against our customs, our traditions and the entire nation. You, Sire, were present when this occurred and I would respectfully request your confirmation.'

The Great King hesitated. 'We are able to confirm your statement,' he finally replied.

'So when he named you his successor, he had already abdicated and no longer had the right to name his heir.'

I was startled by Lord Wickrama Sinha's logic. The Great King was certainly taken aback.

'If any heir were legally named, it was Prince Deva Raja, who was adopted by the late Great King and named in a formal document while the king was functioning as such,' Lord Wickrama Sinha continued smoothly. 'But that heir is pre-empted from the succession too, because the ruler who named him violated our law and tradition in so doing, an offence which of itself could have caused him to forfeit the right to name a successor. If these principles are not followed, a ruler can commit crimes and abdicate in favour of an accomplice to ensure that the accomplice pardons him for such crimes.'

Soft cries of 'Ahey! Ahey!' revealed almost unanimous support amongst the nobles for these statements.

The Great King was searching frantically for answers. Unable to defeat his opponent's logic, he began to glower at Lord Wickrama Sinha.

Totally unperturbed, the young nobleman held up two scrolls. 'This is the original document naming Prince Deva Raja heir to the throne of Lanka and this appoints Queen Anula as the Queen Regent.' His dark, brilliant eyes challenged the Great King. 'Is it your wish that these documents be honoured, Sire?'

The Great King remained speechless.

339

'Only the Council of Nobles can revoke those documents!' Lord Wickrama Sinha's voice rang out. 'Do you, my colleagues, revoke them?'

'Ahey! Ahey!' Again the vote was almost unanimous.

Prince Vidiye leapt to his feet, stood towering over the Council. His great face was taut, the large, staring eyes rolling with anger. He raised a clenched fist and shook it. 'I say, enough of these legal quibbles,' he shouted. 'The Great King Bhuvaneka sits on the throne as the rightful successor of King Wijayo.' He glared at Lord Wickrama Sinha.

The Great King made no move to call him to order. Lord Amara rose abruptly from his front row seat. A short tubby man of middle age, with long black hair tied in a *ksashtriya* knot on top of his head, Amara was one of the most senior lords, well respected by all. 'Sire, you are presiding over a meeting of the Council of Nobles, not a fish auction,' he declared. 'I beg you to use your authority to ensure that the proceedings are conducted in a decorous manner, with due regard for the rules.' He resumed his seat, looked around him for support.

'Order!' . . . 'Order!' . . . 'Sit down Vidiye.' Lord Amara had almost unanimous support.

Prince Vidiye turned angrily to face the hall. Before he could erupt, Lord Wickrama Sinha cut in. 'Prince Vidiye should desist from participating in these discussions because he has a conflict of interest,' he declared. 'He is the husband of your daughter, Sire, and his oldest son could be your successor with Prince Vidiye himself as Regent.'

Angry words were about to erupt against Prince Vidiye when the Great King intervened, a look of resignation on his face. 'Pray sit down, Prince Vidiye,' he commanded sharply.

With a final angry glance all round, Prince Vidiye slumped back onto his seat.

'There is substance in Lord Wickrama's submissions,' the king granted, and I realized that he was trying to placate those present and obtain their support. 'By legal instrument that would pre-empt the traditional line of succession, Prince Deva Raja is the successor to the throne, with his mother Queen Anula the Regent.' A smile hovered around his lips. 'Since the

340

Council of Nobles has refused to accept the instrument, should we not then fall back on custom and tradition?' His voice was now suave.

'Not so, my lord,' Lord Wickrama Sinha demurred. 'The rules of *niyaya*, justice, demand that where there is a conflict, the Council of Nobles must decide on the successor.' He drove home his point. 'Which is why we petitioned for this assembly in the first place.'

Clearly the Great King was casting about for an answer, but he could find none. He could not have anticipated that his authority and appointment would be questioned. Lord Wickrama Sinha, on the other hand, had come fully prepared.

'Let us then proceed to debate the succession,' King Bhuvaneka conceded.

The wrangling and debate went on for three hours, while the dead king's cremated remains still smouldered in the palace burial ground. The ancient custom that the succession was determined only after the explosion of the cracking skull of the corpse was reported did not apply in this case because the dead King Wijayo was not Great King at the time of his death.

At the meeting's end Lanka had been deliberately divided into three kingdoms, Jaya, where King Bhuvaneka would rule as the Great King, Raigam under my uncle Prince Raigam, and Sita Waka under the suzerainty of my father, who thus became King Maya Dunne.

CHAPTER 31
Tuesday, 5 April 1524

As he had promised, Prince Kumara paid his visit to the fort the next day and was conducted to Captain Oliveira's office in the tower. Their greetings over, the captain came immediately to the point. 'Well, Prince, we have already received some news of the proceedings of the Council of Nobles' meeting in the Jaya palace yesterday. Since you were personally present, would you please give us details of what transpired?'

Prince Kumara saw a possible bargaining tool. 'I will give you any other information you desire, Captain, but the proceedings of the Council are confidential. I could only consider divulging them to an ally, if I had one.'

The captain's sharp blue eyes flickered to the yellow eyes of Father Juan, locked for a second then swept back to Prince Kumara. 'Did we not become allies upon your conversion to Holy Church?' he inquired blandly.

'I have not yet been converted.'

'Ah, I thought we agreed the other day that you were already a Catholic by conviction.'

Prince Kumara openly showed his amusement. 'But surely there is no conversion until I'm baptized.' He half turned to Father Juan. 'Is that not so, Father?'

'The act of baptism but consummates the conversion,' the friar responded warmly. 'It is like the consummation of a marriage that has taken place.'

'Does that mean that one can go through life without the baptism, like some marriages that are never consummated, and enter heaven because the marriage with Holy Church has taken place?'

Father Juan, trained to dialectics, as the prince had already discovered, rose to the occasion. 'The captain was not referring to a lifetime without baptism,' he explained. 'He meant only that

342

since you have accepted conversion, you can share your confidences as one of us.'

'But it would be a betrayal of my sacred honour as a prince to do so to anyone but a sworn ally.'

Captain Oliveira clicked his tongue impatiently. 'What do you want, Prince? State your price.'

Such a barbaric attitude to a bribe, something that should be handled with delicacy and grace! Prince Kumara shrugged mentally. 'I have already told you, Captain. I require your military support in Kandy to announce my conversion openly.'

'Is that all?'

'No, that is not all.' Prince Kumara deliberately turned his settle and faced Father Juan. 'The father and I would like to use that support to spread the faith more militantly.' He paused, smiled faintly. 'Of course, if your support is strong enough, we can extend the joint suzerainty of the Church and the Kandyan rule to the sub-kingdoms of Pera and Hangura, making a very solid pro-Catholic, pro-Portuguese kingdom which could free itself from the dominion of the Jaya king and help your own king with his goals in Lanka.'

'Would your father, the king, agree to these moves?'

Prince Kumara turned to face the captain again. 'I don't recall my father saying that he would become a Catholic,' he declared coldly. 'I thought you and I were to be allies as members of the true faith, which we can then propagate?'

The captain shook his head. 'Ambitious little prick, aren't you? You'd even screw your own father.'

'It is in the nature of the organ you just described in such delicate terms to be insatiable when it is lusty.' Prince Kumara grinned, then added with a decisive note, 'Let us stop fencing now, Captain. If you will promise me your support to the extent that I shall require it – and I promise you I will not be unreasonable in my demands – I shall see to it that your forces get to the heartland of the Kandy and central sub-kingdoms which have been impregnable against foreign invaders since the dawn of history. I shall then ensure that the Catholic religion is established by every possible means in the Kandy sub-kingdom. All this provided that you help me to unite the three sub-

343

kingdoms into one, independent of Jaya, under my rule.'

'What would happen to your father?'

The prince shrugged. 'People always fall by the wayside. You know the laws of life better than I because you have proved them in this part of the world, occasionally even shown us how these things should be done.'

'The prince is right,' Father Juan intervened eagerly. 'This is a glorious opportunity for Holy Church and the State to combine at long last.' He paused, his yellow eyes demanding. 'This is indeed the will of God. Prince Kumara is God's instrument. He and I have waited three years for this moment. You cannot deny us, Captain.' The hint of a threat entered his voice. 'I shall clear it for you, after the event, with my superiors, if need be.'

The captain stiffened. 'I shall do my job as commander, taking all factors into account.'

The friar had over-reached himself. The captain was not a man to be threatened. What were the factors the captain would have to consider, Prince Kumara wondered, then could have laughed aloud at his own stupidity. Always discover your opponent's motives and his weaknesses. Trade, that was it. The captain's prime objective in Lanka was trade. 'Once you are in the Kandyan kingdoms, your military power, backed by my troops, will ensure you have a monopoly of our spice trade. We do not have cinnamon, but we have cardamoms, cloves and other preservative spices. Thus far, the Mouro have only been allowed as petty traders into our kingdoms; I would permit their leaders from Colombo to become buyers for you on any scale you desire.' He wondered at the sudden flicker of interest in the captain's sharp blue eyes, ascribed it to greed at the prospect of extended trade for his masters. 'Your profits would be three or four times the cost of the military force you provide.'

'I thought you were to pay the costs of that force?'

For a moment, Prince Kumara was jolted. Then memory enlightened him. 'That was three years ago,' he declared. 'The Kandy kingdom has become much poorer since then because of pressures from the Great Kings of Jaya with their constant demands for tribute. You should not have delayed your support.'

'So much expense for the conversion of one man, however royal his birth?'

'Did not our Saviour say we must leave the flock and go after the lost sheep?' Father Juan cut in piously.

'Besides, the trade prospects will make your outlay more than worthwhile,' Prince Kumara added.

'If I agree, what will be the effect on Prince Maya Dunne and Prince Raigam?'

'If you agree to agree, I shall enlighten you.'

'All right. You're a clever bugger. I'm going to watch your tail. I agree to agree.'

Prince Kumara told them all that had transpired at the meeting of the Council of Nobles. 'So you see, the timing is absolutely perfect,' he concluded. 'While the three western and southern kingdoms are divided and at their weakest, we, your allies in the central kingdoms, will consolidate and grow strong.'

'Divide and rule,' Father Juan urged. He leaned towards Prince Kumara and laughed.

The prince recoiled. I wish you would not divide your horrible breath from your body, he thought silently.

'What of Prince – I suppose I should now call him King – Maya Dunne? Never underestimate that man. He has brains and balls and is dangerous. I shall have his balls some day, but only because I respect his brains.'

'Please remember that my late mother was General Prince Maya Dunne's younger sister.'

Captain Oliveira's grin was cynical. He was getting the measure of the prince. 'What forces do you want?'

Prince Kumara told him. 'We also need a troop of cannon.'

'Cannon!' The word shot forth from incredulous lips. 'How the blue Pyrenees do you think we can get cannon up there? You must be out of your mind.'

'No, I'm not. I know how it can be done.'

Wednesday, 27 April 1524

The mail packet, *Sao Pedro*, on which Fernao sailed for Goa, was a sleek *fusta*, a small, single-masted foist rowed by thirty-five pairs of oars. It made calls at Cochin, Calicut and Cannanore, so it was four weeks after leaving Colombo that the vessel sailed past the headland on which the strong Portuguese fortress guarded the sea approaches to the enclave.

Fernao was thrilled to observe all that his *compadres* had done to Goa since the second Viceroy, grey-bearded Admiral Alfonso de Albuquerque, seized the town of Goa in the year 1510 from the Mouro and made it his capital. He felt especial satisfaction at noting the vast improvements effected during the three years since he was last here. Apart from the fortress, the heart of the colony was now well protected by a massive red-brick wall with gates and battlements. Between the fortress and the wall and along the northern coastline were thriving green vegetable gardens and orchards. The township itself was identifiable by its churches and crosses. All of it, a Portuguese enclave thousands of miles from home, heightened the sense of power Fernao had been developing through witnessing the might and progress of his nation.

His father's flagship, the *Santa Caterina*, was anchored in the strait, and Fernao had himself and his sea chest rowed over. They had parted three years before on a note as close to loving as they had ever experienced, yet Fernao still felt somewhat intimidated by the paternal presence when he took his seat on the chair towards which the admiral gestured with no attempt at physical contact.

In the golden light of the brass lanterns, the stateroom looked exactly the same as when Fernao had last seen it, the same mahogany panelling, shiny brass fittings, framed prints, blue cushions. His father remained standing, an imposing figure in a dark blue doublet rich with gold braid, his carriage erect, the long legs in their white netherhosen still like sturdy masts. The face with its dominant nose and ice-blue eyes was haughty as ever, but the skin had aged beyond the three years since Fernao had last seen it.

'I'm glad to see you, *o filho*, son.' His father's face softened momentarily. 'It's been too long.'

Fernao was concerned to discover how things were between his father and Admiral Vasco da Gama. 'Please forgive my

346

seeming presumption, Sir, but I would like to ask a personal question.'

The blond eyebrows lifted, the ice-blue eyes became sharper. 'You have my permission.'

'Sir, there have been rumours of differences of opinion between you and His Excellency. Are they true?'

His father's brows creased in a frown. Fernao wondered whether he had over-reached himself and was relieved to see the craggy face relax. 'Indeed. The years of prosperity and prestige he spent in retirement as a landed gentleman in Evora, bearing the titles Admiral of India and Count of Vidigueira, on a pension of 2750 gold *cruzados* plus anchorage dues from Goa, Hormuz and the Malaccas, have diminished His Excellency's lust for expansion. It is also possible that he has become embittered towards our class, because not all his wealth and station can make him a prince or a *cavaleiro*. I'd say too that a man of authoritarian attitudes makes a better explorer than administrator.'

'Thank you for your frankness, *o pai.*'

'Well, enough of that,' the admiral continued. 'Tell me, Lieutenant, what brings you to Goa so unexpectedly and without receiving orders?'

'Political events of extraordinary importance in Lanka made Captain Oliveira and me decide that I should report them to you and His Excellency personally, not least because these events most certainly require a reversal of His Excellency's present policies.'

The admiral smiled. He rose onto the balls of his feet. 'It would take an earthquake or a tidal wave to persuade His Excellency to change his mind,' he observed. 'But tell me your story.'

He turned to sit on his bunk bed. It creaked slightly in protest as he adjusted his position, sitting very erect. The ship's bell clanged the end of the watch, its echoes thrumming through the panelling of the state room as Fernao began his story.

The admiral listened in total silence, except once when he grunted his approval of the march to the Jaya palace.

'So I hope you will agree that I did the right thing in coming to Goa personally, Sir.'

'Indeed. I commend your initiative, a sentiment which I am certain the Viceroy will endorse.' The admiral went on to question Fernao in detail as to the political situation in Lanka, trade and what he felt should be Portuguese policy. Finally, he smiled his satisfaction. 'I'm afraid the Viceroy won't like it, but the events you have reported certainly pre-empt his petty trader policy which has confirmed His Imperial Majesty's sorry title of "The Grocer King". We now need more than a continuance of our country's military standing and prestige in Lanka. We need expansion. As a matter of fact, properly handled, there is no reason why that fertile land should not become one of our *conquistas*, overseas possessions, with the Sinhala people subjugated like the *canarim*.'

Fernao recoiled instinctively. The *canarim* were the people of Goa and its neighbourhood. Proud *Konkani-Marathi* by race, of Indo-Aryan ethnic origin, they were fast becoming the servants of Portugal. Their leading families had even begun to ape European manners and customs. 'That would require reinforcing our troops,' he began.

'Indeed.' The admiral sprang to his feet and stood towering over Fernao. 'I shall recommend it to the Viceroy. Since we have already established our sovereignty in this region and the Malabar coast with our ships, we can certainly spare at least another *terco*, infantry regiment, for Ceilan, as we now call the island.' He paused, looked down at Fernao, his expression pleased as if Fernao had personally wrought the miracle of these changes. 'Well, *o filho*, you've had a tiring journey, I'm sure. You shall meet His Excellency first thing tomorrow morning.'

'Thank you, Sir.'

'When do you propose leaving for Colombo?'

'I thought I'd take the *Sao Pedro* back on its return trip the day after tomorrow.'

The admiral's stern features clouded momentarily. 'All too short a stay after such a long journey. H'rrmph.' He paused. 'Well, you had best join me for dinner.'

Men's voices reached them from the main deck, singing an old love song of Spanish Castile:

348

'I shall steal my love in the still of the night,
For her father ne'er lets her out of his sight,
In the turmoil of the day.'

Castanets clacked out the turmoil.

'Before I leave there's a personal matter I'd like to bring to your notice as my admiral and . . . er . . . my father.' Fernao fought to control the butterflies in his stomach. 'With your permission, Sir.'

'What is it, *o filho?*'

The ship lifted slightly on a swell, sank into the trough.

'You may recall meeting the young lady, *a senhora* Julietta de Brito, when you were in Colombo, Sir. She is the daughter of our chief factor, *a senhor* Duarte de Brito, a man of noble blood.'

'Indeed I do recall meeting her. A young lady of great beauty, gentleness and refinement.' The admiral smiled and Fernao's hopes rose. 'It's Navy gossip that you have been spending a great deal of time with her. I entirely approve because it will keep you from the *bordellos!*'

The butterflies settled and Fernao's hopes soared. 'I'm glad you feel that way, sir, because I asked for *a senhora* Julietta's hand in marriage and have received her father's blessing and that of Holy Church. Your own approval will make my happiness complete.'

'What?' The single word shot from the admiral like a musket blast. 'You . . . you want to marry this girl? *Marry* her?'

For a moment, Fernao was stunned. 'Why yes, Sir. With all my heart.'

'But my boy, you are a de Albergaria, of royal blood, and this girl is a *mestico*, a half-breed. You are my only son and it is up to you to keep our ancient, proud bloodline pure.' His father's abrupt tone changed. He began to sound like an adult cajoling a small boy. 'Come, come, *o filho*, you must really think again. By all means go on seeing her, make her your mistress if need be, let her bear your child, but give up any foolish, sentimental ideas of marriage. When people of royal descent marry it must always be to strengthen military, political and economic bonds. There is no room for love and sentiment. It is part of the price we must pay for our heritage, for belonging to old, proud families. You cannot belong and refuse to pay the price.' His voice softened. 'I know how it feels to be young and in love, my son. Remember, the fact that I am your father does not mean that I was not young myself once.'

Fernao was appalled at first, but finally outraged. He could not believe what he was hearing. His father's suggestion that Julietta should become his mistress was obscene. As he fought to hold back an outburst, another thought struck him, left him shaking. He struggled to keep his voice steady. 'Does that mean that you loved someone else when you married my lady mother, sir?' he demanded. 'Did you retain a mistress when you married her, when I was conceived?'

The admiral's ice-blue eyes widened with shock, the mouth and shoulders went slack, but only for an instant. He looked away. 'Your mother and I had a rare and wonderful understanding.' He drew himself up proudly. 'Our relationship does not concern you.'

Of course it does, because I am its product, Fernao thought fiercely. If you did not love my mother when I was conceived, what loyalty do I owe you? Suddenly he felt liberated, a great weight lifted from his mind, the darkness of doubt dissolved. He was coldly calm. 'With all due respect, I'm afraid I find your suggestion intolerable, Sir,' he stated firmly. 'I humbly request your permission to marry *a senhora* Julietta de Brito on my return to Colombo.'

'And if I refuse?' A dangerous edge had crept into his father's voice.

'I am of age and will marry her regardless.'

'Then why ask my permission at all?' The blue eyes were frosty, but angry fires had started to burn deep inside.

'It is a duty I owe you, Sir.'

His father nodded, very calm. 'Ah, duty!' he exclaimed softly. His whole mien chilled Fernao.

'I think you have been too long in the tropics, Lieutenant,' the admiral observed pleasantly. 'You need a change of station. The caravel *Trinidad* sails for Lisbon with cargo in two days. You shall sail with her. On your return, I shall post you to a more

350

temperate climate, Diu perhaps, but you shall have no more land assignments until I am convinced that your period of adolescence is over. How convenient that you brought your sea chest with you!'

Thursday, 28 April 1524

The Viceroy's Residency, built by Admiral de Albuquerque, was a smaller version of the royal palace in Lisbon, right down to the grain of each of the perfectly matched marble squares on its floors. Gilt furniture brought in from Portugal, Dresden china, Chinese and Persian carpets, Bohemian crystal chandeliers gave it all the magnificence of a European palace.

The private study in which Vasco da Gama received Fernao and his father the next morning was no exception. On the wall behind the ornate French-style desk at which the Viceroy sat, a strange round ornament with a gold frame and glass front was hung next to a large banner draped like a tapestry. Beneath the gold frame, four balls attached to thin gold rods rotated.

After the greetings were over, the Viceroy invited Fernao and his father to sit on the other side of his desk, then noticed Fernao's eyes on the wall ornament. 'I see you are curious about my beautiful toy,' he remarked in a curiously husky voice. 'That is a new invention, an instrument for measuring and indicating time. Sundials, hour-glasses and sand-clocks are out, as are timepieces run by wheels. The principle governing this particular instrument is the same as that of the clock installed at St Paul's Cathedral in London three hundred years ago, in which mechanical figures strike out each hour. The difference with this type of clock is that it is driven by a coiled spring so the mechanism can be housed in a small space. Also it can indicate time by the minute. Note that it is now 9.17 am!' The Viceroy seemed so proud of his new toy, so childlike about it that Fernao somehow warmed towards the man.

He and his father had dined together and spent an evening of well-bred charm. The only reference to the crisis had been the admiral's parting words when they bade each other good night. 'If you will promise me on your sacred honour that you will

351

never marry this girl, I shall let you retain your present post. You may then return to Colombo where you can resume the twin careers you have been building for yourself and which have made me very proud to call you my son . . . and of course to your love affair with the girl. Remember though that you owe our family a duty to bear a legal heir of pure lineage who can carry on our name.' He had paused, his eyes unusually reflective. 'For my own part, I must confess that I should like to have a worthy grandson.' He laughed lightly to cover his embarrassment. 'I must be getting senile!'

Fernao had felt only a cold contempt at his father's words. When he promised his father to 'think about it', he did so only to temporize. His iron determination to marry Julietta would never permit him to change his mind. If he gave up his father on her account, Julietta would feel completely obliged to marry him.

Fernao cast aside the reflection to take stock of Admiral Vasco da Gama. He saw a man of middle height, the trunk so long that, seated, he was at eye-level with his taller visitors. His sturdy body was clad in a red silken doublet with sleeves puffed in red and gold, matching the red and gold cross of the Order of Christ that hung from a red scarf round his neck. The same Order was emblazoned on the silk banner which adorned the wall. King Manuel had conferred it on the admiral before he left on his second historic sea voyage to the Indies twenty-one years before, and a Papal bull had guaranteed eternal salvation to all those taking part in that voyage.

Everyone Fernao had met who had sailed with Vasco da Gama counted him the greatest explorer of all time, greater than the Genoese, Cristoforo Colombo, who, they claimed, merely chanced on the New World by accident, opened up its treasures and brought back the pox! The Portuguese, Bartholomeu Diaz, did reach the Cape of Good Hope, but got no farther. In 1498 Vasco da Gama had dared the impossible with a flotilla consisting of four ships, two new square-rigged *nao, Sao Rafael* and *Sao Gabriel*, both having greater cargo capacity than the older ships, the *Berrio* for scouting and a heavy storeship. His naval bombardments had been classic examples of the ruthless exercise of firepower. A harsh, brutal man, he combined these traits of temperament with an excellent sense of international politics which had convinced him that Portugal should establish mastery of the Indian Ocean before the other European countries, whose trade with the Orient was still maintained on the slower and more expensive overland caravan routes.

The Viceroy was almost sixty-four years old, his long black hair, moustache and beard liberally salted white. The close-lipped mouth had a cruel, cynical twist. The nose above was a crag, so high that it rose to jut between the dark eyebrows onto a forehead that seemed low beneath his black velvet cap seamed with tiny pearls. The large deep-set eyes were a remarkable blend of ruthlessness and arrogance underlaid by a strange vulnerability which Fernao sensed rather than saw. This is the face of a man ravaged by success and bitterness, prestige and disease, Fernao decided with a surge of compassion. It is the face of a lonely man.

The Viceroy suddenly fixed him with a glance so penetrating that Fernao knew his thoughts had been probed and discovered. It was an uncanny feeling that left him naked, made him quail. Then the cruel mouth twisted into a smile. 'Pray tell us your story, Lieutenant,' Vasco da Gama commanded.

Fernao recounted the events in Lanka, noting that the Viceroy remained absolutely still, watching each word like a predator waiting to strike. He took care to give the Viceroy every detail and to stick to the facts without vouchsafing any opinion. Only when he had finished did Vasco da Gama's glance drop. For long moments, he toyed with a crystal glass ornament on his desk, staring at it with unseeing eyes. 'What do you recommend, Lieutenant?' He finally inquired without raising his eyes.

Surely God sent this question in answer to my prayers, Fernao thought. It is now or never. 'If I may say so very respectfully, Your Excellency, I believe that your illustrious predecessors in office have made the mistake of linking the military aspects of our presence in Lanka with our primary objective, commerce. This in no way implies criticism of them, because the link was essential at the time if we were to

353

commence trading as preferred customers. The result is, however, that, having well established commercial contacts with the island, the time is now ripe to separate the economic aspects of the two entities, but only after we make certain of the political climate.'

'You are resorting to the euphemisms of diplomacy, Lieutenant.' Vasco da Gama's voice had turned harsh. 'We are plain sailors. Tell us what you mean in plain language.'

Despite the abrupt attack, Fernao proceeded smoothly. 'I suggest that we increase our military forces in Lanka temporarily, for a set period in order to build the coastal forts to which I have just referred and to penetrate the central highlands. We can then withdraw the reinforcements as well as most of the men of the original *terco* in Colombo, leaving only the factory and the factoring staff, supported by skeleton military strike forces, to carry on trade in each of the forts. With your leave, I shall work out the soaring profits we can expect from pure trading operations thereafter, but allowing a period of time for us to recoup the cost of the initial military operations by amortization and to demonstrate that establishing these expanded operations would indeed be worthwhile commercially.'

The dark, deep eyes lightened with interest. 'Spoken like a true factor!' Vasco da Gama exclaimed. 'You have certainly received an injection of golden *cruzados* into your blue blood.' He gave a short, scornful laugh, fixed Admiral de Albergaria with an amused glance. 'How in the name of the blue Alps did you manage to produce such a versatile son, admiral?'

'It would appear that my son has gone beyond his inheritance, Your Excellency,' Admiral de Albergaria stated coldly. 'Your family has a distinguished military history, my own has an impeccable naval record. We are not factors.'

'We should certainly like to see your projections, Lieutenant,' the Viceroy said. 'When can you let us have them?'

'In three days,' Fernao responded. He could have produced the figures within a day, but he wanted to leap over the date on which the *Trinidad* left for Lisbon.

'Lieutenant de Albergaria will not be here three days from

now, Your Excellency,' the admiral growled. 'He has orders from me to proceed to Lisbon for naval duty on the *Trinidad* which sails tomorrow.' His voice was firm and decisive.

The Viceroy's eyebrows lifted. He was about to remonstrate but must have sensed the conflict between father and son, for his gaze shot in Fernao's direction as if he knew an answer must lie there.

'Your Excellency,' Fernao began, then stopped briefly to control his breathing and the beat of his heart. 'Three years ago, in addition to my naval duties, Admiral de Albergaria appointed me the deputy factor of His Imperial Majesty in Lanka on behalf of His Excellency the then Viceroy, who confirmed the appointment. I believe I have discharged the duties of that office with loyalty.' He kept his voice firm, but turned pleading eyes towards the stern figure seated behind the desk. 'I personally desire to remain in Colombo so that I can legally marry *a senhora* Julietta de Brito, whose father, your chief factor, Duarte de Brito, is a nobleman. She is a young lady of great beauty and virtue, but unfortunately she is guilty of a great crime.' He paused dramatically. In the silence, he could hear his father's breathing while the cross on the Viceroy's breast rose to gleam more vividly.

'And what is her crime?' Vasco da Gama inquired abruptly.

'Her mother was a Sinhala woman, which makes *a senhora* a *mestico*.' His voice rose passionately. 'An outcast in the eyes of blue-blooded Christians.' He could see that his words had punched home. 'Your Excellency, I love *a senhora* Julietta truly. I have her father's permission to marry her and the approval of Holy Church. My love is such that, if you would retain me in Lanka as your deputy factor, I shall resign my naval commission to remain with my lady.'

The ticking of the new clock took over the profound silence of the room. Fernao knew that his father was aghast, but one glance at Admiral Vasco da Gama and his guts turned to jelly, his stomach churning. Never had he seen such black fury on a man's face. Then the anger on Vasco da Gama's visage suddenly cleared. A short bark of a laugh escaped him. 'The old tale of tyranny,' he declared. 'You already have your appointment, *a*

355

senhor Fernao de Albergaria.' His glance at Fernao's father was filled with contempt. 'We hope that in this field of your endeavour at least you will be judged solely by your performance.'

Mingling with triumph at the success of his plan, Fernao suddenly felt compassion for his father and an undefinable sense of betrayal and loss deep, deep down. Only when Admiral Lopo Soarez de Albergaria finally smiled, coldly contemptuous of the peasants in the room, his son included, did the mists created by Fernao's love for Julietta clear so that he could identify what it was he had betrayed.

Royalty was a priceless heritage, carefully nurtured both naturally and artificially, a heritage of custom and tradition needed to set standards of conduct for all men, so that the lowly might be uplifted, the poor, even if exploited, might have the comfort and dignity of mannerly conduct. He saw briefly that he had betrayed this heritage. Then the curtain of personal triumph crashed down to hide it. Yet he had only to glance once more at his father's proud face to know that de Albergaria would make no further comment, because he would not permit any vulgar intrusion on his personal and family life.

'This is a very interesting situation,' the Viceroy proceeded, his dark, haunted eyes crammed with malicious enjoyment. 'A de Albergaria of royal blood voluntarily abandons his family heritage and becomes a common trader in pursuit of a different ideal, love.' His sigh was mocking in its ostentation. 'It has ever been so since the days of Samson. Though, by all accounts, we are not dealing with a Delilah in this case, every woman has the potential to emasculate her man.' He shook his head, broad fingers drumming life's warning on his desk.

Sick at heart, Fernao comprehended the extent of Vasco da Gama's bitterness. Was the Viceroy his ally or his enemy? Could it be that to His Excellency, Fernao de Albergaria was merely the instrument for an act of vengeance on the class to which Fernao really belonged, represented here in the person of his father?

Images of Julietta, of her white beauty, her gentle ways, flashed through his mind. She had suffered so many insults

356

because of royalty's addiction to pure blood lines. He could never hurt or betray her. He thrust aside the vagrant thought that subtly coercing her into marriage with him might be another form of betrayal.

'In the context of the present political situation in Lanka, we cannot have a military presence in that country alongside a factor and a deputy factor neither of whom has military standing or military power,' Vasco da Gama declared. 'A *senhor* Fernao Soarez de Albergaria, by virtue of authority vested in us by His Imperial Majesty, Dom Joao III of Portugal, we hereby commission you an officer in the royal Portuguese army and promote you to the rank of full colonel. We place you in command of all our field forces in Lanka, including the *terco* and artillery units presently posted there and such other troops as we shall presently dispatch. You shall move from the flagship to our residency immediately and remain as our guest till the mail packet leaves for Colombo on Tuesday night.'

Fernao knew a surge of delight. He sensed rather than saw his father's immobility. The man had withdrawn from the proceedings but was hearing them with aristocratic contempt. Doubts crept in. An army commission he fully deserved, but the accelerated promotion to such a high rank and responsibility put him, at the age of twenty-one, above Captain Oliveira who had more years of service than he had life. Would he not have to endure his own punishment in the form of Captain Oliveira's lifted eyebrows and the resentment of officers he had suddenly outranked?

Fernao bowed stiffly from his chair. 'Thank you, Your Excellency,' he declared. 'I shall endeavour to justify your faith in me.'

Silently, his tortured mind aflame, he thought, My father and I will probably never talk to each other again. But at this moment, we are more one than we have ever been before, though he does not know it.

CHAPTER 32
Wednesday, 1 June 1524

Departure of the *fusta* was delayed two days by a storm blowing south. Though impatient at the wait, Fernao found compensation in it because he came to know Admiral Vasco da Gama better during the brief period after his projections had been accepted. The ship sailed in the storm's wake, making good speed before its gentler afterwinds, and anchored in Colombo harbour on Wednesday evening exactly nine weeks after Fernao had left for Goa. The last time he had entered this port, it had been as a midshipman on his father's flagship. The recollection brought to his mind the worst moments he had known in Goa, when he returned his father's sword and the gold insignia of his naval rank by messenger and the bleak feeling he had experienced at the end of that first interview with da Gama, when his father departed, bowing gracefully to him and saying 'Colonel', his tone not mocking but coldly formal.

In the golden light of the flares that lined the wharf, Fernao could see that it was alive with people, the murmur of their voices punctuated by the slap of waves against the sides of the wharf and distant sounds of native music from the city. The heavy sea air was punctured by the smell of resin from the flares. The officer of the day, a young lieutenant whom Fernao knew, was present as usual, with a military picket and wagons to collect and transfer the mail and goods from the ship and take them to the fort. Off-duty soldiers and sailors stood in clusters, idly watching the event. Mouro and Sinhala traders, supported by bare-chested labourers dressed in traditional garb, anxiously awaited consignments despatched to them from the vessel's various ports of call. One of the Mouro was a giant of a man, clad in the baggy white trousers and brown waistcoat of his people. The great hawklike face and piercing eyes should have placed him in some fighting line rather than among the ranks of the traders.

'Colonel Fernao Soarez de Albergaria, newly commissioned in the Royal Army of Portugal by order of His Imperial Majesty through the grace of His Excellency the Viceroy, reporting for duty!' Fernao stated, to help the young officer on his way.

The officer sprang to attention again. 'Lieutenant Paolo Gonsalves, officer of the day, Colonel de Albergaria, Sir!' He turned smartly about, then barked orders to his men to form the guard of honour due to officers of field rank. The crowds became hushed as they pressed forward to watch the unusual ceremony.

When his inspection was over, Fernao was escorted by Lieutenant Gonsalves to a horse-drawn buggy. His sea chest was placed in the well.

The horse moved to a click of the driver's tongue and a flip of the reins.

The moment he saw the lights of the fort, Fernao's pulse quickened and his heart started beating faster. He was home again. It brought to mind Vasco da Gama's kindness to him during his stay at the residency, when the Viceroy had revealed a caring, compassionate side to his nature. He had inquired about Julietta, been curious as to the young couple's future plans, expressed confidence in Fernao's career.

'We have a duty to His Imperial Majesty,' the Viceroy had confided during their last dinner together. 'We would not have commissioned or promoted you to such high rank had we not been certain of your abilities.' He had paused. 'After all, many young kings have been generals who have led their men into battle and the only standard by which they were judged was whether they won or lost. For our part, we have yet other standards. How does a man take adversity? Does he acknowledge defeat?'

A swift hand to his heart, quickly lowered, a distending of the Viceroy's nostrils had reminded Fernao that Admiral Vasco da Gama was a very sick man, often in great pain, though he never showed it. An afflicted heart and malfunctioning kidneys had

359

caused those strange patches on the Viceroy's face. Well, you are properly the one to set such standards, Fernao had thought fiercely, for you will never acknowledge defeat from pain or death. 'Your Excellency,' he exclaimed. 'If I may say so respectfully and with the greatest humility, a king is not made *through* birth but *of* birth, of the essence of his being as an individual. You are therefore a king to me, not only a Viceroy.'

The cool darkness, seeming to glide past him as the buggy moved, brought Fernao a distinct image of the look on Admiral Vasco da Gama's face at his words. The dark, haunted eyes had expressed shock, then shone with a strange melting light.

'We would have been proud to have you for a son.' Vasco da Gama's husky voice had been hoarse. He had cleared his throat and called for more wine.

I know the secret of your sorrow, Grand Admiral Vasco da Gama of India and Count of Vidigueira, Fernao thought as the horse clip-clopped over the wooden bridge towards the great gates of the fort. Suddenly he felt affection for the lonely hero.

At that moment, a terrible voice, redolent of the grave-pits and the charnel houses, rang through the balmy night air, seeming to resound so shrill and piercing around the firmament that Fernao clapped his hands to his ears.

On the eve of the Christ child's birth, in this year of Our Lord fifteen hundred and twenty-four, the light of the brightest star of the east, the god who is but a mortal, Vasco da Gama, shall be extinguished.

And defiantly Fernao's heart responded, suddenly unafraid. You may take the mortal flesh and blood of Vasco da Gama, you foul fiend, Death, but his life's achievement will never perish, his memory will live on and be revered for ever.

The officers' orderlies were really military servants. Fernao's was a young olive-skinned *mulatto* seaman named Aires, whose lean, tough face was distinguished by the dark, three-inch knife scar running down his left cheek. Aires had the sharp eyes of a seasoned street fighter, which he had been from childhood in Lisbon until he was imprisoned for manslaughter before being exiled into naval service abroad like the other *degradados*. He was seated on the ground outside Fernao's room, idly picking up pebbles and throwing them at a mark barely discernible in the darkness when the buggy drew up. Not even the barked commands for the guard at the entrance gates to turn out seemed to arouse his curiosity. Only when he noticed Fernao alight from the vehicle did he spring to his feet, stifling an exclamation of pleased surprise. He touched his hand briefly to his dark forelock and rushed forward to take Fernao's sea chest from the buggy.

'It's good to see you again, Aires,' Fernao observed.

The man had removed the sea chest with a grunt, hefted it onto his shoulder. 'I be glad you're back, Sir,' he stated, looked mischievously at Fernao, and added, 'There's more than me will be happy.' He hesitated, then took the plunge. 'Begging pardon, sir, but *a senhora* Julietta be well, you'll be wanting to know.'

Fernao felt a rush of gratitude. He nodded and smiled his appreciation, thanked the driver of the buggy, then followed Aires inside. Lit by a brass hanging lantern, his room smelt musty from being closed up and unoccupied. But it was still home, right down to the narrow truckle bed at the far end, the washbasin on its metal stand, the chamber pot beneath it, the lime-washed walls with pegs for clothes on the left, the wooden crucifix with Christ in bronze above the crude *prie-dieu* on the right.

A look of surprise crossed Aires' face when he noticed Fernao's uniform for the first time, but he was too well disciplined to make any comment on the change in his master's branch of service. 'I be glad they make you a colonel, sir,' he declared. 'There's them as deserves it far less have had it longer. Can I get you summat to drink? Dinner will be served in the mess within the hour.'

'Nothing to drink, thank you. I'll wait for dinner.'

Aires knelt down, opened the sea chest and began to take out Fernao's soiled underwear. 'The dhobi comes tomorrow. Would you like a change of uniform for the evening, sir?'

'I think not.' Fernao unclasped his belt, began unbuckling the new army sword which Admiral Vasco da Gama had given him. 'Please present my compliments to Captain Oliveira as soon as

361

you've finished unpacking and tell him I'd like to call on him in his office immediately, if he is available.' He would have preferred to call on Julietta first. The light in the small window of her quarters had seemed to beckon when his eagerly searching eyes had found it.

Aires paused. 'Captain Oliveira be gone to town, Sir. Expected back shortly though.' He cocked an ear towards the door. 'Ah! That be him right now.'

Fernao caught the bark of orders from the entrance gates. The guard was turning out. He had best speak to the captain before he reached his quarters. 'I'll be back,' he said to Aires. 'Probably after dinner.'

He strode into a darkness filtered by horizontal ladders of light falling from doorways around the inner base of the rampart wall. Above him, the sky was prickled with the bright stars of the Milky Way. The sound of drums from the city blended into the booming of the surf.

Captain Oliveira was standing behind his desk when Fernao entered. He looked up. 'Ah! You're back,' he observed. He hesitated. 'You may be a prick at times, but I missed you.' Then he noticed Fernao's uniform and a look of surprise crossed his chubby face. The browless forehead lifted. 'Now what the blue hell is that get-up, Lieutenant?' he demanded, his voice suddenly raspier than ever. His eyes fell on the insignia. 'Fuck it, Lieutenant. You crazy or something?'

'Not crazy, Captain . . . just something!' Fernao laughed uneasily. 'Our Viceroy, Admiral Vasco da Gama, appointed me a full colonel in the royal army of Portugal. I'm reporting to you for duty in that capacity.'

'That's a lot of shit. How . . . ' Captain Oliveira paused, the blue eyes flashing dangerously. 'What's your position here . . . er . . . Colonel?'

'Still Number Two to you, Captain, but I'm to be in overall command of the *terco* and one other regiment which will arrive on the first available *nao*.'

'Good.' The captain rubbed his hands together in satisfaction, then malice took over. 'What did you have to give for this accelerated promotion? Royal arse?'

362

Fernao flushed, felt a flash of anger. Enough was enough. He drew himself to his full height. 'Captain Oliveira, I'll have you know that I'm not reporting to you for insults but for duty. I'm now the senior ranking army officer in Lanka and I'll thank you to give me the respect due.'

'Okay, Colonel.' The tone was so mocking, Fernao could have erupted. 'I have to respect your rank, but I don't have to respect a rotten bastard who uses his birth and his father to obtain a promotion over a hell of a lot of fine officers, men who've worked their arses off, risked their lives to get where you are.'

It was out, far worse than Fernao had anticipated. He was crushed and dismayed. He had expected resentment, even bitterness, but not from Captain Oliveira. And yet, why not? 'I'm sorry you see it that way, Captain,' he declared. 'I assure you that pride would normally prevent me from divulging personal matters to you, or to anyone, but you and I, the officers and men here will have to work together for the good of our king and our country.' His throat suddenly felt dry and he swallowed. 'I'd like to tell you the facts.'

Captain Oliveira's mouth twisted into a harsh smile. 'You'd better make them good.'

'Far from assisting me to get this appointment, my father refused me permission to marry *a senhora* Julietta.' He eyed the captain intently. 'Do you remember telling me you'd have my ... er ... privates if I played fast and loose with her?'

'I don't merely remember, I'll have them.'

'Good.' Fernao's confidence was mounting. 'As you know, one reason why I went to Goa was to seek my father's permission to marry *a senhora*. He refused it point blank on the grounds of ... er ... differences of blood.'

'The fucking prick, if you'll pardon my Sinhala, Lieuten ... er ... Colonel.'

Fernao adopted a light, bantering tone. 'I thought you'd feel that way, but with due deference, I suppose the action you mention is part of the function of the object to which you refer.'

For a moment Captain Oliveira looked blank. Then his great guffaw resounded through the small room. 'Son of a fucking prick!' he exclaimed. His laugh rang out again at the aptness of the remark, but ended in mid-air so that only the echoes remained. He stared at Fernao, his blue eyes frosted again. 'That's what you are too, Colonel. You feel so high and mighty because you have condescended to treat us as equals. Well, screw that.' He grew quiet, his expression thoughtful.

Fernao was genuinely bewildered. It seemed he could not win either way. Fury suddenly took over and he shook with it, his eyes blazing.

They stared at each other, instant enemies awaiting the first to strike. Fernao looked away. 'I'm truly sorry if there was even a hint of patronage in my words or my attitude, Captain,' he said humbly. 'I beg you to forgive me for it. My love for *a senhora* and my desire to marry her transcend all else in my life so much that I felt I had to resign my naval commission.' He was not about to betray his father.

'You what?' The sharp eyes were bulging with surprise.

'You heard me.'

'Then how is it that . . . ?' Captain Oliveira gestured helplessly with his hands.

'I gave the Viceroy a financial plan for temporarily boosting our strength in Lanka, for continuing to trade with Abdul Raschid as our sole supplier.' Had there been a flicker of interest in Captain Oliveira's eyes? 'The only difference will be that we shall be in substantive military control of the island and therefore dealing with the entire country.'

'Sit down, Colonel.' Captain Oliveira was more amiable now. 'What authority do you propose to exercise?'

'I have no intention of interfering with the affairs of the regiments. The commanding officers must run them while I exercise overall command.'

Captain Oliveira's eyes narrowed. 'That's all right by me, so long as you never forget who is in command over you.' He jerked his fingers inwards to point repeatedly at himself. 'Me . . . me . . . me!' He began speaking slowly and deliberately. 'Take this from an older man who has seen a lot of life, Colonel,' he stated. 'The world, every society, has its classes. You have betrayed your class, walked away from it. The so-called lower classes will always be suspicious of you. Far from welcoming you with open arms because of your grand gesture, they will despise you for your sacrifice.' He paused to eye Fernao as if he were a specimen, yet with a trace of pity in his blue eyes. 'So you are a man without a class, a man in a gap. You had better pray to God, to the blessed saints, to Jesus Christ and to the Virgin Mary that *a senhora* Julietta will be able to bridge that gap for you.'

Wednesday, 1 June 1524

Her father had gone to the wharves, to ensure that space was available for the *fusta*'s cargo. She already knew, through a vessel that had come directly from Goa the day before, that Fernao would be on board.

The best tailor in the city, an Indian, had by now become accustomed to making clothes for the Portuguese ladies in the fort. Julietta wore a new flouncy dress of green silk, very tight at the waist, flaring at the hips, which she had had made while Fernao was away. She could not deny that she hoped for his approval and that she had missed his presence in the fort.

She had lost a little weight during the past nine weeks, because she had had no appetite for food. The momentous decision with which she had been confronted continued to disturb her because she was still not certain as to what she would like. She could not deny that marrying Fernao would make the rest of her life easy, would please everyone, including Menika, but her love for Prince Tikiri clamoured against giving herself to any other man.

She was seated in the parlour on the edge of a settle when she heard the knock on the door. Instinctively she jumped to her feet, gathered her dress. Now why did I do that, as if Fernao were my lover, not just my dear friend, she wondered. With a sigh, she resumed her seat, heard the front door creak open, the murmur of voices, Fernao's deep and resonant. Then came his footsteps, firm on the tiled floor.

'A *senhora*!' His voice was vibrant.

She raised her eyes to his, wanting to remain calm and poised, hiding her pleasure at seeing him, but his gaze was so ardent she could not restrain a blush. He held out his arms to her as if it were the most natural thing in the world. Half reluctant, she let him hold her briefly. Strangely, he smelled of sweet musk and physical contact with him did not repel her any more than when they danced together. Perhaps . . .

He released her. 'I've missed you terribly,' he said quietly.

'I've missed you too,' she replied, truthfully.

His brilliant, pale blue eyes searched her face. He must have thought he found what he was looking for. 'I love you,' he breathed.

'Oh Fernao, I'm so glad.'

A flicker of disappointment crossed his face. It sped to her heart because she did want him to be happy, yes, to make him happy. He was a good man and she would certainly be better for him than those scheming young Portuguese women looking for a husband in the Indies.

A discreet cough brought her back to reality. 'Master, missy, *a senhor* de Brito directed me to chaperone you if you chose to take a walk on the ramparts.' Menika's voice held an apologetic note.

Fernao turned round towards Menika. 'That would be kind of you,' he stated. The sides of his eyes crinkled humorously. 'I hope you have lots of time, because *a senhora* and I have much to discuss.'

They stopped at their favourite spot on the rampart wall. Menika was a shadow some distance away, the night sky above them was brilliant with stars, which cast pale light on a heaving ocean scattered with the ghostly outlines of distant fishing boats. To the right, ships' lanterns signposted the harbour. Below the rampart wall, waves ended their smooth flowing journey, broke against black rocks, hissing, flinging up spray, seethed and receded, leaving behind the familiar dank smell of seaweed.

Julietta noticed Fernao's change of uniform, took in the colonel's insignia for the first time. 'You are a colonel in the army now? What happened?'

She listened in silence while he told her of the events in Goa. He avoided her gaze when he explained how he had resigned his navy commission. Her heart cried in an outrage she could not stop herself from expressing. 'Oh, Fernao, how could you ask your father for permission to marry me when I had not agreed?

'Well, it was my duty to ask my father and commanding admiral first,' he countered defensively. 'Anyway, my father refused his approval.'

'Why?' The foolish question escaped her without thought, then she could have bitten her tongue for asking it.

As he told her, she found her mind spinning back through time to the first day of her shame, when Princess Mala had divulged the story of her birth and heaped scorn on her. That same shame flooded her being now, filling her with a strange feeling of inferiority. Was she a hybrid product of Nature's creation, some gnarled, twisted thing produced by a mating foreign to the earth's genius, the coupling of a bull with a donkey? Somehow the feelings identified with Fernao, made him seem to be the present cause of her shame.

He was staring sadly at her, his face so sensitive in the pale light that some ghost from the past, the desire to wound in order to ease her own anguish, overwhelmed her. 'So your father, the great Admiral Lopo Soarez de Albergaria, of noble birth, thinks his son too good for a mere *mestico*?' she demanded. 'And did you, my noble lord, extend the poor misbegotten creature your compassion and your patronage?' The product of years of suffering and the past weeks of uncertainty, anger and frustration, the words were out of her before she could hold them back.

He looked as if she had struck him. His very vulnerability drove her on. 'I'm sick of being looked down on, discriminated against on account of something for which I was not responsible.' Unusually for her, she could not help spitting out the words. 'The only true class, the only real rank of birth is whether or not a child is the product of true love.' Her voice rose so passionately that Menika glanced curiously in their direction. Julietta no longer cared. 'I have borne this shame for years and years, but I have had enough, Fernao. Men and women mate like beasts, or bear children soullessly to carry a family name. Therein lies the real shame before God, for He

367

intended that mating and procreation should result from love and marriage of body, mind and spirit. My father has told me that I am God's true product, born of his love for my mother and her love for him. I am therefore of the most honourable estate. Are you of the same breed, *a senhor* Fernao Soarez de Albergaria?'

His eyes closed, his brow furrowed with pain. She could not bear to hurt him any more. 'Oh Fernao, Fernao, what have I said?' Her voice dropped. 'I didn't mean it against you, but against those who despise me for being a *mestico*. I had no right to take the years of shame out on you. Please forgive me. Please try to see what it must be like to be Julietta de Brito who must have something to which she can cling?'

He opened his eyes wide. 'But you have *me* to cling to at last.' His voice sounded firm, but the hurt remained on his face. He shook himself. 'My poor Julietta, I never dreamed . . . ' he began, then she noticed an unusual hardening somewhere deep inside him. His eyes flicked past her for a moment as if he was struggling with himself. 'We all have our crosses to bear,' he declared in even, almost formal tones. 'I gave up my father, my naval career to be free to marry you. Is this all you have to offer me in return, unkind words?'

'I'm sorry, Fernao.' She was on the defensive now, still bewildered, an animal cornered on all sides, panting, breathless. Not knowing which way to turn, she still wanted to ease Fernao's pain. 'All that is important is our friendship.' She saw him wince at the word 'friendship', needed to offer him some solace. 'I missed you while you were gone. You have done me so much honour and I have not even shown you gratitude.' Her eyes filled with tears and she looked away to fight them back. 'Please tell me all that happened in Goa.'

He told her, still tonelessly. 'I don't care what anyone says,' he ended. 'I sacrificed all my past life because I love you. I have become a vagrant socially, even spiritually, a man without class in a world that believes in and is regulated by class. I had hoped that you would bridge the gap, be my refuge so none of it would matter. I must say that what could have been the finest moments of our lives have been spoiled.'

'I told you I'm sorry, Fernao.' The tears were streaming down her cheeks now. 'I didn't mean to hurt you.'

'Give me those who deliberately hurt me any day,' he stated firmly, his eyes cold as the gloom. 'I can defend myself against them. The enemies within me are those I love, who are supposed to care for me but assail my vulnerability. A thinking person, an aware person who cares should never plead lack of intention as an excuse for causing pain.'

She had never thought of lack of intention in this way, but immediately knew it to be true. She could not undo the damage she had caused, but she should at least compensate for it. Suddenly her resistance to all the pressures collapsed. Her path seemed very clear. She was not being asked to love Fernao, only to marry him. If she agreed, any infidelity because of her love for Prince Tikiri would remain in the deepest, most secret recesses of her heart. Life would never present the opportunity for her to give that infidelity physical expression, so what was she fighting about?

The crash of the waves beneath them ceased momentarily. In the brief silence, a great calm settled over her. The constant anguish of indecision was over.

'I'm but the weak product of my past life, Fernao,' she said softly. 'I've never had to think of others. I hurt my father deeply through the years because I blamed him for my mixed birth. I failed him when he needed me most. I failed you tonight, but I should like you to give me another chance because my failure has opened my eyes, perhaps my heart. I cannot say that I love you in the way you would want me to. Perhaps the difference is that I love you but am not in love with you. Whatever it be, would you marry me, regardless?'

He faced her squarely. 'I want with all my heart that you should love me the way I desire,' he responded steadily. 'But I am prepared to wait and to work towards it. I believe that marriage would give us both the best opportunity to reach the truest and highest forms of love. It would afford me the right to woo you night and day instead of on fine evenings alone, here on the ramparts.' He smiled wryly. 'It would also give you the chance to be responsive.' He paused. 'Yes, I want to marry you regardless.'

'Do you believe that affection and respect are enough, at least to start with?'

'I know no more about these things than you do, Julietta. After all, I'm only twenty-one. I have been a sailor most of my adult life and have never known a woman. Yet my heart tells me that affection, respect, caring are what married life is about. Of course my romantic soul yearns to hold you in my arms beneath these stars, to have your gaze tremulous on mine while you tell me that you love me. But since that is not to be,' his expression became wistful, 'I can look for it on nights yet to come.' His eyes became brilliant as the stars above, compelling. 'Will you marry me, Julietta de Brito?'

She was caught up in some magic of the night, of the moment, as when she had first danced with Fernao on his father's flagship. 'I would be honoured to marry you, Colonel Fernao Soarez de Albergaria,' she whispered.

Then she was in his arms, regardless of Menika, the men on the ramparts. A wave, more thunderous, crashed against the rocks below, flung up spray that wet their faces as he kissed her lips beneath the stars.

Strangely, she was moved. Strangely, she could not find the kiss distasteful even though it brought back to her that first and only kiss from Prince Tikiri, making her shiver involuntarily.

Fernao must have thought that she shivered from the cold, for he moved his lips away so that he could hold her closer. At that moment, she accepted that he was indeed her refuge, but deep, deep inside her resentment simmered at all the pressures that had brought them to this moment despite the pure, white knowledge of her love for another man.

Julietta and Fernao inspected the mansion barely a week later and were entranced by the two-story structure of local brick and red tile nestling in a spacious grove of coconut, mango and flamboyant trees on the Mutu Vella hill just below the governor's residence. Fernao thought it ironic that the first real home that Julietta and he would share should adjoin the grove into which the *Santa Caterina* had fired on the day of his arrival in Colombo. The gardens were surrounded by a high boundary wall with a path running alongside it for sentries to patrol. A sentry box and guardhouse just within the wooden entrance gates completed satisfactory security arrangements.

The house had been built by a wealthy Goanese trader who desired to rent it out indefinitely so that he could move back home with his family, and it was fully furnished in a mixture of styles. The front verandah, facing the ocean, was scattered with comfortable Sinhala armchairs of *nadun* wood. The entrance foyer had a red and black Kashmir rug on white mountain crystal floors and Indian cabinets of dark wood with filigreed panels. The large reception room to the left of the foyer was furnished in the Portuguese style, the dining room to its right was French with a Persian carpet. Beyond the dining room was a rear verandah opening onto a red brick-paved courtyard with a fountain in the centre, and trellises with trailing vines that hid the kitchen, storerooms and servants' rooms.

The six bedrooms were upstairs, around a sitting area opening out of the upper landing. The two front bedrooms and a studio had a view of the ocean and the harbour, while the remaining bedrooms ran along either side of the house. Each of the front bedrooms had a huge four-poster with a canopy overhead, ornate linen cabinets, pegged screens and clothes horses. Attached lavatories contained a bathtub and a privy with a wooden commode, a washstand accommodating a ceramic jug and ewer, with matching chamber pots in the little lockers beneath.

Fernao rented the mansion the very same day.

CHAPTER 33
Monday, 10 October 1524

Formal notices of the marriage had been sent, as required by protocol, to the Great King Bhuvaneka, King Maya Dunne, King Raigam and all the sub-kings. Fernao also made it a point to ensure that Abdul Raschid, Prince Kumara and Prince Tikiri were informed. The mail packet had sailed for Goa the day on which the first banns were published. Fernao had taken care to send letters to his father and the Viceroy, notifying them.

Captain Oliveira had allotted quarters within the fort to Fernao, as befitted his new rank and station, though he would live in the rented mansion on the Mutu Vella hill, close to the governor's mansion. As with the residences of other officers living outside the fort, it was guarded by men of the regiment. Fernao's guard, consisting of its commander, Sergeant Correa, recently promoted from the ranks, and two sections of six musketeers, each section alternating daily, commenced their duties the week before the wedding.

The wedding took place on 10 October 1524, at a private ceremony in the fort chapel. It was a cool morning of white-gold sunlight. Fernao, attended by a young army captain, Armand Rego, as his best man, awaited Julietta at the entrance to the chapel which was crowded with the officers and their wives. He found himself breathless with excitement. Julietta arrived on her father's arm. Dressed in a white silk gown, wearing a veil and train of Brussels lace, she looked so ethereal that Fernao's heart started to pound. The service was conducted by Father Juan, clad in the brilliant vestments of the Church. They solemnly took their vows, Fernao in firm tones, Julietta tremulous.

There came the moment when Fernao raised his bride's veil to kiss her. The radiant glow on her face startled him. He had been told that this was characteristic of young brides, but had never dreamed of such beauty.

The luncheon feast commenced at 1.00 pm, after Julietta had rested and changed into a new blue outfit. There were Portuguese and Sinhala dishes: *paella*, beef, mutton and vegetable curries filled the air inside the fort with odours of ginger, garlic, cinnamon, coriander and lime. Cask after cask of Madeira wine was broken for the occasion. The feasting, singing and dancing to the fort's band of fiddlers, flautists and drummers went on through the heat of the afternoon.

Before the couple retired to change once more for their departure, they opened their presents at a table set up where all could see. There was a magnificent necklace of natural pearls for Julietta from the Abdul Raschids. A Scindhi bay, which had been at Julietta's door that morning, a gift from the Oliveiras, was paraded around. Then came a surprise package from Admiral Vasco da Gama. Fernao was amazed when he saw its contents.

'What is it?' Julietta inquired.

'It's . . . it's a clock His Excellency had in his office.' Fernao's voice was hoarse. 'It was his new toy, he said, one of his proudest possessions.'

'There's a parchment in the package,' Captain Oliveira volunteered.

Fernao picked up the scroll, broke the Viceroy's seal, unwound the ribbon, unrolled the parchment. The brief letter was neatly inscribed by a secretary and signed with Vasco da Gama's characteristic crowsfeet scrawl.

To Colonel Fernao Soarez de Albergaria and his wife, Admiral Vasco da Gama sends cordial greetings on the occasion of their marriage. We hope this token of affection and esteem will be symbolic of the fact that time has begun for you and that it will continue as a constant reminder of our timeless good wishes for a happy, healthy, prosperous life, blest with many children.

In the spirit that royalty does not belong to birth but to

character, the King of the Oceans salutes the King of the Heart,

Vasco da Gama, Viceroy
Estado da India

Fernao shook his head quickly, bit his lip to quell his emotion.

'Holy sea-cow, Colonel, how did you do it?' he heard Captain Oliveira exclaim. 'You must indeed be the King of the Heart to have discovered one where there was none.'

Hastily, Fernao reached for the next package, a slim rectangular box of thin wood about four feet by three feet in size. He unfastened the clasp and lifted the lid. He heard Julietta, standing beside him, gasp. The box contained a framed oil painting of a young man, obviously a prince, on a black charger, riding to rescue a beautiful young maiden from a dragon. Fernao reached quickly for the accompanying scroll and read it aloud:

To Colonel Fernao Soarez de Albergaria and his bride, Prince Tikiri Bandara of Sita Waka sends greetings.

A *senhora* once painted this beautiful picture. It was held in the Jaya palace for safe-keeping against the day a princely hero would come to her rescue. That day has arrived at last and the painting is delivered where it rightly belongs, with heartfelt wishes for a long and healthy, prosperous and happy married life, blest with many fine children, from

Tikiri Bandara, Prince of Sita Waka

Fernao stood stock still, seized by a spasm of jealousy. Then the simple beauty of Prince Tikiri's gesture swept all else aside.

Captain Oliveira cleared his throat noisily. 'Son of a holy sea-cow!' he exclaimed. 'Today is a day for princely conduct. You seem to inspire it, Colonel.'

Fernao turned impulsively to Julietta and found the aquamarine eyes glistening with tears. 'Why the tears . . . today of all days?'

'I am deeply moved,' Julietta replied slowly. 'Captain Oliveira is right. You do inspire princely conduct, my husband. I feel so humble before you, so honoured to be your wife. I shall dedicate my whole life to your happiness.'

Had she seemed lost for a fleeting moment, or was it his imagination?

Monday, 10 October 1524

Nestling in the dark grove, beneath a night blue sky glittering with stars, the distant lamp-glow from the mansion beckoned invitingly as Fernao and Julietta were driven up in their wagon. Fernao was flushed from the wine and happy from the wedding celebrations, glad to find Julietta excited, yet relaxed. His plan had worked, for Julietta's heart was surely opening out to him. Everything has gone off so perfectly, he thought, from Mass this morning to the reception this evening. I did the right thing by Julietta and me when I organized, even plotted, our marriage.

They were dutifully checked outside the great wooden entrance gates by smiling sentries, holding up flaming torches, who waved them on.

'Oh look!' Julietta exclaimed. He followed her slim, white fingers. 'There are fireflies in the branches of that flamboyant tree.'

'I ordered them specially to light your way home,' he stated gravely.

That low laugh he loved so much escaped her. 'I might have known,' she declared.

'What do you mean?'

'I've married a miserly man. He tries to save on oil by using fireflies.' Her mock-sigh was heavy. 'But . . . it's too late now. I'm trapped.'

This easy bantering between them had developed during the past four months. Surely friends can become lovers once they are married, Fernao thought. 'You are indeed trapped.' He could not resist the urge to pull her to him, holding her so tight that she gasped. 'You are now a prisoner in the Miser's Mansion.'

'Oh Fernao, you're wonderful.' She sighed contentedly, then looked at him, large eyes luminous through the gloom. 'When I was little, we would trap fireflies in a square of thin linen and their tiny glow would throw a ghostly light on our faces and faintly illuminate the darkness.'

'Really, little live torches?'

'Yes. Please, Fernao, can we do it again some night, just you and I?'

'Yes, beloved Julietta.' He felt a fierce urge to triumph over her former background. 'And you will hear birdsongs through your bedroom window once again. When the moon is full, the perfume of queen-of-the-night will be wafted up to you. This is the home you once knew, only much, much more.'

'No, Fernao. *You* are now my home. I shall try to be a good wife to you and for you. I meant the vows I took today. Your patience, your kindness, your understanding, your sacrifice and your need for me have made you my home. I have no other.'

He was moved by her words. 'What a sweet thought. Always remember that you are my home from now on.' And yet, a part of him vaguely missed the poetry and romance her sweet thoughts had denied him.

The wagon wheeled left around the circle and halted at the verandah steps. Aires hastened down, followed by two Sinhala servants in white tunics, pantaloons and turbans, Menika hovering in the background, her eyes shining. The scar running down Aires' cheek seemed to stretch with his smile. The horse snorted and stamped a foot. The servants gave the Sinhala salutation, bending low, clasped hands at their faces. Aires saluted and opened the wagon door. 'Welcome home *a senhor*, *a senhora*! My congratulations and good wishes. May God and His holy saints give you both a long and blessed life.'

Aires had laid out a light supper of cold chicken, bread and *ghee* for them in the dining room, which they nibbled at, to please him. Fernao made Aires drink a quick goblet of Madeira with them, before they went upstairs to their bedrooms to wash and change for the night.

Menika fussed around Julietta . . . 'my poor baby must be so tired,' . . . then, looking pointedly at Fernao . . . 'I hope that she is permitted some rest tonight!'

Finally, Fernao stood by the window of his bedroom,

listening for Menika's tread to announce that she had gone downstairs. Until this moment he had been doing something, with people all around him. Now that he was alone and the moment of sexual consummation was almost at hand, a part of him was afraid. He had never lain with a woman before, nor had he received any instruction. All he knew about sex was from hearing rough gossip or the bragging of officers and men, little gobbets of knowledge.

And what of Julietta? Would she give him a practical mating, to satisfy his carnal desires, or would she create romance for him? Was she capable of responding spontaneously? He remembered what an old family retainer had once told him. Had it been in another lifetime? Perfect love comes from the union of a virgin man with a virgin woman. The thought allayed his apprehension somewhat. Julietta and he were two people, with no knowledge or experience, feeling their way to the ecstasy of the closest physical union a man and a woman could have. Fumbling would not matter, nor was there any question of success or failure, because their entire life lay ahead, sanctioned by man and God. Perhaps the sexual union would even break Julietta completely loose for him.

He heard the adjacent door creak open, then slam. He smiled, knowing that normally neither Menika nor any servant would slam a door. Menika was obviously making sure that he heard her leaving Julietta's room. The beating of his heart became the accompaniment to his mounting excitement.

He turned and crossed the room with eager footsteps, his long crimson robe swishing. A single taper cast a dim light on the deserted hallway. He turned and stood a moment before the closed door of Julietta's bedroom to steady himself. He raised a hand to knock and paused with it upraised. The dark teakwood was a barrier to be crossed. Without any sense of drama, he suddenly realized that once he knocked on that door, a secure past, devoid of sex, would for ever be closed to him and a life of new responsibilities would be opened, satisfying a wife, satisfying himself, fathering children and looking after them. Was he ready for that responsibility? He loved Julietta, but could he play the role and be happy? He remembered Julietta's

377

reaction on the rampart wall on the night of his return from Goa, the night he needed her help, comfort and understanding most of all. Was Julietta ready for her own heavy responsibilities? It was too late now to consider such doubts. He knocked lightly, heard Julietta's husky 'Come in!' and opened the door. He stepped inside, closed the door quietly behind him and stood with his back to it, hands behind him still on the knob.

The bedroom was lit by tapers on brass wall-sconces. His eyes sped through air tinged with the scent of camphor incense from hanging burners, past the creamy silk linen on the great four-poster bed, beyond the masses of flowers in shiny brass vases on the bedside tables and the dressing table.

Julietta had been standing by the window, looking outside. She turned to face him. She wore a white silken robe, tightly belted to reveal her tiny waist and the flaring hips. Her hair looked darker than usual because the light was too faint to throw up its copper tints, so her white skin seemed pure as snow, her whole being virginal. His gaze took all of her in, then sought her eyes. Surely there was love in them. Their glances locked. His breath caught, his nostrils flared, he was dazed by a holy lust, desire he had never before experienced. The intervening space between them began to shimmer, brilliant water linking two islands lightly shaken by some undercurrent of the deep.

All his doubts vanished. He did not know when he took the first step towards her. Suddenly, he was in motion, slow-drawn by some magnetic force within them both.

Eyes still locked in that unwavering gaze, he finally stood looking down at her, conscious of the rise and fall of her white breasts. She was gazing up at him, tremulous now. He breathed the fragrance of her attar-of-roses perfume, then saw her delicate nostrils dilate. The exquisite beauty of it all was more than he could bear. With a half-gasp of excitement, he reached for her. She flowed into his embrace, her body incredibly pliant, her head hidden in his shoulder. He had never held a woman thus before. It was amazing that such firm flesh could be so soft.

'My love, my bride,' he whispered, hardly comprehending

378

either what he was saying or the pounding of his heart. Her thighs, soft against his legs, sent thrills up them, reaching for his penis, hardening it in a trice. He pressed it against her pubis and heard her tiny gasp. He smelled the fragrance of her hair, then her face was uplifted to his and her aquamarine eyes were deeper and more brilliant than any ocean he had sailed. Gaze to gaze, he lowered his face, slowly, slowly. Some sensitive, artistic part of him had taken over so that he knew exactly what he had to do without knowing it. His lips paused above hers and he felt her breath, scented with *valmi* root, upon his face. Her eyelids fluttered and closed as his lips touched hers. A few moments of firmness before her lips melted and his whole being responded. Long moments of fluid, gentle movement, then her mouth opened and he felt the sex-breath emerge from deep inside her. He identified it without ever having known it before and it consumed him.

With a groan, he released her, lifted her in his arms, carried her to the great bed. She lay back on the bed, her chest heaving, her nostrils flared, her eyes great pools.

He unfastened his robe and let it drop to the floor, stood naked before her for the first time, his penis large, so erect, so hard it was hurting him. Her eyes drifted down to it, paused there, inscrutable. This is the mystery of a woman cleaving to a man, he dimly thought. Her eyes returned to his and he bent forward to undress her.

He was filled with holy awe at the beauty of her nakedness, the slender neck, the full breasts with their pink nipples erect above the large circular aureoles, the slim waist, the generous hips and thighs. Like the models painted by Renaissance painters, but the face more delicate. I can adore her while I love her, he thought, before the mists of desire enveloped him and he reached blindly for her.

Their first mating was without any of the foreplay he had heard so much about. He was gentle, gentle, gentle when he entered her, piercing her virginity. She cried out once, but softly. He thrust through the pain to take her to him. He nearly came then, before he could even begin to move, but some miracle of love and determination enabled him to hold back.

379

Desperately at first, lying inside her, all the way inside her, quietly, steadying his breathing to get back his control, his every instinct screaming that this was vital to their mating for ever. Then he began to move slowly, loving her, adoring her.

Love made him control himself so that when he burst forth, it released her own orgasm in perfect climax.

'I love you,' he gasped.

'I love you, Fernao.'

A flood of gratitude and humility swept through him. 'You have given me your virginity,' he breathed. 'But, my beloved, virginity does not end with the piercing of a veil.' He looked deep into her eyes, her very soul. 'I promise you that you will be a virgin each time I make love to you.'

'Oh Fernao, I shall remain virgin for you all my life.'

He wondered why the tears sparkled on her eyelids and rolled down her cheeks, thought they were tears of joy and was deeply moved.

Monday, 10 October 1524

Sergeant Correa had been delighted when he was appointed commander of the detail that was to guard the new home of Colonel Fernao Soarez de Albergaria on the Mutu Vella hill. Perhaps being there at night would bring him another opportunity such as he had experienced over three years ago, when he had murdered that woman.

With a muttered excuse to the sentries about checking the garden, Correa clumped up the driveway alone. Once past the bend in the road, he left it to merge into the shadows. He paused behind a tall bush and stared up to get a closer look at the young woman who stood gazing into the darkness outside. Her face was not revealed, but the contours of her upper body were unmistakable. Sergeant Correa licked dry lips at the thought of those mounds of white breasts, that neat round bottom about which he had fantasized so frequently inside the fort. His very closeness to the scene of his first experience on the Mutu Vella hill, which he had got away with, gave him a sense of security in what he wanted so badly to do, filled him

380

with urgency to satisfy his lust.

He had never stopped to question why he was so different from other men. He was the product of his boyhood and environment. Having run away to sea when he was only twelve, the only way he could satisfy his insatiate lust was with other males. He learned early enough the pleasures of anal sex. Being big for his age, he was soon able to take rather than give.

He was sent to prison for brutally beating a young man who refused to give him sex during one of his spells on land in Lisbon. This was how he came to volunteer for service overseas and became a *degradado*. Before he left on his first voyage, he took a whore in a Lisbon brothel and contracted the dreadful new disease which Cristoforo Colombo and his men had brought back from the New World. The excruciating agony of it generated hatred of all women in him and a compelling lust for vengeance. From then on, he brutalized women whenever possible, avoiding the organ that had given him the disease in the first place. He vainly sought a virgin for it was a popular belief that the disease could be cured by sex with a virgin. Her tightness, he believed, would force out the obstruction that was so painful that each time it manifested itself in his penis he was afraid even to pass urine.

Like most men, he took whatever he wanted, gratified his every desire so long as he could do it without enduring the consequences. As for killing the object of his sex, this was a natural method of temporarily easing the pain in his penis.

A firefly settled on his shoulder in the darkness. He brushed it aside impatiently, continued to stare at the figure at the window, licking dry lips, once again mentally stripping off the woman's clothes, seeing white breasts, protuberant pink buttocks, feeling the soft arse-hole with his finger. His penis hardened, grew erect, pressed hard against his pantaloons. He drew it out, started moving it to ease the pressure, imagining himself up Julietta's rear. At that moment, she turned. By god, you are offering yourself to me, he thought with fiendish delight. His penis hardened so much that it hurt. He started moving it faster. He saw the young woman in the arms of a tall figure that blended with hers.

381

It broke the spell. With a muttered oath, he stopped. You are unfaithful to me, you slut, he gritted, silently framing the words. You have opened your body to another man almost at the moment of my climaxing inside your rear. You will no longer be a virgin after tonight, so you cannot cure me of my ailment. All you can do is satisfy my lust and die.

In searing madness, held back only by the need for self-preservation, he planned his gratification and Julietta's punishment. His penis flaccid again, he turned away to return to the guard post at the entrance to the property.

What was that movement in the shadows between him and the building? Had someone spotted him? His heart sank. He had to kill anyone who discovered his secret. He reached for the knife at his waist.

He pulled back from the bush, circled through the gloom, reached the edge of the building to take the observer in the rear...a good thought, he decided cruelly. He found only empty darkness. His eyes had been playing tricks.

Monday, 10 October 1524

Though worn out by the events of the day and the conflicts that occasionally simmered within her, Julietta could not fall asleep that night. It was strange to have a man sharing her bed, her head cradled on his chest. Now if it had only been Tiki-Tiki... she resolutely cast the thought aside. She had made her vows and would keep them.

Giving herself sexually to Fernao, with no pretence, had been the most difficult thing she had ever done in her life. The tears that had followed her climaxing were involuntary. They had come from a sad heart. She felt she had betrayed her love for Prince Tikiri by giving herself so completely to another man. She knew how she would have felt if the roles had been reversed, gladness for her prince, but desolated in her love. Her lovemaking with Fernao had also marked an emotional turning-point. She had worried so much about it, and when it was over she felt a gush of relief and thankfulness that it had gone well and that her reactions had been natural. Yet some unidentified regret remained.

The wedding night came as a climax to the months of doubt since she had accepted Fernao's proposal. It was one thing to have made the decision, another to sustain it. The questions kept rising. Was she doing right by Fernao? Why had she allowed him well-nigh to coerce her into marriage? How could he have done so if he loved her truly? Did she have the strength to make him happy? How would she fare on her wedding night? She had used those intervening months to accustom herself to the role she had accepted, so that by the time the wedding day arrived, the Julietta of the Jaya palace and the succeeding years was relegated to the unseen, unconscious recesses of her being and only Julietta Duarte, bride-to-be of Colonel Fernao Soarez de Albergaria, existed. Tonight, had she been able to live the role instead of merely playing it? During the love-making she had experienced a curious suspension of her true self, and when it was over, she felt somehow lost, hence too the tears.

Lying in the lamplight, listening to Fernao's heavy breathing, feeling the regular movement of his body, she told herself that a part of her had died so that a new Julietta could be born. She was happy and sad, yet the sadness was no longer because she had left Prince Tikiri in this life, but because she had left herself. As for Prince Tikiri, her God-given love for him would surely be renewed when he met her in heaven. For the present, she would love, honour and obey this good man lying so peacefully beside her. She would give him her all.

She placed a gentle hand on his dark head. He murmured and snuggled closer to her. The comfortable movement made her feel excited at the thought of their honeymoon cruise around the island on the *nao*. She had best get some sleep because the ship was to leave on the morning tide.

CHAPTER 34

Monday, 24 October 1524

Thirteen days later, on a blustery pre-monsoon evening, the great *nao* anchored in the port of Colombo again. For Fernao, their honeymoon, sailing around the island, had been perfect, in spite of Julietta's occasional bouts of sea-sickness, which had been more acute when she started her menstrual period two days before the voyage ended. Now it was back to work in the fort for him, the very next morning. He felt a new man, full of energy, drive and a tremendous sense of power when he entered headquarters.

Captain Oliveira's welcome was cordial enough for a man who had a bad head cold, a huge red pimple on one chubby cheek and watery blue eyes. He blew his nose loudly into a large white handkerchief. 'Fucking weather!' he complained, his voice raspy. 'Pre-monsoon always brings these cursed colds and sore throats.'

'Lucky you don't have the ague,' Fernao volunteered, taking his seat across from the captain's desk.

'Lucky I don't have the fucking pox too!' the captain grunted. 'What I don't have won't cure this shitty cold.'

'Glad I didn't give it to you,' Fernao countered drily.

Captain Oliveira stared at him blankly, reached up and ran a palm once over his shiny, bald head. '*I* should get the pox from you, colonel?'

'No, no . . . ' Fernao began in confusion.

'Let's go back to the beginning, Colonel.' A faint grin crossed the captain's face. 'Did you enjoy your honeymoon?'

'Immensely, thank you.'

'And *a senhora* is well and happy and you are both comfortable in your new home?'

'Yes and she thanks you too.'

'Good, good.' The captain paused. 'Now your report, Colonel.'

'I visited every possible harbour along the coast and prepared a detailed appreciation of their possibilities. Here it is in writing.' Fernao offered the manuscript to the captain.

'Splendid. Anything special in the report?'

'All of it is special,' Fernao responded with a smile. 'Oh, you'll be glad to know that the great stone cross with our royal coat of arms inscribed on it, which Captain de Almeida erected on his visit to Galle in 1505, still stands tall on the Point du Galle, an inspiring monument.'

'Which ensures that this country remains under His Imperial Majesty's divine protection,' Captain Oliveira commented drily.

'I would say our first priority should be to build another fort in Galle, because the southwest coast abounds with cinnamon. There's an ideal location on the north side of the port.' He felt a surge of enthusiasm. 'I have suggested that we also build forts in Negombo, Mannar, Trinco, Hamban and Matara.'

'To what end?'

'First, trade, which would justify the costs. Second, the creation of a ring of steel around the country, with a base at its centre, Kandy.'

'Jesus, you talk like a conquistador.' The captain blew his nose loudly into his linen handkerchief. The sound reverberated through the room, a paean of derision.

'Isn't that what we are? We want uninterrupted trade, riches. The only way to achieve it to the maximum is by controlling the entire country.' Knowing he suddenly sounded like his father, Fernao fell silent.

'What will the reactions of the Sinhala kings be?'

'Do we care when we have the firepower?'

Captain Oliveira gazed intently at him. 'What has happened to make you so...so...' He gestured helplessly. 'I mean, when we first came here, you were full of the Sinhala race, its independence and culture, so desirous of ensuring the rights of the Sinhala people.'

'I was a boy then. Now I'm grown to manhood.'

'Overnight? Can it be that having finally proved your manhood in bed, you are extending it willy-nilly to your official duties?'

Fernao flushed. 'That has nothing to do with it. I admit I now have family responsibilities and intend fulfilling them to the hilt.'

'Have you considered the risks, the human lives involved in what could be a dangerous gamble?'

'That's a strange note of caution to be sounded by you, Captain.' Fernao laughed. 'Wasn't Admiral Vasco da Gama's journey around the Cape the most dangerous gamble of all? Have not the costs, even the thousands of lives lost since then, been worth the gamble?'

'I don't know, Colonel. To tell you the truth, I've never considered it.'

'Perhaps I too will consider the question *ex post facto*.'

'I warn you it may then be too late. If His Excellency approves your plan, it may let loose the hounds of war. Certainly King Maya Dunne and his son Prince Tikiri will never stand for it.'

'Damn them both, I say. They must submit or perish.'

'Especially the prince.'

Fernao felt his eyes grow as frosty as his mind. 'Now what precisely do you mean by that?' he inquired in chill tones.

'You have a sense of predestination about the prince,' the captain answered slowly.

An unexpected flurry of wind brought raindrops, oddly sparkling through sunshine, splattering against the wall of the tower. The smell of new wet soil was wafted through the window.

'And if I do?'

'I understand it only too well,' Captain Oliveira replied gravely. 'I have seen it happen. Men of sensitivity are aware of the source of danger or death long before the event.'

'I shall never let such feelings cloud my judgment,' Fernao asserted.

'I know you won't, Colonel. You are at heart a man of honour.' He opened his desk drawer, drew out a parchment scroll bearing the seals of the Viceroy. He slammed the drawer shut, tapped his desk with the scroll. 'This despatch arrived on the mail packet yesterday. It contains the orders of His Excellency. I am to be in overall command of the vessels and men of this station, but you will have full power to make decisions as to the establishment of new factories, trading stations and forts in the island and as to the disposition and use of all our land forces, asserting our dominion, as needed, for the fullest trade monopoly. You may be sure His Excellency will approve your report, but God help us, for this is far beyond what we ought to be doing. All else apart, there will have to be payment for the horrendous costs some day so we will have to develop an enormous volume of trade.'

'We will establish our forts slowly, their numbers to grow in tandem with the expansion of trade in each area.'

'You seem to have all the answers.'

Tuesday, 25 October 1524

The news Abdul Raschid brought home the next night was excellent. It was obvious that their son, Ali, shared his excitement. Seated on a settle, a slim, erect figure, the boy's gold silk tunic and pantaloons made his olive skin seem to glow in the lamplight. His head, the black hair shining, was alert, the mouth firm.

'So you see, wife, the opportunity presented to us by Captain Oliveira and Colonel de Albergaria, praise be to Allah, is limitless.' Abdul reached for the inevitable sweetmeat, an orange *muskat*, and began eating it with his customary relish, thick lips smacking. 'We shall become the sole supplier of the *parangi* for all their purchases in the coastal areas of the island. We help them build up their trade, they then build forts to protect the trade . . .' he smacked his lips in satisfaction ' . . . and us. Of course, they will monitor the prices, but we can afford to drop our margin of profit because of the volume.'

'The *parangi* want an economic stranglehold over the whole island,' Aisha responded. 'They want to use us because their plan will require a vast organization extending to various parts of the country, which they cannot readily set up because they

387

don't have the connections. We shall have to risk a lot of money.'

'That's what I told the captain, pretending not to be excited over the deal. "Supposing we set up this whole organization and you decide not to trade through us any longer?" I asked him. He replied that they will give a written agreement to carry on with us for a period of five years. I told him all they had to do was get in their ships and leave us high and dry on the land, or even to take over our organization by force. I demanded a large sum of money in gold *cruzados*, payable in advance, as surety against their leaving. If they honoured the agreement, we would use it as payment for the last consignments at the end of the term of the contract.'

'That was very clever. What did the captain reply?'

Abdul's flabby face creased in a pleased grin. 'He agreed. They both wanted the business badly, each for his own good reasons.'

'Father, mother, may I be permitted to speak?' Ali had remained respectfully silent up to now.

'Certainly.' Abdul nodded, reached for a *halva* this time.

'We certainly have our agents, all of them our own Mouro people, in the major coastal towns, but we will need to reinforce them with trusted buyers and inspectors. We will have to build or rent factories and warehouses. It is crucial that we have someone reliable to set the entire operation up properly from the very start, is it not?'

'Of course,' Abdul Raschid agreed.

'You and my lady mother have to stay in Colombo, so that leaves only me.'

'You?' Aisha recoiled at the thought of losing her son from home.

'Why not, revered mother.' Iron had entered the young voice.

'You might be kidnapped for ransom, even assassinated.' The possibilities filled her with horror.

'That's a risk I'll have to take.'

Monday, 7 November 1524

Events were moving so fast they had kept me busy night and day. As soon as we returned to Sita Waka after the meeting of the Council of Nobles, we set in motion plans to convert the township of Sita Waka into a fortified city, as befitted the capital of a new kingdom, with our family mansion the centre of our new capitol, with fortress walls and a moat. It was a pity in a way, for the mansion lost its rustic beauty. Also, it was one thing to decree a new kingdom, quite another to establish it and get it going. But I was glad to throw myself into the achievement of my father's plans, because Juli's marriage to Colonel de Albergaria had almost crushed me.

Meanwhile, Palitha was no Kodi. The twenty-four muskets he had manufactured were not reliable and his attempts to produce the perfect musket were still uncertain. In addition, he nearly killed himself during one of the test-firings of a prototype cannon.

In the days immediately following Julietta's wedding, I received regular reports from my spies on events at the de Albergaria mansion. At first, the news that Sergeant Correa, the beast who had foully murdered the prostitute Lila, had been appointed guard commander of the mansion left me with mixed feelings. Lila's death could now be avenged more easily, but I was uneasy that such a man should be living on the same premises as Juli, that a rapist pervert was responsible for the protection of the girl whom I still considered my own, regardless of her marriage to another man, because my love for her came first and would never die.

During the past three years, we had received reports of the sodomization and murder of several prostitutes in Colombo. It seemed that Sergeant Correa must be responsible, but there was nothing I could do about it. Worse, it was becoming apparent to us that a dreadful, excruciatingly painful new disease of the genitals was spreading among certain classes of men in Colombo. In the process of time, we had realized that it had first occurred only with men who had consorted with prostitutes regularly used by the *parangi* soldiers, who were obviously carriers of the disease. But here again we could do nothing about it. The *parangi* did not take rape seriously. To them, despite the teachings of their Church, sex seemed to be the product of lust and the desire for pleasurable sensations, like eating or passing wind, not of love and marriage. Copulation was something for men to wrest from women, like beasts of the jungle.

I have an uncanny gift. If something impells me to be at a certain place at a certain time, there is always a reason for it. Whether this comes from the *devas*, from my destiny, from hidden processes of reasoning that surface in the form of such impulses, or from some combination of all three, I do not know. Today, this instinct told me that I should go to Colombo without delay.

Apart from instinct, I had received a report from my agent in the de Albergaria residence in the Mutu Vella hill who had observed Sergeant Correa's obscene actions in the garden on Julietta's wedding night. I could no longer shrug off the danger to Julietta by telling myself that her safety was not my business, that my action in returning her painting to her as a wedding present contained my solemn acknowledgement that she now had a new champion. No, I could not cast Julietta off, even though her marriage to Colonel de Albergaria confirmed my suspicions that it was she who betrayed Kodi, perhaps deliberately to curry favour with her lover and the *parangi* commanders; after all, I had told myself, most people who avidly desire a marriage will go to any lengths to achieve it.

Perhaps more than anything, the possible threat to Julietta's safety told me how much and how totally I loved her. There would never be anyone else for me. I had to protect her.

When I learned also that Colonel de Albergaria would be away from home on the night of 10 November, since it was his turn to be on duty in the fort, I obtained leave from my father to visit my uncle Prince Maitri Pala, who was still governor of the port, in his mansion on the Mutu Vella hill.

Thursday, 10 November 1524

Julietta was happy in her married life, with the happiness that comes from giving. The most difficult part had remained the sex. She still had to struggle to separate herself from herself in order to give herself to Fernao as she had done on their wedding night, but she had won through and was now reaping the rewards in Fernao's happiness and her own increasing contentment.

One problem resurfaced. She could not prevent bouts of secret resentment at the way in which Fernao had engineered the marriage. She had discovered the whole truth from a beaming Father Juan and her pleased *o pai* when they greeted her on her return from the honeymoon. Aren't you now glad that you accepted the pressure we put on you at Fernao's instigation? Were the three of us not right to point the way to your ultimate happiness? Shocked, she had asked herself whether her marriage had been made by God in heaven, or by Fernao on earth. Her love for Prince Tikiri had come from God. She could not avoid feeling violated. Well, there was no help for it now. Surely time and effort would get her over this difficulty. Meanwhile, she was becoming more and more dependent on Fernao each day.

The mansion was sheer luxury after the Jaya cottage and the quarters in Colombo. She had so much to be thankful for, especially the host of servants, including her ever-faithful Menika as a maid, Appu, the new *major domo*, a slim Sinhala who ran the household as if it were an army squad, a superb Mouro cook, Fernao's Sinhala valet, several footmen, grooms and gardeners.

Running the mansion and being the wife of Colonel de Albergaria was a full-time job. As soon as Fernao left for work in the morning, she started her day by organizing the marketing and the day's chores for the servants. While shopping for spices would be done monthly under Appu's direction, meat, fish and vegetables were bought twice a day. The fish was especially fresh because it came direct from the night's catch of the boats beached on the harbour-shore below. It was most welcome on

391

Fridays when, as Catholics, she and Fernao ate no meat. All this involved shopping lists and payments to be made daily. Supervising the cleaning of the house and the maintenance of the extensive garden and the laundry lists were also time-consuming tasks, because she would check it all with the meticulousness of an officer's wife. In addition, there was entertaining to be done because of Fernao's position.

Yet with all this, she missed Fernao when he was away at work and her first Sundays in the mansion had been particularly happy because Fernao did not have to go to the fort and they could both attend Mass conducted by Father Juan in a fine new church the Great King had approved their building in the area called Cochin Market on the waterfront. All the Portuguese and their wives had attended, dressed in their Sunday finery, so the mansion had been crowded with luncheon guests after the service, one large happy family united in the true faith.

She had been discovering a stern new strength and an almost harsh new purpose in Fernao since their wedding day. Though it disquieted her somewhat, he was such a wonderfully kind and thoughtful husband that she set her apprehension aside.

Finally, Fernao's duty night in the fort, which she had been dreading, arrived. She felt lost when he kissed her good-bye in the bedroom that morning. 'Oh Fernao, can't you come back somehow tonight, perhaps in the early morning? I could wait up for you.'

'My love, you know that it is my duty turn. I have to sleep in the fort.' He stroked her head. 'How your hair shines in the morning sunlight . . . as it did last night in the lamplight. You are so beautiful. Be mine alone for ever, beloved.'

'Yes, yes indeed. I am yours alone.' She simply could not bring herself to say 'forever', because that was for Prince Tikiri. 'No one else shall touch me.' She clung to him again, this time without knowing why. 'Hurry home.'

Thursday, 10 November 1524

Sergeant Correa deliberately made his presence known in at least two toddy taverns in the city, having violent arguments with the tavern-keepers before ostentatiously making his way in the direction of the street of brothels in the Slave Island. He even taunted the sentries outside the Abdul Raschid home with having to be on duty while he was on his way to a house of pleasure. Finally, he slipped into the vacant lot he had selected and changed his uniform for a black shirt and pantaloons.

Carrying his bag, his uniform and the rope ladder in it, he threaded through the city's dark alleys, avoiding the main streets, and headed for the Mutu Vella hill. He reached the de Albergaria mansion in time to hide in the bushes across the street and observe the changing of guards at the entrance gates. The midnight watch had commenced and it was time for action, a rearguard action! He grinned wolfishly in the darkness.

He removed the rope ladder from his bag, hid the bag in a bush and coiled the rope around his arm. He slipped across the deserted street, climbed the wall and dropped into the spacious grounds of the adjoining mansion, which he knew to be empty. He prowled silently along the exterior of the de Albergaria boundary wall till he came to the spot he had earmarked for his entry. There, he climbed the boundary wall and surveyed the scene.

Not a light glimmered in the mansion. Everyone must be fast asleep. Lying on the wall, he thanked the devil for giving him a dark, overcast night. He knew the layout of the mansion and its routine perfectly. The young bride in her bedroom would probably have that old woman servant sleeping on the floor beside her bed. The adjoining bedroom, being the colonel's, would be empty. You will have another husband enter your bedroom tonight, he thought with fiendish glee. His penis stirred in response, causing the ulcers to throb painfully.

He leapt lightly to the ground. All this was easy work for one who had participated in many a military night assault. A breath of wind rustled the dark leaves overhead as he crept into the inky blackness beneath the trees and cautiously made his way towards the front of the building. He paused at the edge of the grove, keenly searching the lawn. It was deserted; the house was still as a grave. The scent of night jasmine reached his nostrils, intensified his sexual desire. He crossed the lawn flat-footed, reached the wall of the house below the colonel's bedroom, paused to ensure that he had been unobserved. Nothing moved. Only the sound of crickets and the squeak of a rat disturbed the stillness.

He moved the ladder from his shoulder, uncoiled it, threw the end with the grappling hook up towards the windowsill. It clanked and caught with the first swing. A good omen. He pulled, tested for firmness.

With the agility of a great cat, he climbed up the ladder, paused at the sill, gazed long and fixedly into the bedroom to accustom his eyes to the darkness, ready to leap down the ladder at the slightest sign of life. He soon distinguished the outlines of the bed, the dressing table, each item of furniture. Nothing had changed since his first official inspection of the house as the guard commander on the day the detail took over its protection. He swung inside, padded softly across the room, reached the door. He gently felt for the knob, found it, tested. The door was unlocked.

He slipped into the darkness of the passageway, reached the adjoining bedroom. He found the knob, quietly tested again. A thrill of satisfaction ran through him. He opened the unlocked door, heard deep breathing inside. Both women were asleep. The scent of camphor incense hung heavy on the air. His eyes began to distinguish objects in the room. The shapeless bulk on the floor beside the bed would be the sleeping servant woman; he could differentiate between her stertorous snores and the more gentle breathing of the young woman. He imagined the white breasts of his prey moving gently up and down. His penis stiffened, grew erect, the ulcers clamoured to be soothed.

Heart beating faster, he tiptoed across the room, dropped to a crawl and paused beside the sleeping figure on the floor. Wearing a loose cloth, the woman lay on her back. Her arms, folded across her chest, rose and fell with her breathing. She smelt of sleep clothes and stale breath. Revolted, a violent spasm of desire to block out the smell shot through him. He raised his right hand, fingers together, thumb extended. He jabbed the gap in between swiftly at the voice box. With a strangled croak, the figure stretched, the trunk rising. His huge hands immediately reached for the scrawny neck with its broken voicebox, gripped, squeezing ferociously. The woman writhed, struggling for breath. He held her down with his huge body.

The figure on the bed stirred, murmured something. He froze without loosening his grip. Heart pounding he heard the bed creak as the young woman turned over. He waited till her breathing became regular again, then tightened his grip.

When the old woman was lifeless, he released his hold. He quietly rose to his feet, stood towering over the bed. This was the critical moment. He must stun the young woman without killing her. He was not one of those ghouls who entered corpses. He needed the death throes of the sphincter to give him total satisfaction.

He leaned over, touched the woman's shoulder. She jerked on the instant, sat up. 'Fernao?'

The intimacy of her slumber-misted voice nearly drove him wild. He half-turned, leaned over, chopped lightly with both hands on the sides of her neck. She jerked upwards, fell back on the pillows. He picked her up in his arms. Her body was so warm and soft he wanted to enter it there and then. Once again, he restrained himself, recalled his true need, to tear this adulterous bitch apart and execute her in the very same place where he had experienced his first incredible revenge on womankind.

He swung the still figure easily over his shoulder and padded across the room.

CHAPTER 35
Thursday, 10 November 1524

It was strange lying alone in his quarters in the fort after all the weeks of having Julietta's warm, soft body beside him every night. He missed her sorely. Though his work was exciting, especially now that he had added military and trade responsibilities, a part of him never wanted to leave Julietta every morning. Yet the sum total of it all was that he went to bed each night contentedly because Julietta was there, lovemaking was new and exciting, sleeping beside her afterwards was deeply satisfying and he awoke in the morning eagerly anticipating the day's work. Life was indeed good to him, he reflected just after midnight; the thought relieved the dull weight of the twenty more hours away from Julietta. He longed to return home to his mansion immediately.

Aires had brought him his dinner from the mess hall. Knowing that sleep would not come easily, he ate in his office in the tower of the fort and kept working on trade figures until shortly after the commencement of the midnight watch. When he retired to his old room, because his new quarters were occupied by a visiting sea-captain and his wife, he had found the air inside warm and close after the coolness of his mansion on the hill.

He had changed into his nightgown, blown out the lantern and lain down on the narrow truckle bed. It was hard and uncomfortable. He stared up at the darkness, his mind hot, dry and alive, racing with the figures he had been working on that night. He set these aside to allow thoughts of Julietta to trickle through the parched skin of his consciousness, soothing it like cool water. She would be asleep. He wafted his spirit to her so that it could merge with hers through the mists of slumber.

Suddenly, from nowhere, unease sparked so fiercely inside him that it made him jerk upright. The unease immediately flamed into alarm. What made him so afraid? He was not an imaginative person. Here he was, safe in the fort while Julietta was safe at home. He lay back again, yet remained stiff and tense.

He tried to drive away the fear, but it began growing until it was tearing into his mind. His body felt fevered; he broke into a cold sweat. He sat up again, flinging aside the thin bedsheet. He needed fresh air. No, he needed to get to Julietta. He would ride out to Mutu Vella immediately.

He groped for the tinder box, made the flame, took the tiny taper to the lantern and lit it. He reached for his pantaloons and stopped. This was absurd. Colonel Fernao de Albergaria, head of the infantry regiments in the fort at Colombo, sleeping apart from his young, beautiful bride for the first time, leaving his post during his duty turn and dashing to her because of some mad sense of foreboding! He had his duty to perform, a responsibility to fulfil. Above all, he had to be an example to his men. The struggle between the wild impulse of love and the stern call of duty went back and forth for a full minute. Duty won.

He remembered that he had not said his prayers, because he had come to saying them with Juli every night. 'O dear God, O blessed Jesus Christ, O sweet Virgin Mary, protector of women, guard my Julietta this night and always I beseech you . . .'

Thursday, 10 November 1524

At first, Julietta could not comprehend what had taken place. Then memory flooded back. And terror. When she awoke to a touch on her shoulder, she had thought it was Fernao's until the huge shadowy presence registered as an intruder. But it was only for an instant before the impact of blows on either side of her neck sent sharp pain shooting up both sides of her head and stars had flashed into a total blackness.

She was lying on the ground now, in darkness again, the earth cold to her back, stars glimmering through dark branches overhead. Her neck and head ached. Where was she? Panic gripped her. Then she saw the giant figure looming over her,

397

breathing deeply. The knowledge that she had been abducted hit her with stunning force, brought chill terror that engulfed her. Who could this man be?

She lay petrified for a moment before reasoning asserted itself. She had been carried away from her home. Why? It could only be to rape her. The answer smashed into her mind with the force of a cannonball. She had to escape somehow while this man was recovering his breath.

She jerked upright, placed a palm on the ground. A scream welled up in her throat but instinct stifled it. She rose, twisting sideways.

A huge hand grabbed her hair, yanked so hard it was almost torn away. She shrieked with the pain, then was flung to the ground still shrieking. The huge hand was clamped over her mouth. It smelled of sweat. She tried to bite it, but she could not open her mouth. A rough voice growled in Portuguese, 'One more croak out of you, fucking bitch, and I'll choke you to death!' The reek of liquor on his breath smote her nostrils. Vaguely she heard the creak of crickets beneath the pounding of her heart.

Stricken with dread, she stared up at the face above her, trying to identify it through the gloom. All she could see was a pale blur of skin, shining eyes. The man had spoken in Portuguese. Did he know her? O Blessed Virgin Mary, help your helpless child. Oh Fernao, where are you?

The chill certainty that there would be no help seized her. She had to help herself. How? With cunning. First, she must control her fear. Impossible. She decided wildly that she would at least try to identify the man by every means possible, the vague appearance, the sound of his voice, his black clothing, his smell, anything, so she could bring him to justice. If she lived . . .

The man reached down, roughly seized her wrist, dragged her to her feet. 'I gotta look at you first.' He was gloating. 'Try to run away or scream and you're dead.' A short laugh escaped him. 'Better wed than dead, eh?'

A cruel hand seized her nightgown at the neck, ripped it off in one savage movement, the tearing sound eerie in the

398

stillness. The air was suddenly chill on her bare breasts. She raised her hands to cover her nakedness, began to shake with terror. He tore off his shirt. She saw the black hairs matting his chest.

A swishing sound broke the stillness.

Something enveloped her body, a giant spider's web. The ground was swept from under her feet. She fell, the man on top of her. His massive body was crushing her. He stank of sweat and booze. Her flesh crawled at the feel of gross naked limbs pressing closer, closer upon her. Sheer horror brought merciful oblivion.

Thursday, 10 November 1524

A midnight summons from his father, King Wira, could only mean an emergency. This was confirmed when he met Queen Anula also heading towards the king's audience chamber in the Kandy palace. Dressed in pale blue, the bodice tight-drawn over her large breasts, the waist tiny, the hips full, her walk in the flarelight of the verandah was so sexy that he had an instant erection. By the Catholic saints, this woman has a most unsaintly effect on me, he thought. He gave her the salutation due a queen, bowing low, palms together before the eyes.

'You are breathtaking, a part of the mystery of this night,' he whispered so that only she could hear. 'You are light in the shadows.' Aloud he said, 'I see you too have been summoned by His Majesty. Permit me to accompany you, my lady.'

'There is no mystery about where you came from tonight,' she whispered back. 'You smell like a brothel and defile me with the breath of a whore in your mouth.' Aloud she said, 'We are flattered to be included in the royal summons. Pray join us.'

They walked on together, side by side. 'I'd like you for my whore!' he said under his breath.

'Go screw your own whore!' she whispered back.

He could not help smiling to himself as he fell into step beside her. Since he returned from Colombo, the queen and he had fallen naturally into a degree of crude frankness when they conversed alone together. Her downright vulgarity was so totally in contrast to her usual decorous speech that he accepted it as part of the intimacy of sex-play between them and responded accordingly. He had missed her when he had to go to Batti to meet the *parangi* ship carrying the young Colonel de Albergaria and his bride. When he had confessed this to her on his return, she delighted him by admitting that she had missed her *ko-lang kumaraya*, rascally prince. Since then, she had become more open with him about her dislike of his visits to his mistress. 'You service me as Manel does, as readily and superbly,' he now said quietly so that only she could hear, 'and I might consider curtailing my visits to her.'

'I can do better than any whore,' she retorted, still under her breath. 'I'll show you some day.'

'When?' His grin was deliberately taunting. 'Though I warn you it will have to be on a trial basis, for you'll have to prove that you can fulfil your boast!'

Her eyes flashed dangerously. 'If I satisfied an old goat who could not even get it up, I can surely pulverize a callow youth like you.'

'This callow youth needs no help to get it up,' he bragged. 'On the contrary, his problem is to keep it down, because he's no old goat but a young, virile stud bull. It's you who'll have to show that you can keep your end up.'

'I'm no whore to give you my end,' she flashed back. 'If I tackled a Great King, I can surely do better than your fucking whore any day.'

'Ah! Then you are indeed the queen of whores.'

For a moment she looked as if she would strike him, then a well-bred laugh escaped her. 'You are incorrigible,' she had said.

He chuckled inwardly.

The audience chamber smelled of incense. King Wira was seated cross-legged as usual on his favourite settee. He waved Queen Anula to a chair and jerked his head in the direction of Prince Kumara's ebony settle. 'Sit down, sit down,' he bade them. He cast his small, lecherous eyes on the queen. 'You grow younger and more beautiful by the hour, Madam.' He made no apology for the summons at that unusual hour.

A mosquito whining past his head added to Prince Kumara's impatience at his father's *sevala*, slithery, talk. He wondered momentarily how his dead mother, the half-sister of the proud King Maya Dunne, had endured the old man's ways.

The king picked up a rolled parchment from beside him, tapped his knee with it. 'We summoned you to an immediate audience because we have received a very important missive from the *parangi* military chief, Colonel de Albergaria,' he announced grandly, then spoiled the effect by clearing his throat, hawking and spitting into the brass spittoon beside his settee. 'It was brought to us personally by the Catholic priest, Father Juan, who has returned to our capital for a very important purpose.' He bared betel-stained teeth in a devilish grin. 'The baptism of our son and heir.'

Oh no, Prince Kumara thought, I'm not ready for that just yet. Aloud, he said, 'My agreement with the *parangi* is that I'll be baptized as soon as they have enough infantrymen, musketeers and some cannon here to back our plans.'

The king held up the scroll. 'That is exactly what they propose,' he stated, obviously enjoying his son's discomfiture. 'They are sending two companies of infantry and two troops of artillery to Batti. You, Prince Kumara, shall leave first thing in the morning for Batti where you shall meet the *parangi* ship and personally lead the contingent to our capital, as promised. Immediately on your return, you shall accept baptism into the Catholic Church.' He laughed maliciously. 'Maybe having a good Catholic in the family will give us a passport to heaven.'

Prince Kumara realized that the king was taking over his own scheme to get the *parangi*'s military support. It infuriated him, but his pulses quickened when he recalled the political plums that would follow. He ran a quick tongue over dry lips, observed the queen's dark eyes appraising him and responded by assuming an air of urbane unconcern. The seed of a thought, as to how he could get even with his father, entered his mind. 'I'd rather my baptism gave you entry to the sub-kingdoms of Pera, Gampola and Hangura, Sire, than a passport to heaven,' he declared. 'I shall certainly go to Batti and lead the *parangi* here, after which I shall accept baptism from Father Juan.'

'Nothing like a good ducking in the Maha Veli, great sand river, to cool the sexual ardour. Isn't that what Christian baptism involves?' King Wira gave a hee...hee...hee laugh.

'Well put, Sire,' the queen intervened maliciously. 'This means another long trip for your son, and the wrath of the Buddhist people on his return. He is noble indeed to sacrifice so much for the expansion of the Kandy kingdom. It requires a little self-sacrifice for children to grow up.'

The king slapped a fat thigh, laughed so uproariously that a tear ran down one cheek. He wiped it with his palm. 'You always put things so succinctly, Madam,' he commented. 'You are a lady after our own heart.' He looked pointedly at her breasts. 'What a pity that having taken you to our heart we cannot take you to our bedchamber.'

The queen dimpled a smile, gave him an artful look, then sighed. 'We cannot have all we want in life, Sire, neither of us, more's the pity.'

The queen's soft tones spoke volumes that Prince Kumara knew to be fiction. The seed that had entered his mind sprouted to decision. 'What we now need is strong allies,' he stated.

'Such as whom?' Both the king and Queen Anula were suddenly so watchful that the blinking of a moth's eyelids could have been heard in the silence.

'The Kiri Vella clan of Queen Anula is enormously powerful, Sire.'

His father's eyes shot to the queen. 'Upon my *kharma*, the prince is right. Here you are, Madam, a figurehead of the Kiri Vella clan, right in our court. How could we have overlooked it?'

'Because you are so gallant and noble, Sire, that your sole concern has been the protection of an unfortunate woman.' She cast suspicious eyes in Prince Kumara's direction. 'But please remember that we are but a discredited queen.'

'There is one way in which we can re-establish your credibility,' Prince Kumara shot back, his idea now in full growth.

'How?' his father demanded.

'I propose that, after the usual period following the death of her spouse, the Buddhist widow, Queen Anula, should marry me.'

Cool and steady as the night air in the mountains outside, he relished the queen's tiny gasp and his father's dropped jaw.

The king's gaze shifted towards Queen Anula. 'What do you think of that brainwave from our clever son, Madam?'

Her beautiful eyes turned wistful, then were demurely lowered. 'We women have no right to go against the dictates of our men, especially when it is our king who commands. Most especially when the king is as noble as you, Sire. But you well know what a rascal your son is.' She sighed heavily, raised a sad gaze to the king.

How beautifully you have pre-empted my father's approval, Prince Kumara thought with admiration.

'Such is our *kharma*,' the queen continued. 'Perhaps this unfortunate marriage will in some small way repay you for graciously giving us sanctuary in our time of need.' She paused, her gaze on King Wira luminous. 'There is nothing, nothing at all that we can refuse you.'

It did not take much persuasion to make Queen Anula agree to Prince Kumara's proposal. He even detected a certain eagerness in her assent, after the first bitchy demur. '*Aney*, Sire, we shall have to depend on you to protect us from your mischievous son once we marry him, but how can a widowed queen who has the respect of her people wed a known fornicator?' And to make sure of the king's assent: 'Of course, we realize that, like the young, we of royal blood must also frequently make sacrifices for the good of the realm. There can be no questioning the advantages to you, Sire, of such a marriage, despite our plight.'

He was pleased when further sparring resulted in agreement that the marriage would be announced shortly, the wedding to take place after a decorous period from the date of King Wijayo's death.

Following his final positive reaction to the proposal, King Wira became thoughtful, absently scratching his chest, his pig eyes staring. Knowing the way his father's mind was working,

Prince Kumara remarked acidly, 'What a pity you and I are not brothers, Sire, for then, according to our Kandyan custom, my wife could have shared both our bedchambers.'

'Maybe we should marry the queen instead,' his father shot back.

'Sire, we have one last request to make,' the queen intervened, deftly deflecting that line of thought. 'Since we are to take this monster of yours for a spouse, we would like the opportunity of a frank talk with him in our quarters tonight, properly chaperoned, of course, before he leaves for Batti, to try and persuade him to see the error of his ... er ... moral conduct.'

'Since you will refuse us nothing, we shall certainly not refuse you this,' the king responded with a lustful leer.

Once in the queen's chamber, they sat opposite each other as before, the aged attendant, Nona, in the ante-room.

Though the night was dark outside, Prince Kumara caught a glimpse of the sky, lit by a band of glimmering stars, just above the Highland Forest mountain. A bright promise for the future, he thought. Two cats began to snarl at each other close at hand, reminding him of the queen's words. 'Oh save me from this fornicator,' he now mimicked her ... 'There is nothing, nothing at all that we can refuse you.' He glowered at her. 'Well, Madam,' he went on, 'you and I both know that my father wants to lay you. If that will further my aims, I shall certainly encourage you not to refuse him.' Her dusky loveliness in the soft lampglow so enthralled him that he secretly thought, I shall kill any man who tries to take you. 'Since you desire to make our proposed marriage one of convenience, I shall service you and every other woman who needs such services! As you see, your latent promiscuity evokes the most romantic, princely dialogue from me!'

A slim, dark hand flew to her mouth. He delighted in the gesture because it showed that she could not always practise deceit with him. 'Do you think that I could take any other man to bed once I have made love to you?' she demanded quietly, seriously, dropping the royal plural.

In a flash, the words aroused the tender feelings he had for

404

her. He rose to his feet, strode across the room, bent one knee before her, his eyes adoring on hers. 'Madam, beauteous queen, you are the most desirable lady in the realm. I would seek no other woman if you were true to me. Bear with me in the one responsibility I have, towards my unborn child, as I shall help you to fulfil your responsibilities towards the son you have begotten from another man. Then I think you and I can have a truly happy marriage. I need to respect you and your virtue in order to love you. I need to love you truly in order to cherish you. In turn, if I cannot have your respect, I do not need your love, for it is your respect alone that will inspire your fidelity. I would have neither your love nor your respect if I were a cuckold. That is a shame I shall never bear. Hear me now. I love you. Else, I would not have sought to wed you.'

A gasp escaped her, the beautiful dark eyes brimmed with tears. 'Do you really mean that, Prince?' she whispered hoarsely.

'What?'

'That you love me?'

'I do.'

'And I love you, Prince. Otherwise I should have fought against your proposal, whatever the cost.'

Their glances were a merging. For once in his adult life, Prince Kumara gazed on a beautiful woman without lust for her. Love was a totally new emotion for him; he was shaken by it, a little scared, but nonetheless sure of himself. The queen blushed, a slow mantling of forest pools at dusk.

Filled with a great peace, he rose to his feet. 'That is the first sincere speech I have made in my life,' he declared lightly, seeking to cover his emotion. 'Such feelings are dangerous. I must be getting old. Or perhaps you have the capacity to make an old goat out of any man!'

'Our feelings are shared, Prince, for each other alone. Be sure that I shall watch to ensure that you and I remain our cynical, amoral selves towards the rest of the world.'

His laugh rang joyous, free, another new experience. 'You are a lady after my own heart, my queen, my wife-to-be.'

'And you are a man, a prince among men, my husband-to-be.' She paused. Her glance became mischievous, her tone mocking. 'Which reminds me. Your gestures of noble self-sacrifice match my own in marrying you.'

'What do you mean?'

'By becoming a Catholic, you may expose yourself to the odium of Sinhala Buddhists, but you will certainly place yourself in the strongest possible position with your father, because of the *parangi*.'

He grinned. 'The thought had not escaped me.'

'And by marrying me and becoming the focal point of an alliance with low-country Sinhala elements of my clan, you will really put yourself in a position of leverage. Such noble self-sacrifice!'

With a low laugh, he reverted to his normal self. 'My dear lady, the consciousness of nobility alone is a poor reward for self-sacrifice, which belongs to the unctuous, one of the lower forms of human life. You will find, in this category, priests who have only an illusory piety to commend their continence and *brachmachariya* who cannot even have an illusion of sex. All poor dried up creatures, like the barren fig tree that Jesus cursed. Apparent self-sacrifice for personal gain is, on the other hand, a princely virtue. It has a double reward, the realization of a devious purpose and the aura deriving from a pretence of nobility that fills the common people with awe. To rob the ignorant of their illusions as to one's nobility is the ultimate sin.'

'You believe in sin?' She was baiting him again.

'Not against life or some moral code, but against living.'

'Spoken like my prince.'

'What is sin after all?' Her obvious admiration and eagerness to hear his studied witticisms always stimulated him. 'It is no more than the complaint of the weak against the strong, the used against the user, the sufferer against the person inflicting the suffering. The Catholic Church has conjured the original sin. When Adam fornicated with Eve, he didn't know what he was letting himself in for. He obviously showed her how good it really could be without fulfilling her. Otherwise, why should she go on to fornicate with the serpent? Well, the serpent must have known his job, for Adam immediately accused her of something new in the Garden of Eden, infidelity. Since then, the male sex who cannot make good love have that concept to bind women to them, calling sex the original sin. Faugh! The concept has prevented many a delightful liaison through fear and ruined many a delicious adultery through pangs of conscience!'

She laughed, but a little tightly. 'Do you intend pursuing your adulteries, sin or not, after we are married?'

'Only if you are inadequate. As for you, I advise you to give up any thought of it, because I shall love you to exhaustion and have your every move monitored by eunuchs.'

'Balls!'

'They don't have any, my good lady. Or haven't you heard?' He grinned.

'You're very sure of yourself.'

'Isn't that one of the traits you find most attractive in me?'

'Yes, but there's one trait that causes us deep concern.'

'What is that?'

'Your lack of compassion.'

'Ha! I know why it bothers you.'

'Why?'

'Because you have none either.' He directed a level gaze at her. 'In any relationship between two people, if one person has even a mustard seed of it, the person without has all the advantage.' He deliberately injected into his voice the wry note he reserved for his flights of unusual thought. 'What is compassion? We are told by the Christians that it is a godly virtue, by Buddhists that it is one of the attributes leading to Enlightenment. The Hindus and Muslims acknowledge it in its time and place. All very practical, all motivated by the self-interest of those who preach it in the hope that compassion will beget charity. I ask you, how many people are intrinsically good, or naturally compassionate? No one, I venture to suggest.'

Her large, beautiful eyes widened, a strange look in them, a kind of hopelessness. 'You may be right. What does that leave us then?'

'The world at our feet. Our own brand of selfish goodness, shorn of the hypocrisy of the be-gooders. Do you realize that it brings us closer to the godhead concept than any Christian?'

'How so?' That tinge of hopelessness still lurked in her eyes.

407

'There is absolutely nothing compassionate, loving or forgiving in creation, so how then can these be attributes of a Creator? Observe nature, Madam. What is there compassionate or loving in the way the earth and the universe operate? On the contrary, everything is governed by the ruthless efficiency of cause and effect, the triumph of power, direct or subtle, the crashing tidal-wave or the invisible hurricane winds, all of which mean perpetual change. Compassion, forgiveness, charity, were introduced into human society by clever teachers who wanted to give the strong and powerful, the achievers, abstract moral codes so that the poor and weak might capitalize on them. Save for feelings between man and woman, sometimes between parent and child, which have also been carefully nurtured by society, all of it is a meticulously fostered myth.'

She exhaled loudly, half sigh, half expression of wonderment. Then her face tightened. 'You are more than precocious. You are brilliant. We'll not share you with anyone.' She pointed a slender finger at him. 'Not anyone at all. Least of all that whore of yours.'

He relaxed on his settle, well satisfied. 'Now as to that,' he began, happily anticipating the lover's squabble, which would tell him how fiercely this beautiful woman cared for him . . .

CHAPTER 36
Thursday, 10 November 1524

Lying awake, nerves taut, in my bedroom in the governor's mansion on the Mutu Vella hill, it was past midnight when I finally heard the scrape of gravel on my window. Fully dressed, I had been awaiting the signal with mounting anxiety. I leapt out of bed, padded across the room. Peering outside, I noted a shadowy figure on the paved courtyard beneath. The night was so black, I could barely discern the pale blur of a face. My eyes briefly took in the inky carpet of the groves and the Mutu Vella hill, spreading downwards to meet the dark harbour waters relieved by the lights of the *parangi* ships. I remembered another night, nearly four years ago, and a sigh escaped me. I did not know its cause.

I had already tied the coiled rope securely to the centre upright of the window. I uncoiled it, paid it out until it reached the ground. Within seconds, I slid down the rope with practised ease, my black tunic and pantaloons making me practically invisible in the dark. The air was cool, brought back memories of childhood escapades. The rope tricks, as we called them, of my boyhood had been heralds of tonight. I was certainly not a boy any longer, nor was my purpose to go out fishing in secret or to steal mangoes from neighbouring gardens though the trees of the mansion were laden with the fruit.

My feet touched the ground. Captain Sadha grinned at me through the darkness. A guard commander, very familiar with the sentry posts and routines, he was a member of our clan and my man in the mansion. It was an act of the *devas* that he was off duty tonight. 'All's well, Prince,' he said in the undertone of the trained spy. 'You have nothing to worry about.'

The pall of anxiety within me lifted at his reassurance. Eager to know more, I nonetheless followed him silently. We crept across the courtyard, making for the boundary wall of the mansion, my mind buzzing with a dozen questions. We passed through the familiar wicket gate, Captain Sadha still leading. Somehow I was not surprised when he headed for the grove in which the *parangi* cannon balls first fell and Lila, the prostitute, was brutally violated and murdered. Alert for sounds, I heard the creak of crickets and the squeak of a mouse, remembered how much Julietta used to love the sounds of night.

The captain paused at the edge of the grove and faced me. Like most people, he proceeded to tell me his story from the beginning, while I was impatient for its end. We had rightly anticipated that if the beast was going to strike, it would be on a night when Colonel de Albergaria was scheduled for night duty in the fort. Captain Sadha had used his men to keep track of Sergeant Correa without his knowledge. I listened impatiently to the details of the mission and was glad when the captain ended. Then I became impatient to rush to the scene.

'One question though, Prince.' He raised a finger. 'How did you know that Sergeant Correa would make for the grove?'

'Just a hunch,' I replied evasively, not wanting to bring up the subject of my involvement in the death of Lila by divulging my theory that a criminal generally returns to the scene of an unpunished crime. Knowing my intentions, Captain Sadha had placed his men, clad in black tunics and pantaloons, around the small, open glade deep inside the grove to which Sergeant Correa had carried Julietta. In the red-gold light of the hissing torches held by the captain's men, I saw the sergeant standing between two of his captors. The net in which he had been trapped lay on the ground beside him.

Though he was gagged, his hands bound behind his back, his feet manacled, the giant Correa showed no trace of fear. His arrogance surely sprang from the feeling of power created by Portuguese military might. Rage, hatred and a hint of bewilderment make him look like a caged monster. The scar running down his face was livid, his whole being exuded evil.

In contrast, the fair Julietta, still unconscious, hair dishevelled, lay on a cloak on the dark earth, the picture of light and innocence. The men had placed her there, knowing that it was better for her to come to on her own.

How can I describe my feelings at seeing her again after all these years? I longed to run to her, take her in my arms and revive her but I had work to do before she regained consciousness. I was about to speak when I noticed her torn nightgown. A strangled sound emerged from the depths of my belly. Insensate rage such as I had never experienced before consumed me. This filthy beast standing before me had dared to lay his foul hands upon Julietta. But for my intervention, she would be lying dead at this moment, here in this dark grove, ravished, mutilated, broken. I fought down the urge to reach for my knife, rush to the beast, stab him, cut him up. Years of princely training and a more deadly purpose gave me the strength to hold back.

A high wind rustled through the branches. I glanced up and saw it had begun clearing the sky of clouds, leaving patches of deep blue sky spangled with glittering silver stars. I drew a deep breath to regain control of myself. The air was cool.

I stepped forward into the better light. Sergeant Correa recognized me. His eyes flickered with the dawning of knowledge that this was more than the work of thieves or brigands. I sensed the first rumble of fear in his guts like a physical thing. With a muttered curse, he began struggling against his bonds. His captors roughly held him down.

I paused before him. I had to look up to hold his eyes. The acid reek of liquor and the sour stench of his sweat smote me. This filthy creature should never be permitted to lay a breath on any woman. 'I am Prince Tikiri Bandara of Sita Waka, a member of the royal family of Lanka,' I announced quietly. 'You know me?'

He nodded, speechless.

'Remove his gag,' I directed the men holding him. 'If he utters even a single cry, gut him with your knives.'

'You are here on trial, accused of rape, sodomy, kidnapping and murder,' I continued. 'Your captors are the witnesses. I am your judge.' I glanced down at Julietta. 'I shall spare your victim the pain of giving evidence.' I paused, holding his gaze with controlled fury. 'Your first crime against the laws of this land was committed in this very grove over three years ago. Do you remember?'

411

His eyes widened, his throat wobbled, a fleck of spittle appeared at the side of his mouth. His fear had turned to terror.

'I have waited a long time to bring you to justice,' I continued inexorably. 'Also for vengeance.' The words hissed out almost without thought. 'Each of the many crimes you have committed during the past years carries the penalty of death, but I may exercise the prerogative of decreeing some lesser punishment.'

He had begun to sweat in the cool air. He ran his tongue over lips suddenly gone dry. Good, I thought fiercely. You are now experiencing some of the terror you caused the poor women who were your victims.

'Are you guilty, or not guilty?' I demanded.

He remained silent, his face working, trying to control his mounting panic.

'I shall take your silence as an admission of guilt,' I declared. 'Do you wish to make a statement?'

He finally steadied himself, glared at me with fiendish hatred, then spat in my direction.

'I shall take that gesture as your statement,' I said in even tones. 'It is now for me to pass sentence.' I paused, felt my eyes glitter in the torchlight, my mind go icy cold with the penalty I had conceived years before. 'You have been endowed with a human instrument which you misuse in the most gruesome manner. Not knowing its rightful use, you have made it a dangerous implement which governs you although it's your mind that should control it. Muslim law says that if a man steals, his hand is chopped off. Although I abhor such extremes, the principle seems fitting in your case. I hereby decree that your genitals be chopped off, the sentence to be carried out immediately.'

His jaw dropped in a great gasp. He stared at me unbelieving. Then, as the truth hit him, his eyes popped open. The flesh of his face sagged. 'You would not dare!' he whispered.

'I do dare, as you shall see.'

'You ... you ... you fucking barbarian. My superiors, my comrades will have your balls.'

'It would not matter once we have removed yours. And as to your superiors, you may certainly report what I have done to them. Perhaps you will add the reasons for my sentence.' I glanced down at Julietta. She stirred once. A hardness such as I have never experienced before seized me, dilated my chest and my nostrils. 'Colonel de Albergaria is hardly likely to lend you sympathy and support when he hears the story. He is your commanding officer, is he not?'

'But the law...' He was croaking now, gibbering like a maniac.

'At this moment, *I* am the law!' I declared·relentlessly.

The men had been warned as to my intention and were ready to give it effect. They closed in on Sergeant Correa. He began begging for mercy. 'No! No! Please...'

The cry of a beast in mortal agony escaped him. The deed was done. His agonized shrieks subsided into whimpering, as he was dragged away. The animal sounds were taken up by the crescendo of Julietta's cry when she sat up.

I rushed up to her. 'You are safe, Juli,' I cried. 'Everything is all right. We shall take you home.' My heart was stricken by the terror in her eyes. I reached out instinctively, helped her to her feet, held her in my arms.

She clung to me, sobbing uncontrollably, her face against my shoulder, her body cold, the half-naked breasts warm and soft on my chest.

She raised a tearstained face to me. 'Oh, Tiki, Tiki, how... how?' She lapsed into incoherence, her whimpers mingling with some dead echo of the cries of a stricken beast.

I drew her head down on to my shoulder again. 'Don't worry about how, Juli,' I murmured into her dark hair. 'We can talk about that later. For now, just know you are safe.'

She began weeping like a child, a single note that did not end. 'Where is that fiend?' she inquired between sobs.

'You don't have to worry about him. Just hush now, Juli... hush now.' I rocked her gently, a bruised child.

When her weeping began to subside, Captain Sadha came up to me. 'What shall we do with the prisoner, Prince? He's unconscious.'

'He'll probably die.' I felt not a trace of pity. 'Leave him in the grove and let him rot. If he lives, he will meet his final doom at

413

the hands of his own people. Tell them why you apprehended him and that he escaped.'

The captain saluted me, began issuing orders to his men. When he had finished, he came up to me again. 'We shall retire now and await you and the lady at the entrance to the grove.'

He must have known of my boyhood friendship with Julietta and, being a man of great understanding, thought it best to leave Julietta and me alone in the glade for a brief while so that she could recover somewhat from her ordeal with a person she knew and trusted. 'As I have already told you, no one is to know of the part I have played in the rescue,' I reminded him. 'Your men happened to come upon the scene by chance.'

'The *parangi* will claim it was divine intervention, the grace of their God.'

'Perhaps it was, if there is such a God. In which case, we were merely His instruments.'

Captain Sadha saluted, turned away. The light of the departing torches was slowly absorbed by the trees. Julietta made no move to disengage herself from my arms. I could feel the beating of her heart.

The creaking of crickets reached my consciousness. I seized upon it as a method of bringing Julietta back to security. 'Can you hear the sound of crickets?' I inquired gently.

She listened, nodded against my shoulder.

'It's been a long time,' I breathed.

She was silent for a while, then settled her head more firmly against my shoulder, wiped her nose against my black tunic as if it were the most natural thing in the world. I held her closer. The vague scent of her jasmine perfume took me back through the years. My heart started beating faster.

Finally, she raised her tearstained face to me, ethereal in the half-light, the eyes luminous. 'Why did you leave me, Tiki-Tiki?'

I heard an indrawn breath before realizing that it was mine. I felt myself too reticent, fought desperately against the reflex, conscious that this moment was too precious and might never come again.

She did not take her eyes off me while the struggle went on. She seemed to be willing me to speak, and I marvelled at the

414

strength and beauty of a spirit that could want to probe my old wound when her own was so much more grievous and new. Then I perceived that there was within her a deeper wound than those she had suffered tonight, glimpsed that I had been its cause.

I could not look at her as I began to speak, but I knew that she never once took her eyes off me. I told her all, without recrimination. As I kept talking my eyes downcast, I knew that this Juli whom I held in my arms could never have betrayed me; I became more concerned about the impact of my past mistrust of her than of the anguish that I had endured through the years.

When I finished, I awaited her outburst. It did not come. Instead, a long sigh escaped her. 'My poor Tiki-tiki,' she said softly, almost to herself. 'How dreadful it must have been for you. How much you have suffered.'

A groan escaped me. Tears prickled my eyes, but I held them back.

Juli released me gently. 'Let's sit down,' she suggested, turning towards the dark patch of the cloak that had inadvertently been left behind. 'We may never get the opportunity to talk again.'

'What of my men? They will be expecting us.'

She paused. 'They can wait.'

'Your home...' I began, but suddenly recognized a new authority in her voice and manner. She was so calm that I realized that the child had grown up to be a woman, deep and ageless. Filled with the wonder of it, I took her elbow. We sat down side by side on the cloak, she sideways with her legs tucked beneath her. The years rolled back, for this was the way we had sat and talked so often before.

Time stood still while Juli told me her story, how she remained true to me in her heart despite her own hurt and doubts. When she referred to her woman, Menika, she suddenly jerked erect. 'Menika! I wonder how that man got past her!'

I laid a hand gently on hers. 'Menika is dead,' I said. 'Sergeant Correa killed her while she slept, so she knew no pain.'

A single sob escaped her, but she gave no other sign of grief. She would face it in private later.

415

'Menika was the only mother I knew.' She stated the fact so simply and directly that I knew she had indeed grown up. Then she quietly told me about Menika's life, the love the dead woman knew, the single night of consummation that was her lifetime of love.

I listened, moved beyond words.

Finally Juli fell silent. There was so much more to say, but time had gone by. We stared into space, knowing that we were nearing the end.

'Look at me!' Juli suddenly commanded.

My eyes met hers. A strange thrill ran through me, for in the half-light I saw in her gaze a world of tenderness which I cannot speak of.

'Tiki-tiki, I'm a married woman now. I have taken vows of fidelity to my husband, before God and Holy Church, that were both spoken and implied. Yet what you and I once knew, what we still know and will know for ever must have come from God in the beginning, before I ever took my vows. Else why was it you that came to my aid tonight?' She seemed to commune with herself. 'Yes, yes, that's right. You should never have sent that painting back to me, because it is you, not my husband, who are and always will be the prince riding to rescue me from the dragon.' Her eyes began to brim with tears.

I gazed at her dumbly, my mouth dry, my chest and throat aching, my eyes stinging.

'Tonight may never happen again,' she continued slowly. Her gaze became more intense, like that of a woman seer. 'Nor is it a part of my normal life. I need to be cleansed, Tiki-tiki, and only you can do it. I need something that will rescue me from the dragons of fear, uncertainty, anguish and even death.'

'How can I help you?' I inquired hoarsely.

'By making love to me.'

The grove started to spin. I could not believe my ears, but I felt a pounding in them. I had never made love to a woman. My only sexual experience had been the fumbling occasion when I kissed Julietta so long ago. Now this. 'I want no reward for saving you tonight,' I muttered, but still under the wondrous spell of her gaze.

416

'I am offering you no reward, Tiki-tiki. I am only saying that our love has to be consummated, once and for all time, tonight, while I am Juli and you are Tiki-tiki again.'

I understood what she meant.

Juli and I, a virgin woman, no less, and a virgin man, made love to each other, lying on a soldier's cloak in the semi-gloom of a small glade beneath the Mutu Vella stars. There was no fumbling. It was a perfect union, made in heaven.

Heaven. I looked up at the sky and it had begun to pale, the stars fainter, perhaps three more hours to dawn. Juli must be taken home.

A great sadness, a craving never to let her go, the sick knowledge that I must, churned within me, choking me.

Menika, a dead serving woman, and I, a live prince, had become one through the brief span of our loving and the eternity of our love life; for I knew with certainty that this most precious part of my life had begun and ended in minutes. Menika's travail was over; mine had begun.

What I had known was so pure and right that, as Juli and I lay fulfilled in each other's arms, I wondered what I could give back to it, how I could make it right for a married woman who had broken her vows. In a blinding flash of light, I knew the answer. I had to be true to these moments for the rest of my life.

Silently I took the vow of *brachmachariya*. I would never again know a woman in this way, never again, even if I had to marry.

Thus I gave back to Juli and her God the righteousness and purity of our blessed consummation.

CHAPTER 37
Friday, 11 November 1524

Julietta took a deep breath and forced herself to open the door of her bedroom. Though she was bone weary, every part of her shrieked silently as the terror returned. This room which had been her sanctuary, would she ever be able to enter it again without remembering the nightmare of her experience? It was not just herself, but the room, indeed the entire house, that had been violated by the presence of an intruder. Yet the room seemed so peaceful now in the pale light of near-dawn, she could not believe that a stranger had broken in...

Why had Tiki-tiki's men not followed Sergeant Correa inside and prevented the outrage? She knew the answer. This house was Portuguese territory, Fernao's territory...

She closed the door and stood before it, her hand on the lock. She had left Tiki-tiki with a strange numbness, knowing that doubts and longings would emerge later. That numbness had persisted through the daze of her return to the mansion, the first stunned reactions of the guards, followed by uproar, the message to Fernao on pounding hooves that faded into the distance. It had remained when she entered the disturbed household and finally, during the hushed moments when she stared down at Menika's dead body in one of the rear rooms of the house. Only a heartbroken sob had escaped her at seeing the frail figure, the wrinkled skin now grey, lying limp on a mat. Then the determination to act like a princess, to be worthy of Tiki-tiki, flooded her, made her hold back her emotions. Those were probably the easier moments, for the real grief would start to stab when her routine began again and Menika was no part of it.

Standing by the door, Julietta knew that she must gather all her resources of mind and spirit in order to relegate to some compartment at the back of her mind the wonder of what she had known with Tiki-tiki as something separate from her existence. Strangely, she knew that the effort she had put into separating herself from herself during the lovemaking on her wedding night would help her now that she was back home, for conscience, compassion for her dear, kind Fernao and apprehension that he might discover her secret had commenced. It was in this room, on that bed, that she had given a man, her husband, her body for the first time. They were clamorous reminders of the real life to which she had re-awoken from a dream. No part of her, however, regretted what she had done, for she had come to terms with it before she caused it to happen. Now her real love life would be as Menika's had been, but in a way it would be worse for her than for Menika, because she loved Fernao too and was married to him.

A way of life had ended. The finality of it made her shoulders droop; she had to lean against the door for support. Then, some instinct made her straighten up with the fierce resolve that she would never burden Fernao by admitting to what she had done. Nor would she take it to the confessional, because God had already been her witness.

She recalled the rapist's hands on her body and shuddered violently. Tiki-tiki had cleansed her, but had he exorcised the demon? How would she respond to Fernao now? A chill dread streaked through her. Fernao had coerced her into the marriage and on to that nuptial bed with its pink cushions and coverlet. She had not given her body to him through desire for him or for the act, but because she had married him. True, she had finally responded to him, but her act of love with Tiki-tiki whispered that Fernao had, in his own way, been guilty of rape. Was she thinking thus only to allay her conscience?

She became aware of the ache in every muscle of her body. She walked slowly and painfully to the bed, paused, then collapsed onto it. She closed her eyes. Her mind began to whirl, the wheels spun into blackness.

Friday, 11 November 1524

Fernao reached the mansion just as dawn was breaking. His knock on the bedroom door blended with the crowing of the cocks. He burst in before Julietta had time to bid him enter. She came erect with a scream. He rushed to the bed, half sat on it, then took her in his arms.

'Hush, my beloved,' he soothed her. 'It's all right. It's all right.' He rocked her gently back and forth.

For moments, she lay passive in his arms, remembering how Tiki-tiki had rocked her. Dear God, how to separate the two lives? The words came out slowly. 'I screamed just now, didn't I?' She paused. 'I . . . I was dreaming . . . that . . . that it happened again. Oh Fernao, it was horrible, horrible. And Menika is dead. My mother is dead. Oh God, why am I alive?'

'For me, my beloved.' Oh God, why did I put duty before love's warning last night? Will I ever live that down?

She continued lying still in his arms, trying to get his words into focus. Yes, indeed, I am alive for you, Fernao, she thought. You were so good to me that I do have something to live for. I shall be a devoted, faithful wife to you. I shall make it up to you for what I had with Tiki-tiki. Her mind went to the prince. How lonely he must be. Compassion for him reached her throat and a strangled sob escaped her.

Fernao misinterpreted the sound. 'It has been a horrible experience for you,' he said gently. 'Would you like to talk about it?'

Every part of her screamed, No, no, no! I only wish to forget all of it. I wish I could plunge my fingernails into my brain and tear out that memory part of it forever. She trembled at the recollection. Her teeth began to chatter. Her skin felt cold, broke out in goose prickles. She clung closer to Fernao, desperately reaching for security. She tilted her head and gazed into his eyes. His helplessness brought forth a gush of affection. Something told her that he needed to know all. She turned her cheek, resting it on his shoulder. With a desperate determination, she began to speak, the words coming out haltingly at first. She told him all except for her meeting with the prince.

He listened in silence, holding her close, his cheek against her hair. When she had finished, he remained thoughtful for long moments. He finally spoke, sounding uncomfortable. 'You say the rapist was Sergeant Correa, the commander of the guard here.' He paused, swallowed. 'How did you know his name?'

Julietta was confused. She had not expected to be questioned, only comforted. She had learned the name of the rapist from Prince Tikiri. 'He . . . he has been here, I mean, at his post. I've heard the servants talk.' She had a sudden inspiration. 'And Menika once mentioned his name.'

'Oh!' His body tensed. 'Did you know him? Did you ever talk to him?'

'No. Of course not.' She glanced up at him. 'What is the meaning of all these questions, Fernao?'

He avoided her gaze. 'I know you're a virtuous woman, Julietta. If nothing else, you proved it during the years you lived in the fort.' He seemed uncertain, then swallowed again, made a decision. 'But it's so difficult to believe that a soldier would murder a serving woman, abduct the wife of his commanding officer,' the words were coming out in a rush, 'unless he thought, rightly or wrongly, that he had some sort of encouragement.'

'What?' She sat up with a start, pushing away from him, staring at him incredulously, her nerves screaming.

'I chose my words with care. Please try to understand me, Julietta. This has been an even more horrible experience for me, in its own way, than for you.'

She laughed hysterically, steadied herself. His words linked with her secret resentment at being subtly forced into marrying him. Beneath Fernao's love, was there a selfish heart? 'I don't believe this!' she cried. 'I'm woken up in the middle of the night, silenced with a blow and carried away unconscious to a dark grove by a man I've never spoken to. I wake to find myself about to be raped and probably murdered by the brute beast. I'm saved in the nick of time. I'm half-dead with terror. And you say, you . . . you . . . ' The hysteria rose to her throat again. She pointed a wild finger at him. 'You must be joking, Fernao. And it would be funny if it were not utterly tragic. Why, the Sinhala

421

who rescued me showed me more compassion than you, my husband.' She remembered Prince Tikiri and thanked God for him. Then her feelings of guilt instantly made her glad that Fernao had given her cause to take the offensive. 'I wish I could weep but I'm only disgusted.'

Fernao reached out for her then, held her close to him against her tightness and resistance, his breathing laboured. 'I know I have failed you, Julietta. Please forgive me. I did not say you encouraged this monster, merely that he may have *thought* you encouraged him. You are so sweet and kind to everyone. Who knows what goes on in the mind of a man? You don't know men such as Correa the way I do. They are conceited, arrogant, think every woman admires and desires them. You could not be blamed for what might have gone on in his mind when you were merely being your gentle self.' He hesitated. 'Please also try to remember that I have to play a dual role, as your husband and as the man's commanding officer.'

Words, words, she thought. She felt utterly dejected, weary unto death, but she had to play his game of words. She pretended to relax her body. 'I know what you're saying, Fernao. I'm sorry I misunderstood you.' She could not resist a barb. 'It is difficult for me to conceive that it is not my loving husband here in my bedroom, but the dutiful commanding officer of the two regiments, holding me in his arms.' With enormous effort she pretended a smile to make the words seem a joke. 'I assure you I've never spoken to the man, or even exchanged glances with him, in my life. You are a just man and you can have faith in my virtue.' The words seemed to ring as hollow as her life had become.

'There is one more thing that I have to ask you.' He was thoughtful, trying to phrase his question, and Julietta tensed in anticipation of it. 'Are you saying then that he . . . he . . . he did not . . . er . . . enter you, my love?'

'No, he did not,' she hastened to reassure him. 'I was rescued just in time.'

A long pause. She wondered why he did not express relief, gladness. 'Are you sure?' he inquired, apparently solicitous. 'I mean . . . er . . . you're not trying to protect me?'

Her heart missed a beat, her breathing quickened. She suddenly realized that he was intent, almost watchful now. Her instinct told her to be careful. She relaxed. 'I'm sure,' she replied simply.

'How is it then that you smell of a man's emission?' The words seemed to leap out of him involuntarily, their tone almost harsh.

Julietta was suddenly reminded of that day in the fort when Fernao had come to bid her goodbye before the Portuguese contingent left for Jaya and he had shown his jealousy of Prince Tikiri. Why was he asking this of all questions? Had he somehow learned that the prince had been her saviour? This time he had reason to be suspicious, for she *was* guilty. A combination of self-preservation and a desire to protect the innocent Fernao swept over her. 'I can't imagine what it can be,' she stated firmly. 'It may be something from that glade. I couldn't bathe when I got back, because...because...' She fought back the tears, her mouth crumpling, 'Menika was not here to prepare me a hot bath.' She steadied herself. 'If the man had done that I would have no cause to hide it from you, Fernao. I would surely tell you and look to you for understanding and comfort.'

His body tightened at the reminder of her need. 'I'm sorry, my darling. I wanted to be sure that, if it had happened, you would feel able to share it with me.' His voice had become gentle again. He stared into space. 'I was also concerned that you might bear the man's child.'

At that moment, Julietta knew beyond doubt that she had conceived of Prince Tikiri. A strange mixture of emotions flashed through her – panic, fierce joy, pity for Fernao, a feeling of destiny. She knew she had to keep this knowledge from the world, especially from Fernao and her Tiki-tiki. This was her secret, her burden alone. She would do everything, be cunning if necessary, to protect what she had conceived.

Supposing the baby were dark? It would betray her. For a moment, she panicked. No, her mother had been Sinhala. Thank you, dead mother. There was a purpose to your being Sinhala, though you never knew it.

423

'If you have any doubts, you could always check,' she volunteered quietly. 'Would you like me to raise my gown?'

He tightened with shock. 'Oh no, no!' He was almost stammering. 'You know I'd never do that! I believe you. I do believe you, Julietta. You are the most wonderful woman in the world to make such an offer at such a time. It can only come from true love. I'm lucky to have you for a wife.' His arms tightened about her again.

She had known that he would not check. You have had your comfort and caring already, a still small voice within her whispered, so from how many more can you expect it?

'When we catch that monster, Sergeant Correa,' she heard Fernao say fiercely, 'I shall be hard put to it not to chop him into little pieces myself.' He started to rock her gently again. 'My poor, poor Julietta.'

Too late, Fernao. Too late. You have proved to me that the love I feel for you is affection born of communion, common tastes, a desire for a husband and a home. It does not have the magic of my love for Tiki-tiki, which alone is the kind that can never be erased or diminished by such grave disappointment as I have known from you today.

She glanced beyond his shoulder through the open windows. The day had brightened outside. The sun had risen.

Fernao followed Julietta's gaze and stared blindly at the sunshine outside, her dark auburn hair, which he so loved, a mixture of fragrance and sweat to his nostrils. The clamour of birds intruded on his senses, joyous, carefree sounds contrasting with the heaviness in his heart. 'Did *you* do it?' . . . 'Did *you* do it?' 'Here I am.' . . . 'Here I am. . . .' went the whistles.

He knew he had failed Julietta in her direst hour of need, but he had not been able to control the demon within him. God knew he had tried. Yet, however fair he wanted to be, he could not erase from his mind the raw smell that had smitten him, no less, when he first took Julietta in his arms. And the feel of her had been different. That's right, some part of her had been withdrawn, as it had been years ago, when she had held back from him because she loved Prince Tikiri. This as much as anything had triggered his responses to her. The woman he was holding in his arms was the old Julietta and yet someone new as well. Had she been this way when he first entered the bedroom and took her in his arms? His mind felt raw with the effort to pierce that veil and he cast it aside.

Who was responsible, he or Julietta? Perhaps both of them, perhaps neither.

Was Sergeant Correa responsible? No, the monster had merely been the instrument that dug out the hidden springs. Fernao rather suspected that the Sinhala had killed the sergeant but would not admit it for fear of reprisals. Even in rescuing the colonel's wife, they had no right to lay a hand on a Portuguese soldier, who could be judged only by his own superiors.

Thoughts of the Sinhala inevitably brought Prince Tikiri again to mind. That bastard was the one originally responsible, Fernao thought. I am destined to kill him or have him killed some day.

Author's Note

AUTHOR'S NOTE

Many of the events of this novel actually took place, although not always exactly as I describe them. The names of most of the main characters have come from the history books, including *Portugal* by John Dos Passos; the *Rajavaliya*; the *Chula Vamsa* (Wm Geiger's translation); and Father S.G. Perera's *History of Ceylon, Portuguese Period*.

Portuguese characters: King Dom Manuel I; King Dom Joao III; Vasco da Gama; de Albergaria; the de Almeidas; de Albuquerque.

Sinhala characters: King Dharma Parakrama Bahu; King Wijayo; his consort, whom I have named Queen Anula, and her son, Prince Deva Raja; King Bhuvaneka Bahu; King Jaya Wira Bandara; Prince Kumara; Prince Vidiye; King Maya Dunne and his youngest son.

Indian/Moorish characters: The Zamorins of Calicut; Paichi Marcar.

Also some historical events: Vasco da Gama's discovery of the sea route to India in 1498 and his subsequent appointment as Viceroy; the planting of the stone cross in Galle by Lorenzo de Almeida; the establishment of Portuguese forts in Colombo, Galle and other coastal cities; and *Wijayo ba kolla*, the looting of King Wijayo's treasury and his assassination. Rather more actual history is included in the sequel to this novel, *The Last Sinhala Lions*. I have, however, telescoped time, juxtaposed dates, altered actual events, created characters, all in the interest of more readable stories, in both books.

The Aryan Sinhala of Lanka were continually subjected to pressure from the south of India – the Cholas in this novel and in *The Winds of Sinhala*. In the eighth century AD they were forced to move their capital from Anu in the north central region to Polon farther south, and later, just before the time of this story, to Jaya seven miles east of Colombo. Constant fighting against the invader and growth of sub-kingdoms weakened the Sinhala and allowed Moorish traders such as the Raschid family to establish a stranglehold on Lanka's valuable spices and her import-export trade.

Portugal's first contact with the island was in 1498 when the Zamorin – or Moorish king – in Calcutta impounded Vasco da Gama's ships and made it a condition of their release that he should seize a Sinhala vessel carrying spices and trained elephants from Colombo to Ormuz in the Persian Gulf. Five years later, in an attempt to corner trade in the Indian Ocean before his rivals in Europe could take advantage of the new sea route, King Manuel I of Portugal despatched the most powerful fleet his country had ever assembled to India. With it, Vasco da Gama bombarded Calicut and established trading posts at Cannanore and Cochin, proclaiming that in future trading would only be permitted under licence from Portugal. When the Zamorin of Calicut violated this decree a squadron patrolling off Calcutta seized two large ships and twenty-two small dhows belonging to the Zamorin and carrying rice, cotton goods and jars of butter. The crews were treated with great savagery by the Portuguese *degradado* ex-convict sailors, earning da Gama a reputation for harshness and cruelty. Many of the Portuguese traders subsequently took Muslim or native wives.

In 1504 King Manuel named Francisco de Almeida first Viceroy of India and the following year a naval squadron commanded by his son, Lorenzo, was accidentally carried to the port of Galle in southern Lanka, where Lorenzo found Moorish traders operating under the protection of King Dharma. Lorenzo made a treaty with the Sinhala king, who sent King Manuel a magnificent cat's eye ring and four hundred *bahars* of cinnamon.

This was an era of extreme cruelty and ruthlessness. Save for some of the methods, however, it is no different from the modern scene, with the exception that today honour is scorned and even the meaning of nobility unknown to many. I pray that this book will inspire those who still have such ideals to cherish them whatever the price.

Colin de Silva
Honolulu, Hawaii, 1986